PRAISE FOR

the

Unquiet Grave

"McCrumb hears voices from the grave and kindly passes their messages along."
—*The New York Times Book Review*

"Unquiet indeed."
—*Kirkus Reviews*

"In this compelling story, McCrumb continues to relate the dynamic tales of Appalachia and its people."
—*Library Journal*

"McCrumb has a real knack for crafting full-bodied characters and using folklore to construct compelling plots."
—*Booklist*

"Sharyn McCrumb understands the South, and her understanding and storytelling ability are evident in every page of this well-crafted novel."
—Historical Novel Society

"Based on one of the most incredible ghost stories in American folklore. You won't be able to put down."
—*Bustle*

ALSO BY SHARYN McCRUMB

the

Unquiet Grave

Grave

A Novel

Sharyn McCrumb

POCKET BOOKS

New York   London   Toronto   Sydney   New Delhi

Pocket Books
An Imprint of Simon & Schuster, Inc.
1230 Avenue of the Americas
New York, NY 10020

This book is a work of fiction. Any references to historical events, real people, or real places are used fictitiously. Other names, characters, places, and events are products of the author's imagination, and any resemblance to actual events or places or persons, living or dead, is entirely coincidental.

First Pocket Books paperback edition January 2019

POCKET and colophon are trademarks of Simon & Schuster, Inc.

For information about special discounts for bulk purchases, please contact Simon & Schuster Special Sales at 1-866-506-1949 or business@simonandschuster.com.

The Simon & Schuster Speakers Bureau can bring authors to your live event. For more information or to book an event, contact the Simon & Schuster Speakers Bureau at 1-866-248-3049 or visit our website at www.simonspeakers.com.

Manufactured in the United States of America

10 9 8 7 6 5 4 3 2 1

ISBN 978-1-9821-3641-3
ISBN 978-1-4767-7289-9 (ebook)

For Sandra Menders

the
Unquiet Grave

one

LAKIN, WEST VIRGINIA

1930

THE PLACE WAS AS QUIET as it ever got in the hours around midnight, with only occasional screams or sobs from the cells down the corridor to disturb his contemplation. Somewhere, perhaps on another floor of the building, someone was singing.

He was standing at the window, as he always did at that time of night, hands resting on the bars, his face pressed against the wire-reinforced glass, as if the cool night air could waft him away. Perhaps no one cared if he stood at the window after lights-out; there were a hundred patients and perhaps a dozen staff members who were busy enough without having to worry about a quiet man having a sleepless night. Anyhow, even if they did care, chances were that they wouldn't see him. His dark face would not glow in the moonlight and give him away.

He strained his eyes, searching the darkness beyond the treetops, hoping that the clouds would part enough to let him see the shapes of the dark cliffs across the river. That was Ohio, over there. In his parents' day, back when this place was still part of Virginia, that side of the river would have meant freedom, but that had changed now. Now freedom—or the lack of it—was the same everywhere for ordinary people. And for madmen and criminals, there was no freedom at all. Since he had spent most of his life subscribing to, and even enforcing, that rule, it seemed churlish to object to it now, just because its strictures now applied to him. Those who are a danger to themselves or others must be restrained.

He could never see the river itself—it was nearly a mile away, beyond the fields on the other side of the road. Except in the dead of winter, the trees blocked the view, and then the steep embankment obscured the water. At least he knew it was there, though: the broad, dark waters of the Ohio rolling on to the Mississippi and on to its freedom in the Gulf. He would like to have seen that confluence, followed it even, all the way to journey's end. The puny little rivers where he came from, in the eastern part of West Virginia, weren't a patch on this one; why, except in the spring floods, you could wade across most of them. What was the point of being here—so close—and not getting to see the river? What was the point of being here anyhow? It wasn't as if they could help him. If he had been delusional, perhaps they could have led him back to reason, but he always thought that his problem was seeing the world too clearly.

From somewhere down the hall a long scream pierced the stillness. One of the old men was either hallucinating horrors or remembering real parts of his past, perhaps as far back as slavery—it was hard to tell which was worse, because those who imagined them believed with equal fervor. At least he was spared all of that. He spent a long time at night with his face pressed close to the window, and when he finally fell into bed, he did not dream.

He wished he could either become entirely sane or else very much more mad. A delusion that transported you right away from unpleasant realities would be more blessing than affliction, it seemed to him. Let him drift away on a current of madness into a dreamworld where he was young again, where his gentle Eliza or her successor, clever Alice, was still alive and well—or, better yet, some kingdom out of a fairy story, in which the world was entirely different from anything he'd ever known. Let there be talking horses, and penny candy stick trees, and golden rivers of bourbon. He sighed. None of those fantasies particularly appealed to him any more than the real world did just now. He had spent his life in the profession of law—not a discipline that encouraged its practitioners to be fanciful. He had always considered an excess of dignity and a dearth of imagination to be positive qualities in his character, but unless madness conferred its own artistic inspiration, his temperament made him ill-equipped to enjoy the benefits of delusion, and his lifelong habit of reserve would have held him back anyway. He was forever an observer, and one day he had decided that he had seen enough and wanted to leave. Yet here he was.

His own particular form of insanity was to see the world exactly as it was, and to despair in silence.

As he grew older, the truth, unvarnished by hope or illusion, made him desperate to escape life itself. But suicide was considered madness, rather than a shrewd appraisal of one's options, and so here he was in this barred asylum, as desolate and bereft of choices as Shakespeare's Ophelia, but prevented, both literally and metaphorically, from reaching the river.

Odd that, while he could never see the river, there were other things that he *did* see sometimes in the night. A thing with glowing red eyes and leathery wings . . . Other patients had spoken of it, too, but while they had wild imaginations, unmoored from logic, he did not. Precisely because he saw things exactly as they were, he knew that whatever-it-was was real.

Best not to speak of that, though. He couldn't be bothered to try to convince the long-suffering staff of the asylum that this one particular delusion was not one at all. It didn't matter really. The thing was doing no harm, except perhaps to make people who reported it seem madder than they actually were.

It hadn't taken him long to figure out that these people could not help him, even if they wanted to, and that the best course would be to learn the rules of the game that would set him free as quickly as possible. He had been *learning the rules* and *playing the game* all his life, so this was just one more battle of wits, not much different from the others. There were no white people here, but the game was pretty much the same: those in charge versus those who had no power at all.

"You're up late tonight, James."

He stiffened, nettled by the condescending tone, the use of his Christian name. He turned toward the doorway, where a shadow was silhouetted by the light in the corridor. "With all due respect, sir, despite my present circumstances, I am not your inferior, and from the sound of your voice, I do not think myself junior to you in age, either. I am certainly not a child. Please address me as Mr. Gardner."

There was a brief silence while the shadow seemed to consider the matter. "Need we be so formal? After all, you are a patient here. And I am an attending physician."

"If we were on my home ground—in a courtroom—instead of in a hospital, would you willingly allow me to call you by your given name while you addressed *me* as 'Mister'?"

"Perhaps not. We doctors like to stand on ceremony."

"Have we met? Your voice is unfamiliar to me."

"In passing. I have not treated you, but my room is just down the hall here, and I thought since we were neighbors I'd pay a call on you. I couldn't sleep, either."

The prisoner considered it. "So you are our hall monitor. I remember you. You may come in if you like."

"Thank you. Another time, perhaps. I didn't bring the keys."

"How odd that they house you doctors here among your patients. No one quarters lawyers next door to the criminals in the jail."

The visitor chuckled. "I suppose not, but there weren't many alternatives in this case. Point Pleasant is six miles down the road, and its population is mostly white, so it was deemed both inconvenient and awkward for us to try to live there. We're understaffed here, too, so it's helpful to have us in residence in case we're needed beyond our regular working hours. I don't mind. It saves me rent money."

"Your voice makes me think you're mighty young, Doctor, and that last remark of yours clinched it. What's your name again?"

There was a slight pause before the reply. "My name is Boozer. Dr. Boozer, that is."

He laughed. "*Boozer?* That name must have been a cross to bear at times."

"I got used to it. By the time I was ten, I'd heard every schoolyard jest that can be made about it, but after people become acquainted with me they stop noticing. And my parents tried to temper its effects by giving me an ordinary first name—James. Like yours."

"Boozer." Gardner considered it. "No doubt people think the name means you are descended from drunkards. I don't suppose it does, though."

"Well, not in our case. I can't speak for the original owners. I'm sure our surname was a leftover from the white folks back where my parents came from, because its origin is Scottish, and we most definitely are not. I looked it up one time in the library when I was in Pennsylvania. It's a variation of Bousay, but God only knows what *that* means."

"You must spend a lot of time explaining that."

"It's best to get it out of the way quickly, I've found. Anyhow, the staff says that you are an educated fellow yourself, Mr. Gardner, and your conversation certainly bears that out. When you called the courtroom your home ground, did you mean that you were a lawyer?"

"I *am* a lawyer, young man. I still am one. And when I get shed of this place, I shall resume my practice immediately back in Mercer County, so don't go thinking of me as a permanent fixture around here."

"I wish you well, Ja— Mr. Gardner. And we'll do our best to send you on your way. God knows we need the space. They called lights-out a long while back, yet here you are, gazing out the window. Are you having trouble sleeping?"

"I savor the silence in the dead of night. If I had to exist only in the cacophony of daytime here, I would indeed go mad."

"I know. It helps to think of them as injured. They don't have any visible wounds to prove that, but I'm certain they suffer just as much."

"*Canst thou not minister to a mind diseased?*" The mockery in Gardner's voice was unmistakable.

"We do what we can. Some people are easier to reach than others. I'd like to help you, if you'd ever like to talk about things."

"Perhaps one day, young man. But you haven't lived long enough yet to have had much experience of the world. I warn you that the things I say, which to you will seem the sheerest lunacy, will be the plain unvarnished truth."

"Are you standing at that window watching for the red-eyed demon some of the patients claim is out there?"

Gardner laughed. "Perhaps I am, Doctor. And perhaps I cannot tell a hawk from a handsaw. But I'll tell you one thing I did *not* ever see—the ghost of Zona Heaster Shue."

"Who is that?"

"A white lady—just a country girl who died a long time back. I never met her, but she lost a case for me in court. She testified for the prosecution."

"Before she died, you mean?"

Mr. Gardner laughed. "No, *after*!"

two

GREENBRIER COUNTY, WEST VIRGINIA

1896

I WASN'T THERE.

I reckon that's when the trouble started, though, that September day on the farm in the Richlands, where Zona was staying for a while, away from home and enjoying the last of late summer with her cousins and their friends. We hoped they'd keep her out of mischief, but we knew from bitter experience that Zona did as she pleased, and propriety be damned. Well, she was a grown girl, so I had little choice but to let her go. I used to try to make her act ladylike, but she was such a lovely, winsome little thing that her father could never bring himself to rein her in—he will have to live with that.

At the time I was halfway across the county on the farm in Meadow Bluff, tending to the cooking and the washing, and minding the younger children, same as always. Zona was well past twenty, and sometimes I could feel every minute of my forty-six years, so I could have used her help around the place, but Zona wasn't one to be stuck with her folks on a mountain farm in the back of beyond. She'd have hitched her wagon to a skunk, much less a star, just to get away from home and out into the world. She'd already tried once, but that ended in tears.

I heard an account of that fateful day, when it was too late to matter, from Sarah, the oldest of the Richlands cousins, who made a tale of it as country folk do for want of any other entertainment. I don't blame her for what came after. Seems like it was destined to happen, and no one could have stopped it.

"The lady visitor from Lewisburg came hobbling up the lane to the farm that afternoon," she told me. "And she *was* a lady, too. Everything from the cut of her clothes to her air of calm superiority proclaimed that. It came so natural to her that you couldn't even take offense. She was leading a lame chestnut mare, and as soon as she spied me, she asked for a cup of water—or milk, if we could spare it.

"She was smudged with road dust, and damp with sweat, but in spite of that we could tell from her fancy broadcloth riding clothes and those high-polished black boots of hers that she was as much of a thoroughbred as that saddle horse beside her. She looked to be one of the society ladies staying over at the grand hotel folks call the Old White, but that was miles away from us, over in White Sulphur Springs. No society lady would ever have ridden that far alone on an afternoon excursion. Zona was somewhere about the house, but the visitor's arrival had put her right out of my mind, so I didn't call for her. Instead, I hurried down the steps to meet the lady, mainly to be hospitable, but also because I didn't want her in our little parlor with its faded horsehair sofa and the worn rug I'd braided myself from rags. I wasn't ashamed of it, exactly; it was clean and all we could afford, but I was afraid that if I let her in, I'd see it ever after through her eyes—shabby and cheap.

"It turned out she had been visiting folks she knew over in Lewisburg, and she rode out this way past the ladies' academy, down the Midland Trail for a change of scenery. Nobody coming straight from the hotel would happen upon our place unless they'd been to Lewisburg first. We live nearly twenty miles away—too far from there even to sell their cooks some vegetables from our garden for their dining room, or a side of beef or some chickens, the way farm folk who live closer to the hotel do. I wish we did live closer; we could do with the extra money.

"I'll bet those who sell their vegetables and hens to the hotel wouldn't recognize them if they happened to dine there—not after all the tarting up that's done to them in that kitchen of theirs, sauces and spices and I don't know what all. Nobody around here ever does go there, but we hear tales now and again from folks with kin working there. Peculiar food and outlandish clothes; if I had their money, I'd have better things to spend it on.

"I just mostly fry up or boil what we eat, but I've had no complaints about my cooking. We're plain folks, and plain food suits us just fine. I wouldn't be asking this lady guest to sit supper with us, either, that's for sure.

"Said she had borrowed a horse from the people she was visiting, and she had ridden out along the pike for an afternoon excursion, but her horse stumbled and threw a shoe on the stones. She wasn't thrown, but she'd had to dismount, of course. Leading the mare, she'd hobbled into the first lane she came to—you recall that you can see our place from the main road; it's not far. I bade her come on up, and she sank down on our front porch, worn out by the ordeal of her quarter-mile walk. I tried not to

smile as she held forth about her afternoon's tribula-
tions. Why, us farmers' wives walk farther than that
just seeing to the hens and the garden, but it would
have been rude to tell her so.

"I sent our youngest across the pike a ways after
the blacksmith, and then I went inside to get the lady
some fresh milk out of the jug, marveling that anyone could so blithely put complete strangers to any
trouble on their behalf, for it's not a thing that would
come easily to most folks around here."

At that point in her recitation, I nodded at my
cousin, knowing exactly how she felt. Around here
we don't hold with being in debt, and accepting a
favor is simply a different way of owing someone.
Better to grant a favor than to have to ask for one,
though, so I'm sure she thanked Providence that the
situation was not the other way around.

"Our youngest is twelve, you know, and he
chafes at being pent up here on the farm, as he calls
it, so he was glad enough to go on this errand, before
his daddy got back from the fields with more chores
for him to do before suppertime.

"We could spare all the milk our thirsty visitor cared to drink, for, although folks like us seldom
have much ready cash, there is always enough to eat
on a farm, and I gave it to the lady willingly enough,
just for the pleasure of admiring her fine green riding
habit and the black felt hat with a green feather in the
band. We don't get to see colorful strangers all that
often here, and since the fancy hotel is so far away,
she was a rare sight indeed. Mostly I see other farm
wives in homemade dresses in church on a Sunday,
and I know their wardrobes by heart.

"The lady's broadcloth coat and skirt did not
count as finery to her, of course. They were only
clothes for an afternoon ride, but they probably
cost more than everything we had in the house—

certainly more than all the clothes we owned, for I made most of those myself, and I've never had a store-bought dress in my life."

Neither have I, I thought when Cousin Sarah said that. Well, I wouldn't have any use for such finery, anyhow, living out here near Sewell Mountain, but back when I was of courting age, I'd have liked the chance to put on such clothes as the ones my cousin described. Maybe a satin gown would have changed my life.

But I never danced at the Old White, and no prince ever came riding out of a storybook to take me away. I never was the beauty to draw beaux from miles around, so when I got far enough past twelve to think on leaving home to set up housekeeping, I married up with Jacob Heaster, whose folks lived near us over on the other side of Sewell Mountain. He was two years older than me, but I'd known him from church and school all my life, and though there weren't too awful many girls to choose from in our community, I reckon he could'a done worse, and maybe I could'a done better, but we soldiered on and made a family, which is all there is, when you come right down to it. The rest is just trimmings.

The war was on when I was young, but instead of bringing gallant soldiers to our area to charm the hearts of the local maidens, it took all our eligible young bucks away, killed a fair few of them, and sent back a slew of others maimed in body or spirit, so that many a young girl back then ended her days as a spinster. Lucky for both of us: Jacob wasn't but thirteen when the war commenced. He could have gone—there's some that young that did—but my Jacob did not, and so in 1870, after it was all over, I got me a husband, when many a likely-looking girl did without. At least my Zona was born too late to suffer that, though I'll wager she was pretty enough to have beaten out every other belle in the settlement.

If we moved nearer to the county town, I thought, Zona might have landed herself someone besides a poor dirt farmer. A beauty when she's young has that one chance to catch the eye of a gentleman, so I didn't object overmuch when Zona asked to spend a few weeks visiting in Richlands. Chances don't come too awful many times in life.

I was thinking back on all that, wishing Zona could have had clothes as fine as the lady's riding habit, and nodding while my cousin prattled on about what had happened that day. By and by her boy had come ambling back down the lane followed by a tall, strapping stranger.

"I hadn't seen him before," Sarah said, "but he had the look of a workingman, handsome enough, with crinkly black hair and a wide smile, but big, too, and brawny from the heavy work he did at the forge. He carried his tools in an open wooden box, and he wore a leather apron over his shirt and trousers to save them from the mud and sparks when he shod the animals. I was surprised to see a new fellow. I was expecting James Crookshanks, who owns the smithy there on the creek at Livesay's Mill, down a ways and on the other side of the Midland Trail. Crookshanks must have hired on new help quite recently, though, for I hadn't heard tell of this fellow, and from the look of him, the word of his arrival would spread among the ladies soon enough, especially if he was in need of a wife.

"He wasn't all that young, though. Thirty if he was a day, I thought, so if he didn't have a wife, he must have misplaced her. He had strong, even features and a chiseled, square-chinned face that would have looked fitten on one of those statues of Greek gods you see in the history books, but the effect was a bit tainted by his frayed and sweaty work shirt and those grimy britches, going threadbare at the knees. Either he had no one to do his washing and mending for him, or he hadn't many changes of clothes. Probably both, I thought, but he was new to the community; it wouldn't be hard for him to dazzle a hopeful young woman into doing his laundry, for he was uncommonly handsome."

I nodded, knowing exactly what Sarah meant, but even if I hadn't been a long-married woman, I wouldn't have been taken in by that fellow. There's many a woman who would not see beyond a sculptured face, but I had lived through enough hard times to know that beauty and goodness are not always the same thing—especially in a man. I wouldn't put it past such a fellow to find a plump and plain spinster, still young and foolish enough to be hopeful, and to encourage her to show her devotion by doing his mending and making him dinners. He'd get shed of her fast enough, of course, when someone better came along, but you couldn't warn a homely woman about that. It would only hurt her twice.

"Oh, he was all smiles," my cousin remembered, "for handsome people expect to be liked and welcomed, as if the pleasure of seeing them is a gift they give you. I didn't smile back, though. I don't take naturally to strangers, and besides there's many a poisonous plant that's pretty to look at.

"The burly Adonis came up to the foot of the steps, to where the horsewoman and I were standing, still grinning like a wave on a slop bucket, and right off he said how-do to the lady and me, eying the both of us, bold as brass. You could tell he didn't have much use for me, though. My worn calico house dress, my graying hair, and the little lines around my mouth told him I was too old and commonplace to be worth bothering about, though he'd be civil enough, in case he should think up a use for me later on, something to do with a needle or a washboard like as not. His eyes slid right past me, and I could see him taking the measure of that young society woman as if she were a horse he was thinking of buying, instead of the possessor of one. I smiled a little at that, because I was thinking, *She's well beyond your price range, fellow, for all your fine looks*, and I reckon the same thought must have occurred to him, because a moment later, he lowered the wick on his charm and turned away from the steps to give his attention to the stone-bruised mare. He patted her neck, spoke a few soothing words in her ear when she shied, and lifted her damaged hoof with practiced steadiness as if it were no heavier than a china teacup.

"After a few moments' inspection, he dug a little iron pick out of his assortment of tools, and poked at the stone until it came loose and fell into the dust at his feet. He stood up again, letting the horse's hoof fall back gently into the dirt, and mopped his brow with a faded bandana.

"Well, I reckon that'll set her to rights, ma'am, he declared, *but she'll need a new shoe anyhow. And she'll be tender-footed for the better part of a week, so you'd best not ride her.*

"The lady murmured her thanks. *I'd like to get her shod before I take her back, though, as a courtesy to my hosts who lent her to me. Can you take care of that?* She was accustomed to dealing with servants; you could tell.

"He nodded. *Forge is just over the way there. I'll lead her over there and get her shod quick as I can. How far from home are you?*

"She hesitated, as if it didn't seem right to confide any particulars to a strange young man who wasn't even her class to begin with. *I'm visiting some people in Lewisburg. Five miles, perhaps?*

"He mopped his brow again. *I make it closer to six, ma'am. But it would seem like more on a hot day like this. Too far for you to ride her back safely, and I don't reckon your shoe leather would stand the hike. I'd be happy to carry you home, though, ma'am, on one of Crookshanks's mounts, if you don't mind riding behind the saddle. Then, when you get to where you're staying, you can send somebody back for the mare.*

"I put a stop to that quick enough. *We'll see that you get home,* I put in before the lady could answer him. She might be dewy enough to mistake impudence for kindness, but I was not. *When the smith here is done shoeing your mare, one of my sons can take you to town in our wagon, and we can tie the horse's lead rein to the back. She should be all right on that bruised foot if you go slow enough.*

"She had the grace to blush a little, and I knew she had actually been considering taking him up on his offer, but instead she nodded at me and managed to smile. *That might be best. Thank you.*

"The likely-looking blacksmith was still standing there, holding the mare's reins and trying to think if there was anything he could say besides good-bye, when the screen door opened, and there was your Zona, a-standing there on the threshold, taking in the scene."

So that's how it happened, I thought. As random as a lightning strike and just as deadly, but painful or not I needed to hear tell of it.

"She contrived to look surprised. *I thought I heard voices out here,* she said, all innocence. Zona looked at the lady long enough to take in the style of her finery, for, as you well know, that girl was always a great one for fashion and getting gussied up. With barely a glance at the shining chestnut mare, she turned her attention to the likely-looking blacksmith, and he returned her gaze with the same toothy smile you'd see on a hound dog that had figured out that this particular cured ham was hanging low enough for it to reach.

"I confess it: I didn't like the big-eyed stare she was shooting back at him, either."

I could well imagine. My daughter, Zona, was a pert little thing, with wide hazel eyes and a strawberry blonde mane that she tied in braids, loose enough so that wings of shining hair hung down below her ears like a satin drapery. Zona needed watching—we knew that of old—but yet and still she was past twenty-one and there was only so much anybody could do to keep her in the traces. Hindsight being what it is, I wished my cousin had had a broom in her hand at that minute. I would have given anything in the world for her to have swatted Zona right back into the house, to keep her away from that man, but it was too late even then, and it would never have happened anyhow. Such a display wouldn't have been seemly in front of company, and besides the damage was already done the minute those two set eyes upon one another. Having seen her, he would find her again, same as any tomcat would. I twisted my handkerchief as I listened, wishing that fine lady had chosen someplace else to take her injured horse.

The elder cousin took up the tale again. "Zona put her hands on her hips, and gave the stranger a wry smile, eyebrows arched and eyes a-dancing. *Well, mister, I ain't seen you around here before.*

"He grinned back, with his charm at full wick again. *I ain't been here that long, missy, so I reckon that's why.*

"She tilted her head, like she was sizing him up. *Where do you hail from then, Mister . . . ?*

"He grinned, basking in the attention from a pretty young miss. *Name's Erasmus Shue, which I kind'a changed to Edward, on account of it's such a mouthful. But folks mostly call me Trout. How 'bout yourself?*

"That society lady and me, we might as well have been a couple of flies on the porch rail for all the notice those two took of us after that.

"By now Zona was well nigh smirking at him—cat-in-the-cream-jug smug, she was. *Well, Mr. Shue—the name fits the trade, I see—I am Miss Elva Zona Heaster, a visitor to my cousin's house here. How do.*

"He inclined his head, like a little mock bow. *A pleasure, Miss Heaster. It is 'Miss,' is it not? I thought so. Well, I'll tell you what. I'll have my hands full carrying this here toolbox, so if you don't mind giving me a hand with that mare, we'll walk across the pike to Crookshanks's smithy, and you can hear the story of my life. I sure would like to hear yours.*

"When he said that, Zona was off that porch and into the yard like a calf who's found the fence gap. Without a by-your-leave to me or the lady, she picked up the horse's lead rein and fell into step beside the blacksmith, and neither one of them thought to ask my permission. Not for the first time, I was sorry I'd ever agreed to let Zona come over the mountain and stay a spell with us."

Cousin Sarah couldn't have regretted that kindness more than I did, but what's done is done, and there was no use lamenting the fact, so I only asked her what happened after that.

"After that? Well, the lady handed me back the cup of milk, and she had the good manners not to make any comments about what had just gone on under our noses. She looked around her, smiling at the chickens scratching in the dirt a few yards away, and then at the rolling green hills of pasture in front of the house. *How peaceful it is here!* she said. *Nothing ever changes at all.*

"I returned her smile to be civil, and I offered to show her my flower garden while we waited for the horse to be shod, but as we walked across the grass,

I was thinking how mistaken she was. Even if you stayed in the same place and did the same thing day in and day out, everything changed, whether you noticed it or not."

Didn't I know it! Things change while your attention is taken up elsewhere, and before you know it, everything is different. Things looked like they'd stay the same forever where I was born at the other end of the county, over Sewell Mountain way, a patchwork of farms and woods, set among these hills, near about twenty miles from my cousin's farm in the Richlands. That elegant hotel was open then, over in White Sulphur Springs, same as now, but since it was clear at the other end of the county, it might as well have been the moon for all it had in common with our backwoods settlement. Back up Sewell Mountain, we raised our own food in the garden and the stock pen, and I mopped, and cooked, and scrubbed the clothes on a washboard so much that the days all ran together and I'd have to look out the window to see whether it was fall or spring. And since I sewed all the family's clothes, fashion never altered much from one year to the next around here, but things changed all right, even so.

For starters, I had lived in two different states without even crossing the road.

That was on account of the war, of course. Aside from a little set-to in Lewisburg late in the war, and a bigger one in the next county at Droop Mountain back in '63, we didn't see overmuch in the way of fighting in these parts—nothing much here worth fighting over, I reckon—but all the same, a few months before I turned fifteen, I woke up one morning and learned that I no longer lived in Virginia. Some politicians from even farther away than the Old White Hotel had taken it upon themselves to vote to make the western part of the Old Dominion into a whole separate state. I was only a young girl, and it didn't affect me none then—the grass still grew, and the chicken tasted the same on Sunday—but it taught me early on that even if you stood stock-still and did nothing at all, things could change for you completely in the twinkling of an eye. Besides that, every move you did make could work for good or ill to alter the course of your life.

Jacob and I talked a time or two about moving away from Meadow Bluff toward the other end of Greenbrier County, maybe to a farm a few miles down the pike from Lewisburg, and I'd give worlds to know what would have happened had we done that. It looked like a sensible choice back then. Poor people don't often get much in the way of choices. I don't reckon that was Jacob's fault, us being poor, and I married him young, knowing that he had no land of his own and no trade save for farming, so if I was discontent I'd have only myself to blame. I did hope, though, if we worked hard and the country recovered from the war, our fortunes would change. If they did, it wasn't for the better. By the time Jacob and I reached our midthirties, with our children most nigh grown, I knew we had about all we were ever likely to get: four acres of our own, plus what he earned working for other people.

He might have prospered if we had moved down into the valley near town, because the soil was better there, and the farms were bigger. He might have got hired on to work a goodly bit of acreage over near my cousin's place at Livesay's Mill. I told myself that the children might have had more chances in life if we left the hills, and perhaps I was right about that, but the thing to remember about chances is there's bad luck as well as good. Anyhow, I let Zona go off visiting on her own that summer.

All my cousin could tell me about the rest of

that fateful day was that an hour or so after Zona left with the blacksmith, Aunt Martha Jones's boy from over the way brought back the lady's horse, and collected the half-dollar the smith charged for shoeing it, but it was well past suppertime before Zona ever came back.

three

PERHAPS THERE WAS SOME dangerous middle
ground between being too pretty and not being
pretty enough. I had tried to say as much to Zona
once, in one of her tempers, and she didn't thank
me for it. Perhaps it was a cruel thing to say, but
it was my duty to warn her before she ruined her
future with her headstrong ways. Much as I wanted
her to be safe and happy, I never had much luck
talking sense into Zona. She was always dead set
on doing whatever she pleased, and she was always
sure that she knew best. That quarrel between us
blew over, as they always did, but I didn't hold
out much hope that she would remember my
warning, even though I had told her the plain
truth.

"You don't know beans about courting!" she
shouted at me once, in the midst of one of our set-
tos. "You grew up on a mountain farm with precious
few beaux to choose from on account of the war."

"I know well enough," I told her, though it was
true that I had never been the wild girl Zona was. I
settled on Jacob before I turned fifteen, and that was

that. "You'd have to grow up in a root cellar not to know what men are like."

Maybe you could be pretty enough for a man to want to trifle with you, but not pretty enough for him to take the trouble to keep you. Or maybe you could be pretty enough to be worth having, but not the soft, submissive, hardworking little woman that a man generally ends up choosing for a wife. Zona was pretty, and she knew it. That made her think she needn't bother to mind her ways. She saw no reason to be meek and mild, or to wait for some man to choose her. Thought she was entitled to do the choosing herself, Zona did. She was altogether too sharp and outspoken for her own good, and I told her so, but she just tossed her head, shaking that red mane of hers, and said I was being old-fashioned, and that times were changing as we headed into the new century. I don't think I was wrong, though. Times may change, but men mostly don't.

Well before Edward "Call me Trout" Shue came ambling along, with his possum grin and his storybook profile, we'd had trouble with Zona. Living way out near Sewell Mountain hadn't given her too many chances to flaunt her prettiness, but she still found ways to court trouble. She had more than her share of beaux—not enough to fill up a barn dance, as she'd have liked, but a few steady local farm boys—but they weren't to her liking. They were the quiet, steadfast fellows inclined to sow one tiny patch of wild oats afore they settled on a sensible wife and helpmeet to tend the farm. Those young men might have admired a beauty, but there were things that mattered more: a diligent, house-proud, hardworking wife who could get up at dawn to bake biscuits, knock the dirt out of work clothes with hot water and a battlin' stick, and tend the garden and the laying hens. A farmer's helpmeet who toiled too long and hard in weather and sun to keep her beauty much past twenty. Zona was nobody's idea of that kind of woman—not even her own—but sometimes a man can be dazzled by a lovely face, and get himself into scrapes he'll regret later.

To her daddy's way of thinking, she ought to have been married already. Who ever heard of a farm girl as pretty as she was reaching the age of twenty without being wed? She ought to have had more choices than a fox in a henhouse, but for whatever reason, either the young men weren't up to scratch for her or else she didn't suit them. Perhaps the truth was that, on account of her pretty face, she thought more of herself than maybe she should have, and that made her too hard to please. Or maybe she had so many choices that she just decided to postpone getting on with the rest of her life, and she resolved to enjoy every last minute of her youth and freedom. I suppose we should have been stricter with her, and insisted that she give more thought to the future. Her father seldom put his foot down where Zona was concerned. I should have hectored him into being stricter with her, but I'd had a short and lackluster youth myself, and I think I was secretly glad to see her glorying in all the fun that I never had. There's little enough time for a woman to be young in this world.

Lewisburg may be a flyspeck of a town, compared to Cincinnati or Washington or Louisville, and Meadow Bluff was barely a settlement, but I reckon Zona could find trouble in a horse trough if she put her mind to it. And find trouble she did. I don't know where she met that George Woldridge. She wanted to go sashaying off to dances and socials with all the other young people about, but though her looks might have taken her to fancy places, her social class and lack of money kept her out, more's the pity. We lived so far from town that she didn't often get a chance to go anywhere. We were glad of that and thought we were protecting her, but George Woldridge must have turned up somewhere along the way, at somebody else's place, perhaps, or else maybe she just met him on her own. She never brought him to the house. The first I heard of him was when I found her weeping into her apron on the back steps.

"What's got into you, girl?" I said. She would weep as quickly from vexation at being left out of a party as she would from turning her ankle—there was no telling what had put her out of sorts. I was edging past her down the steps with the wicker basket, more set on getting the clothes off the line before those rain clouds let loose than I was about whatever little shadow was darkening Zona's day.

"My monthlies never came," she said, hiding her face in the folds of her apron so that I had to strain to hear the words.

"Your mon—" That sat me down. I let the empty basket tumble on down the steps into the grass, and we sat there without speaking for another minute or two while I tried to take it in. The rain came and I stared out across the yard, watching clouds of mist curtain off the hills, and then pellets of rain began to fall, and the sheets got soaked on the clothesline, but I didn't register it somehow. Or maybe it just didn't seem important anymore. Zona was in the family way. That put paid to all her hopes of a storybook life and to all the fine dreams I'd had of getting to watch it happen.

"What were you thinking of doing about it?" I said after a while, when her weeping subsided some, and when I could trust my own voice to keep steady and not give way to sobs.

She shook her head. "I don't know, Mama. All

this time I've been hoping I was wrong, instead of thinking about what comes next."

"Well, do you know which of the young men . . ."

"Of course I do!" Her voice squeaked a little as outrage overtook her misery. "There ain't been but one. It's George Woldridge. He's wonderful strong, and tolerably handsome, though not too much for brains. Why, he could pick me up with one hand, as if I wasn't nothing but a doll."

I sniffed. "He ought not to have done any such thing. Besides, I don't see that any of that counts for anything. What does he do?"

"He works as a logger now and again, but lately he's been hired on at that farm down by the main road, the one on the right side on the way to town."

I knew which farm she meant. We weren't well acquainted with the people who owned it, not being kin to them or members of the same church, but we'd see them and their hired folk and their families sometimes at community gatherings. I didn't know the man she named, though.

"Can this Woldridge fellow afford to take a wife? Well, I don't suppose that matters now, does it?"

Zona's face was red and her eyes had swollen into squinty little slits, making her look more like a hobgoblin than a pretty farmer's daughter. I thought she'd better learn to govern her nerve storms better than that before trying to face down either her beau or her daddy with her tale of woe. Her beauty was her saving grace, and she'd best not try to do battle without it.

"You must pull yourself together, Zona," I said, though I was close to tears myself. "We've no choice but to tell your father about this, but what he will say about it, I don't know. Thank the Lord he's not a man of violence, or else your young man might be make-work for the undertaker. As it is, I would expect your father to go and have a talk with the fellow at once to see about arranging a wedding at the earliest possible time. Nothing fancy, of course. Just a simple service in the parlor with only family present."

Zona's eyes welled up again. "Talking to him won't do no good, Mama. He's already said he has no intention of marrying me—and I don't know that I'd want him to."

"Not want him to? I don't see that either one of you has much choice in the matter, Zona, not with a baby on the way . . ."

The tears stopped, and her nostrils flared. Zona's temper overcame her grief. "What does that matter? George doesn't own the farm. He just works there. He hardly makes enough money to feed himself, much less a ready-made family. Anyhow, I liked him well enough to begin with, but I've gone off him now. Anybody would, the way he's been acting."

"And just how has he been acting?"

"I went to him as soon as I was sure. Told him I was in the family way. And he acted like I had done it on purpose to snare him into marriage. He as much as said so. The conceited fool! As if he was a prize—him with his no-account job and a gut that'll make him look like a tusk hog in ten years if he isn't careful. He'd be lucky to have me."

"Well, Zona, it seems that he already has."

She flushed. "Anyhow, George was furious with me. Said he didn't give a tinker's dam if I had as many young'uns as a farrowing sow, he'd still not marry me. Said he'd swear before the law that the baby weren't his if I persisted. So what am I to do? Force him to marry me? Would you call that being better off?"

I just sat there on the porch steps, staring out at that curtain of cloud mist that was hiding the hills and wishing that we could pack up everything we owned and head off to the eastern end of the county, where she'd have better suitors to choose from—and wishing even more that we had done it before it was too late.

We ended up waiting a couple of days before we did anything. I needed time to think it over. Zona was more than two months gone by the time she told me her news, so a few days one way or the other wouldn't have made any difference. Finally, when she managed to calm down and I had got used to the idea, we decided to tell Jacob about his daughter's trouble. Even though it wasn't even Sunday, we cooked fried chicken with mashed potatoes and milk gravy—his favorites—for supper that evening, and topped off the meal with a lattice-crust apple pie, to make sure that he'd be in a good mood before we broke the news.

Zona let me do most of the talking. She sat there on the hassock by her daddy's chair, sweet and sorrowful, with a clean white apron over her calico dress and a pale blue ribbon in her hair, looking as pure as Mary in a manger scene. She was our only daughter, and Jacob doted on her, though he thought he didn't let it show. Like most men, he never saw beyond her pretty face, and I was sorry that I had to be the one to make him see the truth.

When I finished putting the facts to him as gently as I could, Jacob just sat there for a moment, staring as if he hadn't made sense of what I'd been saying. Finally he sighed and shook his head. "This here's the wages of that girl's wild ways, Mary Jane. It's no use coming to me with it now."

Zona wept prettily this time, with dewy tears just wetting her eyelashes and making her hazel eyes sparkle. She dabbed at her cheeks with the handkerchief she had stuffed up her sleeve. "Oh, Daddy, there must be something you can do! I don't know what I'll do if you don't help me. Mama said you could make it all right. Find me a better catch, or tell folks the baby is yours and Mama's, or make it go away somehow. Won't you please try?"

I had said no such thing, but it didn't matter. Jacob wasn't to be swayed by his daughter's wiles this time. He gave her a sorrowful look, and there were tears in his eyes, too. The last ones he would ever shed for her. "Daughter, you sowed more wild oats than a decent woman ever ought to, and I own that your mother and I ought to have reined you in well before now. We must accept our share of the blame for what has befallen you. That said, I don't know that I can find it in me to fault that George Woldridge for refusing to burden himself with damaged goods. Why should he buy the cow when the milk was given to him for free?"

Zona looked as if he'd slapped her, and although I could see her father's point of view—if she were somebody else's daughter, I might even have shared it—still, I knew he was only lashing out in the pain of his disappointment. It wasn't right to let a family member suffer, though, even if the trouble was of her own making. Men sometimes put justice ahead of loyalty, but I've never known a woman to do it.

"It seems to me that there's blame to be placed on both sides," I said.

"But her reputation . . ."

"Jacob, the man isn't an English lord." That's an expression I got from my own father. He wasn't a lord, either, but he was an Englishman. "George Woldridge is a day laborer, working now as a stockman on that farm down by the main road. I wouldn't be surprised if he drank his wages the very day he got them. He'd be doing Zona no favor by marrying her. He'd be doing his duty. That's all."

Jacob sighed again. "She ought to have had more pride than to settle for that. I had hopes for the girl."

"Maybe Zona was too free with her favors— I daresay she was—but George Woldridge did not turn down the offer, and that baby she's carrying is the proof of that, so he must shoulder his share of the blame as well. I don't see why he should be allowed to escape the consequences while poor Zona here is burdened for life, both with the child and with the loss of her reputation. Besides, if he doesn't own up to his responsibility for this child, who do you think is going to bear the cost of supporting it?"

We were, that's who, and it was just as well that Jacob be reminded of it. We had little enough money as it was—times were never easy on a hardscrabble mountain farm—and small boys of our own to provide for somehow. Zona was well past the age when she should have been married and settled, leaving us with one less child to contend with. She ought to have been a comfort that we could look to in our old age. Instead, she was proposing to present us with another mouth to feed. Jacob might have been sitting there fretting over fairness and honor, but I had no intention of standing for it, nor of taking the child, for I knew full well that Zona would have done none of the work of looking after it.

"Well, we'll think on it all some more," I said. I would think on it, anyhow. I did not intend to let her get round her father and persuade him to take it in. "Zona, you can come and help me with the washing up, and leave your daddy in peace."

Something had to be done about the situation— I had not changed my mind about that—but right then I saw that it was no use expecting Jacob Heaster to take a hand in it. That same gentle spirit—I would not call it anything harsher—that kept him out of the war as a young man would make him liable to indulge his daughter and likewise unwilling to confront the scoundrel who ruined her. Easier to blame Zona and let it go, he would think, but I was not going to stand for that, knowing full well who would bear the brunt of the burden. I would have to see to matters myself.

A few days later I left Zona to look after her youngest brothers and walked the few miles to the big farm down the road. I put on my second-best church dress and my straw bonnet, for I wanted to impress this Woldridge fellow with the fact that we were respectable people, not to be trifled with and likely to have more influence with the local authorities than he did. It was midmorning when I got there, and I hoped to find him out working in the fields or the barn by himself because I didn't want to advertise our private business to all and sundry.

When I reached the dirt lane that led into the farm, I was dusty and hot from the long walk in the sunshine, and I hoped I wouldn't meet the owner of the place, for I wanted to get this matter settled without providing any grist for the gossip mill if I could help it. The farmhouse was neat and tidy, and they must have had a couple of hundred acres in crops and pasture. If George Woldridge had been any kin to those folks, it might have been a different matter, but I knew he was just a laborer here. I doubt if the owner knew much about him, certainly not what he'd been getting up to in his time off. I wasn't going near the house; my business was with the fellows who'd likely be somewhere in the vicinity of the barn. I quickened my step, scarcely noticing anything around me, because I was busy rehearsing my set piece in my mind. The scoundrel had taken advantage of my daughter; he would not take advantage of me in an argument.

Just before I reached the door of the barn, a rangy man in overalls came out. "How do," I said. "I'm looking to have a word with George Woldridge."

The fellow squinted into the sunshine, trying to place me, but I just stood there, waiting for an answer. It wasn't any of his business what I'd come about. Finally he rubbed the stubble on his jaw and said, "Well, ma'am, last time I seen him, he was headed out to cut brush over that hill yonder."

So he was out working alone away from the farmyard. That was better. I didn't want to have to wrangle with him at the barn with long-eared hired men hanging on our every word. I thanked the fellow and headed off in the direction of his pointing, wishing that I'd had the sense not to wear my second-best church clothes instead of getting all gussied up to have words with a farmhand on a brambled hillside. Another quarter mile of walking alongside the south pasture fence got me within hailing distance of the hill, and I could see a man about a third of the way up, scything the weeds and making a brush pile.

"You! George Woldridge!"

He turned with an obliging smile plastered on his face, but it faded quickly enough. He might have recognized me, for there is some likeness between Zona and me. His mustache quivered, and he looked wildly left and right, like a coon trapped by hounds and searching for the nearest tree. Maybe he was thinking that Jacob must have come with me—surely a woman wouldn't come alone on such an errand as this. Well, he reckoned without a mother's determination there. I could tell that he figured Zona's daddy must be close by, and that a shotgun wedding was in his immediate future, or anyhow a shotgun. I hoped he wouldn't get into such a panic that he'd come after me with that scythe, and then I wished there had been somebody besides me to take him on, but I was determined to stand my ground. I'd do it alone because I had to. Zona would have been no help—like as not she would cry, or else she'd believe whatever lie he told in order to buy himself some time.

Woldridge mopped his brow with a grimy bandana, which he stuffed back into the bib of his overalls. He was a swarthy fellow, with skin coarsened by working in the sun and a gut that promised he'd run to fat sooner rather than later. I wondered what Zona had seen in him—probably nothing except the chance to have an adventure.

"I'm awful busy right now, ma'am. Gotta have this hill cleared by dark." He backed away from me, trying not to look at me at all. Instead he kept staring at the brush pile, as if his work was too important to be interrupted, which was nonsense. This was the sort of chore you gave a man to do when there wasn't much else that needed to be taken care of.

I didn't intend to have a conversation at hailing distance, so I started to thread my way up that little hill, taking care to avoid the loose stones and tree roots that might have sent me tumbling back down again. As I got close, George Woldridge tried to edge away, but I caught hold of his shirtsleeve. Since there was nobody around to see us, I figured there was nothing to stop me from making a scene. I wouldn't have wanted to, in the ordinary way of things, but if that was the only way to get the weasel's attention, I'd not shrink from it.

"Would you rather continue this discussion back at the main house with your boss listening in? Or in a court of law, perhaps?"

He sighed, knowing that he was beaten. "Have

it your own way, ma'am. Let's just walk back down the slope and into the pasture a little ways, so's you won't fall down this hill and go to blaming me for that."

"You can walk me back toward the barn," I told him. I didn't think there was any meanness in him, but I wanted people to be able to hear me scream if it came to that. When we were back on level ground and had commenced to head back to the lane, I said, "You know who I am, don't you?"

"Reckon you'd be Miz Heaster from down the road a piece."

"I am Zona's mother."

"Yes, ma'am. I figured you were. Ah . . . Zona." He hung his head. "She's a pretty little thing, I'll give her that. But the truth is that what was between us was not love and respect, but only high spirits. On both sides. We were sporting, as young people do, and I had a jar of moonshine with me, and I reckon we got carried away. I never figured she was in love with me, and I never said I cared for her. I am real sorry for her trouble, though."

"*Her* trouble?"

"Well, our trouble then, or maybe the trouble of whoever is the child's father. It could be mine—I'll not deny that—but we can't be sure of that, any more than we can be sure which tom fathered the barn cat's latest litter. I was not the first with Zona, and mayhap I wasn't the last, either. I think she got tired of me after a while. I don't think I had enough airs and graces to suit Miss Zona. Not enough money, neither. So I don't see what I can do about it."

I began to wish that I'd brought, if not Jacob himself, then at least his shotgun. I drew myself up. "Well, sir, I had hoped that you'd be man enough to accept your responsibility in this matter. I expected you to be a gentleman by instinct if not by breeding."

He shrugged. "If you're talking about marriage, Miz Heaster, I don't reckon that would solve anybody's problem. I don't have two nickels to rub together, much less the wherewithal to be supporting a wife and baby. And I'm not persuaded that Zona would want such a union any more than I do. She was awful cold toward me, last time I seen her. 'Course I said some things in the heat of the moment that were not altogether kind."

"I heard."

"Well, like I said, I am uncommonly sorry that this has happened, but I don't know what I can do about it, ma'am. I don't think you'd want to see a grandchild of yours raised in poverty without a fixed home."

I wouldn't, but that didn't mean I was going to let him off the hook so easily. "Do you have any kinfolks that might be willing to take the baby? Your mother and father, for instance?"

He shook his head. "None. They both passed a few years back. I have an older sister that got married and moved to Ohio. Or maybe it was Indiana. I ain't heard from her in a couple of years. We weren't what you'd call close."

We had reached the barnyard by then, and I had run out of questions for George Woldridge. I could see as plain as day that he was like a stud Angus bull—good for making babies, and not for any other earthly thing. He hadn't the wit or the drive to make anything of himself beyond what he already was—a hired hand on a backwoods farm. For all I knew he might be a drinker or a gambler in the bargain, for there was certainly no evidence of self-discipline about him. And as a husband for Zona, he could prove worse than no husband at all. A woman can suffer mightily at the hands of a man who does not love her, and even if he did love her, what future was there in being tied to a laborer, trailing after him from farm to farm until her youth was worn away by childbearing and hardship? And what kind of life would it be for a child of such a couple, raised poor in a loveless home? Maybe marriage wasn't the right answer, after all.

I was thinking all this in a practical frame of mind, not worrying anymore about what the neighbors would think. I loved my Zona and wanted the best for her in this world, even if she had been foolish and wild. Zona was beautiful; she might not keep her bloom for very much longer, but as she looked now, she could certainly do better than poor, hapless George Woldridge. At least, she could do better than him if she didn't have the encumbrance of a child.

I set my mind to considering that problem as I walked home that evening. There could be no question of doing away with the baby. I knew that there were women in every settlement who could give an expectant mother a potion of bitter herbs in whiskey that would cause her to slip the child. They say that pennyroyal will end a pregnancy if it is taken in the proper dosage. But we were God-fearing people, and I would not have that sin on Zona's head or on mine. If the Lord willed my daughter to miscarry, I would not grieve for it overmuch, but if He did not, then the child must live and a home be found for it.

But not with us.

Zona had not expressed any longing for the baby. She seemed to think of it as other folk might think of a fever blister: a painful annoyance to be got rid of and then forgotten. That, as much as anything, told me that she had no love for George Woldridge. Perhaps she might change her mind when she was further along or after the child was born, but I thought that Zona wanted her youth and freedom more than she wanted a baby. She never took an interest in her much younger brothers, never wanted to treat them like baby dolls or play games with them. When I was her age, I had a husband and babies already, and I never thought of wishing them away for any other kind of life, but we were edging up to a new century now, and perhaps times had changed. I don't say the change was for the better, but I could see that young people weren't the same as back in my day.

I didn't see any point in talking any more about it to Jacob. He'd as lief pretend that the whole thing had never happened, but even so, it wasn't my decision to make alone. Zona had to be consulted, for it was her business more than mine, and she was no child herself anymore. After an indifferent supper that night, cooked by Zona, who isn't much use in the kitchen, we settled the rest of the family down for the night, and the two of us sat up by the fire, talking until it burned low.

"I went to that farm with the intention of badgering George Woldridge into marrying you," I told her, "but now that I have seen him, I'm having second thoughts about it."

Zona sniffed. "I should think you are." She was brushing her long strawberry blond hair until it shone in the firelight like a tongue of flame. "George is about as useless as teats on a mule."

"There's no call to be coarse, Zona. It behooves you more than ever now to act like a lady."

She made a face at me. "Well, if I married up with old George, nobody would care what I said ever again. I'd rather die than spend the rest of my life with old ham-handed, slow-coach George."

"Then it would be no kindness to him or the child to push for such a union. That leaves us to decide what we ought to do instead."

Zona yawned and stretched. Then she began to

braid her hair for the night. "Anything but raise it as George Woldridge Jr., I reckon. I don't much care."

"I see that. Perhaps you ought to give some thought as to what is best for your child."

"Farm it out, then, I reckon. Like folks do if they can't bear to drown a litter of pups. They find them a home."

"And I suppose you're expecting me to do that?"

"Well, Mama, I sure don't know anybody in want of a young'un. My friends are mostly looking to get married and have children of their own, or else they're happy just as they are. I wouldn't have any idea how to find a home for it."

"No. I didn't suppose you would, Zona. I just wanted to make sure that it was all right with you if I went ahead and took care of the matter myself."

"I hoped you would, Mama. You don't even have to tell me what you did with it. When the time comes, just do what needs to be done."

A few weeks later, I told the family that I was going back to visit our kin and neighbors back up Sewell Mountain way, and I took the buckboard and journeyed alone. I knew folks up there well enough to know which women could keep a secret and which ones could not. I laid out the problem to the three ladies whose kin I knew, those I trusted most not to gossip about our trouble, and with their help, it only took a little more than a day to find a childless older couple who were glad of the chance to raise a child. It was all arranged, and the bargain sealed with a handshake and promises on both sides.

On November 29, 1895, Zona gave birth to the baby back at our farm with Dr. Lualzo Rupert attending, and me helping as much as I could. We all called him Dr. Lualzo because his father, old Dr. Cyrus Rupert, had sired fifteen children, and four of them became doctors. The rest went elsewhere to practice, but Dr. Lualzo married a daughter of the Reverend Sam Black, and he had taken over the doctoring for the Sewell Mountain communities when his father passed away some five years back, at the venerable age of eighty-three. Because the law required it, Dr. Lualzo registered the birth at the courthouse in Lewisburg, but none of our neighbors was likely to find out about that. Ten days later, when the weather turned mild for a spell and the child was fit enough for travel, I wrapped it in its quilt, and put it into a white oak basket. Just at sunup I hitched up the buckboard again, to take it up the mountain. Jacob and Zona were both awake and stirring in the kitchen as I made ready to leave, but neither of them came out to see the baby or to say good-bye.

We never saw or heard tell of that baby again.

four

LAKIN, WEST VIRGINIA

1930

THE SUNNY PARLOR on the ground floor of the hospital had been furnished with small oak tables, ladder-back chairs, and an old mahogany sideboard holding a battered silver-plated tea urn and a mismatched assortment of china cups and saucers. This was the patients' tea room, a quiet place for the least disturbed of the inmates to gather in the afternoons to pass the time and practice normal conversation again in anticipation of their eventual release. For an hour two or three times a week, they pretended to be normal, or at least proved that, like many people out in the world, they could hide the fact that they weren't.

Some of those who attended the tea were not yet able to assume a veneer of normalcy, but the staff hoped that they might gain some benefit from the attempt, or at least from watching their fellow patients. These lost souls sat away from the others, weeping softly or muttering to themselves, and some simply stared at a patch of bare wall oblivious to the company around them. But enough of the others made an effort to emulate polite conversation to make the exercise worthwhile, and so the doctors encouraged the more promising—or prosperous—patients to attend.

James P. D. Gardner, erstwhile attorney-at-law, sat alone at one of the little tables, as oblivious to those around him as a man waiting for a train. He was not delusional, simply uninterested. He could force himself to socialize for business purposes, but among his fellow sufferers he saw no value in making the effort.

Once or twice he lifted his teacup, thought better of it, and set it down again. He was wearing the green cotton uniform of an inmate, but his posture and demeanor clothed him in an illusory suit and tie, which anywhere but here would be his second skin. Even after all this time, he would occasionally reach a hand up to his throat to adjust the cravat that wasn't there.

He glanced at the end tables on either side of the Victorian sofa—both were bare, in need of dusting. Why didn't they provide newspapers or magazines in the parlor, so that he would have an excuse to ignore the other patients? He had never been adept at small talk even among like-minded colleagues, and experience with the people here had taught him that an ordinary, if strained, conversation could suddenly go off the rails when the other person began to babble about Jesus or started to pick imaginary insects off themselves. He shuddered. Really what could one say to them? Even among the tolerably functional inmates, there were so many who could not even read or write that he was at a loss to find any common ground at all with them. Some had never traveled more than five miles in their lives until they were hauled away to be shut up in this brick fortress with their demons. Should he attempt to explain the finer points of property law to a sharecropper?

There was one interesting patient here, but she didn't seem inclined to be sociable, either. She was a fine-boned woman in her early twenties, he thought, with coppery brown hair and the lightish skin that goes with it. Back home, people called someone of her coloring a redbone, light enough to pass for white if you weren't particularly observant. Her eyes were magnified by wire-rimmed spectacles, and she said little, but occasionally as she read she glowed, lit from within by a tremulous smile. She was always serene and solitary, sitting in the patients' parlor with a large leather-bound book in her lap. He had taken a peek at it once, when she had set it down to go to the lavatory, and discovered that it was *The Complete Works of William Shakespeare*. He only knew her name because it was written on the flyleaf of the book: Kathleen Davies. She had a private room on the first-floor hall of the asylum, one of those assigned to well-to-do patients, or those considered well enough to be discharged in the foreseeable future. Each first-floor room had a narrow metal-frame bed, a braided rag rug, a wood dresser and mirror, and a window that looked out on the front lawn of the asylum. First-floor patients were allowed to wear ordinary clothes, and, provided they behaved rationally, they were not subjected to the harsh treatments that more deranged patients endured: icy baths and immobilizing restraints.

Gardner coveted one of those first-floor rooms. He thought he might spend a little more time observing Miss Davies, and then he might try to engage her in conversation to see how she managed to get assigned there. He wondered if she was an educated woman, and if there was some underlying defect lurking beneath her calm exterior. Because she was quite pretty and apparently sane, he was loath to let go of his illusions of her by making her acquaintance and discovering that she was as mad as the others.

Well, after all, what sort of society could he expect here? The Lakin State Hospital for the Colored Insane—lumped together by race as well as by mental defect. He supposed that if the deranged were segregated by education and rank instead of by skin color, he might have found some congenial souls in their number to pass the time with. He had associated with white men in the practice of law, even defended some, and conversing with them in the way of business had never posed any particular problem for him. As long as they confined themselves to discussing professional matters, they spoke a common language. He was as clever as they, and just as formally educated as most of them, because few of his colleagues had attended law school. Most aspiring lawyers simply apprenticed under a practicing attorney and then sat for the bar exam. In his profession he was their equal. Their respect for him might have been grudging, but it was respect all the same.

Well, *there* was a sign of madness, he told himself, scowling at his folly: thinking even for a private fleeting moment that color would be no obstacle among gentlemen. But there had been a time . . . forty years ago, before the century turned, and when he was still shy of forty himself. Back then it hadn't seemed to matter quite so much about color and pedigree. People didn't make such a great distinction between the races, somehow. There wasn't yet a colored part of town, even. It was a small enough place for folks to know one another, and that helped. He'd had a few white clients and some white neighbors, and everyone just got on with the business of living. There were unwritten rules, of course. You knew your place, and you didn't overstep your bounds, but if you behaved according to expectations, most people were decent. It was generally the lower-class whites you had to watch out for—those who were afraid of you because the accident of their white skin was the only thing that allowed them to think they outranked anybody. They were afraid of losing that advantage. He supposed that rich white people already felt so superior to everybody else that they scarcely noticed the difference between their inferiors, regardless of color. Some were kind and others not, but they were that way regardless. He had worked hard, and never gave anybody cause to complain about him. Never really trusted anybody, either, but better lonely and safe than careless and ruined.

Gardner had even thought that race might matter less and less after 1900, as the world progressed. Had it been a precursor of his madness back then to believe that? Would he have been any madder if he had conversed with hallucinated angels?

The odd thing was that while the world did progress—producing airplanes, telephones, an annihilating modern war, and ever faster and more elaborate automobiles—the racial divide seemed to grow wider with each passing year. Ordinary white people suddenly developed their own form of madness, although it was so universal that it passed for normality: they became unaccountably afraid of their dark-skinned neighbors. New laws were passed and old ones more stringently enforced, and there were groups of hooded men who frightened people into obeying strictures without the sanction of the law at all. It seemed to happen quickly—although perhaps he had simply been preoccupied elsewhere. In the early days of the new twentieth century, he'd had a new wife and a great many clients to tend to concerning matters of law that scarcely ever changed: deeds, wills, and mortgages. His clients were mostly of his own race, but it really didn't matter to a will or a mortgage whether you were black, white, or purple—the legal forms never varied. And while he'd had his head down, toiling over the fine print, the world had turned into a harsher place, one he hardly knew at all.

And now, here he was, despite all his intelligence and prosperity, betrayed by the shadows in his mind and banished to the colored madhouse, as if the patients' common race made for homogeneity. As if, camouflaged by brown covering, his culture and education had become invisible, so that he and the sharecroppers were indistinguishable.

The one possible blessing here at the asylum at Lakin was that the physicians and staff members were also of the African race. From one month to the next, you could almost forget that white people even existed, for you never saw one. Perhaps that segregation was best for everyone in these days of ever stricter and stranger laws of racial separation. Even a gentleman lawyer, provided he was a man of color, might be neglected or treated brutally if he were placed in a facility with white patients, one that was staffed by white attendants who might resent his achievements. In such a place he might be the least and last in everything, considered inferior even to the lowliest toothless old madwoman, provided she was white, but here he could count himself a prince.

He was sitting at a table with a clear view of the double windows overlooking the front lawn. The asylum was built on the crest of a hill—or what passed for one in this flat western end of the state—but he could only see as far as the other side of the road. Here on the ground floor of the building, the trees blocked the rest of the view entirely, so that even the riverside fields beyond the trees and the bare cliffs on the Ohio side of the river were hidden from him.

Out of the corner of his eye, he saw a teacup set down opposite him, and he stiffened, ready to retreat, until he saw who had put it there. He nodded cordially to the white-coated young man who had just sat down. "Good afternoon. It's Dr. Boozer, is it not? My neighbor and my jailer."

"Just your neighbor, I hope, sir." The physician nodded and smiled. "Well remembered." Perhaps he had intended the remark to pass as merely a social pleasantry, but the difference in their positions here tinged his words with the hint of a clinical examination: *Patient is able to recall recent events and remembers people he has previously encountered.* Gardner found himself unaccountably annoyed at being evaluated, even as mildly as this.

"It was you who spoke to me upstairs late the other night, Dr. Boozer. I do indeed remember. You'll find that my memory is excellent. I could recite you case law by the hour, until they'd have to put *you* in a cold bath to calm your fits."

Now, in the light of afternoon, he could see the young physician's features more clearly, and they were not as he had expected them to be: he had assumed that Dr. Boozer would have skin like yellow pine, rather than the rich brown mahogany he did possess. That observation inspired a stray thought, a wry mental observation that, while the world prized darkest mahogany in wood and scorned yellow pine as an unsuitable material for fine furniture, their judgment of the worth of human coloring was quite the reverse. Even he had not been immune; he pictured the lovely face of Alice and pushed the thought away again, before he gave way to emotion, which in here was not termed grief but melancholia.

The doctor's hair was close-cropped above a high forehead, and he sported a little Charlie Chaplin mustache, which Gardner thought rather silly, but with his cleft chin and those well-proportioned features, he would be considered handsome by both races. He looked young—everybody looked young to Gardner these days—and yet he had qualified as a doctor. Perhaps it had not been easy for him, but at least it had been possible. When it came to succeeding in this world, even *shades* of skin color mattered. He'd had such an advantage himself, thanks to his light-skinned mother. Lighter skin often meant greater respect and privilege accorded to its possessor—by both races, oddly enough. He had—not altogether unconsciously—chosen wives as light as himself so that this advantage might be conferred upon their children, but no children ever came. He was alone now, and at age sixty-three he seemed likely to remain so for the rest of his life. Melancholia? Or simply a clear evaluation of the facts?

He wondered if the doctor had married yet. Surely not, since he lived in a room on the same hall as his patients. He had no place to bring a bride and set up housekeeping, but perhaps he had left a wife at home somewhere, with his parents or hers, until he could arrange for lodging. He supposed it would be considered impertinent for him to ask. At any other place they might have been equals, he and this slick Yankee doctor, or else his own greater age would have given him the social advantage between them, but here, by reason of his mental instability, he was merely a patient in a green cotton uniform, while the fine-featured young physician was a panjandrum.

He eyed the doctor with the disfavor of one who will not tolerate condescension, no matter how tactfully disguised. "I suppose I should be honored by your presence. And what brings you here this afternoon, sir? Was it your turn to attend this little boiree, or did you lose the coin toss up in the staff sitting room?" Sarcasm was as close as he ever came to wit, but the physician smiled politely at the attempt and ventured a sip of tepid tea.

"Actually, I wanted to talk to you, Mr. Gardner. One of the attendants told me you generally turn up at these afternoon affairs, and I confess that I find you most interesting."

Gardner raised an eyebrow. "You find *me* interesting? In this place? You astonish me, Doctor. Why, among this lot, I think myself *a snowy dove trooping with crows*. You could pass the time here with a modern-day Prophet Isaiah, hear tales of visiting demons from a terrified old harridan, or perhaps you might even persuade the stony woman in that corner yonder to tell you what made her slit her baby's throat and dump him in the hog pen. I fear that as far as diversions go, I am meager fare compared to such a feast of strangeness."

Dr. Boozer smiled again. "It isn't madness that intrigues me. That's common enough around here, and you do get used to it, you know. There's even a certain sameness to it after a while. But your intellect is a rarity here. You quoted Shakespeare—once just now and twice the other night when we spoke. And in general you talk like a gilt-edged, calf-bound book of sermons. That interests me. You are such a singular fellow here that I was afraid I had hallucinated you myself."

Gardner ignored the doctor's self-deprecating chuckle and pounced on the literal statement. "Hallucinated me? Do I worry you? Am I proof to you that intelligence and education are no protection against madness? Are you afraid you might be next?"

James Boozer shook his head. "Just a figure of speech, Mr. Gardner. And don't tell me to *mend my speech, lest it mar my fortune*, because I'm the fellow in the white coat here. I think I am safe from a charge of madness."

"I expect you are. Sanity seems to be mostly a consensus of opinion, anyhow, and since your opinion counts for much around here, you could probably get away with anything short of setting fire to the curtains."

"I would have said the same about a prominent attorney, Mr. Gardner. So tell me: *What are you in for?*"

five

❨ Zona and Trout ❩

GREENBRIER COUNTY, WEST VIRGINIA

1896

I DIDN'T LIKE ANYTHING about it. Not one thing.

After Zona met that slick young stranger—when he came to shoe the society lady's lame horse—and then walked him back across the road without a by-your-leave to them that she was staying with, she and that blacksmith fellow—Edward or Trout or whatever Mr. Shue was pleased to call himself on a given day—had taken to one another like moths to a candle, and everybody said what a handsome pair they made: him tall, dark-haired, and square-jawed and her a porcelain doll with hair like sparks from a flint, dainty and daring all at once.

But it was only September when she met this new beau, and—although she seemed to have forgotten it entirely—on the twenty-ninth of November last, Zona had been busy birthing the bastard of that no-account farmhand named George Woldridge. At least he was no longer a shadow in our lives. He went off logging in the summer before the child came into the world, and he must have drifted on somewhere else from there, because he never turned up again around here. He was probably afraid he'd be made to pay maintenance on his by-blow if he stayed around. Nobody missed him, either, least of all Zona. I think we were all relieved that he didn't have a change of heart and suddenly declare an interest in his son, but he did not. He went off and left it as if it had been no more than an old shirt that he couldn't be bothered to come back for. Much as I deplored his tomcat attitude toward his child, I was glad to see him go.

That baby was better off without either of his parents troubling themselves about him, and after I delivered him to the older couple who wanted him, I never said a word to remind anyone that he even existed. Some things are best forgotten.

But forgetting a mistake once you've made it is one thing, and rushing headlong to make that same mistake again is quite another. To my mind, that's just what Zona was fixing to do. She made no bones about the fact that she was besotted with Crookshanks's new blacksmith, and he was happy to let her fawn over him as much as she liked. In a few hastily written letters, Zona told me all about the budding courtship, which her hostess, my cousin Sarah, approved of no more than I did. Sarah wrote that they made eyes at each other on her porch, and grinned and giggled between themselves until you'd have thought they were drunk. Zona was forever slipping across the road, when she ought to have been somewhere about the place getting on with her chores in payment for her kinfolk's hospitality.

Everybody knew that James Crookshanks would not allow a workman to go off lollygagging with a sweetheart during working hours, but he couldn't very well stop Zona from bringing a packed lunch to Mr. Shue, or forbid her from standing just outside the forge and watching them at work. Many a young boy and a few old men used to congregate there at the smithy when they had nothing better to do. Watching a red-hot horseshoe come out of the furnace and take shape under hammer and tongs was a marvel to behold on a sleepy country afternoon. Crookshanks couldn't very well forbid Zona from watching without making the rest of the crowd scatter as well, and since the old men, at least, might be customers from time to time, chasing them away would have been bad for business.

I expect the smith wished that Jacob and I would come to Livesay's Mill and cart our headstrong daughter off home so's his hired man could work in peace, but Zona had never listened to me, and I think Jacob lost interest in trying to control her when she broke his heart carrying on with George Woldridge. Or perhaps he hoped that the experience had taught her a lesson, and that she might have developed enough sense to mend her ways on her own. She hadn't, though. Perhaps she thought the worst of her misfortunes had come and gone. Anyhow, if the Brown cousins (my mother's people) had turned her out of the house, she'd have found someplace else to stay soon enough. One good thing about her staying with kin was that they kept me apprised of what Zona was up to.

When evening came and Mr. Shue finished work for the day, most times he would hightail it straight across the road to their place, where Zona would be waiting on the porch, big-eyed and breathless as if it had been five months since they parted instead of five hours. Being hospitable people, John and Sarah would let him sit supper with the family when the food would stretch that far and if they couldn't get out of it, for Zona would promise to do all her chores and half of everybody else's if only they would allow him to stay. She always managed to make her plea with him in earshot so that her cousins couldn't very well refuse without giving offense. She never made good on her promises of extra work, though. That didn't surprise me.

It might have gladdened folks' eyes to see such a handsome couple, devoted and inseparable, if they had been two dewy young people finding love for the first time, but that wasn't the way of it. Zona's past was hardly past at all, and when I came to hear of their carrying-on, I thought it more than likely that a downy fellow on the make like Mr. Shue had sown a few crops of wild oats back wherever he had come from.

Finally on Sunday, the first of November, after many stern letters from me and a couple of scribbled postscripts from her father, Zona did consent to bring her new beau out to Meadow Bluff in a buggy borrowed from Crookshanks. They had fixed it up to get married by then, and now that there was noth-ing to be done about it, she came swanning up to Meadow Bluff to show him off. They were certainly a well-matched pair, as far as looks went, but there was an uneasiness about them that made me wonder what we weren't being told, and maybe even what they weren't telling each other. They had only been acquainted for all of a month by then, and if ever a thing looked too good to be true, it was that sleek and smirking groom-to-be, over thirty if he was a day, and trying to act like love's young dream. He was a sight too old for calf-love, if you was to ask me, which nobody did.

Zona was smug about her new beau, as pleased with herself as if she'd discovered gold coins in the chamber pot, but I was afraid that instead she had just come upon exactly what you'd expect to find in a chamber pot. Time would tell.

I brought the matter up with them that evening at the dinner table, thinking I might learn enough about the handsome Mr. Shue to make some inquiries about his past. I'd had enough of no-account men with less than honorable intentions taking advantage of my daughter. If Zona would not look out for herself, then it fell to me to do it for her.

"Where do you come from, Mr. Shue?" I asked him, holding the plate of biscuits just out of his reach.

He gulped down a mouthful of mashed potatoes and glanced warily at Zona, but I just sat there staring him down and holding out the biscuit plate until he answered.

Finally he muttered, "Droop Mountain, ma'am, over in the next county."

Pocahontas County, then. Droop Mountain had been the site of that battle back in '63, but the place hadn't amounted to much before or since, and it was more than twenty miles north of Lewisburg, mostly woods and fields and a few scattered farms. "Hillsboro lies over that way," I said. "Are your people from here?"

He had managed to snare a biscuit, and was trying to focus all his attention on smothering it with butter *and* honey. "They hailed from Augusta County, over in Virginia, and before that from somewhere back in Pennsylvania, but they settled in Hillsboro when I was still a young'un. Just lately, though, I moved on from about six miles this side of Hillsboro. Like I said: Droop Mountain."

"Y'all farm there then?"

I would have appreciated some help in the conversation from Jacob or Zona so that my table talk wouldn't have sounded so much like the interrogation it was, but they were both staring down at their plates, embarrassed at me being so forthright with a guest, and the young'uns were too busy stuffing down their food to hear a word anybody said. They had taken Mr. Shue's measure as a glutton, and decided that they had best eat quickly before he cleared every dish on the table.

Finally Zona spoke up. "His daddy is a blacksmith, too. That's how come he's so good at what he does. Been learning the trade all his life, near 'bouts."

It seemed strange to hear a man over thirty being praised for taking after his daddy. That might account for half of his life, being born with his father's knack with tools and then learning the trade while he was growing up, but what had he been doing with himself since then?

"You only just got to the Richlands this past month, I hear, when Mr. Crookshanks took you on at the smithy. So you were still living with your folks up until then?"

Mr. Shue and Zona glanced at each other, and I'll bet they were both wishing that the other one had the wit to change the subject or the presence of mind to think up a plausible lie, but Zona knew me well enough to be sure that sooner or later I'd have an answer to my question, or else we would all stay sitting there until I did. She shrugged at him as if to say, *Best to get it over with.*

"I had been out on my own a good while, ma'am," he said, through a mouthful of biscuit, "what with one thing and another, but then a year or two ago I did move back in with the folks. This is a mighty good dinner, Miz Heaster. I surely do admire a woman who's an excellent cook."

"I can't think what you'd want with Zona then," I said, "for it's about all she can do to boil water."

He laughed politely at this, as if I had been making a joke, but it was true enough, and he might as well know it. "I reckon she can learn," he said. "A smart young lady like her. Especially since the talent runs in the family. Maybe you could teach her a few things."

Zona never could stand to be criticized. Her frown showed how nettled she was by my remarks, and by Mr. Shue's lack of trust in her ability. In her anger she forgot herself. "I'm good enough at canning vegetables and I'm able to put up preserves as well as anybody, Mama, and you know it." Then she cast a cold eye on her intended. "Besides, I'll bet I can cook as well as Mr. Shue's *other* wives!"

The silence that followed that remark was like the one that comes in a thunderstorm after the shattering sound of a lightning strike close by. For a couple of seconds it seemed like nobody even breathed, much less chewed. Even the youngest one sat still, his little cheeks bulging, not really understanding the conversation, which the boys mostly hadn't been listening to, but knowing from the posture of the grown-ups that something was amiss. We were all staring at Shue and Zona, waiting to hear the rest.

After a little more silence, Mr. Shue looked up with a sorrowful expression, his dark eyes glistening. "Zona was referring to the fact that I lost my precious wife a year ago in an accident, ma'am, though I seldom speak of it."

"You have my sympathy, sir," I said, which wasn't strictly true, because if he was that recently bereft, he had no call to contemplate getting himself hitched again. "How did she pass?"

He paused a good long while, thinking out what to say. "An accident, like I told you. She was out walking one afternoon, and we reckon she tripped over something and hit her head on a rock when she fell. By the time we found her, she was gone."

"Well, that accounts for one. But I believe my daughter here said *wives*. So what about the rest of them? Are they dead, too?"

He gave Zona a look that could've melted an iron bar, and I'll bet he was regretting confiding in her about so much of his personal business, but after a moment, he reined in his temper again and the anger passed. After he took another swig of coffee, he had recovered himself enough to answer me in civil tones. "There was just the one other, ma'am, and Lord knows she's still alive and kicking, but we parted ways nearly ten years ago, and I ain't hardly seen her since. Just a youthful mistake, that was."

Youthful? I didn't say anything out loud, but I was ciphering in my head fast enough. If he was around thirty-three or thirty-four years of age now, then ten years ago he'd have been at least twenty-three. When I was that age, I'd been married a few years and birthed our oldest boy, Alfred, already. I don't remember feeling particularly youthful back then, either, toiling on the farm from sunup until dark and taking care of a fractious young'un besides. It seemed to me that this slick fellow had precious little to show for a life that was nearly half over, for the Scripture says that the life of a man is threescore years and ten.

So Mr. Edward Trout Shue had been in possession of another wife before the one who had recently died. I reckoned that if she was still alive, but they had *parted ways*, it meant they had been through a divorce, and I wondered which of them had transgressed to the point of making that happen. Him, likely as not. If Zona had a lick of sense, she'd try to find out the circumstances behind that—from someone other than him. Butter wouldn't melt in his mouth, but there was bound to be another side to the story. However, Zona had a mulish look that told me she wouldn't hear a word against him, and the more I tried to get her to use cold common sense in the matter, the more she was going to dig her heels in and refuse to consider anything concerning his past except what she heard from him directly.

I got a little time alone with her in the kitchen after that, when we were washing up the plates and putting away the leftover food from dinner, what little there was of it. "He told you he'd had two wives already?" I asked Zona, handing her the chicken platter to dry. I tried not to sound upset, just interested, because if you got Zona's back up, she wouldn't tell you anything.

She shrugged. "Well, he told me early on about Lucy, the one that died last year. There's no shame in that, is there? He said he thought his heart would be forever in the grave with her, until he met me. Said I was his healing angel."

I was thinking that the wound couldn't have been all that deep if he was over it in only a year, but some men cannot bear to be alone, or maybe they just can't look after themselves. I didn't offer any opinion about that, though. "What about the other one?"

Zona glanced back at the open door, but the men had gone outside. "Well, I don't believe he intended to tell me about her, for it looks bad, him having a divorce in his past. I expect he was afraid that he'd lose me if I found out all that about his former life."

So he should have, I thought, but I wouldn't find out anything else about him if I made Zona feel she had to defend him. She was as touchy as a scalded cat at the best of times, so I had to swallow my censure and listen as silently as I could while she prattled on.

"I think he meant to keep it dark that there had

been another wife before his precious Lucy." She laughed, and reached for another plate to dry. "But he didn't have much choice in the matter."

"How was that?"

"Well, last week when we went down to the courthouse in Lewisburg to get the marriage license, who should we meet but *her*?"

I nearly dropped the plate I'd just taken out of the dishwater. "You met his former wife in the courthouse? What was she doing there?"

Zona's eyes sparkled with mischief. "Why, would you believe it? The very same as him! It turns out that after they parted, she had got herself trained to be a schoolteacher, and then she moved here to Greenbrier County to work. But once she got here she met some fellow over in Falling Spring, where she settled, and they fixed it up to get married, too. Funny, she wasn't calling herself Mrs. Shue anymore. She had gone back to her maiden name, which was Cutlip. Allie Cutlip—that's her name. I heard her introducing herself to some other woman there. But soon she's going to be Mrs. Todd McMillion. Once I figured out who she was, I listened as hard as I could."

"How did your fiancé feel about that, Zona?"

She shrugged. "Oh, I don't reckon he cared. He was shaken when he spied her as we came to the clerk's office, and that's when he let it slip to me who she was, but after that he barely glanced at her. They parted ten years ago, so it's all over and done with. Anyhow, she's at least half a dozen years older than me, and not a patch on me for looks."

Zona looked like the cat in the cream jug when she said that, but I didn't like the sound of any of it. *Come a time, there'll be a girl ten years younger than you*, I thought. "And how did the first Mrs. Shue feel about seeing her former husband?"

Zona smiled. "She wasn't best pleased to see him, I'll tell you that. She acted thunderstruck when she first caught sight of him, and I guess her groom-to-be had heard about Trout, too, 'cause he clenched his fists and got all red in the face. He came over and told Trout he'd better stay away from them, and from Gertie, too. I thought the clerk was going to have to call a peace officer to calm them down."

"Who is Gertie?" I said, willing my voice to keep steady, but I felt like shying those plates against the farthest wall. Instead of unraveling his past, I was just hearing it get more and more knotted up.

"Gertie? That's his daughter. She must be a big girl now, nigh on ten, but he don't never see her, so I'll never be bothered with her."

I didn't like the sound of that, either, but it wouldn't do to let Zona know that. "What a thing to happen as you're getting your marriage license!" I said. "Seeing your former wife about to marry another, and then nearly being made to fight in the courthouse. Didn't Mr. Shue seem put out by all that?"

"No, I told you, it didn't seem to bother him much. It's ancient history to him, I reckon. When he first caught sight of her, he didn't seem too happy to see her. They didn't talk or hug or nothin'. After she got her new beau calmed down, she did start over toward us like she wanted to say something to me, now I come to think of it, but the clerk called us over to the desk just then, and after we got our papers, Trout hustled me away. I didn't want to talk to that old frump anyhow. She was probably jealous. Trout said she wasn't a very good wife, and that's why he left her."

"But he had a daughter with her, you said. Surely he wants to keep in touch with the child?"

"I don't see why he should. I reckon by now he barely knows her."

"And what about *your* child, Zona? Does your intended husband know about that?"

She stared at me as if I'd taken leave of my senses. "Tell him about that mistake of George Woldridge's? Not likely! It's no business of his, is it?"

"Most men would want to know about it. A bride having a past . . . that's not something you want him to find out later from somebody else."

"He won't find out! And if we're to have the wedding here in Meadow Bluff, you'd best see that all of those long-eared old cats around here don't go talebearing to Trout at the reception."

I sighed. "A marriage lasts a lot longer than a day, Zona. And it seems to me that the more time that passes before he does find out, the worse it would be."

"Well, then you'd best see that he doesn't find out, Mama, so be careful who you let on to about the wedding. I figure that what Mr. Edward Trout Shue doesn't know about me won't hurt him. And if he ever does find out after we're married, it'll be too late to matter."

I was afraid that Mr. Edward Trout Shue might have felt exactly the same way about his own past. It seemed likely to me that there was another side to the story of his former life as well, but it was plain that Zona hadn't questioned it, and when she went on to talk about the wedding plans, I let her run on about it to her heart's content, but I didn't contribute much to the conversation because my thoughts were elsewhere.

It was already plain to me that Mr. Shue was the spitting image of trouble, and that my girl would likely come to regret becoming wife number three.

I said as much to Jacob that night, as I was brushing down my hair, getting ready to braid it up for the night. Mr. Shue had finally taken his leave of us about dusk, and Zona insisted on going back with him to the cousins' house, for she vowed that she could not be parted from her beloved for an entire week until his next day off, this coming Sunday. They did promise, though, to come back next Sunday again for dinner, to bring us more news about the wedding plans. They were getting married up here in Meadow Bluff at our little Methodist church, Soule Chapel, and they said they planned to invite a few folks over from the Richlands, since they intended to live there after they were married, close to his work at the smithy.

I had always wanted to see my daughter properly married in a ceremony at our home church, but in the end, the prospect of Zona's wedding gave me no joy whatsoever. I just wished that I could stop them from doing it at all, for I didn't think there was a church in the world holy enough to bless that union into happiness and peace.

"That girl is riding for a fall, Jacob," I said, continuing to brush my hair, which is still the rich brown of walnuts, with hardly any gray at all in it, even though I'm nearly forty-seven. I pulled at a stubborn curl that had turned into a tangle, which is what brought Zona back into my thoughts in the first place.

"You mark my words: *riding for a fall*. That daughter of ours is rushing headlong into this marriage with a fellow she barely knows, and who we know next to nothing about. Why, I wouldn't buy a pig from a man I hadn't known any longer than she has been acquainted with this fellow, and it's plain there's more to him than she realizes, or at least more than she's letting on about. I tell you: I don't like this romance of theirs one bit. Him acting like a love-sick calf, despite the fact that he is thirty-two if he's a day. Not only has he been a husband twice before so this isn't exactly a new experience for him, but he has a daughter that he takes no interest in as well. A big church wedding for a thrice-married man and a girl who's already birthed a baby—I ask you! It's nonsense."

Jacob lay back on the pillow, not even bothering to lift his head as I talked. Finally he let out a long weary sigh. "Let her go, Mary Jane."

I laid down my hairbrush and turned to stare at him. He had propped himself up on the pillows, and was staring out through the window at a pale sliver of moon hanging in the sky above the hills. He sounded sad, as if we were talking about something that had happened a long time ago and couldn't be changed now. Something ruined and lost. But Zona had been his pride and joy all her life, and it made me shiver to hear him say that about her with no more feeling than he'd have had for a leaky old bucket that you had to throw away because it wasn't worth fixing.

"It's no use getting worked up over this, Mary Jane. She may be our daughter, but she's no longer a child, you know. She's past twenty-one, and no stranger to men, though it shames me to say it. That incident last year with that no-account George Woldridge was the proof of that. Now, maybe you're right. I don't say I was taken with that sweetheart of hers any more than you were. I'd sooner trust a snake in an egg basket. So maybe this whole thing is just the thundering mistake you claim it is, but at least it will get her settled, before she can bring any more shame upon us. At least she'll get a husband while she's still pretty enough to land one."

"But he's had two wives already. And he's at least eight years older than she is, with precious few prospects that I can see."

"Blacksmithing is honest work, Mary Jane, and as to his age: we both know men with children by their first wife who are older than their new step-mother, so I wouldn't hold that against him. Maybe maturity has settled him down into a reliable husband and a steady worker."

"And maybe it hasn't."

"Well, then, that's Zona's lookout, not ours. All I know for certain is that it is time she went, Mary Jane. If she marries this fellow—and she is dead set on doing so anyhow, mind you—then we'll be shed of her. And it's high time. As old as she is, she ought to have been out and gone a long time back."

"And should we give up on her?" I turned away from the mirror then, because I could see traces of Zona in my eyes and in the angles of my cheekbones. Maybe it's easier for a father to turn away from a child than it is for the mother who gave birth to it.

"*Let her go.* Zona is all grown up, and there's not much we can do for her now except pray for her, I reckon. If you want to worry about a child, you have three sons you can fret about, and I hope for both our sakes that they turn out to be more of a credit to us than she is."

"I don't trust this fellow she's fixing to wed. I don't like him."

"What do you reckon your chances are at being able to stop her? I make them: slim to none. Just let it go, Mary Jane. She'll do as she pleases, same as always."

"But what if this marriage makes her miserable?"

Jacob shrugged. "Then she'll have a lot of company in this world, won't she?"

six

❧ The Wedding ❧

THE MARRIAGE LICENSE that Mr. Shue and Zona got at the end of October in the Greenbrier County courthouse was good for a month, which gave them a few weeks to plan for the wedding—not that they ought to have needed it, if you ask me, for this was no society couple who would have their wedding reception at the Old White Hotel down in White Sulphur Springs. After Zona and her groom said their vows at Soule Chapel, there might be cake and apple cider in the church hall, but nothing more elegant than that, for all Zona's fine ideas about marriage to a handsome man making her into a *somebody*. It wouldn't quite do that, but as Jacob said, it was an improvement, anyhow.

The time between their first setting eyes on one another and their wedding day was both too long and too short, depending on how you looked at it. The interval was too long for the preparations that the occasion would require, which was next to nothing: some branches of fall berries and a basket full of colored leaves to brighten up the sanctuary, and two or three cakes and a jug of cider for refreshments. Why, you could get that put together inside of two hours. But the interval between meeting and marrying was another matter: entirely too short for propriety.

I expected most of the congregation and many of our neighbors in Meadow Bluff to attend. Considering Zona's past and the suddenness of the occasion, it might have been more fitten to have just a small crowd, mostly immediate family, but nevertheless, word gets around in a small community, and the less inclined you are to talk about something, the more inquisitive everyone becomes. Our kinfolk and neighbors in Meadow Bluff were soon wondering about the indecent haste with which Miss Zona Heaster went from nodding acquaintance to bride, and I was questioned about it by all and sundry, with varying degrees of tact, depending upon their closeness to our family and the quality of their manners.

"Heard about your daughter's betrothal." Mrs. Lewis, a stout old biddy in brown calico, waylaid me in the church aisle after Sunday services. "You must count that as a blessing. I reckon you are glad to see her settled, old as she is. But three *weeks* from now?"

At her side her wizened friend Miss Henry, with bright birdlike eyes in a face like a dried apple, nodded sagely. "Yes, indeed, three weeks does seem awfully sudden, Miz Heaster, and late November is such an unlikely time for a wedding. Come to that, I don't believe I've seen Zona here at church lately. Is she well?"

"She'll be back soon. She's been visiting with our cousin Sarah and her family over in the Richlands," I muttered, trying to edge past her, "so I expect she's attending services there." I didn't think any such thing, but I had no desire to be cross-questioned by half the congregation. I was easing toward the door—Jacob had wisely made his escape as soon as the last hymn notes died away, and I had no doubt that he was waiting for me in the wagon with the boys. Before I could reach the door, though, a couple of other older women, who must have overheard the conversation, gathered around me, hemming me in with such eagerness that it put me in mind of a raccoon treed by hounds.

"What's this we hear about Zona's getting married?"

"How sudden! Do we know the fellow?"

"No. He's from away. Now if you all will excuse me, Jacob is waiting—"

Nobody paid my excuses any mind, and the questions kept coming. "Will she be needing a new dress for the wedding? If not, I could help you let out the seams on one of her old ones."

After that remark, the women glanced knowingly at one another, and anybody could see what they were thinking: a hasty marriage meant that a baby was on the way. After what happened last year, I guess I had no cause to take umbrage at what she was hinting at, even though I doubted they'd heard about it. We had done our best to keep it quiet, and once she had begun to show, Zona stayed on the farm and kept to herself. It nettled me anyhow.

"Thank you, but Zona won't be needing any dress alterations. She hasn't put on an ounce of weight lately, and"—I looked the old cat directly in the eye—"she has no cause to. This is a love match, not a shotgun wedding."

What I said was true, as far as I knew, and I was pretty sure that it was indeed a fact, because when we had seen Zona only the week before, she was showing no signs of being with child. If she had been in the family way, I think she would have confided in me, because I was the one who saw her through her troubles with George Woldridge's by-blow, and I think she would have trusted me again if she were keeping any secret. Besides, I had seen her pregnant only a year ago, and I knew how it took her—the weariness, the cravings, the spells of vomiting. She was showing no signs of any of that now.

"But who is this fellow she's marrying in such a hurry?" another one wanted to know. "Who are his people?"

I tried not to groan. There would be no getting away from them until they had found out all they wanted to know, and I'd best smile and try to look pleased about it, or else they'd want to know how come I wasn't. "He is a Mr. Edward Shue, ladies. He comes from over in Pocahontas County, and he's working now at the smithy at Livesay's Mill."

"Over in the Richlands?"

I nodded. "Just off the Midland Trail." I refused to let on that I wanted to know the particulars of who he was just as much as they did. "He's a likely-looking fellow—tall and strapping with curly black hair and a bold chin. They make a handsome couple."

One of them sighed with pleasure at the romance of it all. "That will be a sight to behold, the two of them all dressed up in wedding finery."

The others nodded in agreement. Weddings—anybody's wedding—made a welcome change to the sameness of life in a farming community. "Zona was always a headstrong girl, but no one can say she isn't pretty. She'll make a beautiful bride. When will she be bringing this young man of hers to services?"

I hesitated. "Well, I hope she will, but although they're having the wedding here in Meadow Bluff, it's a long way from here to the Richlands, where he is employed, and he doesn't make the journey over in time for church. They'll be living over there, after, of course."

"Well, that's only to be expected," said the stout old biddy. Her ancestors came from Tidewater Virginia, and a lifetime on a mountain farm had not cured her of her notions of propriety. They hadn't cured mine, either. My father had started life as a Yorkshire collier, but I think the English notions of proper behavior are stricter than ours. "She must live where her husband's work takes him, but a bride always gets married in her home church so that the people she's known all her life can wish her well."

"Yes, they'll be married here. You can all meet him then."

"And his family, too, of course. Surely they'll be coming here for the wedding?"

"I don't believe you can count on meeting the groom's family," I said with sudden inspiration. "They live all the way up in Pocahontas County, and it would be more than a day's journey for them to travel all the way out here to Little Sewell for the wedding. Of course, it's only going to be a small affair, anyhow. Just close friends and family. Zona's not one to make a fuss."

Actually, she was. She'd have had the reception at the Old White and invited the governor if she had the money and the bloodlines to get away with it. At least I had hoped she would wait until spring to have the ceremony, but the groom was uncommonly anxious to get the wedding over with as quick as he could. I was sure that Zona would have preferred months of giving herself airs about her impending nuptials, to dwell on the details of her wedding clothes and such, but she said that she liked a man who knew his own mind, and she let him have his way. She might have wanted to make sure she'd hooked him without delay, in case, given time, he might somehow find out about the Woldridge baby. I had warned all her brothers never to mention it, but there's no telling what young'uns will say if you're not watching them.

The ladies in the church aisle blinked, digesting my explanation, and I thought I had talked my way clean out of it, but then one of them said, "The groom's family? But surely they'll want to see him—"

They might want to if they hadn't already seen him go through it twice before.

I did push past them then. "I have to get home, ladies. Jacob's out there waiting in the wagon, and the boys will be fractious, a-wanting their dinner."

I hurried away before my Bible-toting interrogators could think up any more questions.

In the summertime, the James River and Kanawha Turnpike is like a road through paradise. The wide green valley of gently rolling meadows is bounded north and south by a wall of darker green mountains, dotted in spring by white-blossomed apple trees and the pink flowers of redbuds, and in August by clumps of goldenrod and patches of purple pokeweed. The land is better for farming than out our way, so the fields are rich with crops or full of fat-bellied cows and shining horses worth more than a year's pay to some folks. It was a landscape of peace and plenty in the sunshine of a summer afternoon, but whipped by the harsh winds of late November, the magic was gone. In the gray light of an autumn afternoon, brown stubble fields swept away from either side of the road toward bleak hills, dark with leafless trees. Mr. and Mrs. Edward Shue would find that road a wearying trial on their way back after the ceremony, but perhaps they would be too excited to notice.

We hadn't far to travel, from home to Soule Chapel, and I had quilts wrapped around every one of us, over our coats, but we still shivered in the slow-going wagon while the wind gusts eddied around us, and the gray clouds that seemed snagged upon the treetops threatened to spit rain on us at any moment. I resolved to leave my bonnet in my lap under the quilt until we actually got to the church, because the rain would turn its ribbons and silk flowers into a sodden mess. Jacob and the boys were in their church clothes—the only good ones they had—and if they got soaked, there would be nothing I could do about it except to wrap them in more quilts and pray that they wouldn't catch their deaths of colds from the wet chills.

The only one who didn't seem to mind the weather was the bride herself. She sat on the front seat of the wagon, wedged between her daddy and me, with such an expression of rapture that you'd think she was on her way to be crowned.

It was Saturday, the twenty-eighth of November: Zona's wedding day, and one day shy of the birthday of the Woldridge baby, who would not be mentioned today or ever.

I tried not to think it was a judgment on the coming marriage that the weather was foul and forbidding. After all, there is a reason that most brides choose to wed in the summertime, for then the weather is one less thing to worry about. I had mentioned to Zona that she and her beau might want to wait six months for more clement weather, but by then Mr. Shue's insistence on a hasty union had converted her to his way of thinking, and she stamped her foot and declared that she would not be dictated to by the almanac. I do believe she thought that the day would show fine and sunny simply because she expected it, but like many a woman before her, she learned to live with disappointment.

Zona was with us for the journey from the house to Soule Chapel, and her groom would be meeting us there.

"You'll have to keep an eye on our menfolk," Zona told me that morning. "Else they might come to the wedding looking like nothing on earth. Daddy might try to wear overalls if you don't watch him, and the boys haven't the least notion of what still fits or what's clean. Just make sure they don't embarrass me. I'll be too busy getting ready myself to fool with them."

I promised her that I would see that the menfolk were suitably dressed, although I did wonder who would be there to be impressed, since none of the folks from here would be dressed in fancy clothes, either, but I did my best to make the family presentable with what we had. The food was ready for the reception afterward. I had made three apple pies and a pound cake to take to the church. If it had been summertime, I'd have been able to use berries or peaches for cobblers as well, but at the end of November, about all I could manage were the pies and the simplest of cakes: a pound of butter, a pound of sugar, a pound of flour—they say that's how the cake got its name. I was sure that some of the other women would also bring food for the reception. For births and deaths and weddings, we all pitch in to honor the occasion.

The pies and cakes were wrapped in a clean cloth

and stowed in a crate in the back of the wagon, with
H. C. guarding it so that the younger ones wouldn't
put a foot through it, squirming around.

"A wedding on a Saturday," I said aloud to
Jacob, mostly to have something to listen to besides
the wind. We were waiting for Zona to finish getting
ready and come out. "There's an old saying about
that: *Wedded on Saturday, no luck at all.*"

Jacob toyed with the reins while he thought
about it. "Didn't we get married on a Saturday,
Mary Jane?"

"No. It was a Thursday, Jacob, but most people
don't have much of a choice. The church is in use
for services on a Sunday, and the rest of the days are
taken up with work."

"I reckon rich people could pick any day they
wanted," said Jacob. "So could farmers, maybe,
but the loggers and the shopkeepers and suchlike
couldn't do it, and they couldn't even go as guests
unless the wedding was held when they weren't
a-working, so a weekday wedding wouldn't have
many guests."

I sniffed. "I wouldn't mind not having many
guests at this one anyhow." But Jacob was right, of
course. It wasn't the day of the week that was making me fret about the outcome of the marriage. It
was my misgivings about the marriage that was making me worry about everything else.

There were more buckboards and buggies in the
yard outside the church than I had expected, which
didn't mean that the wedding couple was rich in
friends, just that the occasion meant there was
something to do on a dreary Saturday afternoon
in Meadow Bluff. Strictly speaking, some of them

probably weren't invited, but nobody would turn them away. Our church was called Soule Chapel, named some fifty years ago for the Methodist bishop Joshua Soule, though he never visited here. It was a white country box of a building with big double doors, painted green, and the pointed spire that in these parts marks a church as Methodist. It didn't have stained glass windows, but since the tall side windows looked out on a forest of hardwoods, the view was pretty enough for three seasons of the year, when the leaves were in all their glory. Not in late November, though.

When we went into the sanctuary, we saw that on the table next to the pulpit someone had placed a big salt crock filled with red and gold leaves and branches of red cotoneaster berries, which brightened up the room just as well as flowers would have. There was an old pump organ up at the front, next to where the choir stood, and rows of oak benches instead of pews. The woodwork had been newly polished and smelled faintly of beeswax. It was a simple but pleasant house of worship, and the ladies of the congregation had done well to make it festive. I wondered why the happy couple seemed so hesitant about getting married here. I thought Zona might be afraid that somebody knew her secret and would let it slip, but Edward Shue didn't know that, yet he seemed even warier over getting married here than she was. The only thing I could figure was that he might be shy among strangers, especially since Zona knew everybody here while he was the odd man out.

I sent Jacob and the boys up to occupy the front bench on the bride's side of the church, where his brother Johnson Heaster and his wife were already seated, while I stayed back to be with Zona. There wasn't anyone sitting on the front bench across the aisle, though; apparently no one from the groom's family was coming, or if they were, they were cutting it mighty fine. I did wonder for a second whether Mr. Shue's former wife, or more likely their daughter, would turn up for the ceremony, but I dismissed that thought as fanciful. From what Zona had said about the way they behaved toward one another when they met in the courthouse, I didn't think either of them wanted to come within five miles of the other one.

Anyhow, that bench stayed empty.

Zona made a beautiful bride. She wasn't wearing a long white dress, because nobody around here can afford the foolishness of a fancy dress that you only wear once, and besides the weather in November was too cold to make it practical, but she looked formal and solemn in a dark satin dress with an apron sort of overdress, a high choker collar, and big puffed sleeves. She wore a matching satin bow at the back of her hair. I thought she looked more elegant than that groom of hers, who showed up sporting a bow tie on a white shirt and a slightly rumpled gray suit jacket with wide lapels.

I leaned over and whispered to Zona so nobody else could hear me, "You'd think that after two previous weddings, the fellow would have had something more fitten to wear."

Zona scowled at me. "It's only a half-hour service," she muttered. "It's what comes after that counts."

I didn't hold out much hope for that, either, but they did make a well-matched pair to look at. The minister did his best, but of course he had only just met the groom. During the ceremony, he stumbled over the pronunciation of both their first names—Elva and Erasmus, which neither of them ever used—but they just smiled. The pair of them stood up at the altar and said their vows loud and clear, looking at each other with shining eyes, as if they were alone in the world. They were a handsome couple, and they knew it. There are marriages held together with less, I told myself, but it felt like whistling in the dark.

Zona was all smiles afterward at the little get-together in the church meeting room. She only scowled once, and that was when she looked out the window and noticed the rain pelting down from a sky that looked like a sheet of lead. "I did hope it would be a fine day for my wedding! After all, it only happens to you once."

I pressed my lips together and turned away quickly before I could say what I was thinking: *Maybe your new husband used up his good-weather allotment with his first two tries.*

Zona was mostly surrounded by her cousins and her old school friends from Meadow Bluff, but there were a few new-made friends from Richlands there as well, laughing and talking. Her new husband was standing on the other side of the room, over near the refreshment table, looking as stiff and awkward as any new-married man. He was eating a hunk of my pound cake with his fingers, and he didn't seem much interested in whether anybody went over to talk to him or not, so I made myself stroll over to wish him well. Edward Shue was family now, and it was my duty to try to be civil to him.

"Congratulations, son-in-law," I said. "It was a lovely wedding, but I'll bet you're glad it's over. Men usually are."

He smiled and nodded, with a mouthful of cake.

"That's the pound cake I made. If there's any left after the reception is over, you must take it home with you." I looked around the room. "And you must make us acquainted with your side of the family, Mr. Shue, now that we're all connected. Speaking of being family, what would you like me to call you now? Seems like you have a good many names to choose from. Erasmus?"

"Oh, Trout'll do me," he said, still trying to swallow his cake.

Well, it wouldn't do me, I thought. Who ever heard of such a silly name for a grown man? "I believe I'll stick with Edward," I said. "Such a nice name, same as the Prince of Wales."

He smiled, and I could see that the comparison pleased him, although perhaps it shouldn't have. I was thinking that if he kept on eating the way he was, he'd soon be as fat as the Prince of Wales, who looked like a tusk hog in the recent pictures they printed of him. Talking about English royalty made me miss my father and wish he had lived to see his granddaughter married, but we had lost him nearly ten years ago. I wondered what he would have thought of the groom.

"And your family from over in Pocahontas County? Didn't they make it to the wedding?"

Edward Shue finished his cake in one big gulp and washed it down with a tin cup of cider. "My family? They couldn't make it today on account of the weather. I reckon I'll take Zona up to meet them one of these days."

"Take me where, hon?" Zona came hurrying over, and gave her groom a hug and a quick kiss on the cheek. "I just came over to get me some cake. I didn't eat a thing all morning. Wedding nerves. Could you cut me a big piece, hon?"

He looked her up and down, and he wasn't smiling back. "You shouldn't eat cake, Zona. You don't want to go getting fat, do you?"

Zona went pale and her eyes widened. "But I haven't eaten a morsel yet today. And anyway, you always said I was beautiful."

He glared at her, like he was daring her to talk back to him, and I saw her lip began to tremble. I didn't want them to make a scene in front of a room full of people, so I put on a smile and said quickly, "Now that the wedding is over with, you can begin your life together over in the Richlands."

Zona's sparkle returned, as if a cloud had passed. "Oh, that house my handsome husband got for us is a beautiful place! It's not even a quarter mile off the Midland Trail, and real close to Mr. Crookshanks's smithy. The house used to be the home of Mr. Livesay himself, the man that ran the mill, but Trout's renting it from him. It has an upstairs, and a front porch, and a fenced-in yard, and everything!"

Edward beamed at her. "It's a peach of a place. I can just see Zona here turning that yard into a perfect flower garden with every color in the rainbow abloom from springtime until fall."

He might be able to picture it, but I couldn't. Zona had no more use for flowers than a blind mule unless they were presented to her in a bouquet. She certainly hadn't the patience to weed and water a big garden. She might do some gardening to get vegetables for the dinner table, but not just for the sake of a pretty yard. Zona didn't say anything, though, and I held my peace, but it did cross my mind that they might have been wise to get to know one another better before they tied the knot. That way there would have been fewer disappointments in store.

I smiled. "I'm looking forward to seeing your new place, then."

Edward gave me a wide-eyed stare that looked almost like alarm until he remembered to smile. "Why, you'll want to wait awhile before you visit us, ma'am. We ain't got the place put to rights yet."

"Well, I didn't think you would yet, of course, but I thought I'd come over soon and see if there was anything we could help you with. I could make you some curtains, and Jacob is handy at making furniture—nothing too fancy, but it would serve."

Zona brightened when I said this, and she looked up at her new husband with a hopeful smile, but he was already shaking his head. "I reckon Zona and me will want to see to all that sort of thing ourselves, thank you all the same. I'll buy her some material, and she can sew the curtains by herself. That way she can be proud of making the home her very own. But we'll have you and the family come over one of these days, when the weather turns fine."

"Well, I guess you newlyweds need your time alone," I said, but I was more uneasy than I let on to them. Zona had never made curtains in her life, and I wouldn't hold out too much hope for her being able to do it now. *Riding for a fall*, I thought.

After that, I spent some time chatting with Cousin Sarah while the newlyweds went around and shook hands with everybody and thanked them for coming.

"Mighty fine pound cake, Mary Jane." Jacob's brother Johnson, brushing crumbs from his coat, kissed my cheek. Johnson was a friend and neighbor as well as kinfolk, and I was glad to see him. He farmed fifty acres near us in Meadow Bluff, but he never made us feel like poor relations.

"I'm glad you like the cake, Brother Johnson. It was the best I could do in haste, it being after harvest time."

"It was short notice, I know, but I think the

nuptials went just fine. And Zona made a beautiful bride. She did you and Jacob proud."

I sighed. "I just hope it takes. I'm praying for them."

"Well, he's a nice-looking fellow, that Mr. Shue, and he couldn't want for a prettier missus. What do you know of his people?"

"Next to nothing, Johnson." I lowered my voice. "But Zona's not his first wife."

He smiled. "Let's hope she's his last one, then."

A little while later, Jacob collected me, and said we needed to be starting back, because he didn't want to be on the road after dark, when the cold really set in. "I reckon it's too late and too cold today to go all the way to the Richlands to see where the newlyweds will be living," he said. "We'll have to visit them some other day."

I sniffed. "Don't hold your breath for an invitation."

A couple of weeks went by, and we didn't hear from them. I wasn't too surprised by that—after all, they were newlyweds, and he had a steady job six days a week, which kept them tied close to home. Zona must have had her hands full cooking and keeping house all by herself, too. A spell of winter weather set in about then, and with so many miles between them in the Richlands and us in Meadow Bluff, I didn't think they'd care to brave the journey in an open buckboard. You can't always tell what the weather will be in one end of the county when you're looking at it from the other. No sense trying to visit if you might catch your death of cold from attempting it.

I did think they might come to see us around

Christmastime—not that we made much of a to-do about it. Jacob or one of the older boys would cut a pine tree from up in the woods, and the younger ones and I would decorate it with paper chains and popcorn. On Christmas morning there might be an orange or a stick of penny candy and a handmade toy for the little ones, and not much else, but still, you expect the family to gather around for Christmas dinner. Jacob's brother Johnson and his family came over in the afternoon, but we saw neither hide nor hair of Zona and Edward Shue.

I'd thought that after a couple of weeks had passed, Zona would be eager to show off her new husband, or at least she'd be bored at being shut up in her house day after day cooking and cleaning, while Edward—she insisted on calling him Trout, but I never would—was working at the smithy.

Nobody in the family was much for letter writing, either, so I hadn't expected any long accounts of married life from Zona. I did get a postcard, though, in mid-December. All it said was, "We won't come for Christmas. I have been ill. The doctor here is seeing to me. But I will try to come visit if I can while Trout is working one day. Love to all, E. Z. Shue."

I was still mulling over that message at supper that night, and finally, when I could stand it no longer, I made up my mind to see for myself, else I'd never get another night's rest for worrying. "Will you be needing the wagon every day next week, Jacob?"

He shook his head. "I can't think of any reason I would, unless you're wanting us to lay in more firewood. And even that wouldn't take more'n a day at most. Why?"

"I wasn't thinking about firewood. I was wanting to send H. C. over to the Richlands to fetch Zona back here for a visit."

"Fetch her back?" He looked up from his plate, a piece of ham dangling from his fork. "Why? Did Zona ask to come?"

"No, but we had a card from her. She says she's ailing. I thought I'd better see what's the matter with her."

"Well, if she's feeling poorly, I don't think that an all-day journey in an open wagon in December is likely to help her any, do you?"

Jacob was right; I knew it as soon as he said it.

I didn't say anything, but he could tell I was still fretting about it, so finally he said, "If you're that set on seeing her, you could go over to their house. I could take you over there myself, Mary Jane."

I thought about it. We could work it so we arrived after Trout Shue had gone to the smithy, for I remembered how set he was on not having any company until he had the house fixed up like he wanted it, which was likely to be never, knowing Zona's slapdash notions of housekeeping. Still, I didn't want to be the cause of ructions between husband and wife, and he would surely find out if we had paid a visit. I was content to stay out of his way, but I did need to know what was wrong with my daughter.

"H. C. can take me, Jacob, if you can mind the young'uns and the chickens while we're gone, for we'll have to leave mighty early. I'll write back to Zona, and tell her I'll be visiting with Sarah next week, and bringing her a cooked dinner for the two of them. From what Zona told me, John and Sarah don't live more than a couple of miles from Edward's place at Livesay's Mill. We can have her home before he's done at work, and send dinner back with her. The promise of fried chicken and pie ought to persuade him to let her come for a visit with her kinfolks. I wish I knew what was the matter with her, though."

Jacob nodded. "Woman's troubles? Do you reckon there's a baby on the way?"

I shook my head. "I don't think so. I wish I did."

H. C. is nearly sixteen, and just as much help around the place as a grown man, so I had no qualms about letting him drive the wagon when we went to fetch his older sister. I had written a postcard to Cousin Sarah, telling her to expect me for a quick visit next week, and a letter back to Zona, telling her to be ready on the Tuesday to come visit at her cousins' house, where I'd be visiting for the day. H. C. would fetch her from home, I said, bidding her make sure that Trout knew she'd be bringing him back a good dinner when she returned. I was careful not to allow time for her to reply back to us before the day we were going to visit. That lessened the chances of a refusal.

H. C. and I were fortunate in our choice of the day for travel. We left early, when the morning mist was still wreathed around the trees and over the fields like a down quilt, but after the sun got high enough, it turned out to be one of those bright clear days in mid-December when the weather is unseasonably mild. In these mountains, winter doesn't usually bind us in snow and ice until after the New Year anyway, and sometimes you do get December days that are warm as mid-October. I made H. C. wear his coat and scarf anyway, for you never know how the winds will change over the course of the day, but it looked to stay sunny and pleasant all day, and I expect he was as glad as I was of the change from being shut in on the farm doing the usual round of chores.

"Now, when you go to fetch your sister, you be

sure you can tell me what that house is like, H. C. I hope she lets you see inside, but you don't have much time to linger if we're to make the trip there and back home in one day."

H. C. wrinkled his nose. "What kind of things do you want to know?"

"Oh, just how it looks inside. If they've got curtains up yet, and what furniture is there. Is it heated well enough, and is Zona keeping up with her household chores."

H. C. sighed. "I'm not a great one for noticing things like that—unless she's got a dead horse in the parlor—but I'll do my best. Reckon you'd do better to wait and ask Zona herself when I've fetched her."

If she'll tell me the truth, I thought. We rode on at a steady clip through most of the morning, and the road was clear and dry, so we had no trouble in our travels. I kept my coat bundled up around me and my knitted gloves on—it wouldn't do for me to catch a chill and fall sick with so many folks at home to cook for and clean up after. I don't suppose I was very good company for H. C. on the journey to the Richlands because I was too preoccupied worrying about Zona—not just her illness but also the peculiar fellow she had married in such haste.

We got to my cousins' house just as the sun had finished burning away the mists. I was a Robinson before I married Jacob, and when my daddy got here from England in 1840, he wed Miss Jemima Brown from over in Virginia. Sarah was kin to me on my mama's side of the family, and I never knew any of Daddy's people, as they all stayed back across the ocean. I saw little enough of Sarah these days, since we stayed over in the Little Sewell area, so I was glad of a chance to see her, too, but my thoughts were mostly centered around Zona.

I didn't do much more than hug Cousin Sarah

and bid her how-do before I sent H. C. off again in the wagon to fetch his sister from Livesay's Mill.

"And don't take no for an answer!" I told him. "It's just a short trip from there, and the weather is fine. Their house should be easy enough to find. You know how to get to Livesay's Mill, don't you?"

H. C. sighed. "Sure, I do. There's just the one road through there, and if I was to have trouble finding Zona's place, I reckon I could stop somewhere nearby and ask."

"That's fine, son." I leaned in close to hug him, and said softly in his ear, so that my cousin wouldn't overhear me, "Just don't ask for directions at James Crookshanks's smithy. I don't want to give that peculiar husband of hers a chance to forbid her to go."

H. C. hitched up the reins, and the cart clattered off in the direction of Livesay's Mill. I followed Sarah back inside the house to visit a spell while we waited. She settled me down in the parlor next to the fireplace, and brought steaming mugs of coffee and some fresh-baked pumpkin bread.

Then she sat down in the oak rocker on the other side of the hearth, and took out her sewing to keep busy while we talked. While we ate, we talked about the weather, and the ailments of her various elderly relatives, but my mind was on my own family troubles, and I could scarcely keep up my end of the conversation.

"What do you hear from Zona?" I asked her. "I came because I had a postcard the other day, saying that she had taken sick."

She glanced up from her needlework and shook her head. "Mary Jane, I have not caught so much as a glimpse of those two since the wedding. You'd think they were in Texas instead of just a ways down the road."

"It hasn't been that many weeks, I suppose. Newlyweds and all."

"Long enough, I would have thought." Sarah sniffed, jabbing the needle into the shirt she was mending. "They haven't turned up here at church, and they aren't encouraging visitors, either. Leastways, *he's* not. I sent my John over with a fresh-baked custard pie a couple of days after the wedding, and that new husband of Zona's opened the door a crack, thanked John for the pie, and all but slammed the door in his face. He said he thought he saw Zona peeping out of one of the windows, but it was gathering dark, so he wasn't sure."

"I tell myself they're just lovebirds wanting to be left alone."

We looked at each other.

"Well, I hope I never have cause to feel guilty over the fact that she met him while she was staying with us, Mary Jane."

"You can't change what the Lord intended, Sarah," I told her.

"They are a handsome pair, I'll say that for them. She puts me in mind of you at that age. Let them live in one another's pockets all winter. I expect they'll be glad of other company come spring. She may be well along with a baby by then. Do you think that's the trouble with her now?"

"I hope it is."

We had never told the Richlands kinfolk about the Woldridge baby, and I knew that Zona was too downy a bird to confide in anyone when she was visiting here. Least said, soonest mended. I saw no reason to talk about it now, either; that part of Zona's life was over and done with, and that baby was in a good home and well out of whatever situation she had got herself into now. I remembered that Edward Shue had not shown any interest in his own daughter by that first wife of his, and I could not think that he would have been a kind stepfather to a child of Zona's—more likely it would have stopped their courtship in its tracks. I wish that thought had occurred to me sooner, but there's no profit in trying to second-guess fate. They might be as contented as any other married couple, for all I knew, and if they weren't it still wasn't my business to prevent their union. As Jacob had said, *Let her go.*

seven

LAKIN, WEST VIRGINIA

1930

"YOU WANT THE story of my life, Doctor? Why should I give it to you? Are you writing a book about your adventures among the mad?"

The young man shook his head. "It's early days for that. In fact, I don't know that I ever will."

The patients had finished their evening meal, and instead of returning to his cell like the others, Gardner had been escorted by an attendant back to the now-empty parlor, where he found Dr. Boozer waiting for him in a wing chair next to the double windows. An identical chair had been set facing it, and the doctor motioned for him to be seated.

Gardner eased into the worn old chair and looked inquiringly at his host. "I suppose brandy and cigars are out of the question?"

Boozer laughed. "I'm afraid so. I couldn't even persuade the cooks to let me have a pot of coffee to bring in here. The staff here doesn't rate new doctors much higher than patients. Anyhow, all I can offer you is the dubious pleasure of my company and my undivided attention. I thought you might not mind sitting here where we can admire the view, such as it is. If you're agreeable to it, you can chat with me for a bit instead of returning to your quarters."

The lawyer considered it. "Have I the power to refuse you, Doctor?"

"You do, Mr. Gardner. There aren't many things in this facility that are optional, but this is one of them."

"I've no objection to talking to you, but I've a mind to draw up a contract so that you cannot profit by publishing any tale of mine."

"I'm not proposing to be your biographer, Mr. Gardner. I'm just passing the time of day with you. It seems to me that time is something you have an abundance of just now."

Gardner was gazing out the window, at the green lawn that sloped down to the now empty road. Somewhere beyond those trees lay the river. "I'm not much of a chatting man, Doctor, but over the years I have learned to feign being sociable. It is a requirement in my profession—and the one I find most difficult to practice. I doubt, though, that *you* are being sociable. You are currently practicing your own profession, are you not?"

"I wouldn't put it as formally as that." Boozer made an open-handed gesture, a concession that the other man had seen through him. "I like talking to people. I'm trying to get to know you, to see if there's some way I can help you. The more I know about you, the more likely it is that I'll be able to."

Gardner raised his eyebrows. "The medical equivalent of the third degree?"

Boozer smiled. "Hardly that. Most patients wouldn't have any idea what to confess to, because they don't think there's anything wrong with them. Or to put it another way, they think they are reacting normally given the circumstances."

"How so?"

"Well, to use a classic example: Killing your child may be a terrible thing to do, and it is certainly against the law. But if you sincerely believe that God has commanded you to do it, then if you carry out His instructions you are acting in a reasonable manner."

"That's the biblical story of Abraham."

"Yes, but there's a woman patient here who would tell you exactly the same thing if you asked her why she murdered her baby."

"I think Abraham was crazy like a fox. He didn't sacrifice his son, remember. At the last minute, he claimed that God agreed to settle for a ram instead, so he slit its throat instead of Isaac's."

"Yes. Unfortunately, God hasn't been so accommodating lately. At least, not to the patients I've treated. Nobody stopped them from killing a loved one."

"It would be an interesting defense, though. Saying that the Lord commanded you to kill. Put that argument to a God-fearing jury—"

"Well, I wouldn't bet on an acquittal, Mr. Gardner. They just might charge the Almighty as an accessory before the fact."

The two men laughed at that, the first real accord between them.

"No, I don't suppose I could win the case," Gardner conceded. "If the defendant claims that God commanded the act, and twelve jurors refuse to believe it, the matter is settled right there. In the law, it isn't so much the truth that matters; it's the consensus."

"That's how it works here, too. It isn't what the

patient believes that constitutes reality; it's what the physicians believe."

"So, I suppose it is the patient's task to convince the doctors of the truth in his claims?"

"Or you could agree with the doctor's point of view. That's generally quicker."

"Tell me what to say, then."

James Boozer sighed, and rubbed the fine trace of stubble along the angle of his jaw. "I'm trying to help you really get well, not just pretend to get well. And to do that I need to hear your side of it. There is a new idea going about in medical circles that talking might be a useful tool in treating mental patients. I have wanted to try it. I don't know that I entirely agree with the theory. Some of the poor folks here are too far gone for it to work, I think. At least, I doubt my ability to reach them. But you are an educated man, not prone to violence, and I thought we might have a go at it. Surely you'd prefer such a treatment to the traditional alternatives."

"What would those alternatives be?"

"Unpleasant ones." Boozer shrugged. "You've probably heard about them. Being restrained and left in a tub of cold water for the better part of a day. Electrical shocks. Doing violence to the body in attempt to gain the attention of the mind. My colleagues swear that these methods work—at least sometimes."

Gardner's smile was grim. "If your victim has any control at all over his faculties, I believe he would feign sanity simply in order to escape such horrors. I know I would."

"Now there's rational thought." Boozer nodded encouragingly. "So I propose that we simply talk together every day or so, and see if that accomplishes anything. If, after a reasonable time, it doesn't, then my colleagues here can always resort to the conventional means of treating insanity."

Gardner inclined his head. "A threat, but handsomely stated. I see no alternative but to cooperate. Earlier you asked about the circumstances of my commitment."

"I looked it up in your file, actually."

"I thought you would have. It seemed the logical course of action. So why ask me?"

"Because the file doesn't list reasons, only behaviors. And you seem eminently rational, so I thought that perhaps, you being a lawyer working in the South, you really are sane, and that maybe some of the local white attorneys might have railroaded you in here to get rid of you."

The old man stared at the Northern doctor for a long minute, and then he began to laugh. "I diagnose paranoia, Doctor. Lock yourself in a padded cell."

Boozer shuffled some papers to cover his discomfiture. "Well, you hear about such things . . ."

Mr. Gardner gave him a pitying smile. "Now why would my fellow lawyers in Mercer County bother to get rid of me? My clients were mostly colored and mostly poor—even before the economic disaster this country is sliding into. Sometimes I'd take my fee in smoked ham or by having my grass mowed—do you think the white attorneys envy me that? And if I wasn't around to represent those poor folks, then like as not the judge would appoint one of my more prosperous colleagues to defend them pro bono. Conspire to get me put away? Why, faced with the prospect of working extra hours for canned tomatoes, they might just come over here and help me to escape if I were to ask them to, not on my account but to save themselves the bother of attending to my clients."

"Well, if you say so . . ."

"I'm a relic of the previous century, young man—well past it, in the eyes of your generation. Now if I were an ambitious, up-and-coming Northern fellow—like you—maybe some of them might resent me, but I'm not in anybody's way. Except my own." His smile was warmer now. "But I do thank you, Doctor, for the compliment of thinking me sane."

Boozer held up one finger, qualifying his answer. "It's only a superficial impression, though."

"Is it good enough to get me moved to a first-floor room?"

"Not quite yet. Besides, there's no vacancy there at present. Now let's return to my original question: Why are you here?"

Gardner sighed, and stared down at the threadbare carpet. "Because I tried to kill myself. Technically, that is a crime, but they sent me here instead of to jail. We live in enlightened times."

"Well, your file said as much, but I wanted to see what your side of it was." Boozer scribbled a line on his notepad. "You attempted suicide."

"And you want to know why."

The doctor shrugged. "The conventional thinking in psychiatry is that *you* don't know why."

"Of course I know!"

"Well, you are no doubt aware of the precipitate cause." A wry smile. "Not a phrase I use with most of my patients."

"I can well imagine."

"What I mean is: you probably know the immediate reason for your act, but not the underlying causes, which may stretch back many years. So that's where we must start: many years before the act itself. Do you follow me?"

"Of course I do, young man. You want the story of my life. But before we get to your underlying causes, I'd like to put a question to you. Where are you from, Doctor?"

"We don't usually share personal information with patients. Why do you ask?"

"Because it is relevant. You are a young man, and you speak like a Northerner. I've no objection to telling you about my past, but if you have led a sheltered life, it may take a bit of believing on your part."

Boozer steepled his fingers and thought for a moment. "Fair enough. My parents came from South Carolina, and I was born there, but they moved north shortly after I arrived, so this is as far south as I can remember living. I grew up in a little village called Mount Kisco, a few miles north of New York City. My parents used to talk about South Carolina, though, and they are about your age, so perhaps that will satisfy you."

"And do you consider yourself down South now—in this place?"

"Well, it sure is south of Mount Kisco." Boozer smiled, but then he considered the question. "I suppose technically you could call this the South, but it is sadly lacking in magnolias and mint juleps. I can't imagine plantations existing here, and surely the climate is wrong for cotton?"

"No, cotton is out of the question, but they did have slaves once, same as their southern neighbors. West Virginia became a state in order not to leave the Union, though. That makes some difference."

"Yes, maybe it does. I haven't given it much thought. Although I doubt that any qualms about slavery figured into their decision."

"No." Gardner smiled. "I always took it as a sign of their dislike of highfalutin Virginians. In fact, the most rampant pro-Union supporter I ever knew had owned slaves well into the war years. We'll get to him directly, I expect. Now, young man—college? Where did you study to be a doctor?"

"I went to Lincoln University—still the North— just a ways outside Philadelphia, and I graduated from medical school at Howard University in 1927, where I was a member of Alpha Phi Alpha." Seeing the blank look on the old man's face, he hurried on, "But, look, from here on out, Mr. Gardner, you have to let me ask all the questions. Therapy is not a conversation."

"I thought you said you wanted to talk."

"Actually, I want to listen."

"Will you write down what I say then?"

"I'll make notes, yes, so that I can study them later."

Gardner laughed. "So I am to testify, and you will be the court reporter. I know that form well enough."

"Except that I can't write that fast. I'll rely on my memory, and transcribe the notes before I forget what the scribbles mean."

"But is there no one like a defense attorney to protect my rights in case I say things not to your liking?"

"Protecting your rights?" Boozer shrugged. "I hope you will trust me, but aside from that, in my profession, it's called doctor–patient privilege. Even if you confessed to a murder, I could not report it to the police, nor could I be made to testify against you."

"I know all that. And I have no confessions of murder with which to enthrall you. The worst I can say on that score is that occasionally I have failed to save someone—as his legal representative, you understand. But I am satisfied that the poor fellows I unsuccessfully defended were guilty anyhow, so perhaps it wasn't any great failing on my part to fall short of an acquittal. But I am worried not about criminal matters but about personal ones. What if I confide things to you that convince you that I am indeed insane? Suppose you entrap me with my own confessions so that you can keep me here forever?"

"Well, as we discussed earlier, we're a little short on bed space. Besides, I'd be a pretty poor sort of physician if I did that to you, wouldn't I?"

"Oh, you'd be able to justify it very nicely, I'm sure. *For his own good. To protect him and the community from harm. Pro bono publico.* Suppose I said I saw the thing with red eyes and mothlike wings flapping about in the night? Why, you'd throw the key away."

"A lot of people here claim to have seen that creature. If reality is a consensus of opinion, then maybe you'd be crazy *not* to believe in it."

James Gardner laughed. "Why, you might have made a lawyer, boy. That is as downy a snare as ever I've seen. I will watch my words as carefully as if I were on the witness stand. But it can't do any harm to talk about my past, I suppose—up to a point. How old do you think I am, Doctor?"

"I'm no judge of faces. I think we have you down as being in your early fifties. That seems about right."

"I am fortunate in my looks. I take after my father in that, I think. Anyhow, I was born in 1867. My father was a doctor, among other things."

Boozer blinked at this unexpected piece of information. "Was he white? Or from the North?"

"Neither of those things. Born a slave in ol' Virginny. I don't suppose you'd consider him a genuine physician, young man, not with your fancy degrees, but he was all the doctor that a lot of our folks had to rely on back in Greenbrier County. I guess you'd call him a root doctor. Tonics, salves, poultices."

"Delivering babies?"

"Mostly not. Midwives handled that. A lot of women don't think a man knows much about child-birth. Still, he did a power of good. He was a smart man."

"I believe you." Boozer smiled. "After all, his son became an attorney."

"I was the youngest of five, and none of the rest were conspicuously successful, but my father encouraged me to get an education. I worked my way through Storer College up in Harper's Ferry. It's a teachers college, but it served me well. After that, I read law and passed the bar."

"Your father must have been proud of you."

"I think he took it for granted that I'd make something of myself. He expected nothing less, so he wasn't effusive with praise over my accomplishments. Besides, he wasn't one to sit back and let the younger generation take over. After my mama died, my father rang in the new century, at the age of eighty-one, by getting married again."

"Well, that's not unheard of; elderly men often need a caretaker when they become infirm. Under-standable."

Mr. Gardner laughed. "They had a baby a year later. That little boy must be close to your age by now."

"Really? Well . . . wow . . . whatever those ton-ics were that your father was handing out, I'd like a case of them."

"He always said it was in the bloodline. The Gardners make old bones, which is why I don't expect to die in here. I'm only sixty-three. I don't suppose you think there's any *only* about it, though."

"You wear your years well, Mr. Gardner. Maybe if you would talk about whatever put you in here, we could send you back out into the world to live a long, long life."

Gardner laughed. "I tried to kill myself, and you're trying to entice me with a long, long life?"

"I'm hoping that I can make you want one again."

"There are some things that even doctors can't fix. Too bad you can't bring back Alice again."

"Alice?"

"My late wife. Second wife, to be exact. The second wife I lost to death, and it was just too much to bear. I thought I'd follow her to the grave."

"How?"

"I told the doctor I was having trouble sleeping, and he gave me a bottle of pills. I took all of them. Left a note, too. In hindsight, I know I should not have done that, because afterward it meant I was wasting my breath trying to convince them that it was an accident."

"If you took the whole bottle, I don't have to guess what happened."

"You surmise that I took too many pills, sir?"

"I think you must have. That amount of sedatives probably congealed into a big old lump in your stomach, and your body would have coughed them up like a hairball."

"Noted." Gardner inclined his head. "I shall remember that for next time."

Boozer held up a warning finger. "Don't you think like that. I wouldn't want that on my conscience if we were to let you out."

"I'll keep my own counsel about it then. I think I can promise you not to make any further attempt on my life with nostrums, anyhow. It is not a reliable method."

"No. Overdosing is a chancy business. I suppose you were none the worse for the experience, but if all you did was sleep and vomit—not necessarily in that order—you ought to have been able to conceal all that, so somebody must have found you before you had time to recover."

Gardner scowled. "Somebody did. A foolish interfering woman from the church wondered why I wasn't in my pew that Sunday morning. I had done it on a Saturday night in order to make sure I should not be missed at the office, but I had reckoned without predatory old biddies who see widowers as fair game."

"Tracked you down, did they?"

"The most persistent one of the pack. Sniffed me out of my lair like an infernal bloodhound. I had forgotten to lock the door, and she just barged right in, and found me in my bed, still insensible and soiled from my . . . miscalculations. It might have been all right even then if she hadn't spied the note I'd left propped up on the bureau. The game was up then."

"She raised a hue and cry, of course?"

"Yes, under the mistaken impression that she was preserving my life, and the even more mistaken impression that I should be grateful to her for doing so. But instead of a rescue, she had delivered me into the hands of more interfering do-gooders, who sent me here to recover my wits."

"Well, I can't blame her for pursuing you," said Boozer, leaning over to light a cigarette. "An unattached attorney must be quite a catch in a small town."

"A young, unmarried physician would be a better one. Shall I give her your particulars, Doctor?"

They both laughed, but Boozer said, "Funny, but not quite accurate. I have a wife, or I did."

"Then why are you living here in a small room in the asylum?"

The doctor shrugged. "Well, the marriage

didn't quite take. Dorothy is a nice girl—a doctor's daughter that I met in Huntington two years ago: whirlwind courtship, pretty country girl lands a New York doctor—but we just ended up being too different for it to work. She's gone off to Beckley to teach school now, and I came here."

Mr. Gardner regarded him thoughtfully. "You seem to be bearing up well under the loss."

"Well, I'm a happy fellow. I figure there are more fish in the sea. But you're not as easygoing as I am. You were truly grief-stricken over the loss of your wife, weren't you? That's why you did it?"

Gardner shrugged. "I suppose I couldn't imagine life without Alice. She was a fine woman. Handsome. Educated. She taught school, too, there in Mercer County before I married her, and she was everything the wife of a successful attorney ought to be."

"You make her sound like a Rolls-Royce, Mr. Gardner."

"Perhaps I do, but I can't help that."

"And you say she was your second wife?"

"I was in my fifties when I married Alice. My first wife, Eliza, was just a simple country girl, sweet and capable in domestic matters. She was the wife of my youth, and I regretted her death, of course I did, but I was only in my midforties when she died. Perhaps I wasn't a young man, strictly speaking, but given my father's robust example, I thought I had half my life still before me, and I recovered from the loss tolerably well. The young are resilient."

"I suppose we are. We still have time to fix things."

"I felt that at the time. And I did recover. My law practice in Bluefield prospered, and after a while I met Alice. But when she died, I knew I hadn't the heart to start over."

"You've no children, then?"

"No. That might have made a difference. As it was, I saw long years of loneliness ahead of me, and I didn't want to live through them."

"But why should you be alone? You said yourself that a church full of old biddies were in hot pursuit of you. And look at the example of your father. How old did you say he was when he remarried? Eighty-something? Maybe there's more to come in your life."

"Well, you may be right. Grief makes cowards of people sometimes. I wasn't thinking clearly then. But now I have hope."

Dr. Boozer was silent for a few moments, watching his patient. "Do you mean that, or are you just saying what you think I want to hear so that I'll think you're cured?"

James P. D. Gardner smiled. "Now, would I do that, Doctor?"

eight

GREENBRIER COUNTY, WEST VIRGINIA

1896–1897

I WASN'T KEEPING A WATCH on the time, but it seemed like an hour before we heard the rattle of the wagon that told us H. C. had returned from his errand to Livesay's Mill. I ran to the front door and flung it open, knowing that my cousin Sarah would understand my eagerness to see Zona and not give a thought to the propriety of a guest presuming to open a door. I hurried out onto the porch, and waited while H. C. helped his sister down out of the wagon seat. He lifted her out as if she weighed nothing at all, and set her gently in the grass next to the hedge.

Zona was pale, but then she always was, even in summer, so that was no proof of anything amiss, although I fancied her cheekbones stood out sharper than when I had seen her last, and she didn't look as lively as I was used to seeing her. All the bubbling happiness from her wedding day was gone.

She was wrapped up against the cold in her heavy brown coat and woolen gloves, with H. C.'s blue knitted scarf covering her up to the tip of her nose. She pushed it down when she saw us waiting on the porch, and looked up at us with an uncertain smile. What did that smile mean? I wondered. Was it polite tolerance of the fuss made by her overly concerned relations, or embarrassment at having neglected to visit us, or even a forced smile that she summoned, hoping it would cover up a bad situation, something she didn't want to talk about?

We hustled her into the parlor and unwound her from the coat and scarf. She hugged Sarah and me, murmuring a word or two about being thankful to see us. I thought she felt like skin and bones under that heavy winter dress, but I didn't say anything about it. Her eyes were clear and there was no feverish look about her, and she hadn't coughed a single time, not even when she came in out of the cold. Pale as she was, I didn't think she was suffering from consumption, and that's what I had feared, for it's a death warrant for young and old alike. It had been a foolish worry, though. She'd only been gone for a couple of weeks. Consumption takes longer than that to do its work.

When we had settled her under a lap quilt close to the fire, H. C. said he was going to unhitch the horse and turn it out to pasture for an hour or two, until we needed the wagon again. Then he was going to hunt up Cousin John in the barn, or wherever he was, and see if there was anything there that needed doing. I waved him away, knowing that he was as afraid of women's talk as any other man, and that he would have been glad to split rails or slop hogs rather than have to listen to our chatter.

"Don't you stay away too long," Zona called

after him. "I have to be getting back well before dark."

H. C. nodded, barely pausing, and slipped out the front door. We heard him clattering down the steps, and then silence.

I had heard the worry in Zona's voice when she talked about getting home on time. "But your husband knows you're here, though? You told him that?"

She nodded. "I said you were bringing us some fried chicken and apple pie for supper, and that I'd be carrying it home with me. That cheered him up. I hope to the Lord you did bring it, Mama. I promised him."

"It's right in the kitchen there, in a basket. I'll make sure you remember to get it before you go."

"Good." She smiled, and it looked more like relief than happiness. "I never saw such a one for doting on food as that husband of mine. He's like a starving dog. I'll bet he'll eat that whole pie in one sitting."

"What about your share?"

She looked away. "Oh, I don't have much of an appetite these days."

A little silence fell then, and Cousin Sarah said, "I'll make us another pot of coffee." I started to get up, too, but she motioned for me to sit down in the chair by the fire next to Zona. "No need for you to help me in the kitchen, Mary Jane. You stay here and keep Zona company. Reckon I'll make some biscuits while I'm about it. We made apple butter a few weeks back, and I remember Zona was always partial to a nice hot biscuit with apple butter." Sarah— always my favorite of the cousins—was no fool. She must have had her suspicions, same as I did, but she was willing to give Zona and me the time to thrash it out between us without trying to horn in on the conversation. She wouldn't even eavesdrop, for as she bustled away, the door to the kitchen swung shut behind her.

I turned to Zona, still huddled in her chair, staring into the fire. We were alone, but time was short, and I hadn't the leisure of beginning slowly with idle talk to put her at her ease. "Well, Zona. You said you were ill, and so I came to see about you. What is ailing you?"

She shivered a little and tried to smile. "I don't reckon it's much, Mama. The doctor—it's George Knapp from Lewisburg—has been out and given me a tonic."

"You haven't been coughing, have you? Any blood in your handkerchief?"

She gave me a sad smile. "It ain't consumption, Mama. Of course it isn't! And no, I have not been coughing, nor feverish. I'm just tired, I reckon. Maybe the cold weather is getting me down. There's a draft in that house, too, I do believe."

"Why, today is as fine a weather as you could ask for, this time of year. I believe I could have done without my coat on the way over from Little Sewell." I leaned close to be sure that I wasn't overheard, and whispered, "What *is* the matter? Have you started a baby already?"

"I don't think so." She pushed her hand against her belly, but it was as flat as a boy's. "Ain't hardly had time to know that yet. The wedding was just a couple of weeks ago."

"Yes, but if you didn't wait—"

"Well, I ain't known him all that long, neither. It's like I told you: I'm just tired all the time. Seems like there's nothing I want to do except sleep, and that makes Trout wild with me, because he'll get home of an evening, and I ain't done even half my chores."

"Well, if you're sick, it's no wonder, Zona."

"Try telling that to Trout. That cookstove we have is different from the one up home, and it's taking me awhile to get used to it. I burned the biscuits the other night, and he carried on something fierce. He expects his supper to be hot and ready and on the table the minute he walks in the door, and he's not above raising hell if it ain't."

"Well, stand up to him, Zona. He ought to be made to understand that it takes time to get used to new ways of doing things. And you'd better explain to him that when you're ailing, you can't work as long and hard as if you were well. You need to take care of yourself, especially in winter, or you may never get your strength back. If he's impatient now, what's he going to be like when you're pregnant for nine months and never feel up to doing much?"

"I don't know." She wiped off a tear on the back of her hand. "But I don't think standing up to him is the answer."

"Why not?"

"'Cause he don't like that, either."

I heard the quaver in her voice, and I could see that she was determined not to cry. If we'd had more time, I think she would have told me all that was going on, but Zona was proud, and she would never admit that she'd made a mistake, or that there was anything much wrong with her handsome new husband.

I noticed then that she was wearing the same dress I'd last seen her in—the one she wore on her wedding day, a dark dress of satin brocade with a high banded collar and long puffed sleeves. That dress hid every inch of her below the chin, though it seemed to hang a little looser on her than it had before.

I didn't say anything for a minute or two, hoping that she would come out with the rest of the story, but she just went back to staring into the fire, without saying anything at all.

"Do you like this Dr. Knapp, Zona? Would you like to see Dr. Lualzo Rupert from up home?"

She stared at me, eyes wide and nostrils flaring, and it just about broke my heart to see how scared she was. "I don't want him coming anywhere near us. He delivered the baby, and I don't want him to let it slip that I ever had one. I ain't told Trout."

"Well, you could come back to Little Sewell with us, and see Dr. Lualzo on your own. Your husband need never know. I certainly wouldn't tell him."

"No. I'm all right. Dr. Knapp calls out to see me when he's making his rounds in the Richlands. Everybody says he knows his business. Well, most everybody, anyhow. I reckon he loses a patient every now and then, same as the rest of them, but he's all right."

"Well, what does he say is wrong with you?"

"I don't think he rightly knows. A touch of anemia, maybe. He gave me a tonic that was supposed to help."

"Did it?"

"It hasn't yet." She shrugged. "I'm just as tired as before. Dr. Knapp said it might take awhile for the medicine to start working."

I thought about it. "Would you like to come home for a spell?" I knew that I might have to fight Jacob if she accepted the invitation, and that husband of hers might come out to the farm and raise Cain if she did come, but it worried me that she was all alone so much of the time, and feeling poorly. I doubted—knowing her cooking—that she was getting much in the way of nourishing food, either. I thought it might be a good idea to have her home until I could work out what was ailing her.

She didn't seem a bit pleased by my offer, though. Her eyes got big, and she put her hand to her throat, as if she was having trouble catching her breath. "Go back to Little Sewell? Oh, I couldn't do that, Mama! Trout wouldn't stand for it. He says a proper wife's place is with her husband, no matter what."

I didn't think much of Mr. Edward Shue's opinions on anything, but I forbore to say so, because there was no point in upsetting Zona with something that couldn't be helped. "Would you like me or your daddy to have a talk with him? He needs to understand that you won't be much use to him as an invalid. Better to get you well than to ignore the issue."

Zona wiped away another tear with the back of her hand. "You might as well try to explain geometry to a mule. Trout won't listen. He says I'm lazy."

There was some truth in that, I thought. Zona generally was an indifferent cook and a slapdash housekeeper, but it's one thing for a mother to hold that opinion, and quite another for a husband to be saying so after less than a month of marriage. It worried me.

"And it's best if nobody tries to speak to him about it. Trout's got a temper." When Zona saw the look on my face, she said quickly, "He don't mean nothin' by it. He just lets little things irritate him and he blows up quick. But once it's over, he's awful sorry about it. He hugs me, and tells me he loves me. Then he swears he'll never get mad at me again. One time back before we were wed, he even went out in the field and picked me some wildflowers to show how sorry he was."

"Sorry for what?"

Zona shrugged. "Oh, for losing his temper. I know he loves me. And I love him. I wouldn't want to be married to some pantywaist that let his wife boss him around. I just have to learn to be a better wife, I reckon, so's I won't keep making him mad. I'm working on it."

Cousin Sarah came in just then with the coffee and biscuits, and I didn't get to ask Zona any more about it. We just talked about ordinary things amongst the three of us until H. C. turned up, and said we were burning daylight, and that he ought to take Zona back now.

I went into the kitchen and brought out the basket of fried chicken and apple pie that I had made for Zona and Edward, though now I grudged him every mouthful of it. I hadn't cared for him from the beginning, and I liked him even less after what I'd just heard. A handsome brute is still a brute, and the handsome part tends to pass away a lot quicker than the brute does.

"Are you sure you won't come on back with us to Meadow Bluff?" I said, not wanting to let go of the basket.

Zona laughed. "Trout would go crazy if he came home and found me gone. He's been looking forward to this chicken dinner all week. We'll come see you when the weather's better."

"Today is as fine a day as we're likely to get until spring."

"But Trout has to work today, just like every other day except Sunday. But I'll keep at him about letting me come see you, and I'll write to you every now and then until we can come out to visit."

"Has he taken you to meet his family yet?"

"Lord, no! They live twenty miles and more

over the ridges in Pocahontas County. I may not set eyes on them until midsummer. Trout's not too anxious to visit them anyway."

"Why not?"

"I didn't ask. He seems to be happy with just the two of us. And he works so hard at the smithy, I reckon he doesn't want to waste his time off rushing hither and yon a-visiting relations."

"Well, try to get him to bring you to see us. Tell him we'll feed him until he founders."

Zona laughed. "Well, if anything would work, I bet that would, but he just wants to be with me right now. Maybe come spring, he'll get to feeling more sociable."

I walked her outside and waited while H. C. hoisted her back into the wagon seat. "Now you let me know how you're feeling and tell me anything the doctor says, you hear me, Zona?"

She leaned down and kissed my cheek. "I promise, Mama. I'll see you again as soon as I can."

We headed west toward the mountain, trying to get there before the sun set behind it. As it neared evening and the shadows grew long, the wind picked up, and I pulled the quilt up over my coat, hoping it wouldn't get too much colder before nightfall.

"What was their house like, son?" I asked, trying to keep my teeth from chattering as a cold gust of wind swept past the wagon.

"I don't know, Mama. She must have been looking out the window, a-waiting on me to come fetch her, because by the time I stopped the wagon in front of their house, she was out on the porch waving at me."

"You never went inside? What about when you took her back this afternoon?"

"You said you were in a hurry to get home, remember? She didn't seem too anxious to have me stick around anyhow. I offered to carry the food basket inside for her, but she said she could manage it on her own. Next thing I knew she had jumped down out of the wagon, snatched the basket out of the back, and was hightailing it up the steps. So I let her go."

"Was Mr. Shue back then?"

"Didn't see him."

I fretted at the missed opportunity, but there was nothing to be done about it. H. C. was right: we didn't have time to waste with a long journey ahead of us on a winter afternoon. "Well, what does the house look like on the outside?"

H. C. rubbed his chin, trying to compose an answer. "Biggish, I guess. White frame house—could use a lick of paint. Tin roof, no shutters. And a low porch that goes all the way across the front of the house. Oh, and there's a fence, too. White board. It wouldn't keep chickens out, but I reckon the cows couldn't get past it. Knowing Zona and gardening, though, I doubt there'd be anything in the yard for them to eat anyhow."

I looked out at the brown fields stretching away to the dark shapes of bare trees along the creek. "Well, nobody's yard looks like much in December. Maybe things will be better come spring. We could come back then and help her set a garden."

H. C. kept his eyes on the road and didn't say anything, but I knew what he was thinking. We had work aplenty on our own land without taking on chores for Zona, too.

I leaned back in the wagon seat and pulled the quilt up tighter around me. "Well, we'll see how things stand in March when the winter breaks. Things may settle down between the two of them by then."

"Maybe." H. C. snapped the reins so the horse would pick up the pace. The light was fading. "I reckon we can ask her if she needs any help next time we see her."

But I never saw her again. Not alive, that is.

Christmas came and went, and all we got from Mr. and Mrs. Edward Shue was a postcard with a snow scene of a white steepled church and a sprig of holly printed on the front, and on the back a scrawled message saying, "Hope you all are keeping well, Love from Zona."

"Well, that tells us nothing!" I said to Jacob, slapping the card down on the kitchen table. "And that husband of hers didn't even bother to sign his name."

Jacob picked up the card and wiped off the drops of coffee from one edge. He propped it against the biscuit dish in the center of the table, with the church picture facing out.

"Do you reckon he can?"

I tried to smile. "Maybe she wrote and mailed it while he was at work."

"Or maybe he's about as much family to us as a cuckoo in a dove's nest."

Jacob went on eating stew and didn't say anything more, so finally I said, "I've a good mind to go stay with Cousin Sarah in the Richlands, so I can see for myself what's going on over there."

"Let her go, Mary Jane." Jacob's voice was soft, but there was iron in it. "She's over twenty-one and married. What's done is done. She needs to work this out on her own, and Lord knows no man wants his mother-in-law butting in on his marriage."

I hesitated. "Well, it's early days, maybe. I guess I could wait awhile."

"You've got a houseful of family right here that needs you, Mary Jane. Who's going to cook our Christmas dinner and take care of the rest of the young'uns if you was to leave?"

He was right, of course. I couldn't take Christmas away from the boys just on account of Zona, and I couldn't be in two places at once.

"Besides, the snow clouds are hanging above the ridge like sacks of wool, so don't get any notions about heading over to the Richlands. Let's be thankful this Christmas for what we have and not go chasing after what we haven't any control over."

"Seems to me that Edward Shue could make more of an effort to be part of this family."

"That's Zona's lookout, Mary Jane, not yours. Try baiting that trap with honey instead of vinegar, and see if that helps."

"I made him fried chicken and apple pie, didn't I? And it's more than he deserved, I'll tell you that!"

"And if I was Mr. Shue, I'd have been afraid to eat it in case you had spit in it." Jacob sighed. "It's hard to see eye to eye with somebody when you're on your high horse, hon. Climb down."

"It's hard to see eye to eye with folks who are a dozen miles away, too. Let them come a-visiting, and I'll do my best to be pleasant."

"That would be a fine resolution for New Year's, Mary Jane."

Christmastime in the big city and in fancy places like that hotel in White Sulphur Springs is said to be a wonder of beribboned trees with candles in their branches, and piles of presents wrapped in shiny paper, all tied with satin bows. I heard about it from people who had traveled, and now and then I'd see a picture of a holiday scene, but that's not how things were out in Little Sewell. There was a war on when Jacob and I were children, and families here on the outlying farms had no money to spare then or now for finery or store-bought decorations. Mostly we marked the occasion by going to church, and we sang carols and gave one another useful gifts, like warm socks. Jacob made some money by selling one of the young hogs, and he bought me a lace-trimmed handkerchief and a packet of needles for my sewing.

The wilder young bucks in the community would shoot off their guns in the air on Christmas morning. Zona, when she was little, asked me were they trying to shoot down an angel. I said I didn't think so, but I had no more idea than she did what the purpose of that gunfire was. To people who grew up with a war in their backyards, it certainly wasn't a joyful noise. Women's work went right along as usual over Christmastide, only there was more of it. I always cooked a smokehouse ham and a wild turkey for Christmas dinner to make sure that everybody got to eat all they could hold without having to fill up on vegetables and biscuits. In the afternoon we would all go over to Johnson Heaster's place, and have dessert and carol singing with whichever of the neighbors came to celebrate.

We were content with our simple festivities, and I never wished for more, but I did wonder what would pass for a holiday at Zona's house this year. Maybe her ill-tempered husband would get her a box of candy from Green & Bready's store in Lewisburg to make amends for his demanding ways. Maybe by now Zona would have had enough practice cooking on that stove of theirs to be able to make him a fine Christmas dinner so that he would be happy. If there was a way to that man's heart, it certainly did seem to pass through his stomach. But I had begun to think that Mr. Edward Shue was one of those people who runs after the things he wants, but is never satisfied with them once he gets them. When a person is like that, you can't ever give him enough to satisfy him. Everything they get is like fairy gold that turns to ashes in the morning. You may pursue it forever, but once you touch it, it crumbles to dust in your hands.

It didn't seem right, the two of them spending their first holiday by themselves, with nobody else around, but since Jacob insisted on me leaving the newlyweds alone until spring to fix their own troubles, I vowed that I would. Times seemed to be changing quicker as we neared the new century, and perhaps the old traditions that I was raised with weren't the way of the world anymore. Surely, I thought, if Zona needed me, she would get word to me, and maybe hearing no news from her was all the reassurance I could hope for.

We had an ordinary, pleasant Christmastide, and I was careful not to bring up the subject of Zona any more than I could help it. I did pray for her, though, when we went to church. Sitting there in the pew with my head bowed, while everybody else was rejoicing and singing the jubilant hymns of the season, I was silently asking the Almighty to keep my Zona safe and to give her whatever happiness He could manage. I prayed that He would look after my daughter over these cold, dark months since I could not.

It seemed like a long time until spring.

The New Year came and went, and then the breaking up of Christmas on January 6—Old Christmas—with more shooting off guns in the air and a big get-together at Johnson's farm with all the fiddlers and dancers reveling all night long to send out the season in celebration. We stayed until past midnight, and H. C. and Joseph would have been glad to stay longer, but Jacob told them that until they each turned sixteen, they would have to go home when the rest of the family did. Jon is only ten, and he was falling asleep against my arm, and the night air was getting colder, so we left before the revels ended.

"I wish it weren't the dark of the moon," I said, shivering under my quilt in the seat of the wagon. "It's good that we haven't far to go. If it weren't so cold and dark, I'd as lief have stayed longer so the boys could enjoy the music."

"It's foolish to stay up all night," said Jacob as we drove away.

"Well, I reckon your brother Johnson could have put us up for the night, if we had asked him."

"The whole point of the breaking-up party is that the holidays are over now, and come sunup work resumes in the ordinary way." He raised his voice to be heard over the rattle of the cart, and I had to shush him lest he wake the boys. "That would call for a good night's sleep if you ask me, and I'd rather sleep in my own bed at home."

"But you're a farmer. This is a slack time of year for you, regardless. And it makes no difference to me, because women's work is the same no matter what else is going on in the seasons, except, I'll grant you, that there's more to do in the holidays, so

I welcome the end of it all because I could use the rest."

He laughed at that, and said, "I wonder if Zona and her husband have found a party to attend in the Richlands. Bet you if they did, they'll see the holiday out by dancing until dawn."

I sighed. "I hope she is well enough to manage it."

Two weeks went by in a haze of cold that set the snow like stone into the fields and roads of Greenbrier County. We did our chores around the farm, and fed logs to the fires to warm the house. I tried to make sure that everybody got enough hot food to keep them from falling sick, and kept an eye on the boys as best I could so that they wouldn't do some tomfool thing like falling in the creek and catching pneumonia, or breaking their necks sledding down a steep ridge. I didn't hear from Zona, but I knew that spring was just over two months away, and there wasn't any use worrying about her now when the weather made it a misery to travel. Let the world warm up again, and then we'd go over and see how she was faring.

January 23 was an ordinary winter Saturday, cold and clear with a sky that seemed bluer than it ever does in summer. I made a breakfast of hotcakes and syrup to fortify us all against the cold, and made sure that everybody was wrapped up to the eyes in scarfs and coats and blankets before they went out to see to the livestock and cut firewood. They came back in the midafternoon, staying past dinnertime so as not to waste the daylight. I heard them stomping snow off their boots on the porch, which told me that it was time to start cooking. While the boys brought in a load of firewood and

tended the fire, I went into the kitchen to fry up a
chicken for their dinner. I had just floured the last
piece when Jon called out to me from the parlor,
"Company coming!"

I dropped the drumstick onto the cloth and hurried out of the kitchen, wiping my hands on my
apron. I was thinking that Zona and her husband
must have come to pay us a surprise visit, and at the
same time wondering if the chicken would stretch to
feed two more people or if I needed to cut a slab of
cured ham as well. I rushed to the window where the
boys were already peeping out at the visitors. Jacob,
in his chair by the fireplace, affected not to care if we
had company or not.

"It ain't Zona," said Jon, edging aside a little to
let me look out. "See? It's two fellows on horses. I
don't know who they are, though."

"I do," said H. C. "I talked to them at Zona's
wedding. They're friends with our cousins, live over
in the Richlands."

"What are their names, son?" asked Jacob.

H. C. shook his head. "I forget."

"Well, I wonder what brings them all the
way out here on a day like this." I was untying
my apron and patting down my hair. "Do you
reckon Edward and Zona are with them? Maybe
coming along directly in the buckboard?" We
would have to kill another chicken for certain, I
was thinking.

"Guess we'll find out," said Jacob, who got out
of his chair and headed for the door as soon as he
heard their footsteps on the porch.

I shooed the boys away from the window and
went to join Jacob at the front door. When he
opened it, an icy gust of wind hit us in the face, and
Jacob grabbed the nearest fellow by his coat sleeve
and pulled him over the threshold, nodding for his

companion to follow. The two young men were red-nosed from the cold, with bits of snow clinging to their hair and eyelashes. We led them over to the fireplace and made them stand near the hearth until they felt revived enough to divest themselves of their coats and gloves.

I turned to H. C. and Joseph. "See to their horses, boys. It's too cold for them to be standing out in the elements today. Put them in the barn and see that you give them hay and water, too."

They looked a little disappointed at being sent off before the strangers could say what they'd come about, but they knew better than to talk back in front of company, so they retrieved their still-damp coats from a ladder-back chair near the fireplace, and made as long a business as they could of donning scarves and gloves, but they were still bundled up and ready to leave before the strangers thawed out enough to say what they had come about. In fact, they didn't seem at all anxious to do so, but they looked relieved when H. C., Joseph, and Jon went outside.

We stood there, looking at them expectantly, trying not to let curiosity win over hospitality. The two young men looked at each other, as if each one hoped the other would take the lead, but finally the shorter, sandy-haired one said, "Mr. Heaster, Miz Heaster, I'm sorry to be the bearer of bad tidings, but we promised Trout we'd ride out here to let y'all know."

"Let us know what?" Jacob looked from one to the other of them, more puzzled than alarmed, but I knew.

"Mrs. Shue is dead, sir. She was found at the foot of the stairs this afternoon. We reckon she must have fallen."

I turned away then, because they were

probably expecting tears, but they wouldn't see any from me. All I felt was a cold rage somewhere beneath my ribs. Jacob put his hand on my shoulder, but I jerked away. "That devil has killed her!" I didn't mean for them to hear me say that, but they did.

nine

AFTER THE TWO STRANGERS came out with their terrible news, they looked askance at me, as if they were expecting me to fall down in a faint at their feet, but all I could do was stare at them and wait for my mind to catch up to the truth of their message. I kept trying to feel the sense of those words—Zona, dead. Maybe I wouldn't really feel the weight of them until I saw Zona for myself, for sometimes seeing is the only way to believe. But even then—even when the terrible import of their tidings reached my mind— did they suppose that I would give way before strangers? Not likely! I inherited a full dose of British reserve from my English father, and I'd already lived through a war and enough toil and hardship over the years on our mountain farm to destroy a weakling, so it's just as well that I wasn't one. I don't do my grieving in front of other people, and I don't give way to sorrow when there are more urgent matters to consider.

"How did it happen?" I asked, searching their faces for some sign of doubt or shame. "Was that husband of hers at home?"

"No, ma'am," said the sandy-haired fellow. "He was working at the smithy, but aside from that we don't know anything but what we were told. We didn't find her or nothin'."

"Are you fellows friends of Mr. Shue?"

They glanced at each other, and I thought they looked wary, though it was an innocent enough question.

"Not to say friends," said the tall one. "The Richlands ain't a very big place, so we all pretty much know one another. 'Course Trout hasn't been there that long."

"Aunt Martha Jones asked us to come. Said you ought to be told. She is by way of being a neighbor of theirs."

I turned to the sandy-haired fellow. "Your aunt sent you?"

He blushed. "Well, no, ma'am. She ain't no kin to me. She's . . ."

I understood then. "Aunt" and "Uncle" were what some folks called the elder, respected colored folks in the community. "I see. Well, it was kind of her to think of us."

"It was her boy Anderson who found Mrs. Shue. I think Trout had told him to stop by and see if she needed anything, and when he did he found her at the foot of the stairs, so he ran to tell his mama, and she sent him off to get word to Trout. They sent for the doctor, but it wasn't no use. Mrs. Shue was gone afore ever he found her."

The other one chimed in. "When Aunt Martha Jones told folks what had happened, Sam and me, we volunteered to ride out here. She said somebody ought to let you all know that poor Mrs. Shue has passed."

Jacob didn't make a sound during all this, but then he recovered himself well enough to remember to be civil to those two well-intentioned strangers who could not be blamed for the painful news they had brought. "Thank you for your trouble, boys," he managed to say, patting the nearest one on the arm. "We are obliged to you for making the long cold ride out here to let us know. Can we offer you some dinner?"

There wouldn't be any problem now about having enough food to go around. They could have it all. I wouldn't touch a morsel, and I doubted that Jacob would care to eat, either, but to be hospitable, we would sit at the table, make civil conversation, and push the food around on our plates to make the visitors feel at ease.

They must have known that the offer was a hollow gesture, though, and that, in the presence of our grief, the food would be likely to stick in their throats, because they exchanged stricken looks and, without an instant's hesitation, they both began to stammer out excuses to leave.

"It's awful late for a winter afternoon, sir," the tall one said. "We'd best be on our way while it's still light. For sure it's a long cold ride back to the Richlands."

"We thank you for the kind invite," said the other man, "but we just wanted to add our condolences before we started back. And to let you know that Trout asked that the funeral be held tomorrow, after he brings her body back here, on account of its being Sunday. He says that way he won't miss work."

Before I could say what I thought of that, the other one spoke up. "We didn't mean to intrude on your grief, or burden you with having to entertain strangers at a time like this. We'll just be getting our coats and be on our way." As the sandy-haired fellow started to pull on his still-damp coat, another thought struck him. "Have you folks any message that you'd like to send back to the widower?"

Jacob gave me a warning look, knowing full well what sort of message I'd be likely to send back to Mr. Edward Shue. Before I could open my mouth, he said, "You tell him it's fine for him to send her on home, and we will see to the burying. I reckon she ought to be laid to rest up here with her own people."

He glanced over at me as he said that, making sure that I agreed with him, but of course I did. *Mrs. Edward Shue* she might have been when she died, but for all that, Zona had known her husband for less than six months, and as far as we were concerned, he was a stranger.

As soon as the two men left, we called the boys back into the house and told them the news about Zona. They were pale and silent, but prepared for bad news, because solemn strangers riding up to the house on a late-winter afternoon usually meant that something was wrong. They sat there in a row close to the hearth, but still shivering as they took in the news. They looked up at us, waiting to hear the rest, but all Jacob said was that Zona was dead.

"Was she that sick then?" H. C., who was nearest to his sister in age, knew her best of all the boys. He looked distressed but not overcome, because they never wrote or confided in one another, for there was little enough that a twenty-two-year-old woman would have in common with a boy of sixteen.

"All we know is that she fell," Jacob told him. "They're bringing her body home tomorrow."

"How did she fall? Where?"

Jacob bowed his head. "We don't know the particulars, son."

I added, "But we aim to find out."

After supper, which nobody felt much like eating, we sent H. C. over to his uncle Johnson's place to give the news to the rest of the family. I spent the evening cutting armbands out of black cloth for Jacob and each of the boys to wear for mourning. We couldn't afford new clothes in the proper black for bereavement, so the armbands would have to do. I had a dyed-black dress already—Death is afoot often enough in every settlement for a woman to have need of a black dress many times a year. My funeral outfit was cotton, and not warm enough for winter wear, but if I put on two pairs of knit stockings and tucked a woolen shawl and scarf underneath my coat, it would serve to get me through the funeral and the burying.

I sat by the fireplace, sewing in silence. The boys had all gone upstairs to bed, but Jacob sat in his chair, just staring into the flames. He had the Bible in his lap, but after turning a few pages, he closed it and didn't open it again. I could have asked him to read aloud to me as I worked, but I was busy with my own thoughts. I sat there stitching by firelight, dry-eyed, saying nothing.

Finally Jacob leaned back with a sigh, and said, "I don't reckon there's anything we could have done."

"If it pleases you to think so." I stabbed the needle into the seam of the armband. "You said to let her go."

"Do you think we could have talked her out of marrying him, Mary Jane? When did she ever listen to us?"

"He killed her, Jacob. Sure as I'm sitting here, that man killed our daughter."

He shook his head. "We don't know that. You said she had been sick, seeing the doctor. Maybe she had female trouble. Maybe she came over faint and pitched down the stairs."

"You'll never make me believe that, Jacob. She was murdered, all right. I just pray to the Lord that there's some way to see that her killer is punished."

"Well, you mustn't go wasting the county officials' time making wild accusations you can't prove. I doubt they'll set much store by women's intuition."

He was probably right, but it wouldn't stop me from trying. I'd just have to think carefully about it before I set my case before them. I meant to be heard.

The weather cleared up to blue skies the next morning, but it was still cold as blazes. I had barely closed my eyes all night, bedeviled by thoughts of Zona, wondering if she had suffered, if she had died afraid. I had no doubt that Edward Shue had killed her, but I doubted if I would ever find out why.

I put a cake in the oven well before dawn, before I even started on breakfast, for I knew there'd be visitors in the house later that day.

At sunup I woke the rest of the household so that they could finish their morning chores in time for church. The folks at Soule Chapel would have to be told, and we needed to get there early so that we could speak to the preacher and set a time that afternoon for the burying. Then we'd have to hurry home to receive those members of the congregation who'd be kind enough to come to call.

We told the news to some of Jacob's other kin-folks first thing when we reached the church, and before long the whole congregation was abuzz with questions, and the boldest of them coming up to one or another of us asking for the particulars. We couldn't give them any satisfaction on that point, though.

"We don't know. They told us that she died from a fall." I must have said those words to every single person in the congregation. "They are bring-ing her home this afternoon."

Jacob touched my arm. "I've had a word with the reverend, Mary Jane. He says he can oblige us this afternoon. He will announce the funeral time to the congregation once services commence. Is that all right with you?"

I nodded, and turned away so he wouldn't see me cry. Poor Zona's life had been crowded into such a brief span of time: a birth, a wedding, and now a funeral, all within the space of little more than a year. And who would remember her? Not the child she gave away; not the husband, who had already had two other wives; and the community?—not for long, for she had left Little Sewell and she still would have been more or less a stranger in the Richlands. We would tend her grave and try to keep her memory green, but when we were gone, there would be no trace of her left—not even a headstone, for Jacob said that we could scarcely afford one, and besides that, a marker ought to be the responsibility of her next of kin, the man who married her, but I knew that her worthless husband wouldn't waste a penny on a dead wife.

I took my seat on the wooden bench next to Jacob, and sat still and staring while the preacher delivered his sermon, but I didn't hear a word he said.

The journey from the Richlands to Little Sewell with a laden wagon would take three or four hours, I judged, and I didn't look for them to arrive until early afternoon. I was right about that, for the wagon bringing her body home rolled up into our yard shortly after we returned from church. We weren't there alone because our neighbors and kinfolk had followed us home from church, and they would return with us for the burying later in the afternoon.

We were all sitting around sharing the sorrow—men in the parlor, women in the kitchen, and young'uns playing outdoors. The cake wouldn't stretch far enough to feed a houseful of people, so some of the nearer neighbor women had stopped at home to fetch a couple of winter apple pies to serve to the visitors today. But for the suddenness of the burial, there ought to have been food aplenty after the funeral when the people who came back to the house afterward would have brought fried chicken, casseroles, bowls of mashed potatoes—all tokens of their sympathy for us, for words come hard to most of the folks around here; they'd rather do you a kindness than have to talk about delicate matters. There hadn't been time for any of them to cook today, since they'd only just heard the news. As the pies warmed on the stove, we sat in the kitchen, shedding a few tears and talking softly, trying to pretend that we weren't just passing the time, dreading the waiting.

"They're here!" One of the neighbor boys came to the back door and poked his head in just long enough to let us know the group from the Richlands was coming, and then he was gone again, running back to join the rest of the children in the yard, watching the doleful procession.

Three men on horseback rode alongside the wagon, and one of them was Edward Shue himself. When I caught sight of him he was laughing and talking with the nearest rider. When he saw the door open and people spilling out on the porch, he broke it off, trying to look all solemn and bereaved in case anybody had noticed him. After a minute or two he seemed to forget to be mournful, and went back to talking with his companions again. Some of the men from the house went out to help take the coffin out of the back of the wagon, and Edward Shue was right there with them, telling them not to jostle it too much and trying to take hold of the front end of the box himself. He kept right close to the coffin, like a herding dog, as they brought it up the porch steps and into the house. He shook hands with one or two of the men on the porch, and suffered himself to be hugged by some of the neighbor women, but neither Jacob nor I wanted to say anything to him until we could govern our tempers, for it wouldn't do to quarrel in front of a houseful of people.

We had put the two kitchen chairs in an open space in front of the parlor window, and Jacob directed the bearers to set the coffin there. I wished that we could have put flowers out beside the coffin, but in late January, there were none to be found, so I draped an old baby quilt over a stool and set a candle and the Bible on top of it, to remind us all that Zona was in God's hands now.

The coffin lid had only been lightly nailed down, for safety's sake during the journey, but now one of the men took a crowbar and prised it open. When two of them lifted off the lid, Edward Shue, who was hovering close by, turned his face away so that he wouldn't have to look at the body. Then he composed himself, and commenced to talk in a low voice to one of the men who had come with him from the Richlands, but he never left the side of that coffin, not for an instant, and when anybody else tried to get close, he would become agitated, as if he was determined to protect his wife even in death.

I had gone through the ritual of sewing the mourning bands and preparing food for the visitors, but the fact of Zona's death would not really hit me until I saw her for myself. That time had come, and I steeled myself not to show grief—not that I would have anyhow in front of so many people, but also because I was mindful that Zona's killer was only a few paces away, pretending grief like a possum feigns death. But I'd not succumb to such cheap theatrics. Living through a war teaches you everything there is to know about sorrow. Real grief is silent as the grave.

When I felt able to do so without giving way, I went up to the coffin for a last look at my only daughter, but she was so wrapped up that I could scarcely recognize her. Zona was dressed in that same dark, high-necked dress she had worn when she married Edward Shue back in November—well, I couldn't fault him for that; it was the best she had—but he had also wrapped a scarf around her neck, one that didn't match the dress at all. A pillow and a bundle of cloth were placed on either side of her head; I had never seen anyone dressed for burial so outlandishly. Zona seemed lost in all the padding in the coffin. Her whole head was covered in a black veil tied under her chin in a big bowknot. I leaned down to untie the bow so that I could take a last look at my daughter's face, but as I reached out, her husband grabbed my hand.

"Please don't touch her! I can't bear it."

I stared at him, shaking away his grasp. "Don't touch her? But I'm her mother. I only wanted to see her one last time."

"Let her rest in peace, ma'am. Please." His eyes were pleading. "She has suffered enough, and we must not disturb her."

Had it been anybody else, I'd have thought he must be out of his head with grief, talking like that, though he certainly showed no other signs of bereavement, but as it was I decided it was just part of the show. "Surely she has been disturbed already. Someone had to prepare her body and dress her."

He shook his head. "I did that myself. She would have wanted me to do that for her. And now no one else must touch her."

"Did you put that scarf around her neck, too?"

"It was her favorite, ma'am. She would want it laid to rest with her."

"What about the pillow and the roll of cloth?"

There were beads of sweat on his forehead, but he managed to smile. "You'll think me foolish, Miz Heaster, but I wanted my Zona to rest easy in the coffin. I didn't want her to be jostled around on the wagon coming out here. She had such trouble sleeping these last few weeks, and I just thought the pillow might . . ." He shrugged. My expression must have told him how crazy he sounded.

I drew back my hand, but I fixed him with a cold stare that held not an ounce of sympathy. Every word he said made me trust him less. I wondered if he had also prepared the body of that other wife, the one who died year before last, and whom he seemed to have forgotten so easily, as he would no doubt forget Zona. "Tell me what happened."

The room got quiet just then, as if everybody present had been waiting for just that question. No one turned around to stare, but everything was suddenly still, and all the conversations seemed to have stopped midword. I kept my eyes fixed on Edward's face, daring him not to answer me.

The grieving husband didn't seem to notice the tense silence that had befallen the room. He was watching me carefully, as if trying to make up his mind what to say as the stillness stretched on. Finally he sighed and shook his head. "I wasn't there when it happened, Miz Heaster. So I don't know. I left for work that morning, same as always, and she was just fine then. On my way to the smithy, I stopped by Aunt Martha Jones's house and asked her boy to look in on my wife, to see did she want any help with anything around the house. He's a good fellow, not good for much in the ordinary way of things, but willing enough to lend a hand if you make it plain what you want him to do. Well, he says he finally got around to going over to the house about eleven o'clock, and when he went in, he found Zona sprawled out at the foot of the stairs. He called out to her, he said, asking did she need any help, but she was already gone."

Jacob was hovering near my elbow, listening in on Shue's explanation. "She fell then?"

He nodded. "It must have been an accident. I won't think otherwise, though Dr. Knapp did ask me if I thought she had made away with herself."

"Why would he ask that?"

"She had been low in spirits these past few weeks, and he had been treating her for that. But I won't believe she would do such a thing on purpose."

"Neither will I," I said.

By late afternoon the day of the burying had turned cold and misty, with a leaden sky that muffled the tops of the mountains, as if the clouds were intent on burying the world. The wagon crunched over dead leaves and through puddles crusted with ice as we made our way in cold silence to Soule Chapel to lay Zona to rest. Our nearest neighbors followed behind us in their buckboards and buggies. Our boys were riding with neighbors one wagon behind us, for the coffin took up too much room in the back of our wagon for them to fit, too.

I sat up front of our wagon, on the seat beside Jacob, staring straight ahead at the muddy road, edged by bare, wet trees. I had stayed awake all night, so I was as numb from weariness as much as from cold, but I wanted to be. That would make it easier not to give way during the funeral, not to faint when they put my daughter in the ground, and not to cross words with the devil who killed her.

Soule Chapel looked like a cloud itself, hovering there in the mist on a little rise about the dirt road. There were a goodly number of folks already there for the funeral, for the space beside the church was already filled with all manner of horse-drawn conveyances. Some familiar rigs—like Dr. Lualzo Rupert's one-horse shay with his fine black gelding in harness—told me who had arrived. Most of the church congregation seemed to be present, though most of them had been driven indoors by the sharp winter wind. I wondered which of them had come in sympathy to our family, out of friendship to Zona, and which were there out of morbid curiosity because of the tragic circumstances surrounding her death. I was sure that by now word would have spread through the settlement that Zona's sudden death was mysterious.

Jacob jumped down and secured the wagon, and then led me inside the church. He'd had a word with our neighbors, and five of them—and H. C.—had agreed to serve as pallbearers. They brought Zona inside and out of the cold, one last time.

I sat on the front bench close to the pulpit, trying to keep my mind on a silent prayer for my daughter's soul, but I kept trying to remember who I had seen on the benches as I made my way up the aisle. The opposite front bench was empty—just as it had been at Zona's wedding.

There was a clattering at the back of the sanctuary, and then a gust of icy wind. I turned to see what the disturbance was, and lo and behold, it was the widower himself, muffled to the eyes in a scarf and overcoat, making a belated appearance at the funeral of his wife.

The congregation, after a brief glance back out of curiosity, turned around again, pretending that nothing was amiss. Tongues would wag later, of course, but here in church they would preserve the decorum required by the solemn occasion. Edward Shue stamped the mud off his boots on the woven mat just inside the door, and made his way to the bench at the front of the church, while the minister waited in silence for everyone to settle down so that he could begin.

Edward nodded to us and then smiled at the pastor, but when he caught sight of Zona's coffin set up at the front of the sanctuary, his smile faded, and he folded his arms, looking more grim than solemn, preparing to endure a trying afternoon.

The music began to play then, and at the pulpit the pastor opened up his Bible, so I paid no more mind to Edward Shue, but as the service went on, I stared out the window at the clabbered sky, remembering my words of last night and finally repeating them as a silent prayer: *Lord, give me a way to know what really happened to Zona. Give her justice, so that she may rest in peace.*

The service wasn't long. The most momentous events in life—baptisms, weddings, and funerals—don't seem to take much time, but the effects of them bind up the whole of your existence. It seems like life doesn't take much time, either, although some days can seem to last forever.

A few sentimental old souls in the congregation shed tears, because Zona had been so young and pretty that it seemed a waste for her to have had such a brief life, but her widower shed no tears for her, and none of our family wept, either. I suppose Jacob didn't think it fitten for a man to grieve in public, but I was willing myself to be strong, because I had no time for the weakness of self-pity and sorrow.

When the last hymn had ended, we all stood up as the six pallbearers hoisted the oak coffin and marched slowly down the aisle to deliver Zona to her final resting place. We followed them outside into the feeble sunshine that leaked through the gray clouds, and walked the few paces to the burying ground at the back of the church.

The grave had been dug earlier that morning, before we got there. It was perhaps a hundred feet from the back of the church, past the older graves and midway between the woods that lay at the foot of the gentle slope and the dirt lane that ran along the side of the church. The mourners hung back a little, and Edward Shue started over to stand with us, but I gave him a look, and he thought better of it and contented himself with staying at the front of the crowd, but he stayed well away from the casket.

Our family gathered around the open grave, shivering in the wind, and I thought: *We'll all be here beside her by and by, but when I see her in heaven, I want to be able to tell her that I got justice for her here on earth.*

The graveside service was brief—a prayer and a few words of consolation to us. There was no more to be said, and the numbing cold was a warning that lingering here might cause some of us to follow her to the grave. The crowd encircling the open pit stood with heads bowed, solemn and still. We were mindful that a short, imperfect life had ended in disturbing circumstances that none of us understood, and there seemed to be nothing that we could do about it except to consign her body to the earth and her soul to the Lord. We stood there in silence as they shifted the ropes to lower the wooden coffin into the ground. Two or three of the congregation members picked up handfuls of damp earth and tossed them down onto the top of the coffin, but I didn't follow their example. The casting of dirt clods into the grave was a sign that the mourners were releasing their hold on the departed one, but I was not yet ready to do that. I could let her body go into the cold ground, but I hoped that her spirit would stay earthbound for a while longer.

I had to know.

When it was over, and in groups of two and three people began to walk back toward the church, I hurried to catch up with Edward. He had showed no inclination to linger beside the grave, and I thought that there was more than the weather to blame for that.

I put my hand on his arm to stop him, and he stiffened as if I'd put a knife in him. He spun around, saw it was me, and began to stammer, something about how sorry he was, but I had no patience for his excuses. I just wanted to be done with him.

"I have something to return to you, Edward."

When they had opened the coffin back at the house, I saw that Edward had stuffed a sheet into the casket, and I'd thought that such a contrivance was silly and undignified. When the men went out to fetch the wagon to take the coffin to the church, I had eased that sheet out from around her shoulders without disturbing her restful pose. I thought I'd give it back to Edward Shue, because as a newly married man with little money to spare, he couldn't have owned many bed linens, and burying a perfectly good one struck me as a waste. He might as well have this one back and get some use out of it. When we went out to go to the funeral, I tucked it under my blanket in the wagon, so that I could give it back to him at the funeral, for I doubted that any of us would ever set eyes on him again after that.

When I said I had something to give him, he stopped babbling and stared at me. Then he glanced over my shoulder at the casket, still resting there in the open grave. "I've just now recalled that I have something to give to you as well, ma'am." He dug in the pocket of his trousers and pulled out a little gold ring with three discolored pearls set in it. "I reckon she'd want you to have this."

I stared at it, for I had never seen it before in my life. "A ring? But that didn't belong to Zona. Where is her own ring? The one she was wedded with. I want that one, not this old thing."

He sighed and shoved the ring back in his pocket. "I'm sorry, ma'am."

"Will you give me my daughter's ring?"

He just shook his head. "I think you said you had something for me?"

I had no mind to do him any favors, but now I wanted nothing more than to be rid of every trace of him. "When you put Zona in her coffin, you rolled up one of your bedsheets in there alongside the pillows, and I thought maybe you'd be needing that sheet. You can't have too many to spare, and it was practically new. Anyhow, I took it out just before we left the house to come here. I've brought it to give to you. It's under my lap blanket in the wagon yonder."

A gust of wind hit us just then, and that might have been why Edward suddenly commenced to shiver. He pulled his coat tighter around him and backed away from me. "I don't want it back, ma'am. Thank you for the offer, though, but I couldn't take it. If you'll excuse me, I have to go off home now so the fellows can return the wagon to Mr. Crookshanks. It'll be gathering dark afore we get there."

I nodded. "You go ahead." We hadn't so far to go ourselves, but night would surely overtake Edward Shue before he reached Livesay's Mill.

He nodded, and raised his hand in a tentative farewell. "Don't reckon I'll be seeing you all again."

I gave him a long stare, colder than the wind. "You might, one of these days. You just might."

That night I went to bed when the rest of the family did, and I should have been exhausted, as much from dealing with a houseful of people as with grief and toil, but I found that I couldn't sleep anyway. I got up again, telling Jacob that I had remembered more things that needed doing before I could go to bed, and that was true enough. The ash and soot from a fireplace constantly puts dust out into the room, so that no matter how many times you sweep the room and run the feather duster over the furniture, it still has to be done again all too soon. Visitors track in mud on the floors and drop bits of food on the carpet. I was determined that the house should be in good order, so that we could put the memories of the funeral behind us and get on with the business of living.

After I tidied up the mess that everyone had left, and made sure that the rest of the family was fast asleep in their beds, I sat up beside the fire in the parlor, keeping vigil, except that there was no coffin to keep it for. Over by the front window, the coffin had sat, balanced on two kitchen chairs, the lid on the floor behind it, until they nailed it in place when we set off to church for the burial. Perhaps it was just as well that she was gone, so that I couldn't look at her again, for I'd had my fill of seeing her that afternoon when they brought her in.

She had been so veiled and covered that I barely had a glimpse of her face, but her very stillness had seemed more peaceful than I ever remembered seeing her in life. Zona always had a restless air about her, as if she didn't know where she wanted to go but wanted to get there as quick as she could, never satisfied, never still. It seemed to me that she had spent her life like an orphaned calf, pushing against the fence and trying to get someplace else just because it *was* someplace else. And now she had reached her destination, the last place she would ever go, and I didn't think she had ever known a moment's peace until she got there. I hoped the end for her had come fast and unexpected, so that she wouldn't have had time to reflect that it had all been for nothing.

I wish Edward Shue had taken the sheet I'd tried to return to him, for I wanted no trace of him in the house. He wasn't family anymore, if indeed he ever had been. Some in-laws keep on being part of the family, even after the death of the relative they were married to—Abigail Heaster, Johnson's wife, was a friend as well as a relation, and she would go right on being kinfolk to us even if he passed before she did— but with Edward Shue, things were different. None of us could bear to look at him.

There was also something else I had to do.

Even though Zona was already consigned to the earth at Soule Chapel, I needed to honor her memory in the old ways, for my sake as much as hers. I didn't want the rest of the family to see me doing it, because they might think me backward and foolish. Certainly Jacob would say that what I was doing was only a worthless superstition, and perhaps that was so, but these things were also a custom in the community, going back further than anyone can remember, and we did them as a sign of mourning. Tradition can be a comfort in difficult times. It gives you something to hold on to when everything else is falling apart.

I went into the kitchen and took down the box of salt that we kept next to the stove. I poured a handful into a small glass plate. *Salt of the earth.* Salt is cheap and we seldom take much notice of it, but nevertheless it is salt that binds us to life. Even our blood tastes salty. We use salt to preserve the hog meat so that it will keep through the winter. We throw it into the frying pan in case of a grease fire on the stove, and keep it close to the sink to scour the pans with, to clean them after cooking. We gargle with salt when we're sick, and sprinkle it outside in the winter to keep the snow from sticking to the steps and walkways. It purifies and protects us in a hundred ways—and maybe that's the reason for this last, solemn use for salt. The one that nobody talks about.

I carried an oil lamp in one hand and the dish of salt in the other into the parlor, where Zona had lain hours earlier, muffled and shrouded in her oak coffin. She was gone now, so perhaps the ritual was useless, but I knew I would feel better for doing it. Perhaps rituals are for the living, anyhow. I went to the front window, set the dish on the windowsill, and pulled up the window, but only an inch or so, because the cold night air was fierce. My hand shook a little as the wind rushed in under the crack, but I stepped back without spilling any of the salt.

Then I thought about what I was doing. When there is a death in the house, you stop the clock, cover the mirrors, and tie a bit of crepe to the bee-hive. And then you put a dish of table salt on the sill of an open window. For what purpose? To free the soul of the departed one.

Nobody ever explained the whys of it, but I thought that stopping the clock might mean that for the dead, time had ceased to matter. The covered mirror would keep the deceased from seeing their own reflection and trying to hold on to who they were on earth. And the table salt kept evil spirits from getting into the house, so that they could not take hold of the soul of the dead, but yet the departed one could pass through that open window, over the salt and into the hereafter, leaving all their earthly cares behind. It was all meant to ease their passing, and to help them find peace.

I rushed back to the window, dumped the salt outside, where the wind took it, and slammed down the sash.

I didn't want Zona to slip from this world in peace. She had died in violence, in fear and pain, well before her time, and her killer stood a good chance of getting away with it. I wished that the Lord would grant her a way to let me know what had happened to her. It was too late to save her, but at least I could get justice for her.

"Come back, Zona," I whispered. "Don't leave this world until you tell us what happened."

ten

JOHN ALFRED PRESTON always read the local
newspaper, the *Greenbrier Independent*, to keep abreast
of happenings within the county, but today he was
also checking to make sure that his announcement
had appeared on the front page, as he had requested.
Sure enough, there it was in a little box on the left
side of the front page, ahead of the ads of three other
local lawyers: "John A Preston Attorney at Law Lewisburg WVa will practice in the Circuit of Greenbrier
and Adjoining Counties."

He wasn't new in town—far from it: born and
bred here—but it never hurt to remind people that
he was available, should they need legal representation. There were a good many attorneys to choose
from these days, and he couldn't say that he approved
of all of them. He scanned the rest of the front page.
There had been a time not all that long ago when he
hadn't needed spectacles to read the unbroken columns of fine print. Now he couldn't even read the
headlines without them. Well, he would be turning
fifty in May; perhaps it was time to stop fighting the
inevitable. One of these days he might even have to

use a magnifying glass when he perused the paper. Not that there was much worth reading on page one—no news at all to speak of. Some aphorisms on the right side of the page ("Take care of your plough, and your plough will take care of you"); a poem at the top of the page, beginning "On life's rugged road . . ." The author of that bit of doggerel was not named; he wouldn't have claimed it, either. Most of the rest of the front page was taken up with a number of stories and anecdotes having nothing whatever to do with Greenbrier County, West Virginia. He supposed they didn't generate enough news locally to fill up a weekly newspaper, or else they couldn't afford the reporters to go out and find it. Actually, quite a lot went on in little Greenbrier, as it did everywhere else, but he suspected that the local citizenry generally knew more about it than the *Independent* did. He often thought that the locals merely read the newspaper to see who had been caught. In the matter of personal tragedies, when misfortunes occurred in area families, they didn't care to see them plastered all over the local newspaper for all the neighbors to see.

As for the civic news, much of the business— both commercial and political—was conducted behind closed doors, and the results were only presented to the citizenry as a fait accompli. Maybe the average man didn't even want to know all the minutiae of local government and business. Certainly the witty stories and bits of trivia on the front page were more entertaining than the long hours of small talk, punctuated by wrangling, that constituted local politics. Preston didn't mind the *Independent*'s deficiencies. He got the real civic news from those directly involved, and Lillie kept him informed about all the other particulars of Lewisburg so that he was always aware of the births, deaths, and marriages in their social circle, often in greater detail than he considered strictly necessary. It was useful to know such things; so much of business consisted of not talking about business at all.

His late first wife, Sallie, had also been wonderfully adept at managing the social currents of their lives, but of course she came by it naturally, being the daughter of the lieutenant governor of Virginia. Ambition and being socially adroit ran in the Price family, but he came from a line of clergymen, and so he had relied on Sallie—and now her successor, Lillie—to manage that side of his career. He wondered if Sallie had ever been disappointed by the fact that he had not shared her family's ambition and skill at dealing with people. Perhaps, when he was her father's assistant and her suitor, she might have thought that she would become the wife of a governor or a senator. But John Alfred Preston, though wellborn and well educated, could find in himself no attraction to the rough-and-tumble life of a career politician. At the age of seventeen he had gone to war, and that experience had provided him with enough uncertainty and excitement to last him for the rest of his days. Somehow in military life he had come to associate manipulating people with sending them to their deaths, and to this day he shrank from it. By his own standards he had led a good life: pillar of the local community, elder of the church, respected member of the legal fraternity, devoted husband and father. That was enough.

He had thought all that as if he were trying to convince Sallie of the rightness of his choice, but she had been laid to rest in the churchyard these past fifteen years. What had made him think of her now? Perhaps it was because he would soon resume the post of county prosecutor, which she might have mistaken for a stepping-stone to greater things—

wishful thinking, of course. In truth, though, the local attorneys passed the office around amongst themselves like a hot potato. Already he had been prosecutor three times running, then Henry Gilmer had succeeded him, and now Gilmer was leaving office and Preston would come in again. There was no more rhyme or reason to the appointment of county prosecutor than there was in the games of tag that James and Samuel, the two older Preston boys, once played on the lawn. They were Sallie's boys. John and Walter, his sons with Lillie, would be playing there soon, but Walter was barely two and not up to it yet. Preston hoped all his sons would grow up to be successful men that their mothers could be proud of. His chief regret was that Sallie had missed seeing her boys grow up.

Preston had spent his youth in that war. He lived through the final months of it with the 14th Virginia Cavalry under General McCausland in a haze of danger and privation, although he had been only seventeen years old at the time. He had dropped out of Washington College over in Lexington in order to join the army. Just as well that the war ended three months later, before his widowed mother could lose yet another son in battle. Six months before he had enlisted, his older brother Walter had lost an arm in the battle at Spotsylvania Courthouse, and a few months after that—in July of '64—his eldest brother, Thomas, had been killed at Monocacy. Nine months later the war was lost, the region was in shambles, and young John Alfred Preston was the hope of the family.

To finish his education, he returned to Washington College, where Robert E. Lee spent the last three years of his life serving as president. He was proud of having known the general, both at the college and in Greenbrier County. Lee had often sojourned there at the Old White Hotel, startling fellow guests, who would encounter him unexpectedly on the hiking trails around the hotel grounds. Lee was a gracious, somber gentleman, patient and courteous to his well-wishers but preferring to avoid the limelight. Preston could think of no one he would rather emulate.

In due course, Preston got his law degree and went home to Lewisburg, now and forever located in the state of West Virginia, for the region's separation from the Old Dominion had been sanctioned by the Union, and they had won the war. Virginia had been the only state in the union to lose territory on account of the war, but all the state's lawyers and all of Lee's men could not put the two states together again. In time he had grown used to the division, but sometimes even now he felt a pang of nostalgia for Virginia.

As a newly fledged attorney he had entered into practice under the tutelage of the Honorable Samuel Price, whose daughter Sallie he would marry four years later.

Marrying the boss's daughter after four years' acquaintance was hardly the storybook idyll most women would consider romantic, but John Alfred Preston favored practicality over passion. People had thought the war was romantic, too. He had thought so himself, at seventeen, seduced by stirring anthems, banners, gold braid, and the thought of military honors, but the mud and carnage of Petersburg had cured him of his delusions. He emerged from the war impervious to myth and sentiment.

Sallie Price, who was his own age and nearly thirty when they wed, had been a sensible and appropriate choice for a wife. Mawkish love-at-first-sight romances were all very well in Tin Pan Alley melodies, but, lawyerlike, he thought of marriage as more of a contract wherein two people entered into an agreement for their mutual benefit; each was expected to keep his or her part of the bargain, working together for the good of the community and the benefit of the family. As the daughter of a lawyer, Sallie knew what to expect when she married one, and he thought that they had suited each other well. The alliance had been successful—two well-bred, self-disciplined people had joined their lives together, and each had profited by the union. It was unfortunate that poor Sallie would die so soon. She was only thirty-five, and her sons were still toddling boys who would barely remember her, but Preston believed that one had to trust in the ways of Providence and not question God's will.

Strange to think that she had been dead these fifteen years—three times longer than they were married. Perhaps if Sallie had lived, she might have persuaded him to aspire to greater achievements than those of a simple country lawyer. When she died in 1882 and left him with two sons who were little more than babies, he had given up all thought of higher office beyond the bounds of Greenbrier County, with unspoken relief that he should now have a perfect excuse to rise no higher. Better to raise his motherless boys in his hometown, and to devote his surplus energy beyond his ordinary law practice to their care and education. His own parents were long dead, of course—he had barely known his father—but here in Greenbrier County he had a lifelong store of friends and colleagues and a church full of kindred spirits to sustain him as he carried on with his career and tended to his motherless boys for another decade.

He supposed he might have sought another wife sooner to help him raise the children, but John Alfred Preston did nothing impulsively or in haste. He had waited ten years to marry again. Miss Lillie Davis, the daughter of a Clarksburg attorney, was sixteen years his junior. At twenty-nine—nearly the same age that Sallie had been as a bride—she was certainly old enough to be the stepmother of two adolescent youths, but perhaps too young and inexperienced to question her husband's career decisions. She didn't seem to mind that he had no aspirations to be a congressman or even a judge. Well, he was past forty by the time they married—not old, perhaps, but the war had seemed to last forever, and then in its aftermath the world had changed so much over the decades that he sometimes felt that he had lived a hundred years.

Lillie was too young to remember the war, and much of the time he succeeded in keeping the memories of it at bay. She was also a lawyer's daughter, and their union was as calm and cordial as the first one had been. The careful, unsentimental practice of marrying the daughter of an attorney had served him well. He thought he had proved a good husband, honoring his part of the contract to the best of his ability, and he had chosen well in both of his matrimonial endeavors: prudent, sensible wives who were an asset to his position in the community.

He glanced down at the list of marriages on an inside page of the *Independent*, wondering how frivolous, empty-headed women managed to snare a husband. Youthful prettiness, he supposed, but if they outlived that girlish charm, their husbands would repent their choices, perhaps for decades. He sighed and turned a page. Love was a form of madness. It was too bad they couldn't be committed for it, but he supposed there was no cure, anyhow.

He looked at the little box on the page with the newspaper's advertisements: "Greenbrier Official Directory." Every week the *Independent* listed all of the county's personnel from the judges and officers of the court all the way down to the notaries public and the overseers of the poor. There was Henry Gilmer, listed as the county prosecutor, right after Judge McWhorter and ahead of the county commissioners, but in another issue or two Preston's name would replace Gilmer's in the box. The appointment was no less an honor for the fact that he had held the post several times before. Perhaps he had never been called to any higher office than that, nor frequented the seats of the mighty, but he had occupied a place of importance in the affairs of Greenbrier County. He had led a quiet, ordinary life perhaps, but a placid existence could be considered an achievement in this uncertain world, and after the chaos of war in his youth, a quiet, ordinary life was not to be scorned. It was a gift that had been denied to many of his contemporaries. He was mindful of his good fortune to have survived to enjoy a placid old age.

Now that he had reached his fiftieth year of living, he had no need to wish for any sensational murder cases or headline-making scandals. A peaceful, well-ordered county would suit him just fine, and if no one committed a crime or needed prosecuting, he would consider that a blessing, but of course it was past praying for. No matter how peaceful and bucolic a place was, there would always be transgressors—thieves, drunken brawlers, even killers. He didn't know that he felt particularly sorry for the lawbreakers themselves, for in his experience it was their families who suffered and who paid even more dearly for the crime than the felons did. He might pray for them on a Sunday morning in the Old Stone Church, where he was an elder, but there was little else he could do to ease their pain.

He had to squint to read the fine print of the newspaper. You'd think, with so little news to report, that they could take out some of the silly poems and irrelevant items of trivia, and print what was worth reading in a larger typeface. He sighed. He was getting old, not just his eyes but also his aching joints and his dyspeptic stomach. That was all right, though. He had fought the good fight, stayed the course, acted well his part, and he was still in his prime professionally, still striving, still achieving, at least locally.

There was nothing in the newspaper about the county's change of personnel, but everyone who mattered knew. The announcement would be made public within the next few weeks: John Alfred Preston would succeed Henry Gilmer as the prosecuting attorney for the county. The only notice the newspaper was likely to take of that would be to change the wording in the Greenbrier directory in the middle of page two. To most of the law-abiding citizens of Greenbrier County, the change would make no difference. Nor would it affect the feloniously inclined, because the law was the law, set down in books from time immemorial, and it hardly mattered which well-dressed gentleman carried out its directives. Thieves and killers would still go to prison, and their victims would still have their day in court, hoping to receive justice.

For John Alfred Preston, personally, the appointment meant a steady income, not that he needed such financial security. He led a quiet, unostentatious life, preferring to impress his fellow man with his good works—his service on the advisory boards of two local schools, and his long tenure as an elder in the Presbyterian church—rather than with material possessions. He was proud of that. He felt that his character had much to do with his being regularly entrusted with the job of county prosecutor. There were a number of other lawyers now in Greenbrier County, but some of them seemed little better than the rascals they represented in court.

Preston continued to peruse the *Greenbrier Independent* until an ad on an inside page brought him up with a start. *Rucker!* Exactly the sort of attorney he had just been thinking of, as much a scoundrel as the local felons. What was the old devil up to now?

Suing somebody. There was the legal notice, tucked in the column between the ad for the Lee Military Academy and Green & Bready's Grocery. Commissioner Withrow was announcing that on February 20, he would make his ruling in the case of W. P. Rucker versus Lewis Skipper and others. Some civil matter—a squabble over money, of course. Rucker seemed to bring lawsuits against people for sport, much as another man might fish or hunt. He might even have become a lawyer for that express purpose, because it was hardly the man's only profession. He was also a physician, a tavern owner, and Lord knew what else.

Or, rather, the devil did.

William Rucker had been courting trouble in one form or another for forty years. Nobody mentioned it in his presence these days, because he seemed to have turned respectable as he aged, but his past was as colorful as a dime-novel outlaw's.

Rucker had missed almost as much of the war as Preston had, but for a different reason. Rucker was a rabid Union sympathizer who didn't let a little detail like owning slaves himself stand in the way of his political preferences. After he directed the destruction of the railroad bridge over the Cowpasture River, he was captured in Summersville and sent to a Confederate prison. He might have been hanged if President Lincoln himself had not authorized detaining a Confederate surgeon to use as a bargaining chip to win Rucker's release. The negotiations went back and forth for months, but finally Rucker resolved the matter himself by escaping, and when he eventually managed to attach himself to another Union command, he went back to his old ways, and succeeded in getting Union troops to burn another railroad bridge.

Perhaps William Rucker felt that the long years of peacetime were dull after all his youthful escapades. He seemed to have boundless energy, despite his age, and he spread himself thin amongst all his various enterprises. While Preston practiced law solemnly, a priest to his civic duty, Rucker was a gadfly, acting as if each case were a battle, setting fire to legal bridges when he could.

You had to be polite to the man. He was, after all, a member of the legal fraternity, no matter how unorthodox, but Preston could not bring himself to consider William Rucker a colleague, still less a friend. He was at best a colorful diversion from the ordinary business of law, and at worst a habitué of the court on the other side of the process—as a defendant. Members of the county bar still murmured about the time Dr. Rucker ended up in court when his own wife sued him for getting money from her under false pretenses and then using it to pay his gambling debts. People laughed about it, but it made Preston shudder to think of a man swindling his own wife, and a union so acrimonious that the spouses must conduct their battles in court. There was also talk about Rucker's irregular moral conduct. About fifteen years ago, he had fathered a child with one of his household servants. Since it was common knowledge that Margaret Scott Rucker had come into the marriage as a wealthy woman, and that she still owned most of the couple's property outright, it was a wonder that Rucker had not found himself on the receiving end of a suit for divorce. How could anyone trust a man so lacking in loyalty and principles?

Preston supposed that sooner or later he would

be facing Dr. Rucker in the courtroom, prosecuting some hapless wrongdoer who had hired Rucker as his attorney. Appearing against the flamboyant old scoundrel was not a part of the job that Preston was looking forward to, but it would be his duty to do so, and Preston was never one to cavil at duty or to shirk an obligation. As always, he would behave as a gentleman, even when dealing with those who were not.

eleven

WHEN THE FUNERAL WAS OVER, we went back home and got on with our lives. I took the sheet from Zona's coffin out of the wagon and set it in the willow basket with the rest of the soiled laundry. Another couple of days went by before I got around to washing it, but it never occurred to me to throw it away, because it was almost brand-new, and there was no sense in wasting it. By the end of the week, the weather cleared up, and although the sunny day wasn't any warmer than the drizzly ones, at least I could be sure that the washing would dry if I hung it outside on the clothesline.

I heated up water on the stove and set about washing the sheet, first thing. I didn't want the house tainted any longer by traces of Edward Shue. When I unfolded it to dunk into the hot water, I noticed a foul odor coming from the sheet. What could have caused that? It was only next to Zona's body for a few hours, and her death had been so recent that there should have been no smell of death attached to it, but whatever it was, hot water and soap ought to get rid of it. I pushed the sheet into the water, and reached for the soap to give it a good scrubbing, but when I looked down into the wash water, I saw a red stain spreading over the water, seeming to come from the middle of the sheet. Blood? I didn't see why there should be any blood on the sheet, for if Zona had fallen down the stairs, there shouldn't have been any blood, and if he'd wrapped her a few hours after she died, there would have been no bleeding at all—dead things don't bleed. As I stared at the reddening water, I began to wonder why Edward would put a dirty sheet into his wife's coffin—it seemed a disrespectful thing to do, from someone who professed himself to be heartbroken over his dead bride. I put the soap directly onto the red blotch on the sheet and scrubbed as hard as I could, but the stain stayed put.

Maybe it will go away when the sheet dries, I thought.

When I finished scrubbing it, I wrung out the water and carried it out in the yard to dry on the clothesline. The cold wind whipped around me as I fastened the clothespins to the edges, and I knew that between the sunshine and the fierce breeze, the sheet wouldn't take long to dry.

I went back into the kitchen and poured out the tainted water I'd washed the sheet in. After I'd fetched more water and heated it up on the stove, I got on with washing the family's socks and underwear, trying not to think about that stained sheet flapping outside on the clothesline. Half an hour later, when I went back outside to hang out the rest of the washing, I looked again at the sheet. It was whipping back and forth in the pale sunshine, but although the wind had dried it completely, the stain—the pink blot like a faded bloodstain that I had scrubbed so hard in near-boiling water with lye soap—had come back. *Blood will out*—I remembered my father saying that. I couldn't remember the story, exactly. Something about a custom back in the olden days in England—that to find the real killer the authorities had him touch the victim's body at the wake, and if he was guilty, the corpse would begin to bleed. Blood was a sign.

Now, I am not a fanciful woman, nor a superstitious one. I'm not afraid of black cats, or the number thirteen, and I don't think you can tell anything about the future by looking at tea leaves in the bottom of a cup. But I am a God-fearing woman, and I do believe that the Lord doesn't want murderers to go unpunished. For those who call out to him in prayer, He might well send a sign to help move justice along in the right direction. That's not superstition, believing in that; it's faith.

I had prayed for a sign, hadn't I?

This must be it: the Lord's way of telling me that my suspicions were right. Zona had been murdered.

But it wasn't enough.

I believed, but earthly justice requires more than a stain on a sheet as proof that a wrong has been done. I could see myself going into the sheriff's office, carrying that pink-stained bedsheet and claiming that it was the Lord's way of telling me that my daughter had been murdered. Like as not, instead of arresting Edward Shue, they'd clap me into a lunatic asylum.

I looked up at the bright blue sky—what Daddy called the cope of heaven—spread out above our old oak tree and stretching so far beyond Sewell Mountain that it felt like you ought to be able to see all the way to paradise. "I thank you, Lord," I said. "I thank you for this sign, and I believe it, but if you want me to see that this murderer is brought to justice, you will have to give me more evidence than this. I fear that lawmen have hard hearts, and they will need more convincing than this."

I waited for a moment, standing there by the clothesline, bathed in winter sunlight and hearing only the sound of the wind rattling tree branches against the tin roof. I don't know what I was expecting. An angel to appear in the yard next to my bedraggled flower bed? A voice from the clouds? But all I got was a brisk wind carrying the faint smells of wet leaves and wood smoke. The Lord's time is not ours. After another minute, I took that stained sheet off the clothesline, and went back to hanging out wet socks and underwear.

Another week went by, and I didn't say anything to anybody about the sheet, or about my hopes for more solid proof that Zona had been murdered. Jacob had not so much as spoken our daughter's name since the day of the funeral, and the boys seemed to be done with grieving already. They got on with their chores and their schoolwork as if nothing bad at all had happened. The young don't take things so much to heart, I reckoned. Zona hadn't lived here in the last months of her life, and so for them it was easy to forget that she was no longer living at all. My only companion in grief seemed to be the weather, for it turned bitterly cold the week after the funeral, and the trees glittered with crystals of ice. We were cooped up in the house, except when we had to venture out to feed the animals or chop more firewood. I tried to keep myself busy, scrubbing floors and polishing the furniture with beeswax, but it doesn't take much thinking to clean a house, and that left my mind free to dwell on Zona and that devil who had killed her. Every time we ate dinner, I'd picture him shoveling food into his mouth without a care in the world, maybe going to a social over in Livesay's Mill to get likkered up and dance with all the young women, looking for wife number four, like as not. There's many a flighty young miss who would be only too happy to console a handsome brute like Edward Shue. Zona had been foolish to take up with him. She knew about his other wives—knew that the one before her had died from a fall. Still, it's common enough for a woman to die young: fevers and childbirth and accidents carry them off well before they're three score years and ten. Many a man is on his second or third wife before he finally goes to his grave, and no one thinks he is a Bluebeard on account of it. Having two wives die within two years might seem like extraordinary misfortune for Edward Shue, but it wouldn't necessarily lead folks to conclude that he had made away with them.

He had, though.

The more I scrubbed, and swept, and shined, the more my anger grew. I'd catch sight of my reflection as I polished the mirror, and think how grim and hard I looked, as if all my feelings had curdled in the pit of my stomach like soured milk. The only thing that would bring me back to the warmth of the world was seeing that Zona's murdering husband got what was coming to him. Smiling, handsome Edward Shue was like a farm dog that had got away with killing a chicken. Nothing would stop him now that he'd a got a taste for blood, and he'd go right on killing chickens until he was put down.

I wasn't sleeping any more than I was eating. Lately I had even given up trying, for lying there wide-awake in the darkness gave me no distraction from the thoughts that kept circling in my mind, and my restlessness was robbing Jacob of a sleep that otherwise would have come to him easily. Finally, I moved into Zona's old room, empty now except for a bed and dresser. We were going to move H. C. into the room come spring so that he wouldn't have to share a room with his younger brothers. We should have moved him already, when Zona left home for good, but what with one thing and another we hadn't got around to it. I'd sit up there nights, mostly thinking but praying a lot, too. Sometimes I'd stare out the window, looking at the bare tree branches silvered in moonlight or watching the clouds scudding across the sky between little puddles of stars. A week or so went by, and I acted just the same as usual, doing my household chores, and being there in the kitchen with breakfast cooking before any of the rest of the family got up. They never asked me how I was feeling, or whether I was getting any rest, and I never told them anything about what I was going through.

Finally, though, one day I did. I waited until I had set eggs and fried bread on Jacob's plate, and while he started shoveling it in, I said, "I'm going to town today. Over to Lewisburg, that is."

His fork stopped midway to his mouth, and he gave me a wary look, as well he might. Lewisburg was the county seat, but it is twenty miles away, and we hardly ever went there. Folks like us have little need for stores, and little to do with the local officials who are situated there. "Lewisburg? Whatever for, Mary Jane?"

"Going to see the prosecutor. It's time we got Edward Shue put away behind bars."

"The county lawyer? You want him to arrest Zona's husband?"

"I want him to arrest Zona's killer."

"I doubt he'll listen to women's intuition." Jacob gave me that *foolish little woman* smirk and went back to spreading honey on his bread, as if that remark had settled the matter.

"You could come along with me, and help me convince them that she was murdered."

He shook his head. "I don't believe I care to do that."

"You don't want your daughter's killer to be punished?"

"I don't want you to go making a big fuss in front of the whole county, and then see Edward Shue get off scot-free when they can't prove anything against him. Then everybody would think you were a bitter old woman who had taken leave of her senses. It's better if we just get on with the business of living. Zona made her bed when she chose to marry a fellow she hardly knew, and now she is dead and buried. There's nothing we can do that will help her— probably never was."

I folded my arms and gave him a squinty-eyed frown. "*She* thinks otherwise."

He just stared at me for a couple of moments. *Ask me*, I thought. *If you care at all about our lost daughter, ask me what I mean by that.* He opened his mouth, and I waited for the words, but after a moment or two, he shrugged, and went back to eating his bread. "Lewisburg." He sighed. "Well, I haven't got time to take you all the way to town. It would waste the whole day, and I've got fencing to mend."

"That won't stop me from going. I'll get there one way or another, Jacob."

"That's your lookout, then. If you want to go stirring up trouble, I'll have no part of it."

There was no shifting Jacob once he had set his mind on a course, but I didn't need his permission or his company in order to get to town. He was probably right about the lawyers not being willing to listen to a woman's claim without any physical evidence, but I thought I might stand a better chance if I took along someone that they would pay more heed to. The best choice, I thought, was Jacob's older brother Johnson

Heaster. His farm was ten times bigger than ours, which made him a man of substance in the community. They'd hear him out, anyhow. Whether or not they'd believe him—or me—was another matter, but I was determined to try.

After breakfast, when Jacob and H. C. went outside to make a start on mending the fence, I packed lunch pails with ham biscuits and winter apples, and saw the younger boys off to school. Then I put on my hat and coat, and set off down the road to Johnson and Abigail's house. It would have been quicker to cut across the fields, but I dreaded winter mud and icy puddles more than a little extra distance, so I took the long way. It gave me time to think up what I was going to say to my brother-in-law. If I could convince him that I wasn't crazy, maybe I had a chance of winning over the county prosecutor.

"I need a ride to town."

Johnson was surely surprised to find me on his doorstep on that cold February morning, without a wagon or a horse in sight, but he tried not to show it. Like everyone else in the community, he was treating me gently on account of my having lost a daughter a few weeks back. *When he hears what I've come for*, I thought, *he may think I have taken leave of my senses, but it probably won't surprise him.* Grief sometimes spirals into madness. He'd be relieved if I didn't take on like Salome seeing the head of John the Baptist on a platter. I was taking it hard, and everybody knew it. But I had to convince him that I hadn't lost my reason. I had good cause to be upset—not just by the death of my daughter, but by the wherefores of the matter, too.

My brother-in-law Johnson was by way of being

the Heaster family patriarch since his and Jacob's parents were long dead. He was a good half a dozen years older than Jacob, and he had married Abigail toward the end of the war, thirty-three years ago this month. They had more of everything than we did— more children, more land—but we didn't begrudge them any of it. It was a comfort to know that we had family we could count on in time of trouble, and they weren't so prosperous that they didn't have misfortunes of their own to plague them every now and again.

Johnson took a step back and almost lost his hold on the door as a gust of wind hit him. "Why, Mary Jane, you must be frozen out here in this weather. Where's Jacob? You didn't walk here, did you?"

I put my fingers over my lips and nodded. I had breathed in so much cold air that if I had tried to say any more, the sound would have come out in a fit of coughing.

It hadn't been a long walk to Johnson's farm— at least, it wouldn't have seemed so in any season except winter. Their white farmhouse was bigger than ours, but not any fancier. It had a wide one-story porch, but no elaborate Greek columns or painted shutters. Most people in Greenbrier County are content to be plain folk with simple ways, and the only sign of prosperity was the fact that the house was well cared for and encircled by fifty acres of rolling meadows. It was nestled amid a stand of hardwood trees, set on a little rise above the valley, so that the view of distant hills and patchwork fields was as perfect as an oil painting. I always found that house a reassuring sight, one that, except in the dead of winter, would make a visitor feel warm and safe and at peace with the world. My sorrow was too great and the weather too harsh for me to take solace in it then, but at least I was sure of a kinfolk's welcome and a sympathetic listener to the tale I had not yet decided how to tell.

I stood there on the porch, still bereft of speech, my breath coming in clouds and my hands so numb from cold that I had scarcely felt the surface of the door when I knocked. Johnson, spurred into motion by the cold, bundled me into the house, calling out to Abigail to let her know that company had arrived. Just inside the door, I pulled off my wet shoes, so as not to track clumps of mud on the polished oak floors of the parlor. My sister-in-law is a heavyset woman, mother of seven, and four years older than I. She was a winsome girl in her youth, not above putting lampblack on her eyelids and rice powder on her face, but now she has plain scrubbed cheeks and her eyes are sunk in the folds of fat surrounding them. Her hair, mostly gray and wispy now and pulled back into a tight bun on top of her head, does nothing to flatter that reddish moon face. Abigail may not be vain of her appearance, but she is house-proud to a fault, and not even her sympathy for my bereavement would save me from her wrath if I tracked mud onto her shiny polished floor. The parlor always smelled of beeswax, and no escaping bit of wood ash from the fireplace ever stayed put for long on any surface in the room. Abigail's furniture was not store-bought, but it was walnut and cherry, made by local carpenters who were skilled woodworkers, whereas what we had at home was mostly handmade there on the farm out of oak and pine.

Abigail had a mahogany table, instead of an oak one, and a gleaming bureau of imported rosewood—the one store-bought piece—stood against one wall. A Turkey carpet, which Johnson had bought at auction after the war, swirled with intricate designs in dark red and deep blue against a fawn-colored background. The rug in our parlor was an old braided one that I had made myself by twisting rags from old sheets and clothes, and while it was sturdy enough and colorful, Abigail's fine Oriental carpet put it to shame. I couldn't help but envy her the wine-colored draperies that hung at the windows, matching the deep red of the horsehair sofa. My greatest glory—indeed, my only one—was my children: three strapping boys who would be a credit to us one day, and a beautiful daughter who might have married a rich and prominent gentleman. I could scarcely bear to look at that beautifully appointed room now, for while it was too late for me to care about such splendor for myself, it reminded me of all that Zona might have had, if she had been wiser in her choice of a husband. Abigail still had her splendid parlor and her Turkey carpet, while Zona had only a box and a cotton shroud.

None of that was the fault of Johnson and Abigail, though, and I didn't begrudge them any of what they had. They had been friends and neighbors as well as kinfolk to Jacob and me, and we couldn't have asked for better ones. They had known their share of sorrow, too. About ten years back, they had lost a child themselves, a summer baby who had barely lived to the beginning of autumn. Privately, I thought that the death of a three-month-old, the off-spring of parents who had seven other children still alive, was not as tragic as losing a grown-up daughter, but that might have been only my selfishness, for my bereavement was new and it felt to me greater than anything anybody else could have suffered. Johnson and Abigail had shared our grief at Zona's passing as if she had been one of their own, though I had not confided in them our disapproval of Zona's choice of husband, nor my opinion about the cause of her death. Perhaps they sensed it, though, for they knew me better than anyone.

Johnson and Abigail were the people I trusted.

Jacob might have let me down, hiding his pain under a show of indifference and refusing to countenance my suspicions for fear of looking foolish in front of the county gentry, but I was counting on his brother and sister-in-law to trust me, and to help me do what had to be done.

At her husband's hailing, Abigail came downstairs, broom in hand, for it seems that every waking moment she must be setting something to rights about her house. When she saw me, red-nosed and shivering by the fireplace, she professed to be equally horrified that I had walked all the way to their house in the fierce February wind.

"You will catch your death, Mary Jane," she declared. "It's not that I'm not glad to see you, dear, but you've no call to go bringing more tragedy upon this family by courting pneumonia, no matter what the trouble may be. Now warm yourself before I send you upstairs to bed and call the doctor. Johnson, hang up her wet things, but mind they don't drip on my clean floor."

They made me sit in the green chesterfield chair by the fire, while Johnson took my coat, and wrapped me up in a quilt that Abigail fetched from a cedar chest. He hung my scarf and gloves close to the fireplace so that they would dry—and so they'd drip only on the hearthstone—while Abigail fetched me coffee from the pot on the stove. Johnson didn't ask me any more questions just then, but I could see that he was still worried. I was not fanciful nor given to displays of emotion. It wasn't like me to walk all the way there alone in a fierce wind. I had tried not to make a show of my grief, but sorrow isn't easy to hide, and I think the family was worried that I would waste away or take foolish chances—like walking abroad in foul weather—in hopes of shortening my life. I had no intention of dying, though, because if

I were taken, there would be no one left to see that Edward Shue got what was coming to him.

I sipped the hot coffee from one of Abigail's flowered china cups, and stretched out my feet above the warm hearthstone until I could feel my toes again.

When the coffee had warmed my throat enough for me to find my voice again, I tried to smile reassuringly at their looks of concern. Then I answered the unspoken question. "There is no fresh trouble at our place. The boys are fine, and I'm as well as can be expected."

Abigail, back from the kitchen with her own cup of coffee, sat down on the sofa nearest my chair and gave me an appraising stare. "You're looking scrawnier than a March groundhog, Mary Jane. You ought to be drinking buttermilk instead of coffee."

I tried to smile. "The coffee is warming me up, though. I haven't had much of an appetite. Haven't slept much, either, lately. But if you'll help me, I hope to get past it."

They glanced at each other, and Abigail said, "Where's Jacob, hon?"

"Jacob's at home. He knew I was headed here, and I told him why, but he wouldn't come with me. So I set off alone. Jacob will not help me. I was hoping you would."

Johnson took a long look at me, and I knew he was seeing how pale I was, and how thin I'd grown. The dark pouches under my eyes showed how many days now I had spent sleepless nights pacing and grieving. I expect he thought he was looking at a woman losing her hold on reason. "Are you sure you aren't in need of a doctor, Mary Jane? We can keep you here and send for Dr. Lualzo so you won't have to go out in the cold again."

"No. There's nothing wrong with me that a doctor can fix. I'm looking for a lawyer."

Johnson had pulled a ladder-back dining room chair over to the hearth, and now he sat down in it and stared at my face, not even venturing to guess where my grief had taken me. Abigail sighed. She brushed away a tear with the back of her hand, and got up from the sofa. She likes everything to be neat and peaceable, so I wasn't surprised when she bustled off to the kitchen, muttering something about having washing up to do. That was fine. I didn't need consolation; I needed practical help, and for that my business was with Johnson.

After she left there was a long silence, and I didn't say anything more because I knew that Johnson was mulling over what I had said. At last he rubbed his grizzled chin and murmured, "And you need a ride to town so you can find a *lawyer*? You'll excuse my mentioning this, I hope, Mary Jane, but . . . lawyers . . . They don't come cheap."

I smiled. "I don't reckon I'll have to pay this one, Johnson. He's hired out to the county government."

He had to think it over for a moment, and I could see him trying to hide the fact that he was relieved I hadn't come to him for money. He knows that his brother and I have none to spare, though we have too much pride to act like poor relations, and to Johnson's credit, he never boasts of his prosperity. He was doing all right for a mountain farmer, but there's men at the other end of Greenbrier County who could buy and sell him for the price of one of their horses, so he wasn't as high and mighty as all that. Finally he worked out what I had meant by a lawyer I wouldn't have to pay. "The county prosecutor? What do you want him for?"

"Why, I want him to do his job, of course—prosecute somebody." I was tired from the long walk and lack of sleep, and I wished we could dispense with the explanations. But I was asking him for a favor, so I reckon he had a right to know. "That worthless hound Edward Shue murdered my Zona, and I mean to make him pay for it."

"You want Zona's husband arrested." Johnson was struggling to balance sympathy with common sense, but he had known me all my life, so he knew that I wasn't a fanciful woman, just a stubborn one. "I'm not saying he didn't do it, Mary Jane, because he acted mighty peculiar at the funeral, but it seems to me that if they could have charged Shue with killing Zona, they would have done so by now."

"They couldn't charge him before now because they didn't have any evidence, but I do."

"What evidence could you have? Zona has been in the churchyard for a couple of weeks now."

"Her body may be there, but the rest of her isn't."

"Well, of course I know she's in heaven, poor girl, but—"

"No. She's not in heaven. I reckon she's earth-bound, waiting for justice. And I know that her devil of a husband killed her because she told me so!"

Despite her distaste for messes, physical or otherwise, Abigail had been lingering in the doorway, not sure whether or not she was supposed to hear what I'd come about, but when I said that Zona had told me she'd been murdered, she let out a little scream, and then clapped her hand over her mouth and stared at me, round-eyed with horror.

Johnson looked grim. "Have you been having nightmares, Mary Jane?"

"I haven't been sleeping. And I haven't taken leave of my senses, either."

"No one thinks you've lost your mind, but you have suffered a great loss, and such a blow might make anyone . . ." He hesitated, searching for a benevolent word. ". . . fanciful."

I shook my head. "Not I. I've never set any store by old wives' tales—walking under ladders, black cats being bad luck, and such foolishness. And remember when we were young and people took to table tapping for a while, trying to contact the spirits for a lark. I never held with that, did I, Abigail?"

Still in the doorway, she shook her head no, but her eyes were wide, and she looked as pale as a ghost herself.

"This isn't a tale about crystal balls or haint stories told by candlelight. It's about the Lord answering a mother's prayer."

Johnson was solemn, still worried but willing to hear me out. "What prayer was that, Mary Jane?"

"When they told us Zona was dead, right off I said, *That devil has killed her.* There wasn't a doubt in my mind. But that husband of hers wouldn't let anybody get near the body, and so they buried her without anybody asking him any questions. Did you know he had another wife who died the year before he married Zona?"

"I hadn't heard that, no."

"Well, she fell and hit her head and died in November '96."

"You think he killed her, too?"

"Like as not, but I doubt you could ever prove it. Still, it made my suspicions all the stronger. So I prayed about it. I asked God to give me to know what had really happened to my Zona. And a few days ago He did." I saw a worried glance pass between Johnson and Abigail, and I willed myself to stay calm and dry-eyed, so they wouldn't take me for a hysterical woman spinning moonshine out of sorrow.

"What happened a few days ago, Mary Jane? Your answer to prayer—what was it?"

"I had taken to passing the night in Zona's old room so as not to disturb Jacob with my sleeplessness. I'd sit there hour after hour, staring out the window, praying every now and again, or just thinking back on all that had happened. And one night—I was wide-awake, I tell you—I looked up from my reverie, and I saw Zona standing there, right in front of me. Just standing there, looking mournful."

Johnson's face was a careful blank, and I couldn't tell if he believed me or not, but at least he was listening. After a moment he nodded. "Go on."

Abigail had crept a little nearer, wanting to hear my story in spite of her misgivings. "Weren't you afraid, Mary Jane?"

I shook my head. "Why should I be? It was only Zona. She was my daughter. Nine months under my heart I carried her. I reckon I knew her before she came into this world, so it seemed only right that I should keep on knowing her after she left it. No. I wasn't afraid."

"Could you see through her, though? Did she speak?"

"She did speak. She told me what happened to her. And she looked just the way she always did. She was wearing that bibbed satin dress we buried her in. There was one thing she did, though, that was different."

"What's that?"

"She turned her head all the way around to prove to me that her neck was broken."

There was a little moan from the doorway, and we turned in time to see Abigail slump to the floor in a dead faint.

twelve

WE DIDN'T TALK MUCH for most of the journey into town. The wild wind made me want to hunker down inside myself and keep as still as I could to hold on to what little warmth I had. We had to set Abigail to rights before we were able to hitch up the buggy and head to the county seat. We left her sitting in the kitchen drinking sugared coffee and dabbing at her forehead with a wet handkerchief. She had recovered, though I thought she might be beset with nightmares for the next couple of days. Johnson was holding up well enough. I should have told him in private, but then she might have got her feelings hurt by being excluded, so there was really no right way to have handled it, but I was sorry for upsetting her without warning.

Johnson hadn't asked me any more questions about seeing Zona after that. After we got Abigail into a chair, and I set about getting her coffee and a wet cloth, he stood there quietly for a bit, waiting to make sure that she was all right, and then, without looking at me, he said, "I'll go and hitch up the buggy, Mary Jane. Whenever you're ready."

He was going with me, and that was all I cared about. I figured I'd have to tell the whole story in even more detail to the prosecutor when we got to town, and Johnson could hear it all then. I was glad he wasn't asking me any questions on the way, because I was sure that the lawyer would ask me a barrelful when we finally got to see him. Then I got to wondering who the prosecutor was and what kind of man he might be, so I broke the silence. "Johnson, what do you know about this fellow who is the county prosecutor?"

After a moment's cogitation, for Johnson never made up his mind in a hurry, he said, "I've never had cause to cross paths with the gentleman, but his name is John Alfred Preston, and he's a local man. He just took office a few weeks back, but he was practicing law here all along. Just changed sides of the table, I reckon."

"Have you heard anything about him?"

"Not to his detriment. And whether he believes in ghosts—I guess you'll have to find that out for yourself."

I had never been in the courthouse before. We had not been to Lewisburg many times in my life. It's too far from our settlement in Little Sewell for us to travel there on a whim, and it's not a very big town anyhow. If you wanted to make an excursion, and if you could afford to, you might take a train west to Charleston or east to Roanoke, or even all the way to Washington, but Lewisburg didn't have much more to offer than a few stores, a couple of academies for educating the children of the well-to-do, and the county government. The lawmen came to us if we ever needed them, and the tax collectors came whether we needed them or not, so there was generally no cause to go to the county seat at all on government business. I had never set foot in the courthouse. I was not afraid, though. Talking to a small-town lawyer isn't very daunting when you have been speaking with the dead.

The courthouse was on North Court Street, appropriately enough, and it had been there for at least half a century. The war cut a swath of destruction across much of the South, especially in Virginia, but maybe because it didn't amount to much, Lewisburg was spared. The courthouse, built of the red brick they make around here, stood three stories high, a simple and dignified building, which I thought was a fitten way for a little country courthouse to look, as if they dispensed justice in a businesslike way, without putting on all the airs and graces of big-city bureaucrats. The narrow front porch, level with the sidewalk, was held up by four white wooden pillars under a triangular roof that projected out from the main building. There was a cupola on top, with a dome above an open area enclosed by waist-high railings. I liked the look of that. The view from that cupola would be a fine sight in more clement weather. You'd be able to see past the storefronts of the town to the surrounding mountains in all their glory. Today, though, I could only shudder at the thought of being at the mercy of the fierce winds whipping across the valley.

I hurried inside while Johnson saw to the horse and buggy, but I waited for him in the lobby so that we could approach Mr. Preston together. I hoped that by the time Johnson came in the redness would have faded from my nose and cheeks and the feeling would have returned to my fingers and toes. I huddled there just inside the door of the lobby until Johnson appeared, and then I followed him up a flight of stairs to the lawyer's office, a little surprised to see that he knew the way without having to ask anybody.

"I hope he's in," I said softly as we walked down the upstairs hallway.

Johnson considered it. "Well, he ought to be. It's business hours, but this here's a small town, so I reckon we could find him and rout him out if we had to."

Johnson tapped on the door, and a quiet voice said, "Come in."

The office was just big enough for a desk, a bookcase, and a couple of chairs for visitors to sit in. A map of Greenbrier County took up half of one wall, next to a little wooden shelf divided into compartments and stuffed with papers. The bookcase held row after row of identical leather-bound volumes—law books. And the plain wooden desk, also littered with papers, held an assortment of inkwells, a long-handled contraption for notarizing documents, and half a dozen pens and pencils set upright in a glass tumbler. At least he had a window, looking out on the back lawn of the building, but I doubt he got much comfort from it on bone-chilling days like this one.

The man himself looked much the way I'd pictured a county lawyer. He was closer to Johnson's age than mine, maybe a year or two older—it was hard to tell, for being stout and bewhiskered makes a man look older than he is. I couldn't fault him for his manners, though, for he stood up when I entered his office, and waited until I had settled in one of the visitor's chairs before resuming his own seat behind the desk.

Johnson introduced us, ending with, "My sister-in-law here, Mrs. Jacob Heaster, has a serious legal matter to take up with you, Mr. Preston, and the details of it are most unusual, so I ask you to keep an open mind as you listen to her story. She is not a fanciful woman; I will vouch for that."

Mr. Preston did not smile, and I was grateful for that, for I think a prosecutor ought to be a solemn man, and mindful that an entire county looks to him to see that they get justice.

"At your service, Mrs. Heaster," he said, nodding for me to begin.

I stammered a little at first, bashful to be talking about private family matters with a stranger, but I told myself that he was sort of like a doctor in that you had to tell him things in order for him to be able to help you. "Well, sir, I lost my daughter last month . . ."

"You lost— The child died, do you mean?"

"She wasn't a child—she was a bride of less than three months. And the reason she died is because her worthless husband murdered her."

He had been watching me closely, but when I said that, he gasped and looked down at the stacks of papers on his desk. "I don't know of this case. Was it here in Greenbrier?"

"Livesay's Mill. My daughter's husband— Edward Shue is his name, or one of them anyhow— works as a blacksmith there with James Crookshanks. My daughter's name was Elva Zona Heaster—until she married this Mr. Shue, that is. They lived over in Colonel Livesay's old house near the smithy."

"And how did your daughter die, ma'am?"

"Well, at first we thought that she had come over faint, and taken a tumble down the stairs at their house. That's what Dr. Knapp said at the time. He was the one they called to examine Zona after she was found."

"And he said that she had died of natural causes?"

"I don't believe he had much of a chance to do a

thorough examination. Zona's husband hovered over her body and kept everybody away from her as much as he could. He even dressed her for burial himself."

"But you went ahead and buried her."

I nodded. "Well, we didn't know any different then."

Mr. Preston nodded. "I see. But later you found out that this was not the case?"

"He killed her. He wrung her neck like a chicken's and put her at the bottom of the stairs to make it look like an accident."

"He admitted it?" He sat back in his chair now, regarding me with astonishment. "Your son-in-law told you this?"

"No, sir. It was my daughter that told me."

The light faded from the courthouse window as we sat there, the three of us, on that gray February afternoon, going over and over the circumstances of Zona's death and how I came to know about it. I know that my story must have sounded fantastical to Mr. Preston, but to his credit he did not laugh at me or turn me out of his office. I had been afraid he would dismiss me as a hysterical old biddy, but I couldn't let that deter me from doing my duty to seek justice for Zona. He took me through my story over and over, asking questions six different ways, trying to see if I would contradict myself or change my story, but I held fast.

"Your daughter's spirit appeared to you—when?"

"Late at night, there in our house."

"The night of the funeral?"

"No, sir. It was sometime afterward."

He thought for a moment. "I suppose you had

been brooding day and night over your daughter's death."

"No, sir. I wouldn't say that. I was grieving, of course, that she should be taken so young, but that was God's will. I just prayed to the Lord that Zona should be allowed to come back and tell me what had happened."

"And you dreamed that she did just that?"

"I wasn't asleep. I know what dreams are like. This wasn't one."

"How can you be sure, Mrs. Heaster? Sometimes dreams can seem very real."

"I haven't slept much since Zona died."

"A hallucination then. Back in the war, I remember that after soldiers had stayed awake for too many days—night marching and that—they would start to see things that weren't there. It might have been that."

"No, sir. I was wide-awake, and I saw my daughter standing right there in the room with me."

"Could you see through her? Was she enveloped in a bright light?"

I shook my head. "No. None of that."

"Too bad. In the tales you hear, ghost stories and such, the dead always come back filmy and insubstantial. And sometimes people say that they seem to glow with an inner light." He peered at me watching to see how I'd take to his suggestions.

"Well, I couldn't see through her and she didn't glow. She was just like she always was—mostly."

He seemed pleased by that. "All right. Was she wearing something like a choir robe? You know, the way you see angels dressed in paintings."

Zona was no angel, nor likely to become one, but I thought it best not to go into that. "She was wearing the dress we buried her in. And when she spoke to me, she sounded just the same as ever."

"I don't suppose you touched her, did you, Mrs. Heaster?"

"I did. That first time she appeared, I reached out from the bed and I touched her. I wanted to know if people came back to the living in their coffins, but there was no coffin around her. It was just her, same as ever."

He leaned back and stared at me, and I could tell that my answer hadn't been what he was expecting to hear. "You knew that she was dead, and yet you reached out and touched her?"

I gave him a tight smile. Men give themselves airs about being braver than women, but I never could see it myself. "She was my daughter, sir. I had no cause to be afraid of her, alive or dead. And I had prayed for her to come, remember. It was a blessing—nothing to be fearful of."

"So you conversed with her, just as you would with any ordinary person?"

"That first night when I saw her, she didn't have much to say. It seemed like she couldn't bring herself to tell me what happened. Four times she appeared to me, all told. It was the second time she came to me that she was able to talk more about it. That's when she told me that her husband had killed her."

Mr. Preston made a little note on the paper in front of him. Then he leaned back and thought for a moment. "Did she say why?"

I nodded. "She said he came home from work starving that evening, and when he found out that she hadn't cooked up any meat for supper, he got so angry that he choked the life out of her."

John Preston gave me a rueful smile. "You're claiming he murdered his new bride over a complaint about *dinner*? Really, Mrs. Heaster, does that seem likely to you?"

I happened to glance at Johnson, in the chair

beside me. We had been closeted there with Mr. Preston now for several hours, and I knew Johnson had been restless, worried that nightfall would overtake us and afraid of missing his own supper, but now he was also red with embarrassment. I sighed. "I know it sounds foolish, sir, but I cannot help that. No meat for his supper—that's what she told me. And the man does eat like a famished wolf; I can testify to that. There ought to have been enough food for his dinner, though. She had potatoes in the cellar, and late last summer, we'd put up beans and tomatoes—"

"Never mind about that, Mrs. Heaster. If a man has a murderous temper, it doesn't take much to set him off. Still, it isn't proof that he is guilty of murder."

"There's one other thing, Mr. Preston. As Zona was taking her leave of me that second night, she turned her head all the way around—to prove to me that he had wrung her neck."

Mr. Preston turned pale and blinked a couple of times, but he didn't ask me anything else. After a moment, he made some more squiggles on his paper, and then he clasped his hands together, leaned back in his chair, and looked lost in thought. Johnson was making restive motions, hoping that we had been dismissed, but I hadn't got an answer yet, and I was willing to wait all night for one if I had to.

Finally Mr. Preston seemed to come to a decision. He leaned forward and gave me an earnest stare. "Mrs. Heaster, I must believe you. You strike me as a God-fearing woman who would not make such an accusation frivolously or out of spite. But it is a story to confound any court, and I don't think we can indict a man—much less hang him—on your word alone, but what you have told me gives me cause enough to look into the matter further. There may be proof, after all."

I nodded, relieved that he had not dismissed my story as foolishness. "What must you do to prove it?"

"You said that Dr. Knapp attended the body, but that he hadn't made a proper examination?"

"Edward Shue wouldn't hardly let anybody go near her. Now that I think back on it, it seemed like he was covering up for something."

"Let me talk to George Knapp, then. I'll see what his impressions were, and then I think we'd better give him a second chance to examine the body."

"Dig her up, you mean?"

"Yes, ma'am. It's the only way I can think of to get proof that she was murdered. I can understand that you would find this distressing . . ."

I stood up and started putting on my coat. "My daughter was murdered by her own husband, Mr. Preston. Nothing beyond that is going to distress me as long as it furthers the cause of getting justice for her. You do what you have to do. We'll stand it."

Dr. George Washington Knapp was forty-four years old, too young to remember the carnage of the war and too far removed from large cities to see much in the way of clandestine murder. Oh, there were sudden deaths in the county, of course, many of them violent. Farmhands and loggers cut themselves on sharp blades and bled to death where they fell; horse-drawn conveyances overturned and crushed their passengers; people died of snakebite, or tetanus, or they fell off cliffs or out of trees. There were even murders every now and then, but they usually didn't amount to much more than a drunken altercation that got out of hand, one that ended in gunfire or at the point of a knife. But the causes of those deaths were easy to divine—you needed little more than a glance to know what had killed the victims of such tragedies.

Besides that, there were the expected, inevitable deaths: childbirth, strokes, heart attacks, pneumonia, consumption. He saw them all, year in and year out, as a matter of course, and did what he could to delay the inevitable result. But in a community mostly composed of simple, straightforward people, what he mostly did not look for were the secret ways of dispatching an enemy or an inconvenient loved one. If frail old ladies died from foxglove leaves mixed in with their helping of salad greens, or a brutish husband had a side of rat poison with his dinner, Dr. Knapp might catch it—or he might not. In the ordinary way of things, he didn't attend his patients expecting them to be murdered.

Mrs. E. Z. Shue, a newlywed in the Livesay's Mill community of the Richlands section of the county, was no exception. She was a new patient of his, calling on him only after her recent marriage. He remembered her as a pert, handsome woman who had enjoyed good health for most of her life, but suddenly, after her marriage, her good fortune had ended. He had treated her for several weeks for what he had privately considered a female complaint, perhaps a pregnancy, some imbalance in her reproductive organs, or possibly just hysteria. Then, on January 23, he was called to the house because she had been found dead at the foot of the stairs. The occasion was sad, but not suspicious. The distraught husband could scarcely bear to be parted from the body of his young wife.

It had seemed logical to conclude that the poor woman had come over faint and had fallen down the stairs, breaking her neck in the process. A sad ending for a young life, but not unprecedented, and not cause for suspicion. Women did faint, even when they weren't suffering from female complaints. They starved themselves to stay thin, and laced themselves into corsets that constricted their internal organs until the very configurations of their bodies were altered. But those aberrations mostly occurred among the society women that you might find staying at the Old White; he didn't suppose that a blacksmith's wife in Livesay's Mill would have indulged in such foolishness. She had fainted in the wrong place, at the wrong time, and it had cost her her life. There was nothing he could have done, so he signed the death certificate and went back to worrying about the living.

Now this.

A month after the patient went to her rest in the churchyard, John Alfred Preston called on him at home one evening to say that there was some doubt over the cause of Mrs. Shue's death. Thinking back on it, Preston asked, did it strike him as in any way suspicious?

Dr. Knapp wasn't offended by the question. What profession doesn't make mistakes? Cooks cover their errors with sauces; architects, with ivy; and doctors cover theirs with sod. He had been in practice too long to think himself infallible. Against all expectations, healthy young people died, and patients he had given up on got well just to spite him. So, without resentment, he thought about it. He remembered the widower hovering at his elbow, begging him not to disturb "poor Zona." Well, that might have been grief—he had thought so at the time—but it might just as well have been something else. There was no denying that the husband's overwrought behavior had hindered his examination of the deceased. It wouldn't hurt to take another look at the remains, just to see if there was anything he might have missed.

Preston seemed satisfied with his response. He

had promised to secure the proper legal forms to permit the exhumation. Dr. Knapp mustn't perform the autopsy alone, of course. In order for the results to be official, there needed to be witnesses to the findings, both laymen and medical men.

"Witnesses, yes, I concede the point, Mr. Preston, but I expect you will arrange for us to have more onlookers than a presidential inauguration."

Preston smiled over his glass of the doctor's excellent port. "The law believes in being thorough, Dr. Knapp."

"I only hope you know what you're doing. Cutting up a body in an empty schoolhouse with an audience of rubberneckers is asking for trouble. Like as not, they'll be fainting or vomiting on their shoes, and then I'll have to leave off what I'm doing and attend to the living."

"Let's hope they're made of sterner stuff, then. Of course, we've agreed that you won't be the only physician present, so perhaps, if need be, you could take it in turns to administer first aid."

A few days after his meeting with Dr. Knapp, Preston appeared before Judge McClung and argued that rumors pertaining to the death of Mrs. E. Z. Shue warranted an exhumation of her remains so that they could put an end to the speculation once and for all. The woman's family did not oppose an autopsy—indeed, they welcomed it—and the widower, under suspicion of her murder, had no standing with which to object. McClung granted the request of the new state's attorney. To put the rumors to rest, they would disturb the repose of the dead.

So there they were on a bitterly cold Monday, the twenty-second of February, at a remote country church twenty miles from town, ready to get on with the gruesome work of exhuming the body. They had made a grim procession that morning, a line of various horse-drawn conveyances and riders on horseback, all heading west out of Lewisburg toward Soule Chapel, the little Methodist church near Little Sewell.

Justice Homer McClung himself had come to observe the proceedings he had ordered, accompanied by the five members of the jury of inquest. Dr. Knapp and Dr. Houston McClung rode out together, and the third physician, Dr. Lualzo Rupert, who had attended Zona before her marriage and lived at that end of the county, met his colleagues at the church. Lualzo Rupert was still a young man, but three of his siblings were also physicians, and his father, old Dr. Cyrus Rupert, had tended to the medical needs of that end of the county for at least half a century. Because his siblings had taken their medical talents elsewhere, Lualzo had inherited his father's practice, so the tradition of being tended to by a Dr. Rupert continued uninterrupted.

Besides the grand jury, the assorted spectators, and the church members who had dug up the grave, there was one other witness to the proceedings: Edward Shue, the husband of the deceased. He had been ordered to attend, perhaps on the logic that he must witness the proof, if any, against him. Shue had seemed indignant at being compelled to watch the autopsy, and missing a day's work on account of it, but when the proceedings got under way, he appeared to be as indifferent to the sight of his wife's remains as if the trio of doctors had been butchering a hog.

Despite the cold, the churchmen had begun their work early. They had excavated down to the coffin itself by the time the procession arrived from the county seat. Everyone got out and circled round the grave to observe the exhumation. One of the diggers jumped down into the pit to slip the ropes around the coffin so that it could be hoisted up.

"You're not going to find anything. Can't you leave her in peace?" The widower sounded more aggrieved than grieving, but in any case no one paid him any mind. The legal formalities had been set in motion, and no objection, sentimental or sinister, would be allowed to stop the process.

When the coffin had cleared the pit, the churchmen—pallbearers in reverse—carried it to a wagon waiting to haul it a few yards up the road to the log schoolhouse where the autopsy would be performed.

George Knapp led the procession, following the wagon on foot. It was only a short distance to the schoolhouse. "I hope there's no one there to be expecting us," he remarked to the group at large.

Lualzo Rupert, whose territory this was, shook his head. "We had a word with the schoolteacher this morning when we got here. She agreed that letting the children have the day off was the best course. Some of the little devils begged to be allowed to stay and watch, of course, but we were firm, and they finally gave up and left."

"Someone ought to keep an eye on the window," said Houston McClung. "I wouldn't put it past some of those rascals to sneak back and try to watch. At their age, I might have."

Knapp watched his breath make clouds in the air as he spoke. "I hope they kept the fire going in the woodstove. Even a dead patient deserves a doctor with steady hands."

John Alfred Preston caught up with them. "Some of the jurors were asking how long this is likely to take, gentlemen."

Knapp looked at the portly lawyer, wrapped in a great coat, gloved and muffled with woolen scarves. "You'll be thankful you wore all that before it's over, I'll warrant. I wish we could do our work wrapped up as you are. I suppose you can figure on two or three hours, wouldn't you say, Dr. Rupert?"

The younger man nodded. "About that, if we're to be thorough."

"And we *will* be thorough, Mr. Preston. This may be your party, but make no mistake, I am running the show. And we will take as long as we have to until we are satisfied that we know how this poor woman met her death."

The churchmen slid the box off the back of the wagon and carried it into the schoolhouse, followed by doctors, lawmen, and jurors. Two of the jurors made sure that the woodstove was well stocked and burning properly while the medical men divested themselves of their overcoats and scarves and prepared for the task ahead.

When they had pried open the coffin lid and slid it back to reveal the body, Judge McClung thanked the pallbearers for their efforts and hurriedly dismissed them, with a reminder that they should come back by late afternoon to reinter the body. The rest of the laymen remained, but kept at a safe distance from the autopsy table, with handkerchiefs at the ready, in case the smell of decay should become overpowering. George Knapp gave them a sardonic glare and turned back to the business at hand.

Besides the woodstove, the one-room schoolhouse had a stack of firewood, a few lanterns to light the room, a chalkboard, and one north-facing window, under which a long worktable—now empty—had been placed. The students' wooden desks were all pushed against a wall to make room for the observers. Even on a bright summer day the small window would not have afforded enough light for the purposes of an autopsy; on that overcast winter day, it barely cut the gloom. Anticipating this, Rupert, who was familiar with the school building, had brought three more kerosene lanterns, and he had set a pan of water atop the woodstove for the necessary ablutions. Despite the cold, the three physicians removed their suit coats and rolled up their shirtsleeves.

Dr. Houston McClung draped a sheet over the wooden table, and Dr. Knapp and Dr. Rupert set the body down on it. The skin of the dead girl's cheek, as pale and cold as ham in a winter smokehouse, gleamed in the lamplight.

"Hard to believe that she has been a month in the ground. She is uncommonly well preserved," Rupert observed.

George Knapp grunted. "We have the bitter weather to thank for that. She might as well have been kept in an icehouse. I would wish that the cold would abate, but then there'd be the smell to contend with, I suppose."

Reaching into his bag, he took out a scalpel and bent over the still-recognizable remains of Zona Shue, but before proceeding he turned back to the little knot of spectators huddled against the opposite wall. "Speaking of smell, gentlemen, if any of you finds that the experience of witnessing an autopsy brings up unpleasant associations"—he smiled—"or if it brings up your breakfast, please have the courtesy to remove yourself from the premises, lest you inspire the others to similar transports of nausea. We have no time at present for ministering to the living. Thank you."

"I brung my wife's smelling salts," one juror called out, holding up a small cloth bag.

"Good. Share it with those who need it." He

nodded to Dr. Rupert. "Let's get that infernal high-necked dress off her. She seemed to have been partial to that style. She was wearing a similar garment when I was called to the scene at her death."

"Did you remove it then to examine her?" One of the jurors called out the question.

Knapp paused again and turned to look at Edward Shue, who stood near the other spectators. No one seemed to want to stand next to him, and they carefully avoided looking directly at him. Shue seemed angry and apprehensive rather than sorrowful. "Did I remove her garment when I examined her at the time of her death? I tried, gentlemen. But her widower there"—he nodded toward Shue—"he was like a mother hen with one chick. Flew at anybody who tried to get near her. Said he didn't want her disturbed." He scowled. "Well, I reckon we're disturbing her now. Go ahead, Dr. Rupert. Bare her throat."

"Will you tell us what you're doing, Doctor?" asked the judge, edging forward for a better look. "The jury needs to understand the proceedings."

"Certainly, sir, if you wish it. As you know, my initial diagnosis—an everlasting faint, I termed it—was that the unfortunate lady lost consciousness at the top of the stairs and pitched forward, falling to her death. We will look for evidence of some disorder—a blood clot or a tumor, for example—within the young woman's brain that might have caused such an occurrence. First, of course, we must examine the neck itself to determine the nature of the injury."

He turned back to the table, watching closely as Dr. Rupert unfastened the high-collared dress and eased it down to the shoulders of the deceased. Then, with gloved fingers, Lualzo Rupert began gently to probe the neck. When he lifted the torso an inch or two off the table, the head lolled as if it were barely attached to the rest of the body.

Another of the jurors—a farmer—spoke up. "Looks like a chicken what's had its neck wrung, boys." Several of his companions nodded and murmured their assent.

"Inelegantly put, but he is correct," Knapp murmured.

"The neck is broken all right, gentlemen." Rupert looked up suddenly. "Here! Dr. McClung, bring one of those lanterns closer, please."

He waited while Houston McClung stepped closer to the table, holding the kerosene lantern aloft so that its light shined on the head and upper torso of the dead woman. The three doctors leaned forward to examine the white throat. "Do you see that?" asked Rupert. He pointed to the neck just beneath the ear.

McClung leaned closer, lowering the lantern and positioning the light so that it illuminated that part of the body. He nodded. "Plain as day."

Dr. Knapp turned to the knot of spectators, motioning for them to come forward. "Approach the table, please, gentlemen, if you've the stomach for it. We are by no means finished with the autopsy. Certain things must still be ruled out. But before we do any further disarrangement of the body, I should like you to look at the area on the side of the neck that Dr. Rupert is pointing to."

The officers of the court and the gaggle of jurors edged closer to the table, but the widower stayed back against the far wall, arms folded, staring at the floor. James Shawver, one of the deputies who had accompanied the party, glanced at the corpse and immediately took up a position within arm's length of Edward Shue, his hand hovering over his holstered pistol.

The others crowded around the table, peering at the still form of the dead woman. Finally one of them said, "There's dark spots on the side of her neck."

"Finger marks?" asked another.

"That is correct," said Dr. Knapp, pausing to glare at Shue. "The marks show up better now than they would have at the time of death because the blood has pooled in the bruises. Although I don't say that I wouldn't have noticed them if I had been given half a chance."

"He wrung her neck!" muttered one of the witnesses.

Dr. Knapp nodded. "That seems to be the case. Now, as I said, we will continue with the autopsy as planned so that we can rule out cerebral hemorrhages, tumors, and the like, but you may take that as mostly a formality. At this point I believe the cause of death is clear to all of us."

His words took a moment to sink in, and when they did, the observers turned as one man to stare at the defiant widower in horrified fascination. All three lawmen placed themselves within arm's length of the widower, as if expecting him to make a run for it, but he sneered at them and stood his ground. When he saw that the stricken onlookers were all staring at him, Shue leaned back against the wall and scowled back at them. Narrowing his eyes, he set his jaw in a mulish pout. "You'll never prove it."

One of the jurors muttered, "We'll see about that."

Three hours later, when the rest of the body had been examined, and when, with the aid of a hacksaw, the dead woman's brain had been removed and probed for signs of growths or hemorrhages—none found—the three physicians called for the pan of water to clean their hands and their instruments, put the body to rights again in its coffin, and sent one of the observers to summon the burial detail and fetch the wagon to transport the sad little corpse back to its final resting place.

A quarter of an hour later, Dr. Rupert walked out into the pale winter sunshine, shivering a little as a gust of wind caught him broadside. He surveyed the crowd who had waited outside the schoolhouse, mostly local people whom he knew. They pressed closer, as if expecting him to announce the results, but he glanced back over his shoulder at the closed door of the schoolhouse, as if to indicate that it was not his place to declare the findings of the autopsy. Dr. George Knapp had been the man in charge. But as he turned to leave, he caught sight of Mary Jane Heaster, a little off to the side, dry-eyed but watchful. Their eyes met, and with no more than a flicker of an expression, he told her what she needed to know.

The door opened again then, and the rest of the group filed out. They were solemn and silent, perhaps shaken by the grim ritual they had been duty-bound to witness. Edward Shue, handcuffed, accompanied by the three lawmen and flanked by scowling jurors, stumbled on the threshold, but quickly righted himself and met the crowd's gaze with a defiant glare.

The crowd's satisfied murmur turned to a roar as they realized that their cold vigil had not been in vain. They had seen a killer unmasked and arrested, and they had a tale they could tell for the rest of their lives.

Mary Jane Heaster stared at the prisoner as they led him toward a waiting wagon, and then she turned and walked away without a word to anybody.

The *Greenbrier Independent* newspaper,
February 25, 1897, Lewisburg, West
Virginia

FOUL PLAY SUSPECTED

Mrs. Zona (Heaster) Shue died in the
Richlands of this county, on the 23rd of
January, and her body was taken out to
Little Sewell and buried. Since then rumors
in the community caused the authorities to
suspect that she may not have died from
natural causes. In short, her husband,
E. S., commonly known as "Trout," Shue
was suspected of having brought about her
death by violence or in some way unknown
to her friends. An inquest was accordingly
ordered, and on Monday last before Justice
Homer McClung and a jury of Inquest,
assisted by Mr. Preston, the State's
Attorney for the county, Mrs. Shue's
body was exhumed, and a post mortem
examination made, conducted by Drs.
Knapp, Rupert, and Houston McClung,
Shue being present and summoned as a
witness. From one of the Doctors we learn
that the examination clearly disclosed the
fact the Mrs. Shue's neck had been broken.
We hear too that Shue's conduct at the
time of his wife's death and when she lay
a corpse in his house was very suspicious.

The jury found, in accordance with the
facts above stated, charged Shue with the

crime of murder and yesterday afternoon he was brought here by James C. Shawver, John N. McClung, and Estill McClung and lodged in jail to await the action of the grand jury.

thirteen

LAKIN, WEST VIRGINIA

1930

DR. BOOZER BLEW ON HIS HANDS and moved his chair closer to the fire. "This cold is a miserable thing for the old folks in here. Makes their bones ache."

Mr. Gardner smiled. "It may not be good for live folks, Doctor, but it's certainly useful for preserving dead ones."

Boozer looked up in surprise. "What put that into your mind?"

"Oh, don't worry. I wasn't thinking of killing myself. It just brought back memories, that's all."

"I'm relieved to hear it. Aside from this foul weather, how are you faring?"

"Tolerably well, I suppose. I've been passing some of the time chatting with Miss Kathleen Davies in the parlor. We found common ground in the works of Mr. Shakespeare."

"I'm glad you found congenial company to pass the time, if not a clement temperature to do it in.

Now, what were you saying about this weather? Something about preserving dead bodies?"

"Oh, that. This cold snap reminds me of a murder case back in my salad days, in Greenbrier County. My part in it came during the trial in high summer, but the tale itself began in a week colder than this. In fact, if it hadn't been so infernally cold, there might not have been a case at all. And the particulars of it would give anybody chills."

The dinner hour was over, and they had the dayroom to themselves, but there was no sunset to watch that evening. The pewter sky seemed to hover just above the treetops across the road, and it had been spitting rain all afternoon. Since their previous session three days earlier, the weather had turned cold, and Boozer had found Mr. Gardner huddled in the chair by the window, clasping his arms against his body in an effort to keep warm. When he saw the old man shivering in a moth-eaten cardigan over his cotton patient's uniform, he retrieved a thin woolen blanket from the linen storage closet and draped it over the sweater. He even managed to sweet-talk one of the kitchen helpers into giving them a pot of coffee and a pair of white china mugs.

Once he had wrapped the blanket securely over Mr. Gardner's thin shoulders and placed the mug of coffee in his hands, he closed the curtains to shut out the darkness. "That's more like it," he said with forced cheerfulness.

"Better anyhow," the old man conceded. He stifled a cough. "Let me warm my throat a bit before you get me ruminating about the past."

"Take your time," said Boozer, sipping his own coffee. "Quiet is at a premium in this place."

A few minutes passed in companionable silence before Boozer spoke again. "So you were about to tell me about a murder case?"

"That's right. I'll never forget it. You don't get too awful many murder cases as a country lawyer. This one happened back in Greenbrier in 1897."

"Early in your career, then?"

"I was nearly thirty, but perhaps it took me longer to qualify for my profession than it took you."

"About the same, Mr. Gardner. I just turned thirty myself. But doctors have a lot of preparation to get through even after college, interning and all. But at least I had the peristalsis of medical school to push me along. But you didn't go to law school, did you? No, of course not. People read law with an established attorney, didn't they? You had to go it alone."

Gardner nodded. "Well, I was proud as Lucifer. I suppose that spurred me on."

"Pride and obstinance always help in an uphill battle, I think. So, it was 1897, and you were just becoming successful in your profession?"

The lawyer shrugged. "I don't say I was rolling in fields of clover at that point. I had not established my own law practice yet. I was still working under another attorney, for bread crumbs, but looking back now, I can see that I was well on my way. I had something to show for having attained my thirtieth year, by dint of hard work and prodigious self-discipline. I had a diploma from Storer College in Harper's Ferry, and it was becoming apparent that I would manage to make something of myself. If you are not impressed by that, Dr. Boozer, with your medical degree and your fine New York manner, then you ought to be. You weren't even born in 1897, were you?"

James Boozer shook his head. "September of 1899. I've always wished I could have delayed my arrival by a few months, so I wouldn't have been a remnant of the previous century before I was even out of diapers."

Mr. Gardner smiled. "If you chose to lie about your age on account of that trifle, would they call you crazy?"

"I'd try to plead it down to oversensitive. Even though I didn't spend much time back in the last century, certainly not enough to know what it was like, my folks were from South Carolina, if that counts for anything with you."

Gardner gave him a mirthless smile. "I can't say that it does."

"Okay, I'll admit that I don't remember any of the nineteenth century. I think my first memory is of a birthday cake with three candles on it." He sighed. "Why am I telling you all this? This is the sort of question I usually ask the patient."

"I suppose it is, Doctor, but if you insist on listening to my story, we might as well make sure you understand it. You are now the age that I was then—back in 1897 during that murder trial. Seems funny to think of it that way. Sometimes it chafes me to be outranked by a young pup like you, but then I remember that back when I was your age, I thought I knew it all, so I'm sure our relative positions don't seem strange to you. You must see me as a doddering old man whose time has passed. And, mostly, it has. It was a different world back then."

Boozer shrugged. "Not all that different. The white folks down in Point Pleasant won't let any of the staff here live in town, not even the doctors. I have to live here in the hospital, same as the rest of the staff."

"Oh, I don't think people ever change much. There's always a peck order, same as with chickens. You thought being a doctor would put you close to the top tier, which it would if white skin wasn't trumps, but when I was in your shoes, starting out as a lawyer, I had no such illusions of importance.

We were less than forty years from slavery back then, and no piece of paper, not even a certificate to practice law, was going to make white Greenbrier County forget that previous condition of servitude. I don't know that I minded all that much, though. My expectations were lower, maybe. Back in those days we lived in separate societies, and as long as you stayed on your side of the fence and went about your business, things generally went along fine. So, while even with my lawyer's credentials, I might never be counted by some citizens as the equal to an illiterate white sharecropper, I was nevertheless a prince among my own people." He chuckled. "And I was a hell of a catch back then. Those were my courting days."

"Well, I don't see why you think I should find the concept of two societies hard to grasp, Mr. Gardner. Here we sit in West Virginia's asylum for the *Colored* Insane. And the white folks' mental hospital is at least a hundred miles away in Weston. Doesn't sound like things have changed."

"Maybe *you're* the change, Doctor. You chafe at things that we never thought to question. Anyhow, the world in general has changed for everybody. Electric lights. Indoor plumbing. Airplanes." He laughed. "I'd like to see you spend a week in the wilds of the West Virginia mountains, wearing overalls, chopping wood, and hauling water. Yessir, I believe we could sell tickets to that performance."

Boozer shrugged. "It's still like that when you get away from the cities, even in upstate New York. Or so I've heard."

"*So you've heard.*" Mr. Gardner laughed. "Well, to be scrupulously fair, the separation between the races was not absolute, either. Perhaps they tolerated us more then because we did expect less. Have you ever treated a white patient?"

"A few times. On a charity ward when I was a resident, and every now and then after that. Why?"

"When I was your age, I defended a white man on trial for murder."

Boozer had been about to light a cigarette, but he paused so long to stare at his patient that the match burned down until the flame touched his finger-tips. He dropped it on the wood floor and stamped on it, swearing. "Sorry. That'll hurt tomorrow. But did you really? In 1897? You were in charge of the defense of a white man?"

"Not in charge. I was second chair. In capital cases, the law requires that the defendant be represented by two members of counsel. And I guess I don't need to tell you that, although he was a white man, the accused was poor and socially negligible."

"Well, sure, but still—why you? Was the victim colored?"

"White as the driven snow—though somewhat less pure, as rumor had it. The murder victim was the defendant's wife, and they'd only been married a few months. I didn't know either of them from Adam, of course. They lived miles from the county seat in a little farming community, and I lived miles from town in the other direction, in White Sulphur Springs. Based on our respective races, you'd think it would be the other way around, for White Sulphur Springs is the location of the Greenbrier resort—it was called the Old White then—so there was quite a bit of the gentry there, and certainly a lot of wealth and power, especially in the summer months."

"The Greenbrier. I've heard of it. Not all that far from Washington."

Mr. Gardner nodded. "Eastern Seaboard money coming to the hills for comfortable summer temperatures. But the hotel had a need for porters and maids and cooks to pamper the gentry, so a little community grew up in the shadow of the prominent one, and I lived there. The defendant was a blacksmith residing halfway across the county."

Boozer took a long sip of coffee. "So the white defendant was a blacksmith, and you—the colored attorney—lived near the society folks at the Old White. Seems like everything in that case was all turned around. Contrary to expectations."

"Life is mostly contrary to expectations, don't you find, Doctor?"

"I suppose it is. What was it like, working on that case?"

"Like falling down the rabbit hole. Never a dull moment. But if it was a bad year for the white blacksmith, it was a good year for yours truly." The old man raised his coffee cup in a mock toast. "Ol' Trout Shue did away with a wife in 1897, while I managed to acquire one."

"You managed to court a sweetheart while you were working on a murder trial?" Dr. Boozer smiled. "Lawyers must keep better hours than physicians."

"Oh, shoot, I'd have welcomed long hours, but I didn't get them. I told you the defendant was poor. Didn't have two nickels to rub together, which makes for a speedy trial. My courtship of Miss Eliza Myles took months, but the blacksmith's trial lasted barely a week. It was memorable, though."

"I expect it was." Dr. James Boozer took another sip of tepid coffee and leaned back in the frayed armchair. "All right, Mr. Gardner. Let's talk about that."

Everybody said, "You're reading law with a white gentleman, that Dr. William Rucker? Why, you must be awfully grateful."

James Gardner, who saw no reason ever to tell

anyone what he thought or felt, would always lower his eyes modestly and agree with the speaker, black or white: "Oh, yes, indeed. I'm no end of grateful to Dr. Rucker. He is a fine, generous gentleman." As far as he was concerned, though, the operative word in the comment was *must*. If everyone says that you must be grateful, then it takes the shine off the sentiment. He would never by word or deed show resentment, but it rankled him to be thought the object of charity, when he thought that at least some of the gratitude ought to be coming the other way. People never seemed to realize that the more they praised Dr. Rucker's supposed generosity, the less they seemed to value James Gardner's ability and worth.

There was no harm in telling people what they wanted to hear, though, and since pride in a struggling young man was often mistaken for arrogance, he wouldn't risk being suspected of that, not even among his close associates. They might have been surprised to learn that he thought of them merely as associates, but although he might have referred to those people as friends, he did not think of them as such. A favorite maxim of James P. D. Gardner's was *He travels fastest who travels alone.*

The truth, never expressed but deeply felt, was that William Rucker lost nothing and gained considerably by taking on a bright, ambitious, hardworking young man whose only defect was being the wrong color. Because of that, the fledgling attorney had to work cheap, and so his supervising lawyer got twice the work for half the money he would have had to pay a white man. If you asked him, Rucker was getting a bargain—and he was well aware of it, too. William Rucker was not conspicuous for charity or kindness. Or sanity, if it came to that. In later years, James P. D. Gardner would contemplate with rueful amusement on the irony that he should end up in a

lunatic asylum, while William Parks Rucker, madder than a mattress full of bedbugs, should have been
presumed sane and remained free for the whole of
his charmed life.

They didn't lock him up, his worthy colleagues
in the Greenbrier legal fraternity, but they didn't
admire him, either. Associating with a nonwhite
employee wouldn't cost Rucker any esteem in the
eyes of the public, either, because he hadn't much
to lose in the way of reputation as it was. James had
tried, diplomatically, of course, to explain this to the
solemnly pretty Miss Eliza Myles when he took her
out for an evening stroll, which was about all there
was in the way of courting activities in rural, sleepy
Greenbrier County. Eliza was a quiet, handsome
woman, a good listener, and not given to gossiping or
to frivolous ways in dress or deportment. So, without in any way complaining or showing resentment,
James tried to explain to her the true circumstances
of his position in the law office of W. P. Rucker. He
was thinking of making Miss Myles his wife in due
course, and as a show of good faith, he had begun
to confide in her, although such revelations did not
come easily to him. He found, though, that he liked
the feeling of having someone who was always,
unquestioningly, on his side.

One Sunday afternoon after luncheon with their
respective families, they had met near the church to
enjoy a stroll, admiring the flowers and glorying in
the gentle weather of a mountain summer. Eliza,
slender and solemn, with a fine straight nose and
well-chiseled cheekbones, was a handsome woman.
Beyond her sedate beauty, though, her correct and
dignified suitor prized her deportment. She neither prattled nor giggled. She was not educated past
eighth grade, but she was bright. She listened with
calm attentiveness, and her few comments were

always intelligent and well expressed. James felt at ease with her, as much as he could with anyone. One key thing he had to consider in choosing a wife was whether she would help him to advance or hold him back. Eliza Myles, he thought, would suit him well.

They sat down on a fallen log at the edge of a meadow, where the smooth expanse of grass sloped gracefully downward, revealing a far-off vista of hazy blue mountains topped by white clouds like cotton bolls against an even bluer sky.

Eliza settled her skirts decorously to cover her ankles, and gave her full attention to her beau. "You were telling me about Dr. Rucker, James. You don't consider him a kind soul for taking you on as an assistant while you qualify? But surely for a white lawyer to take on a gentleman of color—"

James scoffed. "It isn't charity, I assure you. He gets excellent work for far less money from me, and he loses nothing in reputation. As far as the rest of the legal community is concerned, Dr. Rucker is a loose cannon."

Eliza looked up at him, but his expression gave no sign of his own feelings in the matter. "What is he like?"

James hesitated. "Well—nothing much to look at. Medium height, long white beard, and not much hair on his head. He's not a young man—in his middle sixties if he's a day. But nobody mistakes him for a sweet old grandfather. Do you know why I think he practices law? Because he enjoys suing people."

Eliza laid her hand gently on his arm. "You're joking, aren't you, James? Surely no one would choose his life's profession for such a frivolous reason."

"No one but William P. Rucker. He's a medical doctor. He is. Graduated from a proper medical college in Philadelphia back before the war. He may even have practiced medicine back then, for all I know, but he seems to have become distracted by politics and abandoned the sick."

"A doctor and a lawyer? Well, he sounds like a brilliant man to me."

"You know that old saying *Genius borders insanity*? Well, sometimes I think Dr. Rucker has crossed over that border and come out on the other side. Have you heard about his escapades in the war?"

Eliza shook her head. "All that was before my time. All I know about Dr. Rucker is that you are reading law with him. From that, I assume that he favored the Union side in the war."

"Well, he did back the Union, but nothing with Dr. Rucker is ever pure and simple. The man also owned slaves."

"Did he really?" Eliza's eyes widened. "Well, what did he think they were fighting about?"

"Lord knows. But he married a wealthy woman, one of his distant kinfolks, I believe. Her maiden name was Scott, so all these colored folks around here who go by the last name of Scott likely belonged to her family sometime back and came with her to Greenbrier County. They can spin a tale or two about the Scotts and the Ruckers when the spirit moves them."

"And yet he took you on to read law with him."

"He knows a bargain when he sees one. And I'll bet he justified his slave holdings as a matter of economic necessity. Back before the war, he owned businesses—a general store and a tavern, that I know of—and as I told you, his wife came from money, so I suppose they used slaves to operate these various commercial establishments."

"Did he tell you all this, James?"

"No, but some of the colored Scotts had a word

with me when I first signed on to read law with Dr. Rucker, and the other Greenbrier attorneys aren't shy about discussing him, either. I make it my business to listen."

"Does it worry you?"

"What? That he owned slaves? So did most of the well-to-do men over fifty around here. As fellow attorneys, we all contrive to overlook the fact nowadays. As for Dr. Rucker, I take care to keep on his good side. The fact that he is a qualified, licensed attorney in the state of West Virginia is all that matters to me. If he can sign the papers and get me certified, he can sue the queen of England for all I care. And I wouldn't put it past him. There was a notice in the *Independent* back in January concerning him—did you happen to see it?"

Eliza shook her head. "I don't recall. Was it an article?"

"Legal notice. He was suing a man named Lewis Skipper in Circuit Court. Some business deal gone sour. I know the details, of course, even though I didn't assist him in the case, but it's hardly worth discussing with you. I only mentioned it to bolster my point: the man enjoys bringing lawsuits. I think he considers it a form of sport."

"Well, perhaps he is a little eccentric then. I suppose he can afford to be. They say that if you're rich enough, you can get away with murder."

"Oh, he did that, too."

"Got away with murder? Surely not, James."

"It's true. You can ask one of the Scotts. They told me he killed a man in the early days of the war. Not as a soldier, I mean. He was a civilian. This killing was personal."

"Oh, James! And to think you have to work with such a man. Do you know the circumstances?"

"Only what I've been told. I overheard a

conversation about it once around the courthouse, and then Dr. Rucker himself elaborated a bit on the subject one evening when we were working late. I don't know how we got off on it. As I recall, we were drawing up a witness list, or some such bit of routine business. I don't know what set him off, a name on the list perhaps, but he just started talking about it, and I sat back and listened, like I always do.

"He said it happened over in Covington in the summer of 1861. Rucker was proud of the fact that he was against secession. And he wasn't going to keep quiet and hope nobody challenged him. Oh, no! He was belligerent about it. Proud of it. And they kept hauling him into court, trying to make him take the oath of allegiance to the Commonwealth of Virginia. Virginia, of course, was part of the Confederacy by then, so swearing fealty to the state meant supporting its departure from the Union. Dr. Rucker was dead set against that. On that day, they took him to court over it yet again, but the only oath he took was to swear at them. He refused to cooperate. That didn't surprise me. The harder you push Dr. Rucker, the more he digs in his heels and resists whatever you're trying to get him to do."

"That was brave of him to refuse to swear the oath, though. I suppose they could have put him in prison."

"Knowing him these days, I'll bet he enjoyed being contrary back then as well. And he ended up in prison, anyhow, but I'm getting ahead of the story here. Where was I?"

"He was in court, refusing to take the oath of allegiance."

"Anyhow, he said he was on his way home from court that summer afternoon, after trying to post a letter reporting the postmaster for being a secessionist—that very postmaster refused to accept the letter, by the way—and he was indignant about that."

Eliza began to laugh. "Oh, no, James, no. You are just plain making that up."

James Gardner shook his head. "Nobody but the good Lord could make up Dr. William Rucker, and I expect it taxed His powers of invention to accomplish it. But I've known the man for a fair few years now, and all I can say is that story doesn't even make me bat an eye. Dr. Rucker goes through life like a crosscut saw."

"The wonder is that somebody hasn't tried to do him in."

"I'm coming to that, Eliza. After he left the post office that afternoon, he ran into a mob who were out looking for him. Some of them had probably been there in the courtroom when he refused to take the oath, and they were angry that he wouldn't renounce the Union. Maybe they'd been drinking, too, but that just fueled the anger. He says he counted twenty-three men in the crowd, led by a hulking railroad man who had a loaded weapon in one hand and a weighted stick in the other."

"Oh, my, and Dr. Rucker was unarmed?"

"Of course, he was most certainly armed! He is no fool, and he knew what a dangerous game he was playing. The war had already started, and tempers were running so high that it wasn't safe to talk politics with anybody. Dr. Rucker knew that, and he was carrying both a pistol and a bowie knife. When he saw those men coming at him, he pulled out the knife—either to get the mob to leave him alone or else to stir up more trouble. My guess would be the latter."

"The wonder is that he's still alive thirty years after the war."

James laughed. "Hell doesn't want him. He'd

try to take over. Now this railroad man—his name was Michael Joice—bandied words with Dr. Rucker for a bit, both of them getting madder by the minute, and he ended up by asking what Dr. Rucker would do if he called him a traitor. Well, Dr. Rucker claimed he brandished that bowie knife and told Michael Joice exactly what he *would* do under those circumstances."

Eliza shook her head. "My lands. They must'a all been likkered up to be acting like that."

"I believe you. So then this Michael Joice took the dare and called Dr. Rucker a traitor outright. He prefaced it with profanity, which is not fit for your ears, Eliza, but you can imagine the gist of it. And he swung that heavy club at Dr. Rucker, but Rucker was smaller and more wiry, and apparently he managed to dodge the blow and set on his attacker with that knife."

"Well, that's self-defense, isn't it, James?"

"The first stab was. The problem was that Dr. Rucker didn't stop there. He kept sticking his knife into Joice's body over and over, even when the man was lying helpless on the ground."

"What about the rest of the mob? Didn't they try to help him?"

"Well, I expect that Dr. Rucker was aiming his pistol at them by that time, and after what he'd just done to their leader, there couldn't have been a doubt in any of their minds that he would blow them away without a second's hesitation. One of them must have got away, though, to fetch the law, because someone in an official capacity took charge at that point, and ordered the bystanders to carry the injured man into a nearby hotel to receive medical attention."

Eliza clapped her hand over her mouth. She whispered, "Not from . . ."

"Yes, indeed." James could not suppress a chuckle at the irony of it. "Dr. Rucker. He was a medical school graduate, you know. And he swears that he wasn't ordered to do it. Said he considered it his duty to try to save the fellow."

"Do you think he really did try to save him? Did the man live?"

"Well, he may have tried. I guess if you've had medical training, your instinct might come into play, regardless of your personal feelings. He didn't elaborate on that, but I wouldn't be surprised to learn that he was as pigheaded fighting against Death as he was fighting against everything else in creation. But the railroad man died of his wounds the following day."

"Surely they arrested Dr. Rucker?" Eliza sighed. "I keep having to remind myself that the man is a lawyer himself now."

"And I wonder if that isn't partially in consequence of this incident. Anyhow, you are correct, Miss Eliza. The day after his patient died, they arrested him."

"Well, at least they waited until his patient died." She looked up at him, eyes sparkling. "And what came after that is the part of the story that you understand perfectly, isn't it, James?"

"It's in my line of country, certainly. I know court procedure the way you might know the variations on a . . ." He searched for some feminine equivalent that she might comprehend. ". . . a recipe."

If her smile was mischievous, he didn't notice, so intent was he on his recital of the particulars of the case. "Well, Mr. Attorney-at-Law, how would this legal recipe go, then, sir?"

"Standard procedure. They arrested Dr. Rucker after the death of his opponent . . . victim." He shrugged. "How I would refer to the deceased would depend on which side of the case I was representing. Anyhow, they brought Dr. Rucker before a coroner's jury, who viewed the body, heard some testimony about the circumstances, and decided that Dr. Rucker should stand trial for the man's death. He might have got away with self-defense on just one stab wound, but the fact that he kept knifing the fellow repeatedly—in front of a host of witnesses, mind you—made the matter more complex. So he went to trial."

"Did he defend himself?"

"He never said otherwise. I don't think you could fault Dr. Rucker for a lack of self-confidence. He got his trial a month after the incident, and there were a good number of witnesses called, but no jury. A panel of justices heard the case. They acquitted him."

"They never!"

"The way Dr. Rucker tells it—and I am inclined to believe him, because I don't see how else he could have got off—Michael Joice made a deathbed statement exonerating his assailant. Said the fight was his own fault, and that Dr. Rucker was not to be blamed for his death. There must have been witnesses to that statement. I don't think they would have taken Dr. Rucker's word for it."

"Well, I reckon that poor man went to heaven, anyhow, forgiving his enemy like he did, even knowing he was going to die."

"Perhaps—assuming that last act of charity canceled out the rest of his sorry life."

"So Dr. Rucker got off on the charge of murder and went off to practice law himself. Like the Good Book says: *Go and sin no more.*"

James shook his head. "Not Dr. Rucker. A year later he was back in court for burning up bridges."

fourteen

"WAIT," JAMES BOOZER SAID. "Just wait." He laid a restraining hand upon the old man's arm. "What do you mean, *he was back in court for burning bridges?* I thought the man was a lawyer."

Beyond the curtains in the patients' parlor, a dark sky spangled with stars spread out above the bare branches of the trees across the road. He could imagine the broad expanse of the river silvered by moonlight. But James Boozer had been too captivated by the past to care about the present beauty of the present night. Gardner smiled a little to himself and turned away from the window.

He noted the discomfiture of the young doctor. "Well, before we get to that, I wanted to ask you about another matter. I have received letters from colleagues back in Bluefield, and they are concerned about my continued confinement here. Who should I tell them to write to about that?"

The doctor hesitated. "Why are they writing? Are they concerned that you are being ill-treated?"

"No. I haven't complained about the hospital, per se. It's just that I don't think staying here longer will make any difference. Either I'll soldier on, or I won't. So I'd just as soon be going about my business, and my colleagues back home have offered to speak out on my behalf. But they want to know whom to write to. You?"

James Boozer shook his head. "Not if you're talking about pulling strings. I'm low man on the totem pole around here. They're welcome to write, though I don't know that it will do any good. Dr. Barnett has the final say-so in here, of course."

"I know that Barnett is the director here, but to whom does he report?"

Boozer shrugged. "Somebody in the state government, I suppose. But I hope that I would be consulted before anything was decided. As your attending physician, my recommendation ought to count for a lot."

Mr. Gardner smiled. "Then I hope to stay on your good side, Doctor."

"Now, you were telling me about your mentor, Dr. Rucker, the bridge burner. And he was a lawyer back then?"

"Perhaps not during the war, but he was indeed a lawyer when I was acquainted with him thirty years ago. But thirty-odd years before *that*, he was—according to his lights—a fire-eating patriot. Mm-hmm, yes, he most certainly was. Back in the war. I wasn't born until two years after it ended, but it seems to me like people didn't talk about much of anything else the whole time I was growing up. The way I understood it, there were soldiers on both sides who got conscripted into the army with no choice in the matter, but a goodly number of other men with strong beliefs joined up with one army or the other to fight for their cause. Dr. Rucker would rank high among those with strong beliefs, but he never was much of a joiner, not being conspicuously blessed with friends, and maybe feeling that it would be difficult to consort with his peers when he didn't think he had any. He always insisted on going his own way, no matter what it cost him. I'd say that when it came to the war, his beliefs cost him a few years of his life. It was even harder on his family, I'll warrant, but he wouldn't have taken that into consideration."

"So he turned to the law in later life."

"Not all that much later. In 1870 he became the Greenbrier County prosecutor."

"That was quick. When did he have time to qualify as a lawyer?"

"Lord knows. The man was bright enough, though. I'd say he was a quick study. And as for becoming the county's prosecuting attorney, remember that in Reconstruction, only people who were loyal to the Union got to hold government positions. He probably didn't have too much competition in Greenbrier County back then. He only served two years, though. After that, he either got fed up with the job or else it was back to business as usual among the local politicians."

Boozer smiled. "So old Rucker became part of the established order. Do you take that to mean he learned the error of his ways from his war experience?"

Mr. Gardner laughed. "William P. Rucker? Why, I don't believe that man ever regretted a single thing in his entire life, no matter the consequences. On his moral compass, whatever he took a notion to do was true north. Old enough to know better, too. When that war came along, he was older than you are now, Doctor. Old enough to have had some sense. Had a wife and four sons, too, but that didn't slow him down in pursuing his own peculiar notion of service to the war effort."

"Thirty isn't old in wartime. Why wasn't he conscripted into the army? You said he was a physician. Lord knows they must have needed them on both sides."

"Well, I think he got up to his shenanigans before they passed the conscription act, and by the time they did pass it, he was unavailable."

"How did he get mixed up in burning bridges?"

"I think one thing must have led to another. Early in 1862 he left Covington, where he was none too popular, and went over into West Virginia. He had a plantation there on the Gauley River, and the Union Army had stationed an Ohio Infantry regiment nearby. Dr. Rucker fell in with Colonel George Crook, the commander. *Crook*." Gardner considered it. "His name is hardly an improvement over yours, Doctor."

Boozer sighed. "We've already had that conversation. I'll bet he got tired of hearing the name jokes as quick as I did—about age ten."

"There are those in the area where Crook was headquartered who might disagree with you about the appropriateness of his name, though. Confiscating property was quite a pastime with occupying armies. By the way, that's the same Crook who became a general later on, but this was still early in the war. Anyhow, the two of them—"

"No. Wait. Go back. You said Dr. Rucker owned a *plantation* over there?"

"That's right."

"A plantation. With crops and cows . . . He didn't own *slaves*, did he?"

Gardner sighed. "A plantation is a big farm, Dr. New York City Boy. Of course, he owned slaves. How else was he going to run that place?"

"Well, you said he was pro-Union, so it seemed logical. Besides, if he was consorting with a Union

Army commander, shouldn't they have insisted on his freeing his slaves?"

"Not then. Not even later in the war, because the Emancipation Proclamation did not apply to border states like West Virginia. Early on the Union officers concerned themselves with military strategy, as if they were sheepdogs trying to round up the straying states. I never did ask Dr. Rucker why he chose the Union side in the war. It hardly mattered by the time I got to know him, but as you may have noticed, he certainly had things in common with the other side in that conflict. Illogical, I know, but there it is. I know it's your job to expect people to make sense, Doctor, but I gave up on that endeavor a good long while ago."

"Well, tell me more about him, and let me see if I can make sense of it."

"All right. Good luck to you. He never made sense to me. I don't know what made Dr. Rucker hunt up a Union commander, but it is the sort of thing he'd have been likely to do. Thought he'd be invaluable to the war effort. Never was a diffident man." He peered slyly at Boozer. "Apparently, doctors are never in doubt about their own importance."

"All right, Mr. Gardner. Point taken. So Rucker makes himself an adviser to the local military commander. I suppose he knew the surrounding area, which *would* make him useful."

"So he did. He and the colonel got to talking about what a good idea it would be to destroy a bridge over the Cowpasture River."

"Cowpasture River, huh? Sounds like it's out in the middle of nowhere. I don't know much about the war as it played out away from the major battlefields—Gettysburg, Antietam, we studied those in history class—but why would they bother to blow up a bridge in the hinterlands?"

"Because that railroad bridge was located a few miles from a railroad depot, and the most important commodity that was sent to that depot was salt."

"Salt? Table salt?"

Gardner smiled. "We don't think much about salt these days, do we? Here in 1930 we have lost our dependence on the old ways, with our cars and telephones and refrigerators. Time is like that big slow river over yonder, and you just drift along, thinking about your own concerns, and then one day you look up and realize how far you are from where you started. By then there's no going back. I started out in those simpler times, but even I take it all for granted sometimes. You're too young to know what a different world it was seventy years ago."

"Don't sell me short. I have studied history, even a course in college."

"It's the little things that trip you up, though. Things that wouldn't cross your mind, that seem too commonplace to ever have been missing from ordinary life. Corn flakes. Toilet paper. Tomatoes in December. And salt. Nowadays, you can go to the grocery store and buy all you want for pennies a box. It's hard to think that once upon a time it was a vital necessity, worth fighting over."

"Well, it is hardly a rare commodity."

"Oh, but it was then—at least in much of the South it was. There weren't many salt deposits available for mining, and salt was something the population could not do without. Back in the days before refrigeration, people salted meat to preserve it through the winter. They salted vegetables to preserve them. Added salt to butter to keep it from spoiling. Used it for tanning hides to make leather. The army needed it for that, and for adding to gunpowder. For medical reasons, too. They used to put salt in wounds—"

"Thank you. I went to medical school, you know. People have been treating wounds with salt since Roman times. I know that salt is a necessity for more than just seasoning your dinner; I just didn't know there was a shortage of it anywhere that mattered. I take it that destroying that bridge had something to do with cutting off the supply of salt to some critical area?"

"That's it. The railroad bridge was a covered structure, about two hundred yards long, situated maybe eight miles from the train depot. Loads of salt would be sent regularly to that station from one of the few salt deposits around—some brine wells over near Charleston. Apparently Rucker and his officer friend decided that if they destroyed the bridge and stopped the salt shipments, it would help the Union war effort."

"I expect it would, but if that army commander had a whole regiment of troops at his disposal, what did he need Rucker for? Local geography?"

"Probably. Dr. Rucker knew the area and the political sympathies of all the local residents. Besides, I expect the whole thing was his idea in the first place." The old man smiled. "His job was to guide the soldiers past local pockets of Rebel sympathizers and get them safely to the bridge. Of course, Dr. Rucker being who he was, he took it upon himself to do more than that. And if you think people hated him before then, you should have heard them talk about his exploits in the Cowpasture campaign of '62. He had done some doctoring in those parts, on account of having a residence nearby, and apparently he'd held some local bureaucratic position at some point in the past. He told me all about it once, but I have long forgotten the rights of it. Anyhow, those two activities enabled him to acquire a good bit of local knowledge about the area residents and what they owned. They say he ended up with more than a thousand soldiers accompanying him around the county, although not that many later on the actual mission. So as a prelude to destroying that bridge, Dr. Rucker took it upon himself to tell the soldiers which farms belonged to Rebel partisans, and who owned good horses, and where they might find some wagons, stores of grain—whatever supplies might be useful to an army or might constitute a tragedy to the families who were losing them. They burned a few buildings while they were at it."

"Was the doctor settling old scores, by any chance?"

"No one ever doubted that. The local folks forever after called that campaign Rucker's Raid, and there was no doubt in anybody's mind that he was motivated as much by personal spite as he was by patriotism for the Union. Remember, this was his own stomping grounds. He knew all these people, and I suppose this would have been a perfect opportunity for him to retaliate with impunity. In Greenbrier County, people were still muttering about his iniquities in the 1890s, when I knew him. The wonder is that nobody ever tried to bushwhack him. They never forgot it, I promise you that."

Boozer nodded. "Understandable. So did the soldiers succeed in burning the bridge?"

"You should have heard Rucker tell it. In his cups, he'd wax long and loud about the twenty-mile march over backwoods trails in the pouring rain. I question that part of the tale."

"Seems like it would be hard to burn a bridge in a rainstorm."

"That's what I thought, but I never did voice my objections to Dr. Rucker. He didn't like being cross-examined, and since he was my boss, mostly I just listened and acted like I believed every word he said. The Rebels were guarding the bridge, of course, but Rucker's forces outsmarted them. The bridge-burning expedition consisted of fewer than a hundred men, but the locals had seen a thousand soldiers in the previous days' raids. So when Rucker and his party got close to the bridge, he—or some actual Union officer, more likely, but he claimed it was him—sent the whole force charging the bridge, in order to make the defenders think that Crook's entire army was coming at them."

"That must have been some battle."

"Well, no, he said it wasn't a battle at all. The bridge defenders just turned tail and ran without firing a shot, so Rucker's party had a clear field to burn the bridge at their leisure."

"I wonder his neighbors didn't hang him."

"They'd have given worlds for the privilege, I understand, but he spirited his family away in a confiscated carriage and dug in on his plantation near Summersville, where the nearby Federal forces afforded them protection."

"And there he lived quietly until the end of the war?"

Gardner laughed. "Rucker? Why, trouble was meat and potatoes to him. He was more likely to seek it out than to shrink from it. Two months after the bridge burning, he got an invitation to go to a place in Shenandoah County to meet with General Frémont. He must have thought that another chance for mischief like the Cowpasture caper was on offer, because he hurried on over to Summersville to report to a Lieutenant Colonel Starr, who had recently replaced his buddy Crook as commander of the forces in that area. Starr was supposed to provide a safe escort to get Rucker over to Mount Jackson, where the general had his headquarters. He got there about dusk. Starr had taken up residence in a fine house in Summersville—confiscated, of course. Since the colonel had already arranged a birthday celebration for himself, they decided to delay their departure to Mount Jackson until the following morning. They also delayed their retiring for the night until the wee hours of the morning, because the drinking and story swapping went on quite late. Just about dawn, when they had finally settled down to sleep off the effects of the festivities, they were rousted out of bed by a band of Rebel cavalry, who arrested the whole boiling of them—including Colonel Starr and Dr. Rucker."

Dr. Boozer chuckled. "Boy, that must have been some hangover."

"I have no doubt that it was."

"Well, if you hadn't told me that you read law under him in the 1890s, I would have hazarded a guess about how this story ended."

"Oh, it's a daisy of a tale, and part of it stretches all the way to the 1890s, so hear me out."

Dr. Boozer glanced at his watch and waved for him to proceed. "It's late, but I'd still like to hear it. All I have waiting for me in my cramped little room is a new medical journal."

"And I'd just as soon wait until the nightly serenade of my fellow patients subsides before I retire."

"Anyhow, it'll be a couple of weeks before we can talk again. I worked over Christmas and New Year's, so they're letting me take my time off next week."

"Are you going home?"

"Back to New York? Yes, indeed. There's a new play on Broadway, and an old college buddy and I are going to see it—unless I can find a date. *The Green Pastures.* Bible stories dramatized as folktales, with an all-colored cast. Yessir, I am anxious to see that. Wouldn't miss it."

Mr. Gardner frowned. "Never heard of it. Who wrote it?"

"A white man named Connelly. Some people don't like the way he plays fast and loose with our spiritual beliefs, but it sure is giving a lot of our acting folks a chance to work. It opened back in February with Richard B. Harrison in the starring role—playing God. I'm an admirer of his. That's one good thing about living close to the city. Getting to hear all the latest music and see the new plays."

Mr. Gardner sniffed. "I'm surprised you want to hear my little backwater tales about Greenbrier County."

"But yours are true stories. Not even the best theatre can hold a candle to real life."

"Besides, talking to me is your job, right, Doctor? In case I let something slip about what ails me? Well, never mind. Now where was I? Oh, yes, the raid on Summersville. The Confederate troops, the 14th Virginia Cavalry, to be exact . . ."

"How in the world do you remember that?"

"Because most of them were from Greenbrier County, and they were mighty prone to telling war stories in later years."

"I'm sure they were. These days it's stories of the Great War that I mostly hear. Go on."

"The cavalry was guided to Starr's roost by a Rebel spy named Nancy Hart."

Boozer grinned. "—who was young and beautiful and in love with Dr. Rucker."

Mr. Gardner sighed and shook his head. "You watch too many movies, Doctor. I saw the lady nearly thirty years later, and even allowing for the passage of time, I cannot believe her ever to have been beautiful. She had sallow skin, gooseberry eyes, and teeth too big for her mouth, as I recall. I don't say that Rucker was a saint, but judging by their wartime behavior, neither she nor my mentor felt anything except a mutual desire to annihilate one another. But the story is remarkable, nonetheless. As an aside, I should note that this might give you an idea how muddled things were in that war. Nancy Hart was a staunch Confederate sympathizer, but she and all her family were opposed to slavery. You recall that the rabidly pro-Union Dr. Rucker owned a goodly number of slaves."

Boozer grinned. "As a psychiatrist, I'd offer them a two-for-one deal for treatment."

"Oh, they both thought they were sane—and in the service of the Lord Almighty himself." He sighed. "I suppose that doesn't differentiate them from anybody locked up in here at that. But I reckon a lot of folks back then were crazy in one way or another, so those two hardly stood out from the crowd."

"Did they know each another?"

"Miss Hart and Dr. Rucker? I don't believe they did, but she knew Colonel Starr right enough because he had captured her two weeks before that raid took place."

Boozer laughed. "Sounds like he made a hash of it if she was able to capture him back."

"I think it helped that she was young, and apparently passably attractive to lonely soldiers. She had been put in the town jail, but after a few days, they moved her to the attic of a nearby house, which happened to be the one that Colonel Starr had commandeered for his own use when his troops took over the town. I'm sure that Miss Hart made every effort to charm her captors, and they fell for it, giving her books to peruse and allowing her to stroll around the grounds of the house while she chatted with the men on duty. She behaved like a perfect little lamb, I expect."

"Why didn't she try to escape?"

"She wasn't reckless, and her captors mistook her prudent behavior for cooperation. It was only later that they realized she had been doing reconnaissance, memorizing all the details of the colonel's headquarters. She must have been having a fine time. One of the soldiers even arranged for a photographer to take her portrait, and they say he borrowed the colonel's hat to make her a fetching bonnet for the picture."

"And yet, despite all that pampering, she didn't stay there enjoying Yankee food and hospitality? I'm amazed."

Gardner turned solemn. "That's when the tale ceases to be an amusing idyll. Of course, it all happened sixty-eight years ago, so I don't suppose it matters so much anymore. They're all dead by now."

"What happened?"

"After she had won the trust of her captors, most of whom were probably no older than she, Miss Hart invited one of the guards up to her attic room and beguiled him into giving her his weapon—on the pretext that she wanted to compare it to the gun she used to hunt with back home."

"And the poor sap fell for that yarn?"

Gardner nodded. "The male sex has learned nothing since the Garden of Eden, Doctor."

"I don't guess we have. So she held him at gunpoint while she made her escape?"

"Oh, no. She shot him dead. Then she ran out of the building, stole the colonel's favorite horse, and rode bareback all the way to Confederate lines—a distance of some thirty or forty miles, I believe."

"God Almighty."

"Mr. Kipling was correct. *The female of the species is more deadly than the male.*"

"You don't suppose she was . . . er, defending her virtue when she shot the guard?"

The old man sighed. "You're almost as much of a romantic fool as those besotted puppy soldiers were. No, I do not think Miss Hart's virtue—if she possessed any—was in any danger from those uniformed adolescents. The men of that time and place would have made a pet of her, chivalrously thinking themselves defending a pure and helpless female. She had encouraged them to think it. She had a female companion with her, by the way, and the ladies stayed together. So after beguiling them into regarding her as a harmless country lass, she acted the part of a soldier, same as a man would. Maybe they had forgotten that she was an enemy agent, but I'll warrant *she* never did."

"But you said she came back two weeks later. Surely, she was avenging—"

"There was *always* avenging to be done in that war. Decades later people on both sides were still talking of the wrongs they had suffered. I heard and read their accounts until it became like rain on a roof. As for Nancy Hart's motives: early in the war her sister's husband, a Confederate sympathizer, had been taken from his home by Union soldiers on the pretext of making him give a speech in town in favor of the Union. He was later discovered, still a good ways from town, shot in the back. I expect that incident hardened Miss Hart's partisanship considerably."

"Yes, if you look at it in that light . . ."

"And there may have been a dozen other grievances she either saw or endured to fuel her rage against the army. But her actions toward Starr and his soldiers were reasonable. Judging her as a combatant rather than as a delicate female flower, you would conclude that she acted with cool and strategic logic. She availed herself of the opportunity to reconnoiter the enemy's headquarters, and when she felt she had sufficient information, she escaped and made use of that intelligence. It was Dr. Rucker's bad luck to be caught up in her reprisal. They must have been delighted to get him. There could hardly have been a more hated man in the area."

"Did he put up a fight when they tried to capture him?"

"No. He tried to outsmart them. Well, some say he hid first. But a soldier noticed his boots sticking out from under the bed, and they hauled him out. Then he claimed to be a Confederate sympathizer, and offered to show them spoils they could take, and suggested that they burn down the house since it was a Union hole."

"I thought they had confiscated the house from a local citizen."

"They had. I suppose these finer points of ownership become obscured in matters of war. Anyhow, his ruse came to naught. The soldiers herded all their captives out into the street, and one among them immediately recognized Dr. Rucker, which ended his pretense of being an innocent bystander. They knew he wasn't that, but they had some trouble deciding what he actually was—prisoner of war or captured spy. The rest of the captives got sent to prisons around Richmond, and the Union got them out on prisoner exchanges a few weeks later, but Dr. Rucker was another matter. They kept him in irons and moved him around here and there, to places you'll have never heard of, Doctor: Salt Sulphur Springs, Christiansburg, then Lynchburg for a while. He told me that people came to see him there as if he were a zoo animal, which outraged him mightily. Then he was sent to Richmond, too, to Castle Thunder prison."

"That sounds like something out of a novel by Dumas."

"It was just a converted brick tobacco warehouse, but it held deserters, spies, and political prisoners for most of the war. From the little Rucker ever said about it, I gather that it was a hellish place to be shut up in, but he wasn't there for long."

"So his Union comrades got him out?"

"No, the Confederates kept moving him. He must have seen the inside of more prisons than a professional burglar. But the Federals did keep trying to effect his release. Six ways from Sunday they tried to put together a deal to exchange medical prisoners that would include him, but they did not succeed. The first thing they did—to prevent him from mysteriously dying in captivity—was to take four hostages in Lewisburg as insurance for his safety. Colonel Crook—Rucker's bridge-burning associate—let it be known that if anything happened to Dr. Rucker, the hostages would be hanged. That move did nothing to endear him to Greenbrier County, I assure you."

"Were they hanged? No, wait—Dr. Rucker lived through the war, so I suppose not. But you said that he moved to Lewisburg after the war. That must have made for some awkward moments on occasion."

"I expect it did, but I never knew Dr. Rucker to care very much about what was awkward and what wasn't."

"When did he get out of prison? Didn't you say that they got Starr and the soldiers back from the Confederates in a matter of weeks?"

"They did, but nobody cared much about them. That was just wartime business as usual. Rucker was a different matter altogether. He was local, and the animosity toward him was entirely personal. In fact, he said there was a catfight among authorities over the privilege of trying him. The provost marshal of his home county claimed the right to indict him

for treason, and the governor of Virginia thought
that the Commonwealth ought to have that honor.
I suppose the Confederate government itself might
have tried him if they had cared to. In the end, they
referred the matter to Jefferson Davis, and the Confederate government agreed to let Virginia try him
on three counts: treason, murder, and horse-stealing.
All of which he denied. He claimed he hadn't joined
the Union army, hadn't stolen anything, and didn't
burn the Cowpasture bridge."

"But he did burn it, didn't he?"

"Well, somebody did, and he was one of the
party that day. Whether or not you could hold him
responsible for the actions of an occupying army is a
question for lawyers to wrangle over in court."

"A sly old fox, then, equivocating. But what did
you think of him personally, Mr. Gardner?"

"That's like asking what I think of the weather,
Doctor. It all depends. It all depends."

"How so?"

"Dr. Rucker was nice enough to me, according
to his lights. I might not have made a lawyer if he
hadn't taken me on. There's many a white man who
wouldn't have done it then and now, but it doesn't
do to look too closely to certain aspects of the old
rascal's life or to speculate on his motives."

"You mean, like burning bridges and stabbing
people in street brawls?"

Gardner rubbed his chin while he considered the
matter. "I don't know that I was thinking precisely
of those particular examples. The war years were
tumultuous times, and desperate people did things
they might not otherwise have done. What troubles
me most is something that happened shortly after he
went to prison—but on his orders, I have no doubt."

"What was that?"

"Well, after the Confederates locked him up,

Mrs. Rucker might have been worried about having enough money to live on while he was away, or maybe she figured she couldn't manage all his various properties and enterprises on her own. Anyhow, she and the children decided to light out for Union territory—Ohio—where, presumably, they would have fewer enemies." Mr. Gardner paused for a moment and stared out the window toward the cliffs of the Ohio border, only a mile away, but invisible in the darkness.

"Mrs. Rucker sold the tavern in Covington, the plantation near Summersville, various bits and pieces of real estate—and she sold their slaves."

Dr. Boozer stared. "She sold— But he was a *Union* sympathizer. You said he helped the Union soldiers burn the bridge. And she was headed for Ohio? Union territory."

"That's right. All the more reason."

"When was this again?"

"Fall of 1862."

"So . . . wait . . . Lincoln issued the Emancipation Proclamation at the first of the year in 1863. Surely people knew it was coming. And two months before the president would set those people free, the Ruckers *sold* them?"

Gardner nodded. "I told you: the Emancipation Proclamation only freed slaves in the Confederacy, so in West Virginia, it did not apply."

"But surely . . . morally . . ."

"I guess Rucker was a shrewd businessman first and a patriot second. His wife was going to Ohio, and if she took the slaves with her, she would have had to free them. He probably reasoned that he stood to lose thousands of dollars if he still had his money tied up in human stock when his wife relocated to Union territory. So he liquidated his assets."

James Boozer was pacing now. He patted his

pockets for cigarettes, but found none. He turned to look at the old man in the chair by the window, pointing, as if he'd caught him in a lie. "But that man claimed to be loyal to the Union. Surely he recognized Lincoln's general intent . . . Surely he'd feel honor-bound to conform to the moral tenets of the country he chose to support. After all, he had a choice, and he chose the Union over the Confederacy, even when, geographically, it would have been more convenient and less dangerous to do the opposite. So why—?"

Gardner laughed. "Well, Boozer, you're the psychiatrist, aren't you? Isn't it your job to figure out why people do things?"

Boozer sighed. "Most people behave more consistently—I'd even say more *logically*—than your former mentor. It's hard to figure out where a loose cannon is going to roll. But morally, Dr. Rucker seems to be all over the place. He sells slaves, knowing that the side he favors opposes slavery, and then he takes you on as an apprentice, or whatever it is they call a lawyer-in-training."

Gardner motioned the doctor back to the other chair. "Yes, but remember that more than a quarter of a century elapsed between those two incidents. The one consistency that I can see is that Dr. Rucker was first and foremost a keen businessman. It made financial sense to sell those people while he could be sure of recouping his investment, and it made sense for him to take me on as an attorney, because I'd work harder and for less money than a white lawyer would." His smile was grim. "*With malice toward none*, Doctor. It was just business. In both instances he got his money's worth."

"And you knew all this when you went to work for him?"

"Not all of it. Once I became associated with

him, I listened more carefully to everybody's tales about his actions in the war. But I was never tempted to quit on account of his moral shortcomings. I figured that a qualified colored attorney was the least that Dr. Rucker owed the world, and I resolved to become a good one."

Boozer shrugged. "All right. I hope the old scoundrel suffered for selling those folks down the river, that's all. How many of them were there?"

"Not more than half a dozen that I know of. And his wife took a few more with her when she and the children went to Ohio under a Federal escort. She had to free those she took with her, of course, which is why they sold the rest of them, but that was the price she paid for safe passage. There were people in Greenbrier County—former slaves themselves—that remembered them, which is how I heard about it."

"All right. So Rucker sat out the war in a Richmond prison, did he?"

"Not quite. As I said, his captors kept moving him, while the other side fired many rounds of legal documents at the Confederate government, attempting to argue the matter. It seemed to boil down to a difference of opinion. The United States considered Dr. Rucker to be a physician—and both sides seemed good about exchanging doctors—but the Confederates claimed he had committed crimes that were not authorized by the Federals, and that he wasn't acting as a military doctor anyhow. The paperwork flew back and forth for a good while, I understand. And they still had not given him a trial. Finally he broke the diplomatic impasse himself in the most expedient way. In October 1863, he escaped."

"Did he really? How?"

"They had shipped him to Danville by then, and although prisoners weren't supposed to have reading materials or writing paper, I gather that Dr. Rucker's captors were somewhat in awe of him. Maybe he did a little doctoring to impress them. Lord knows there ought to have been plenty of maladies in need of treatment in a military prison. He always claimed that he was well-informed on the news of the day, and that he carried on a wide and varied correspondence during his confinement. Anyhow, he never really said who helped him escape, although someone must have. Maybe he managed to bribe a guard. All he said was that he slipped out of the prison in the dead of night, wearing a Rebel uniform, and that a friend—name withheld, but believed to be a woman—was waiting for him outside in a buggy to spirit him away. Apparently they left Danville at a fast clip and headed for Lynchburg, Dr. Rucker's hometown."

Boozer grinned and hummed a snatch of a tune. "How does that go now? *It's a mighty rough road from Lynchburg to Danville . . .*"

"They weren't traveling by train, Doctor, so the 'Wreck of the Old 97' has little to do with the matter. I'm surprised you know that song, being a New Yorker. I'd have pegged you for a jazz man myself."

"Yes, but I'm trapped here in the Back of Beyond, West Virginia, same as you, and if I want to listen to the radio in my off-duty hours, I'm limited to whatever stations we can get out here, which is mostly the ones that play hillbilly music."

"Well, you seem to have become infected. Physician, heal thyself."

"Why, Mr. Gardner, I believe you made a joke just then."

"Only a small one. Especially compared to that prank of Dr. Rucker's, when he managed to hoodwink the entire Confederacy. I imagine he had quite a number of friends orchestrating the escape."

"Wherever did he find them? I thought he was generally hated in the area."

"He was a man of contradictions, Doctor."

"I don't suppose he switched sides once he escaped from the Danville jail?"

"No, indeed, but he didn't rusticate in the country somewhere and wait for the hostilities to cease, either. He went right back to looking for trouble."

"It couldn't have been hard to find in those days. What did he do?"

"Well, he spent a couple of weeks skulking around Greenbrier and Pocahontas Counties, dodging the Rebel troops who were bent on his recapture, but friends always managed to warn him when any soldiers were near, and he would leave one bolt-hole and find himself another before they caught up with him. He finally made it to Union lines, and was presently whisked off to Washington because the secretary of war wanted information from him in order to correct the maps the military was using. In early 1864 he fell in with his old friend Crook again—by now Crook had been made a brigadier general, which Rucker took the credit for. Dr. Rucker said that Crook's promotion came on account of the blowing up of the Cowpasture bridge, which he claimed to have planned and carried out. Apparently, both of them thought it would be a good idea to blow up some more bridges."

"Sure. Why mess with success. Any bridge in particular?"

"One in southwest Virginia. The New River bridge. He managed to get himself commissioned as a major in the Union army in the spring of '64 on the strength of the local knowledge he claimed to have about the western part of Virginia—which until the war had included West Virginia. So there they were, based near Charleston, when Grant sent word, wanting to know if General Crook thought he could mount an expedition down to Dublin Depot—that's close to two hundred miles away—and destroy a Confederate base at Dublin and burn the big railroad bridge nearby. There was more salt involved, by the way. Saltville, Virginia, was a major salt works for the Rebels, and they intended to destroy that as well as the means of transporting it."

Boozer stifled a yawn. "Really?"

Mr. Gardner stood up. "Well, it's getting late, just as it was late in the war by the time all that transpired. Rucker was around for the Battle of Cloyd's Mountain, which probably didn't make your history books, either. Anyhow, the Union would have won the war just as easily without him. But I'm tired, and you have to go to work in the morning, so let's leave it at that. Next time we meet, I'll tell you about the sequel to the Nancy Hart story, and perhaps I'll have more news soon from my influential friends in Bluefield. Or I could follow Dr. Rucker's example and plan an escape on my own. Good night, Dr. Boozer."

fifteen

GREENBRIER COUNTY, WEST VIRGINIA

1897

EVER SINCE ZONA DIED I had wanted to go back to Livesay's Mill, but winter is a hard time to travel in. I was already beholden to my brother-in-law for taking me to see the prosecutor in Lewisburg, because I had no other choice, but people here don't ask for favors lightly, not even from family. I didn't want to impose on him again for something that wasn't strictly necessary. Walking would cost me nothing except a wearisome day and some shoe leather, but I had to wait for clement weather before I set out. Finally, about three weeks after they took Zona up out of her grave, the March rains stopped and there was a string of warm sunny days. It wouldn't last, of course. April snows are not uncommon here. When the third straight day dawned clear and mild, I made up my mind to go.

"You need to take the boys into the field with you today," I told Jacob as I dished up breakfast.

"I'm fixing to go over to Livesay's Mill. I'll be back around suppertime."

Jacob shrugged and turned his face to the wall. He didn't even ask how I was getting there or why I was going. He would never say a word about Zona. Maybe he thought about her, but her name never passed his lips. Of course, he never had much to say, anyhow. I put on my coat, and stuffed a scarf and wool gloves in one pocket in case the wind picked up. In the other pocket I had stuffed a couple of ham biscuits from breakfast, for I knew I'd be walking most of the day.

As I set off down the road toward the pike that wound east to Lewisburg, I thought about Jacob and all the years we had been together. When had the silence between us taken root? Or had it always been there, but in my younger days I hadn't noticed it, because when we were young and loving, there hadn't been so much need for words? Now and then, though, I missed my own family. There were six of us: my two older brothers, William and Thomas; then me and my sister Joanna, two years younger than me; and the littlest ones, George and Martha. Daddy was a coal miner, same as he'd been back in England, and then he turned to farming, so we were no better off in material ways than Jacob's family, but we laughed and sang, and on winter evenings, we'd all sit close to the fireplace while Daddy told us stories he remembered from his boyhood—tales about kings and outlaws, ghost stories and fairy tales. Even though I never left Greenbrier County, I felt as if I had traveled far and wide on the wings of those stories. But the Heasters seemed too ground down by toil to be fanciful, or maybe they thought the Lord wouldn't approve. So as the years passed, Jacob and I talked mostly about chores and the weather, while the spaces between conversations grew longer and longer. I had almost forgotten how to be sociable.

This visit to Livesay's Mill was no social call, either. I wanted to see what else I could find out about Zona's death. Maybe Mr. Preston had enough evidence to convict Edward Shue of the murder, but if I could find anything else to put a nail in his coffin, I would.

It took a good four hours to get all the way down to Livesay's Mill, but I was enjoying the warm sunshine and I passed the time looking for the beginnings of spring in the fields and woods. I ate a ham biscuit as I got close to my destination because I could tell by the sun that it was right on dinnertime. I went to the house first. I knew it was empty now, with Edward Shue in jail and Zona in the churchyard, but I thought I could look around on my own, and maybe talk to some of the neighbors.

The house didn't look deserted yet. It was still too early in the year for the weeds to overtake the yard. Mr. Livesay would probably rent it out again before summer. Everybody knew that Zona had died there, but there's hardly a house anywhere that hasn't seen a death sometime or other, so that wouldn't matter to the new tenants.

I went up on the porch and peeked in the windows, but all I could see were plank floors and a narrow staircase. Dust motes floated in a ray of sunshine.

"Did you come to see where the lady died? Ain't nothing there to look at anymore."

I turned from the window. Just beyond the fence a colored woman stood looking up at me with a look of stern disapproval. I was glad to see it. She didn't know who I was, of course, but I was grateful to her for trying to keep people from making a sideshow of my daughter's death.

I hurried down the steps, thinking that this

woman might also be an answer to prayer. "I am Mrs. Heaster—Zona Shue's mother," I told her. "Thank you for looking out for her, even now. You were one of her neighbors, weren't you?"

She looked at me for a few moments—confirming the resemblance, I thought—and then she nodded. "I'm Mrs. Reuben Jones, but folks mostly call me Aunt Martha. We live over the way." She nodded toward a small frame house in the distance.

"Were you acquainted with my Zona?"

A careful nod this time. She was wondering what I'd come about. "Can't say I knew her well. They hadn't lived here long, and they kept to themselves. But I talked to her a time or two, when she was ailing."

"Thank you for your kindness to my daughter. I'm glad she had someone to turn to."

"You never came to visit her yourself, though?"

"No. He wouldn't allow it. Kept telling us to wait until they got the place fixed up."

Aunt Martha's eyes flashed, and I could tell from her expression what she thought of Edward's excuse for barring visitors. For the hundredth time I wished we had come anyhow.

"He was a hard man, that husband of hers. It was my son that found her. I reckon Mr. Shue meant for that to happen. He still has nightmares over it."

"Edward Shue never cared who he hurt. And I mean to see that he gets what's coming to him."

"Reckon I'd feel the same if it was one of my girls. But I don't know what help you'll find here. Once they put Mr. Shue in jail, Mr. Livesay ordered some of his men over to clean out the whole place and lock it up. Nothing left to see."

"I walked all the way here from Meadow Bluff. I can't give up now." I thought for a moment. "Is there some kind of shed anywhere on the property?

A place to store provisions? She said it was down by the fence. In a rocky place."

Aunt Martha's eyes narrowed. "*She* said? Who?"

I sighed. Come the trial everybody would know, so I might as well get used to talking about it. "My daughter came to me—after she died. She told me her husband had killed her."

I could see the astonishment in her dark eyes, and she blinked a few times, trying to think of something civil to say, I supposed.

"That's how we knew to open the grave and let the doctors examine her. Zona told me he had broken her neck."

"And the law believed you?"

"They did. They ordered the examination, and that's how they found the proof to arrest Mr. Shue."

Aunt Martha Jones let out a long breath, shaking her head in wonder. "Well, if the fancy lawyers up in Lewisburg believed you, who am I to doubt it? Anyhow, you're right. There is a little shed down by the fence, and since you ain't been here before today, I don't see how else you could know that."

Thank you, Zona, I thought. "I need to see it. Can you take me there?"

We walked around to the back of the house, past bare trees and through the high brown weeds to where the ground sloped downward toward a weathered fence. There, jutting out of the rocky hillside, was the front part of a shed—just a few feet of boards and a door under a tin roof. We made our way to the door, and just as she put her hand on the doorknob, Aunt Martha turned to look at me. "You really saw your daughter's ghost, ma'am? For sure?"

I nodded. "Just as plain as I can see you. Four times she came to me. Told me what her husband did to her. And she told me to look here."

"Did she tell you what heaven was like?"

"I forgot to ask her." I edged past her and pushed open the door.

Steps led down into a small hollowed-out room lined with shelves. A few glass jars of preserved vegetables stood on the shelf next to the door. It might not have been enough to last out the winter, but it did outlast their need for it. I looked at all those jars of tomatoes, pickled cucumbers, apple butter, beans . . . and I thought about those hot days in the kitchen last summer . . . not even a year ago . . . when I'd corralled Zona, who'd have rather been elsewhere, and made her help me with the canning. I remembered how impatient she'd been, and I wondered what would have happened when she was expected to do it on her own. Probably just what did happen, I thought. Edward Shue was a brute, and it wouldn't have taken much to spark his rage.

"What's that on the floor yonder?" Aunt Martha, who had been behind me in the doorway moved aside to let in more light, and then I saw what she was pointing to: a dark stain on the floor next to an empty shelf.

I knelt down and ran my finger over the dark patch, but it had dried long ago. "Is it blood?"

Aunt Martha bent close to the stain and sniffed. She shook her head. "No telling now. It's been here a long time, from the look of it. Maybe it is blood. Maybe so. But it could be rabbit blood, or chicken, or hog. Did your daughter tell you to look for blood?"

I hesitated for a moment. "She didn't say what to look for. Just said to come to this place. And it's just like she said it would be. But she never told me why I was supposed to come here. Maybe she wanted me to see the bloodstain."

Aunt Martha made no reply, which meant she didn't agree with me. If I couldn't convince her, there wasn't much chance of Mr. Preston taking any notice of it, either. Nobody could prove that stain was human blood. I'd tell him about it before the trial, but I didn't think it would alter the case.

We looked around the storage room for a few minutes after that, but there was nothing out of the ordinary. I'd been there an hour, which is all the time the daylight would allow me, but I didn't think spending any more time would make any difference. A wild goose chase and a wasted day. I thanked Martha Jones again for her help and her kindness to Zona, and she wished me Godspeed. Then I started back up the road toward Lewisburg, hoping to make it home before dark.

sixteen

HE HOPED THAT DR. RUCKER was not planning to attend the funeral. There would be enough bad memories stirred by the occasion without Rucker appearing as the specter at the feast, reminding everyone of dark times best forgotten.

After breakfast John Alfred Preston slipped on the jacket of his good black suit and studied himself in the hall mirror. Perhaps it was a bit warm in May to wear a coat of such heavy material, but it was the most appropriate garment he owned for the solemn occasion of a funeral, and that consideration far outweighed any thoughts of personal comfort. He would have to attend to legal matters in his office for a few hours in the morning, wearing his unseasonably warm attire, but at least he hadn't far to walk in the morning sunshine to reach the site of the funeral.

The service was taking place in the Old Stone Church, not two hundred yards from his office in the courthouse. Since he was a Presbyterian elder in that church, he probably would have attended any funeral held there, unless some legal business prevented it, but this one was a personal obligation as well as a parochial duty, for he had known Austin Handley all his life. He would attend the service alone, though. The card on the funeral wreath (decorous, not too large) would say it was a tribute from both of them, but Lillie had been an infant during the war. She did not remember Austin Handley from the old days, and young Walter, who was a baby now, was too young to be trusted to behave at funerals, so perhaps it was best for his mother to stay at home with him and John. Preston had decided that he would prefer to concentrate on the loss of his friend without having to worry about a bored wife and a fretful child.

The Handleys were a prominent family in Greenbrier County, one branch of which handled the local undertaking business, ensuring that Austin would be ushered out of the world by his own kinsmen. He had been a farmer, though, tending to the vast and fruitful acreage that had been valued back before the war, in his father's time, at more than ten thousand dollars. He'd had a comfortable life, but there had been a dark side to that prosperity when the war came. No doubt that was why— But he didn't want to dwell on the past, especially not when those memories inevitably led to William P. Rucker, whom he would face in court in a few weeks' time. He would win the case, of course—there was no doubt about the defendant's guilt—but that was little consolation. He would still be forced to endure that arrogant, self-righteous little man in court for the better part of a week. This funeral only served as a bitter reminder: one by one, they were all dying— all the brave men from the old days—while Rucker, who should never have survived the war, lived on and on.

Well, it had been a long, full life for Austin Handley, very nearly the three score years and ten ascribed by the psalmist, and Handley had been vigorous to the last. Preston wondered if the minister would be able to resist the phrase *He died in harness*, for it was entirely appropriate. On the last day of April, the old man had been working on his farm, harrowing an already plowed field to provide a finer tilth for the sowing to come, when he had been stricken with a sudden and mercifully brief affliction of the heart. His farmhands had carried him back to the house, and a doctor was summoned, but he was gone before nightfall. Preston could not claim that his old friend had been taken before his time. Perhaps his quick, painless death was the sort that anyone should wish for, instead of a slow descent into senile infirmity. Still, for Preston's own sake, he regretted the passing of Austin Handley as the severing of yet another link to the past, to his own youth. It was also a reminder to Preston that he himself had recently reached the half-century mark, and not many decades hence, he and all his memories would also be swept into oblivion. Just now, though, those memories were all too clear.

It was hard to believe that the war had ended more than thirty years ago. A whole generation of adults had come of age since then—Lillie among them—with no memories of it at all, yet for those of his generation, the time spent in war was often clearer than the recent past. Perhaps that was because cold, and fear, and the constant presence of death had formed an acid that etched the war memories indelibly in the mind. It had taken a long time for everyday life to override the stories of past battles that had once dominated the conversation whenever his old friends gathered.

He slipped into the church and took his place in the accustomed pew, noting with satisfaction that the coffin at the front of the church was laden with flowers. The funeral was well attended, a tribute to Austin

Handley's long life and his standing in the community. Preston's thoughts drifted in and out as the obsequies went on; he knew his old friend's achievements and virtues as well as anybody there. His eyes and his thoughts strayed to the rest of the congregation. The 14th Virginia Cavalry was well represented, although sadly older and grayer than he cared to remember them. He would see them in the churchyard, and for a few minutes, savoring memories with those who shared them, they could all be young again.

After the chords of the last hymn trailed off into silence, the mourners followed the coffin out into the churchyard, where an open grave banked with flowers awaited the mortal remains of Austin Handley. John Alfred Preston stood beside the church door for a moment while his eyes adjusted to the bright May sunshine.

"It's a sad loss for the county, isn't it, Preston?" said a voice behind him.

He turned, recognizing the voice of Samuel Feamster, whom he still thought of as Lieutenant after all these years. They had both served in the 14th Virginia Cavalry—though Preston, who had only turned eighteen in '65, a month before the war ended, had only managed to serve for two months, while Sam Feamster, the elder by a decade, had been in for most of the war. His lean hawk face with its long patrician nose had aged now into gauntness, and his hair was sparser now, but he still held himself with the erect bearing of a soldier, showing no signs of the infirmity of age.

Preston smiled as he shook the hand of his old comrade. "How are you faring? And the family?"

Sam Feamster smiled. "We're all in the pink, thank you. Ann is expecting another baby. We have two boys and two girls, so I reckon this will tip the balance."

"You'll outlive us all, Lieutenant."

Sam Feamster shrugged. "I don't know that I'd care to. The world is changing at a dizzying pace, some of it good but not all. More and more I find myself in a world full of strangers. Seeing Austin Handley off to his eternal reward today sure does bring back memories, though. Sometimes I wonder how any of us managed to survive that infernal war. I reckon Handley was lucky to get another thirty-two years past the end of it. I thought he was done for when the Federals took him hostage back in '62."

"He thought so, too, as I recall. You know my father-in-law—the first one, Samuel Price—was another one of the men they took to guarantee Rucker's safety after he was captured in Summersville. Of course, Lieutenant-Governor Price wasn't my father-in-law at the time—I was only fifteen then—but in later years, after I married Sallie, I used to hear him speak about it." He glanced past Feamster toward another part of the churchyard, where Sallie Price Preston had rested in peace for the past fifteen years—three times longer than the span of their marriage. It wasn't as if he'd forgotten. He could see her sometimes in the faces of their two sons, and of course he attended church every Sunday there at the Old Stone Church, so he passed within sight of her grave often, but time had closed the wound, and he had been married to Lillie now for a decade, so he seldom paused to think of Sallie, except at times—like now—when the past clouded his thoughts.

"I hear that Dr. Rucker is defending that scoundrel who murdered his wife over at Livesay's Mill, so I reckon you'll be squaring off against him in court come June."

Preston nodded. "So it seems."

"He didn't come to the funeral, did he?"

Feamster looked around the churchyard, tense and scowling.

"Dr. Rucker? I don't believe so. I didn't see him."

"One murderer defending another. That's ironic, that is. They ought to take turns defending one another."

"Well, the law decrees that even the lowliest wretch is entitled to a defense."

"I suppose the fellow could claim that his lawyer is a bigger villain than he is, though I don't suppose that would get him off on the murder charge."

Preston permitted himself a tight smile. "I must admit I don't envy Dr. Rucker this particular case. He has little enough straw from which to fashion the bricks of a defense." Preston was still looking over the churchyard, at the scattered knots of mourners talking quietly now among themselves. "I believe that's Dr. William McClung over there, isn't it?"

Feamster squinted into the sunshine. "So it is. Another old comrade from the 14th. He's looking well, isn't he? Perhaps a fair few of us will live to see the new century. I wonder how many of those hostages Dr. Rucker will outlive? There was poor old Handley there, and Senator Price, your late father-in-law, but I disremember the others."

"Colonel Crook must have been partial to Samuels. Besides my father-in-law Samuel Price, he made hostages of Samuel Tuckwiller and Samuel McClung—but don't ask me how the latter is kin to Dr. McClung over there, because you can't throw a rock in this county without hitting a McClung."

Sam Feamster smiled. "You must ask my wife to sort it out for you sometime. She was a McClung afore I married her."

"I had forgotten. She has been Mrs. Feamster for a good long while, hasn't she?"

"She has. Our oldest girl, Pattie, will turn twenty next year."

"And that hostage business was more than thirty years ago, too, so perhaps we ought not to dwell on it, especially as regards Dr. Rucker. It matters less every day." He nodded toward the open grave of Austin Handley. "Little by little the past is fading away. Let's go and say our good-byes to another piece of it."

seventeen

LAKIN, WEST VIRGINIA

1931

"HOW ARE YOU FEELING these days?"

Mr. Gardner squinted into the bright afternoon sunshine, and made out the form of his doctor standing on the dirt path near the bench. The winter had been bitterly cold and the asylum's heating system proved unequal to the task of combating the chill. Patients and staff alike had crept along the corridors dressed in all the clothes they could fit on, some of them swaddled in blankets as well. Finally, though, in early March the weather broke—at least for a while—and the thankful residents of West Virginia's Asylum for the Colored Insane ventured outside to bask in the sun or wander around the grounds under the watchful eyes of attendants. Some of them were tending the flower beds, in hopes of finding more tangible evidence of the fine weather to come.

James Gardner had borrowed a magazine from one of the nurses—a frivolous offering whose subject matter he disdained, but it was better than idleness. Wearing his black overcoat and a white silk scarf, he had planted himself on a wooden bench in full sunshine. He was squinting at the fine print of an article on the film star Dolores Del Rio and her colorful collection of shawls when Dr. Boozer hailed him from the path.

Abandoning the magazine without regret, Mr. Gardner patted the bench and nodded for the doctor to join him.

"How am I feeling, Doctor? Still cold. It takes warmer weather than this to heat up my old bones."

James Boozer, wearing his white physician's coat over a tweed jacket, smiled indulgently. "Being raised in New York helps a lot. I wouldn't notice the cold until you could walk across that river over there."

"I wish I could see the river. I've been here for months, and I've never caught a glimpse of it." A gust of wind hit Mr. Gardner full on, making him shiver and rattling the pages of the magazine. He frowned, stuffing the offending paper into his overcoat pocket. "The Ohio hasn't frozen around here for twenty years, Doctor, but my blood may freeze at any minute out here, and you couldn't light a cigarette in this wind. I'm going to the parlor. If you can acquire a pot of coffee, you're welcome to join me in a warmer venue."

Boozer helped the old man to his feet. "I'll see what I can do."

"How was your trip to New York?"

"Mighty fine. I saw *Green Pastures* twice. Enjoyed it so much that I ended up taking my parents to a Saturday matinee. How about you? Any news from Mercer County?"

"I had a letter from my fellow attorney in Bluefield. He has agreed to handle any of the legal paperwork necessary to effect my release. They don't report much progress yet."

Dr. Boozer considered it. "Well, you don't want to be too hasty. I want to be satisfied that you are well and no longer a danger to yourself before I see you go. Just who are these influential friends of yours anyhow?"

Mr. Gardner hesitated for a moment, but finally he said, "They're my fellow Masons, Doctor. And somewhere up the hospital chain of command there's bound to be another one."

They headed up the steps and into the main building. Dr. Boozer told his patient to wait in the first-floor parlor while he went in search of coffee, but when Mr. Gardner started to enter the room, he found that one of the staff nurses was holding a sing-along with some of the older patients there. When Boozer, with coffeepot and white china mugs in hand, emerged from the kitchen, he found Mr. Gardner still waiting in the hallway outside. He was standing beside the closed door, with his finger to his lips, grimacing at the strains of "Down by the Old Mill Stream" played on the tinkly upright piano, accompanied by wobbly off-key voices. Without breaking stride, Boozer jerked his head toward the main staircase, indicating that Gardner should follow him upstairs, where the staff had a private lounge of their own.

"We'll probably have the place to ourselves," Boozer called out as he trotted up the stairs. "Everybody else is either on duty or out enjoying the sunshine."

The staff lounge was not conspicuously grander than the downstairs parlor for the mildly disturbed patients. Its red velvet upholstery was worn and shiny, and the carpet, while reasonably new, was a nondescript shade of brown that added nothing to the character of the room. A coal fire was burning merrily in the marble fireplace. Its mantel bore a display of Edwardian ruby glass vases and tarnished silver-plated candlesticks—breakable objects and potential weapons, and thus forbidden in the patients' area, but not an aesthetic improvement over the spare décor downstairs. The room's best feature was a glass-fronted bookcase of carved walnut, containing a selection of novels, cast-off biographies and textbooks, and tattered copies of *National Geographic*.

Mr. Gardner wandered over to the window. "You can't see the river from here, either."

"No, sorry. It faces the wrong direction. Have a seat. You've been telling me about the adventures of the infamous Dr. Rucker. As I recall, you said that there was a coda to the tale, some twenty years after the war?"

Mr. Gardner strolled over to the bookcase and stooped down to examine the titles behind the glass. "Wish I could borrow some of these."

Boozer shook his head. "I'm not a big enough dog around here to let you. Maybe I could take one, though, and quietly lend it to you. Let me think about it."

"Don't get in trouble on my account, Doctor. I know what it is to be a young man in a new profession, trying not to make waves. Will they mind your letting me in here?"

Boozer grinned. "I'll tell them it's part of your therapy. Normalization."

Mr. Gardner moved a Queen Anne chair nearer the fire and sat down, stretching out his legs to receive the warmth of the blaze. Boozer set the coffeepot on the marble-topped coffee table, and filled the two mugs. He handed one to his patient.

"I break the rules when I think there's a good reason for it," he said, "but as a new staff doctor, I try not to be too much of a nuisance to my elders."

"I suppose it's natural for the young bulls to test the strength of the fences."

"Perhaps—provided that you can do it without hurting your career. Do you think we grow out of it as we age and become the authorities ourselves? Had your boss calmed down any by the time he took you on?"

"Well, the fact that the war was long over when I knew him meant there were fewer opportunities to make mischief."

"Bridge burning would be frowned upon."

"But I suppose he still delighted in doing what was least expected of him. Taking me on, for example, despite my race and the objections of some members of the bar. In fact, I wonder if those objections were part of the appeal for him. I was smart, I worked well and cheaply, and my position as his assistant was one in the eye for his colleagues. He liked to shock people, I think. That may be why he agreed to defend Kenos Douglas. That trial is the postscript to Dr. Rucker's war escapades that I alluded to, although really the wonder is not that he took the case, but that he was *offered* it in the first place."

"Kenos Douglas? You haven't mentioned him. What was he in trouble for?"

"It was a murder trial. Nothing particularly exciting—just a drunken brawl that ended in tragedy, as such incidents are wont to do—but still the fellow's life was at stake, which meant that every effort had to be made to give him the best possible defense."

"And you're surprised that Rucker was offered the case because he wasn't a particularly able lawyer—just did it as sort of a hobby?"

"That, incidentally, but that isn't the main thing. Remember Nancy Hart, the Confederate spy who got Dr. Rucker captured along with Colonel Starr at Summersville in '62? Well, Kenos Douglas was her son."

"*The son of the spy who sent him to prison?*" James Boozer shook his head. "Is *everybody* in West Virginia crazy?"

Gardner chuckled. "That would be your call, Doctor. I'd say some more than others."

"Nancy Hart gets the man arrested and jailed for more than a year during wartime, in peril of being executed for treason, and then, a few decades later, when her son is on trial for his life, *that's* who she hires to defend him?"

James Gardner nodded. "That's about the size of it, but I wonder if either of them thought about it in those terms. After all, when she retained Rucker's services as a lawyer, more than thirty years had gone by since the raid that had led to his capture. Perhaps by then she thought of him as just another Greenbrier lawyer, maybe even the only one they could afford. And, of course, he was in the business of defending people, and hardly in a position to turn a client away on account of his pedigree. I don't know. That was before I joined his practice."

"And the son killed someone in a drunken brawl? Didn't you say that his mother shot a soldier in the face while she was escaping from detention in Summersville? I guess the apple doesn't fall too far from the tree."

"I'm not sure there was any malice intended in either case, though. Do you want the particulars?"

"Yes, indeed. I remember your saying that Nancy Hart was a plain woman with lank hair and gooseberry eyes, but apparently, despite these deficiencies, she managed to find a husband."

"Yes, but if beauty were required for matrimony, Doctor, there would be considerably fewer of us on earth."

"Touché, but so many men died in that war that thousands of women stayed spinsters. You'd think that the surviving soldiers could have afforded to be choosy."

"Well, perhaps Josh Douglas was. Take it from an old man: Beauty isn't everything in the long haul. Nancy Hart took care of Mr. Douglas when he was a wounded soldier—a Confederate soldier, of course—during the war, and after the end of the hostilities, he hunted her up and married her. They settled on a farm in Greenbrier County, and in true mountain fashion they mostly kept to themselves thereafter."

"I take it Kenos didn't follow their example?"

"Well, he was young—and drunk. It was Christmas Eve, as I recall. 1893. A fellow named Thomas Reed was giving a Christmas party that evening for those of his friends and relatives who had helped him in wood chopping that day. Apparently, Kenos Douglas was not one of their number, but after getting himself inebriated, he wandered over to Reed's place and barged in on the festivities. For some reason, he fired off a pistol, shooting through the ceiling, and Reed quite sensibly ejected Douglas from the party. I believe there were children asleep upstairs. After Reed pushed the interloper outside, he shut the door and stood pressing against it to prevent Douglas from getting back in. Angered by this treatment, Kenos Douglas fired his pistol through the closed door, mortally wounding Reed."

"Did he know he had killed the fellow?"

"Well, he hadn't—then. Thomas Reed died three days later. By then Kenos Douglas, accompanied by his brother, George, had headed for the hills. The county court set a five-hundred-dollar bounty for his arrest, and a week later one of Greenbrier's expert trackers, a fellow named Dawson—or 'Tall Sycamore,' as folks called him—had followed the Douglases' trail to the headwaters of Anthony's Creek, up in the mountains. He managed to get the drop on them, and they surrendered without a fight. So Dawson let the brother go, and took Kenos Douglas off to jail."

"Did he get the five-hundred-dollar bounty?"

"I suppose so. I never heard anything to the contrary. Anyhow, Kenos Douglas was installed in the jail in Lewisburg to be tried in the court term in April, which gave his family ample time to secure representation for him. Mr. Henry Gilmer prosecuted. I knew him well enough. He was the prosecutor for a term in between the terms of John A. Preston. It was the two of them that Dr. Rucker and I went up against in that murder case I told you about. We'll get around to it directly. This Douglas case I only knew about the way all the legal community gets to know about what cases are being tried in a given term of court. Murders were rare enough to be fodder for discussion."

"What kind of a defense could you mount in such a case? Insanity? Impairment through intoxication?"

"As I recall, Dr. Rucker claimed that Douglas didn't do it. He maintained that some unidentified third party had fired the shot through the door as Douglas stood by watching."

"In which case Douglas could clear himself by telling the court who did fire the shot, right?"

"Unless it was some heavily disguised stranger unknown to him. I believe that was the theory."

"Then what became of this stranger after the shot was fired?"

"Vanished as mysteriously as he appeared." Dr. Boozer laughed, and Mr. Gardner permitted himself a wry smile, but then he added, "Remember that the defense doesn't have to prove anything. They can offer an alternative explanation for what is alleged by the prosecution. *Reasonable doubt.* If you can convince the jury that there was another possibility, they may vote not guilty just because they're not sure. That was Dr. Rucker's plan. He didn't even confine himself to one theory."

"Throw everything at the wall and see what sticks, huh? What was his second hypothesis?"

"Well, if they didn't care for the mysterious-stranger theory, then he offered them the chance to believe that the shooting was purely accidental. Maybe Kenos Douglas was just going to fire off a shot into the air or at a tree, but at the last second somebody nearby jostled his arm and the bullet went astray—through the door and into Thomas Reed. Remember you're dealing with a bunch of drunks in the dark here, so who's to say?"

Boozer looked thoughtful. "I suppose it could have happened like that."

"And had you been a juror, Doctor, that conclusion would have prevented you from voting guilty, wouldn't it?"

"I don't know. It might have. Especially since he was on trial for his life. I'd want to be absolutely certain before I voted to condemn a man. Did that strategy work with the jury in the Douglas trial?"

"He got a hung jury in the April trial. Apparently a couple of the jurors were of the same mind as you are about being completely sure before sending a man to his death. Finally, the judge gave up and dismissed the jury, ruling that they'd start over with new ones in the November term of the court. So the following fall, Dr. Rucker went through the whole scenario again before a new audience."

"Did it work that time?"

"Juries are peculiar, Doctor. They are the variable in the legal scheme of things. I suppose for those of you in the medical profession the equivalent would be the disease that might kill one strong young person and not another, with no apparent reason for the difference in outcome. So while that April jury was befuddled by Dr. Rucker's efforts in misdirection, the November jurors would have none of it. They came back with a verdict of guilty of murder in the first degree, but they called for a sentence of life imprisonment instead of the death penalty, so Kenos Douglas went off to the state penitentiary at Moundsville, which should have been the last of him."

"Should have been?"

Gardner smiled. "This is where *your* profession's variable comes into it. In 1899—I was still practicing law in Lewisburg then—we heard that Kenos Douglas had come down with tuberculosis during his five years' imprisonment in Moundsville—and no wonder. The men were confined to tiny prison cells without heat or light for fourteen hours a day, and fed on rations that were little better than pig swill. The wonder is that they didn't all contract it. But Douglas did, and in view of his medical condition—and perhaps to keep him from infecting the rest of them—the prison authorities granted him a compassionate early release and sent him home to die." Here Mr. Gardner paused with a laugh that ended in a coughing fit. "Except he didn't."

Boozer fished a linen handkerchief out of his pocket and handed it over. "He didn't go home?"

"No. He didn't *die*. The pure mountain air of Greenbrier County revived him, and he got married, raised a brood of children, and went right on living. The government couldn't take back the pardon, though, so he finished out his life as a free man, and as far as I know, he never got into any trouble again."

Boozer thought about it and shook his head. "People don't usually recover from tuberculosis—at least not by just going home and not getting treatment. There are clinics in places like Switzerland . . . Do you suppose Douglas was misdiagnosed?"

"I always figured it was the mountain air. That's what brings rich people to the big hotel in White Sulphur Springs. They said it was healthier there in the mountains, especially in the summer fever season."

"It's possible, I suppose, but medically speaking, I find it unlikely." Still frowning, Boozer stared into the fire, scanning pages of medical texts in his mind. "If I had to bet on it, I'd put my money on a misdiagnosis. Squalid, overcrowded prison; second-rate doctors with rudimentary equipment and too many sick prisoners to treat—it would be easy for them to make a wrong guess when they were examining him, especially if tuberculosis was prevalent in Moundsville, which I'm sure it was. It's what they would have expected to find."

"And you think it was something else?"

"You said he was a drinker, didn't you? And the food in that prison was bound to be vile, so I'd expect him to be physically run down. It's not uncommon for heavy drinkers and malnourished persons to develop a lung abscess, and my guess is that your Mr. Douglas was both of those things, and that a lung abscess is exactly what he got."

"How do you get a lung abscess?"

"Well, it's a microbial infection. Sometimes you can get it from aspirating your own vomit, which a drunk has been known to do. When you do that, some of your own mouth bacteria enters your lungs, causing an infection: inflamed tissue, dead patches in the lungs. But the symptoms of a lung abscess would easily fool an overworked doctor: a spiking temperature, a cough that brings up blood and phlegm, chest pain. So they assume that he has tuberculosis and send him home, and when his environment changes for the better, he gets well."

Gardner shrugged. "That disease doesn't sound like much of an improvement over TB, if you ask me. Recovering from it could be a miraculous occurrence, too."

"Maybe so. Death is more random than we'd like to think. Some people die in days from an infected finger, while others live for decades with some malady that ought to have killed them. Every profession has its miracles, I suppose. If you want to give God the credit, call it a miracle. Do you think that fellow Douglas deserved his?"

"Miracles have always struck me as random happenings, Doctor. If they go by merit, then the Lord must have a different scorecard from mine. If I was in the business of handing out miracles, I believe I would have given one to Thomas Reed, the man standing behind the door, not to the fellow who shot him."

"Maybe it was a sign that Douglas didn't do it after all—or that it was an accident."

"I've buried two wives now, and both of them died young, and both deserved better treatment than they got out of life. If I didn't believe that such judgments were random, I'd figure that either I was crazy or else God was."

"I suppose that brooding on the inequities of life could lead one to despair."

Mr. Gardner smiled. "Then don't brood on it, Doctor. Philosophers have been grappling with that question for centuries; I don't suppose that psychiatrists are likely to find the answer."

eighteen

GREENBRIER COUNTY, WEST VIRGINIA

1897

SPRING CAME BACK TO THE WORLD in the months since Zona died, but it was still winter in my mind. In a couple of weeks the trial of her killer would begin, and Mr. Preston said that I was to be called as a witness. Just me. Not Jacob or anyone else in the family. We didn't talk about the trial at home. Every time I mentioned it, Jacob said, "Will that bring her back?" I didn't know if he was angry at Shue for killing her, at Zona for the foolish life she led and threw away, or at me for not letting her rest in peace.

The other day over dinner I said to him, "By the time of the trial it will be six months since we laid her to rest. The ground will have settled by now. We ought to be thinking about getting her a headstone."

Jacob looked up at me with a spoonful of beans halfway to his mouth. "Now why should we do that, Mary Jane? Didn't you already prove that Zona ain't there anyhow? Isn't she strolling around the county, paying calls on folks?"

Perhaps he meant it in jest, but I answered him with a cold stare. "Just to me. Just after it happened. Not since. And that appearance was a miracle God granted me in an answer to prayer."

Jacob grunted. "Well, maybe you could pray for a grave marker then. Those things don't come cheap, and we have better things to do with what little money we have."

I didn't bother to ask him why he didn't think our daughter was worthy of a grave marker, for I knew his excuse would be the expense of it, but that wasn't the real reason. I didn't know if he was ashamed of her foolish choices in men, or if he was angry with her for being murdered. He might not even have known himself what the real answer was, but it was plain that he had set his sights on forgetting her, and it would be easier to push her out of his mind if there wasn't a stone in the Soule Chapel churchyard to remind him of her every Sunday.

Every time we went to church, I would take a few minutes before the service and stop by her grave. The grass had started to grow there, and once spring came, I began to take what flowers I could find to mark the spot—snowdrops, then jonquils in March; later on I would take the shaggy pink blooms from the rhododendron bushes that grow in the shade of the woods up the mountain. I wished Zona could see them. She had to make do with berries and dead leaves for her wedding decorations—maybe that was a sign, now that I think back on it—but it's sad to die in the bleakness of winter when the world looks dead as well. Only the world comes back to life in April, green and beautiful and crowned with flowers, but for Zona winter will last forever, with precious little happiness to take with her in remembrance of her life on earth.

I prayed for her, too. I knew that she had been foolish and intemperate in her ways, but it seemed to me that she paid for whatever wrongs she did. *The wages of sin is death*, they say, and she paid that price in full. Surely God would not punish her further in the next world after all that she suffered here. I wish now that I could have asked her about where she is now—is it heaven? And what is it like? But in those weeks after she died, I was so eaten up with the desire to expose her killer and avenge her death that all I could think of was knowing the details of what had happened so I could make him pay. When people asked me, I said I got what I asked for. I was told how and by whose hand she died. But in a way Jacob was right. That knowledge, and the trial that was the result of it, didn't bring my Zona back, and it wasn't bringing me peace because I still didn't know that she was all right, and it haunts me.

nineteen

LAKIN, WEST VIRGINIA

1931

"SO YOU ACTUALLY got to defend a white man in a court of law—in 1897." James Boozer shook his head. "I marvel, Mr. Gardner. And in the South, too. I am still amazed."

The days were warm again, and they had found a west-facing bench in the sunshine.

James Gardner shrugged. "Well, bear in mind that the client was a no-account fellow, new to the county, and that everybody knew for a fact that he was guilty."

"Guilty of what?"

"Oh, homicide. First degree murder. His bride of three months was found dead at the bottom of the stairs in their home, and he went to great lengths to prevent the doctor from doing a thorough post-mortem examination. They finally dug her up a month later, and found she had a broken neck and finger marks on the skin around her throat. But even if he was a heartless monster, he had to have a defense, and we were it."

"Is that why you were allowed to defend him?"

"I was only part of the defense team, and that was because Dr. Rucker, who was chief counsel, appointed me. Maybe some of the people in the community would have said the wife-killer didn't deserve any better lawyer than the likes of me. But never mind that they would have been misjudging my ability, the fact was that in court I was not the face of the defense. William P. Rucker was. In court he sat there beside the accused at the defense table, looking like a Sunday school image of God, with his beetle brows and his long white beard. Most of the time I was just a young fellow at the far end of the table, scribbling notes while the witnesses talked.

"I did contribute to the efforts for the defense, though. Such as it was. Indeed, how can you defend a man when the whole community believes his dead wife herself accused him of murdering her? We did try, though. We rounded up what witnesses we could—mainly other men around Livesay's Mill who would say that Trout Shue was a genial companion and a hardworking employee for James Crookshanks, the blacksmith. All of that might even have been true, for all I know, but of course being a capital fellow doesn't prove that you didn't choke the life out of your missus, though I'm blessed if I ever could figure out why he did it."

"So you did believe that he was guilty?"

"Well, I tried to keep an open mind there at the beginning. You don't want to go thinking you're telling lies in court, or abetting falsehood. I *hoped* he wasn't guilty—I can't put it any higher than that. I didn't know any of the people involved in the case. They all lived miles away from White Sulphur Springs, and even if they hadn't, we would not have run in the same circles. But I had the chance to interview two of the prospective witnesses. Dr. Rucker thought they might tell me things they wouldn't tell him or the prosecutor."

"Really? How come?"

"On account of their color, Boozer. Remember that the youth who found the body of Mrs. Shue was one of our race, a neighbor named Anderson Jones who used to run errands for Trout Shue. Jones and his mother were neighbors of the Shues, and knew them tolerably well. About nine weeks before Edward Shue's trial for murder would commence in Lewisburg, we began to think about framing a defense, and so one afternoon in April, Dr. Rucker sent me over to Livesay's Mill to see what the Joneses could tell me. The accused wife-killer had been in jail more than a month by then, since the day of the autopsy in late February, and judging from the public sentiment concerning the case, we hadn't much hope of getting him off, but we had been retained to defend the fellow, and we took the view that if we could save him from the gallows and get him only a term of imprisonment, we might count that as a victory.

"I rode out from Lewisburg to Livesay's Mill that afternoon in my buggy. You wouldn't think it any distance at all these days, what with paved roads and fast motorcars, but at the turn of the century, when it was all dirt roads and mudholes, you had to go at a slow pace if you didn't want your horse to go lame or keel over from being pushed too hard. Anyhow, I got there by midafternoon, and although the weather was still cool and windy, and the roads muddy, at least it was not bitterly cold or snowing. I guess by now you've learned that spring can behave any way it wants to in West Virginia."

Dr. Boozer nodded. "I don't pack my winter clothes away until May."

"So I rode out there and found where they lived without any trouble—out in the country everybody knows everybody; you only have to find somebody to ask. Aunt Martha Jones was the wife of a farm laborer named Reuben Jones, and they lived in the settlement that had grown up around Livesay's Mill, in a modest rented house with a brood of children. It's hard to tell how old Mrs. Jones was. I remember thinking she was a woman in late middle age, but I was thirty then. Maybe I would have seen her differently if I had met her now. There was quite a young child as well as five older ones, as I recall. In fact, three of her offspring were adults, although they lived at home. Mrs. Jones must have been a little over fifty, but her wrinkled face and plump, shapeless body proclaimed that she had taken a hard road to get there.

"Anyhow, she was a respectable married woman, apparently trusted and well liked in the community. The fact that the white folks called her Aunt Martha ought to tell you both that and the fact that she was too old to cause anybody's heart to flutter. Mostly, they meant it as a term of affection and even respect."

Seeing Dr. Boozer's upraised eyebrows, he added, "It was a different time. A different century. I suppose they lived up to the light they had, most of them. I don't suppose she minded it, though I'm thankful that no one except my sisters' children has ever ventured to call me uncle."

Boozer was smiling. "I can't imagine it happening, Mr. Gardner. You're not a comfortable sort of person. Do you wish you were?"

"No. I should hardly know how to respond."

"Just as well, then. So, to return to the tale of

your murder case. You were saying that Mrs. Jones's husband worked on a nearby farm, and that the son in question ran errands and did odd jobs. Was that enough to support a houseful of children, or did she work, also?"

Mr. Gardner thought for a moment and shook his head. "I think she did, but I forget—if I ever knew. But remember that three of those children were adults themselves. The Jones family was quite large—then. I'm sure that they all kept busy earning a living. Mr. Jones worked on a farm. And the others? Doing chores for white folks, I guess. Laundry, cooking, mending, cleaning houses. I can't think what else any of them would have done in that time and place, but it's likely that I did not bother to ask. I wasn't concerned with the family members personally, except as possible witnesses for the case, because the Joneses were neighbors of the Shues, and because their son had found the body. Trout Shue had only lived in the community for a few months, but the Joneses lived close, and they should have known Trout and his bride as well as anybody. So I had to find out what they knew.

"I must have looked like a peacock in a hen yard in that little backwoods settlement that afternoon. I wore my good dark suit, a new white shirt, and a red silk necktie. I was going out among strangers, and I never wanted anybody to mistake me for a laborer. It must have given Martha Jones quite a turn to see me there at her front door, for when she opened it, she stared at me as if I were an apparition. She was a short, stout, dark-skinned little woman, wearing a white apron over a long blue dress. She was holding a colander of peeled potatoes, so I surmised that I had disturbed her dinner preparations. She peered out at me with dark eyes as expressionless as marbles, waiting, I suppose, to see what bad news I brought, for in her world, men in suits nearly always meant misfortune of some kind."

"Good afternoon, madam," I said as pleasantly as if I had been effusively welcomed.

"My husband ain't to home right now." She looked as if she were about to close the door. "He'll be working over to the farm until sundown."

I forced a smile. "That's all right. I am not bringing you any troublesome news. I'd just like to talk a bit, if we may. My name is James P. D. Gardner."

She stared at me. "That's a mouthful, for sure and certain. What do folk call you?"

"Mr. Gardner," I said, and then, thinking that she might consider my truthful response officious and uncivil, I finished lamely, "Or just plain Gardner, if you prefer. I wonder if I might have a word with you, and with your son if he is on the premises."

She studied me carefully, still as blank-faced as a sphinx. "Is you selling Bibles?"

Mr. Gardner broke off his narrative here and looked at his companion. "I won't attempt to render the dialect of her speech overmuch, Dr. Boozer. It isn't necessary to the tale, and I find there is too much mockery made of that dialect by comedians these days, in blackface and otherwise. She was a simple, careworn but dignified woman who spoke in the normal patterns of her time and place. Perhaps she would sound comical to you, Doctor, but I did not find her so then."

James Boozer nodded. "I understand. They

never did get South Carolina off my mama's tongue, either, but she was no less sharp and genteel for that. Tell me, though, how is it that you don't speak that way yourself? You are Southern-born, and surely your parents were born into slavery?"

Gardner considered it. "Partly my training at Storer College and partly determination, of course. My father was a freedman, and he educated himself. Good at anything he turned his hand to. Raised horses, did some rudimentary doctoring. He taught me to read and to use books, and he encouraged me—pushed me, really—to become whatever I wanted to be. Not that I needed much pushing. I craved position—respect—like some fools crave opium. Did your people push you, Doctor?"

Boozer thought about it. "No. They knew I was bright, of course. Seems to me like I just fell upwards. How did you manage?"

"It's true that the village in which we lived was populated by simple country folk, but remember that it also boasted a fine, exclusive resort full of wealthy, well-traveled people."

Boozer nodded, with a knowing smile. "Who wouldn't give you the time of day, would they?"

"Oh, some of the most aristocratic ones were kind enough. They thought they outranked everybody, so from the heights of their eminence they could discern no appreciable difference between me and a local working-class white man. And they were generally civil, because they had no fear of anyone scaling their castle walls, socially speaking—it simply couldn't be done, regardless of your creed or color. It's mostly fear makes people rude, and as they had not the one, neither did they have the other. I don't say they hailed me as a brother in humanity, but they found no sport in humiliation. Or if they did, they practiced it on more pertinent targets: the social climbers and the pretentious nouveau riche of their own race."

"So those aristocrats constituted your finishing school? How did you get close enough to study them?"

"I worked some at the hotel there when I was a boy, and I listened. Those people were my Bible, and I learned chapter and verse of their speech and manners."

Boozer looked at the old man sitting ramrod straight on the weatherworn wooden bench. He might have been in the witness box or meeting with the governor, so formal was his speech and demeanor. Looking at him, one felt that he missed a necktie the way other people would miss trousers. "You didn't feel like you were being phony?"

"Phony?" James Gardner shook his head. "I was young. And once I learned, I never spoke or acted any other way, not around anybody. I found that people treated me as the person I presented myself to be. It soon became second nature, and not long afterward I *was* that person. There was no one else that I could be anymore. That mold was set forty years ago. By now it is unbreakable." He looked around at the other patients shuffling across the lawn, and at the dark shape of the brick building on the slope above them. "Even in here."

"But your speech and your demeanor made you a stranger to your own people. You just told me that the countrywoman Aunt Martha Jones asked if you sold Bibles."

Mr. Gardner shrugged. "At least she didn't mistake me for a field hand. I would choose respect over camaraderie any day."

"But being so isolated can contribute to despair, which may be part of the reason you ended up here. Don't you want people to like you?"

"Doesn't matter what I want. They generally don't like me, so I've learned to settle for respect. If I tried to be hail-fellow-well-met with all and sundry, then you would be justified in branding me a phony."

"All right. Have it your way. I don't know that I'm in any position to disagree with you. I am particular about my status as well. I introduce myself as *Dr.* Boozer, even to store clerks and small children."

The two men shared a brief smile of perfect understanding.

Boozer took another sip of his coffee. "So you were saying that when you went out to question the neighbor of your client, she mistook you for a Bible salesman. What did you say to that?"

The old man settled back in the chair by the window, and cradling his coffee cup in both hands, he took up the tale again.

When I recovered from the unexpectedness of the question, I replied, "Why, no, ma'am, I'm not selling Bibles, nor anything else. And since you strike me as a God-fearing woman, I doubt that you are in need of one."

"Can't none of us read, mister, excepting Margaret, though Samuel and Sarah be learning. But we all know the scriptures well enough, just from going to preaching."

"I'm sure you do, but religion is not my vocation. I am an attorney from Lewisburg."

She stiffened a little at that, and I think she would have preferred a Bible salesman, because in the battle between good and evil, those in the legal profession are generally thought to represent the other side. Attorneys bearing pieces of paper often augur incomprehensible bad news.

Her expression became mulish. "You got no call to put us out of this house, sir. We pay our rent, smack on time, every month we can."

"You and your family are not in trouble of any kind, Miz Jones." (I had learned to say "Miz" to keep from having to decide whether a woman is married or not, and especially to spare her feelings if she ought to be married but isn't.) "I have come to talk to you about Mr. Edward 'Trout' Shue. You may be aware that he is charged with murder. He will be on trial for his life in June."

"Well, if that's all you're after, I guess I can talk about that." She opened the door a little wider and nodded for me to come in. "You're letting all the heat out," she said, to temper the cordiality of the invitation. "I reckon you better come in. Sit at the table there while I finish peeling the rest of these potatoes."

I followed her into a small room with a rough pine floor and beadboard walls. A small woodstove warmed the space tolerably well, though the warm weather made it an easier task. A young woman and an adolescent girl, both resembling Mrs. Jones, were in the little parlor. The younger sister was on her knees, a dozen straight pins held tightly between her lips, hemming a long dress that the older one was wearing. The garment was evidently under construction, as one sleeve was not yet attached and some lace at the neck was stitched only on one side. They stared at me for a moment, when I came in, and I ventured a reassuring smile.

"These are my girls Margaret and Sarah. Their older sister, Mary Ellen, is getting married the first week in May, so we're getting the wedding clothes together. Margaret is the maid of honor, and I reckon Sarah will be the bridesmaid."

She paused, and I suppose she expected me to express congratulations, but I was too preoccupied with my witness questions to rise to social pleasantries. Finally I murmured, "A happy occasion, I'm sure."

That seemed to satisfy her, because after a short pause, she went on, "Mary Ellen is out working this afternoon. The two older boys are on the farm with their daddy. Sarah, put down your sewing, and take this gentleman's hat and coat."

I removed my overcoat and handed it over along with my new felt hat, hoping that they would be returned to me in the same pristine condition in which I surrendered them. The house was tolerably clean, and if it was somewhat untidy, that was not to be wondered at, because it was a small dwelling to contain so large a family.

Sarah gave me a shy smile as she accepted my coat and hat.

"Thank you, Miss Jones," I said, and she giggled as she hurried away with my coat. She was about fourteen, and I knew from the behavior of my own sisters that she was still young enough to be flattered to be called Miss instead of her first name.

"Mr. Gardner here is a lawyer from Lewisburg, Margaret," said Mrs. Jones, addressing the older daughter in meaningful tones.

The young woman's response was a quick nod, but although she glanced at me with somewhat more interest, she did not speak. She looked to be well past twenty, not that much younger than myself, in fact, but I did not inquire as to why she still resided at home. She seemed a nice enough person, but she was plain and apparently on her way to becoming the spitting image of her mother. I became even more circumspect than ever, if that is possible, because I did not wish to encourage any match-

making instincts among the Joneses. I was not vain
of my own attractiveness, but I knew full well that a
bachelor lawyer would be a pearl beyond price to a
laborer's family with several spinster daughters.

At a nod from her mother, Margaret Jones picked
up the sewing box and some scraps of material and
carried them into some other part of the house. I followed Mrs. Jones through an open doorway and into
the kitchen area, where the rest of the potatoes for
their supper sat upon a scarred pine table.

"Mind the young'un," said Mrs. Jones, and then
I noticed a chubby, wide-eyed child in a homemade
calico dress sitting on the floor near the stove, on
which a big pot of soup beans bubbled merrily. In
front of the child sat a bowl of freshly plucked brown
feathers, probably the by-product of the chicken that
would constitute the evening meal to come. The
child—I could not tell its sex, for all small children
back then were dressed more or less alike—had a
smear of honey on the palm of each pudgy hand, and
it was engaged in transferring a brown tail feather
from one hand to the other and back again, so rapt
in concentration that it did not even look up when
I passed.

"That's our sweet baby," said Martha Jones,
nodding toward the child. "No trouble at all."

I tried to think of something to say. Mrs. Jones
looked fifty if she was a day, and her daughters were
all unmarried. I did not like to ask whose child it
was, so I simply said, "A pretty youngster. What is
its name?"

She beamed proudly. "Reuben, same as my husband. I done birthed eight young'uns myself, and
we are blessed to have most of 'em still alive, and all
under our roof—at least until Mary Ellen weds her
sweetheart, Lomie, in a few weeks' time. You'll meet
the menfolk directly. Samuel and Anderson will be

back close to nightfall, same as their daddy. You may as well take a chair there and talk while I get on with my work."

I sat down as bidden and waited until she settled in again and began to attack the potatoes with a paring knife before I took out my pen and my notebook, preparing to make a record of the interview.

"So you're wanting to talk about Mr. Edward Shue," she said, shaking her head. "A most peculiar man. Are you fixing to convict him at this jury trial?"

"That would be the task of the county's prosecuting attorney, Mr. Preston," I said, hoping I would not have to explain the intricacies of the legal system to a farmwife. "But anyone accused of a crime is entitled to have someone represent him to offer a defense. The jury will listen to both sides, and then decide on his guilt, or lack of it."

She looked at me scornfully. "I don't imagine they'll have to think too long and hard about that."

"I couldn't say. But perhaps I ought to tell you that I am representing Mr. Shue. That is, we will be defending him in court."

"Oh, *are* you?" Martha Jones scowled at me and hacked at the potato. "You think it's all right to go around murdering wives, do you?"

I had been a defense attorney long enough to be ready for that question. When tempers run high about a case, people are always quick to blame lawyers for defending someone unpopular. "Since the man is on trial for his life, everyone wants to gather as many facts as possible so that we can all rest assured that justice is done."

"Fair enough." She scraped at the peel of another potato.

"But from your question, I take it that you think he is guilty?"

She shrugged. "I didn't see him do it, mind you. But he was acting mighty peculiar after it happened. Wouldn't let nobody go near that lady's body. I offered to help with the laying out and dressing the corpse, same as any neighbor would, but he insisted on doing it all hisself. I never saw the like of it. Acted like he was all tore up with grief over her death. But then we saw him two or three days later, and he was grinning and cracking jokes like he didn't have a care in the world. Mighty strange if you ask me."

"So it sounds," I murmured, trying to think of a counterargument in case this should be brought up in court.

"And the day it happened, Mr. Shue was dead set on Andy going over to see if Mrs. Shue wanted any help. Stopped by to ask him three different times. Now Andy has been known to be forgetful, but I was here. I would have reminded him and made sure that he went. Mr. Shue was never that particular before. It was my boy that found Mrs. Shue at the foot of the stairs. Well, I expect you know that. It's why you're here, isn't it?"

"Partly."

She half rose from her chair, wide-eyed and alarmed, and I saw that her old mistrust of my profession had returned. "You're not going to try to say my boy did it, are you?"

"No," I said quickly, more to allay her fears than from any certainty about the strategy of Dr. Rucker's defense. It seemed far-fetched, though. "I think you knew Mr. and Mrs. Shue as well as anyone else in the area, didn't you?"

"We live close, that's all. We obliged now and then."

"Were either of your older daughters by any chance friends with Mrs. Shue? Would she have confided in one of them?"

Mrs. Jones laughed. "Mrs. Shue wasn't a great one for having lady friends, black or white, and if she had been, she wouldn't have chosen my Mary Ellen or Margaret as a chum. My girls didn't have much in common with Mrs. Shue. Thank the Lord for that."

"What do you mean?"

"Well, Mrs. E. Z. Shue was a pretty little lady—didn't she know it!—and she was civil enough to me, but I met her before the rest of the family did, and right off I had my doubts about her."

"How so?"

"Well, first of all, because the pair of them got hitched in such a tearing hurry. It didn't seem fitten to me. They hardly knew one another. And then she took sick a couple of weeks after she and Mr. Shue got married. Since he had to work—not that men are any use in a sickroom, anyhow—he asked me to look out for her. I went over one morning in December to see how she was faring, and to give her some soup. I went in and did a little tidying up in the kitchen and gave the floor a lick and a promise, because we all knew how particular Mr. Trout Shue was about housekeeping. I did that, and then I took her up some chicken broth and a slab of bread I'd baked that morning. While she was eating the soup, I sat there with her, just making conversation to cheer her up because I could tell she had been crying. I didn't say nothing about that. Figured she'd tell me if she wanted to. But I did ask her if she thought her illness might be the sign that she was starting a baby. *Oh, no!* she says. *I know what that feels like.* She blushed, and changed the subject real quick after that, and I think she was sorry she had let it slip, but I knew then that she wasn't the innocent young bride she wanted folk to think she was. She had a past. I don't say I hold it against her, like some people would, but all the same, I thought there might be trouble coming from it someday. I don't say I expected what did happen, though. No, sir, I never figured on that."

All that was news to me. As far as I knew, no one had impugned the virtue of Zona Heaster Shue, and the implication that she had borne a child meant that there could be another person in the story. I wondered if there were more to it than just a past connection. "Did you notice any visitors going to the house?"

Martha Jones shook her head. "No, I did not. I know what you're thinking. You're wondering if Mrs. Shue had a man on the side, but she did not. Nothing like that was going on."

"You're sure?"

"I am. Those folks didn't have any visitors at all—not any social callers, that is. No friends. One of us might do the odd chore for them now and again—chop some wood, do some washing or a little cleaning, especially after she took sick, that kind of thing—but we weren't being sociable. I reckon we were neighborly, but Mr. Trout Shue paid us what he could. They always kept to themselves, though, even more than you'd expect newlyweds to do."

"But your son Anderson is reported to have found Mrs. Shue's body, so he was inside the house."

"You'll be wanting to talk to him about that, I expect, though much good it may do you."

She had a peculiar expression on her face when she said that, but I didn't question her about it. I'd see Anderson Jones himself soon enough, because I wasn't heading back to town until I did.

"Andy will be back before long. He's been out with his daddy for most of the day, but by now he may be out helping another one of our neighbors with some wood chopping. He was supposed to do that this afternoon, but he'll be back directly. I suppose I could keep talking to you until then. I got biscuits to make. You better scoot back a ways from the table unless you want to get flour on that fine black suit of yours. Mind, I don't think anything I can tell you will help that man you're defending."

"I understand, ma'am. I'll settle for the truth."

"I can give you that, best I know it. And a glass of spring water or a cup of coffee, before I get started, if you're in need of either one."

"Coffee, then, if it's no trouble." While she busied herself with the coffeepot and the white china mugs, I told her I didn't want to put words in her mouth, but if she knew anything that could help our defense, I needed to hear it. Until I'd heard what she could tell me, I didn't know if she'd be any use as a witness at the trial or not, but I did have to talk to the boy who had found Mrs. Shue's body. It seemed sensible to pass the time by having a pleasant chat with her. She might tell me things she didn't know she knew.

When the coffee was ready, she called for Margaret to start the chicken frying and to put the potatoes on to boil. When that had been accomplished to her satisfaction, she sat back down again. "We don't have no sugar," she told me. "Though I reckon I could get you a dollop of cream if you were wanting it."

"Thank you, no," I said. "I'll take it as it comes. Now you were telling me about Mr. and Mrs. Shue."

"Yes, sir, they were civil to one and all, but they kept to themselves right much," said Martha Jones, pouring the coffee. She stood up at the table opposite me and set a thick white cloth on top of the table, sprinkling it with flour. She bustled about, getting a bowl for more flour and milk, and began kneading the dough for the biscuits. I watched at a safe distance as little puffs of flour flew here and there while she worked.

"Yessir, they kept themselves to themselves. We didn't think anything odd about that at first, since they were newlyweds. He was friendly enough, always wanting my Andy to do some trifling errand for him. They never had family to visit, though, neither one of them. I reckon none of the kinfolk lived close enough to come calling."

"I believe Mrs. Heaster's family live out in Meadow Bluff, and his people are over in Pocahontas County, so perhaps you're right about distance being the difficulty."

"It was wintertime." She thumped the mound of floured dough on to the white cloth, and looked up at me with raised eyebrows. "I wouldn't say that was the whole of it, though. I did wonder why he came over here in the first place. I believe his daddy is a blacksmith over in Pocahontas County. Why didn't he stay put and work with him?"

"I don't know. Sometimes people have to leave the family to grow up, I think."

She laughed. "Him? He's past thirty, and I've heard tell that he'd had a wife before. Seems to me like he ought to be plenty grown up by now. But never mind him. What about his wife? Her family is in the county, over in Meadow Bluff, like you said. I think a new bride's mama would want to visit her, at least to have a look at her daughter's new home. When my Mary Ellen gets wed in May, I certainly intend to visit her in her new home. And we'll all be invited to supper after the first week or two, you mark my words. Mary Ellen will still be part of this family, even after she becomes Mrs. Lomie Lewis. And Mrs. Shue was younger than my girl. What could her parents be thinking leaving her alone for so long with a man none of them hardly knew? Meadow Bluff ain't all *that* far from Livesay's Mill. But Mrs. Heaster's family never once set foot in that house."

"Are you sure?"

She shrugged. "You could ask them yourself, if they'll talk to you. But when she was ailing and I went to look in on her, we got to talking about canning beans and 'maters, and I asked if her mama had seen all what she had stored away in the pantry. And she said her mama hadn't come to visit. Turns out she brought most of that food from home, though."

"Yes, they married in late fall, so there wouldn't have been much on hand for canning purposes by then."

Martha Jones gave me a knowing grin. "Well, if you know that much, I reckon you didn't grow up on the moon after all, Mr. *Gilt-Edged* P. D. Gardner, but you sure are a rare bird for these parts."

I did not correct her about my name, nor did I offer her any information about my origins, and sure enough, after a few more moments of cutting dough into the shapes of biscuits, Mrs. Jones picked up the thread of her story again.

"I knew that she couldn't have canned all those vegetables, but I wouldn't have called her on it if she had claimed she had. That wouldn't have been courteous, and we take care not to have ructions with any of our neighbors, especially the white folks."

"Very wise," I murmured. The origin of the canned goods mattered little, but I wanted to encourage her to continue her narrative. "So the Heasters did not visit? Perhaps the winter weather kept them away."

"Or maybe they knew they weren't welcome. When Mrs. Shue said her mother had not come to the house yet, she sounded kind of sad about it. She allowed as how Mr. Shue had been set on them getting adjusted to married life and getting the house fixed up before he was willing to entertain guests. Curtains and more furniture, I understood her to mean. They didn't have overmuch in the way of household goods. It was a hasty marriage, that's for sure, and he didn't bring nothing much with him from Pocahontas County. I reckon the family might have let her take a few things away with her when she went back to Meadow Bluff to be married. One wagonload is all they could have managed. He didn't make much money at Crookshanks's smithy, not enough to fill up a house with furniture right away. But nobody would have expected them to. And as for not wanting guests to see their unfinished house—now, me, I wouldn't call close family *guests*, would you?"

"I suppose not," I said, but I was thinking, *It would depend on how well I liked the family.* Mrs. Jones was correct, though, in the main. Most people in that place and time associated almost exclusively with family connections, and it never would have occurred to them to stand on ceremony with close kin. It might have occurred to me, but then I had always known that I was a changeling, and I never assumed that my own reactions were in any way a reflection of the norm.

Mrs. Jones flattened another biscuit between her palms, deep in thought, remembering her erstwhile neighbors. Finally she said, "I told you that the Heasters never visited their daughter, and that's the truth, but I have met Miz Heaster since then."

I tried to contain my surprise. "Did you?"

She nodded. "She came here back in the early spring, looking for something. There's a little cabin down behind the house here, across the meadow amongst some rocks. And Miz Heaster came and asked could she go look into that shed, for her daughter wanted her to find something."

"What was she looking for?"

"She didn't rightly know. She said she had

plumb forgot to ask when her daughter told her to go, because she was so surprised to see her."

"Mrs. Shue called upon her mother? When?"

"Well, that's just it. It was a couple of weeks after she passed."

I turned the words over in my mind, trying to put some other construction on their meaning, but there wasn't one. Finally I said, "Do you mean that the woman claims to have seen her daughter's ghost?"

She nodded. "That's what the lady said, and I may as well tell you that according to her, Miz Shue told her that it was Trout what killed her. Wrung her neck, she said. What's more she believes it. Just so you know."

"Thank you," I said, repressing a smile. "I don't believe the law is allowed to recognize the testimony of deceased persons, but I'll include it in my report to Dr. Rucker. Did Mrs. Heaster visit you before the autopsy or afterward?"

"Afterward, though I don't recall exactly when. It was after the weather got warmer, anyhow."

Of course it was, I thought. "And did the lady find what it was that she was supposed to be looking for in the shed at the end of the pasture?"

Martha Jones shook her head. "I helped her look, but we didn't find nothing, except some stains that might have been blood. Hog's blood, for all we knew. Didn't prove anything one way or t'other. She was mighty disappointed, and I thought she might ask again if her daughter's ghost came back, but I guess it never did. Anyhow, I ain't seen her since."

"I wonder if Mrs. Heaster got on well with her daughter. It seems odd that she did not visit the newlyweds."

"I think Mrs. Shue wanted her to come. She acted like she would have welcomed anybody's company, especially when she was ailing, but it seemed to me like Mrs. Shue wasn't given any say in the matter of visitors. It was all about what her new husband wanted. He was particular about his food, I'll tell you that."

I was about to ask her more about Mr. Shue's habits when a dog barked somewhere outside and someone called out from the yard, "Martha, we're back! Sarah, come get these shoes!"

"That will be Reuben and my boy." Martha jumped up from her chair, her smile tinged with relief. She scooped up the baby and hurried to the door to meet them, followed by Margaret.

I trailed along after them, because it seemed discourteous for me, a stranger, to sit there alone in the kitchen while the family gathered elsewhere. Through the open door I could see a wiry, grizzled man and a boy of perhaps twelve stooping to remove their mud-caked boots before they entered the house. At the door, the youngest daughter, Sarah, was waiting to collect their footwear to be cleaned outside. Mrs. Jones, I surmised, did not allow mud to be tracked through her tidy house.

Her husband was not much taller than his wife, but considerably thinner. His farmwork had kept him fit, though the outdoor labor had turned his face to wrinkled leather. The fact that he had hugged his wife upon entering the room, and that his offspring crowded joyfully around him, led me to think that Mr. Jones was a naturally mild and genial fellow, but he regarded me with grave courtesy that hinted at a distrust of strangers, or perhaps of well-dressed strangers whose presence did not constitute a social call.

I introduced myself to Mr. Jones, and solemnly we shook hands. "And is this young man Anderson?" I asked, ready to shake hands with the boy as well, but he hung back and eyed me with solemn reserve.

Reuben Jones and his wife exchanged a look that struck me as both wary and awkward. After a moment's pause, Martha Jones said, "That there is Samuel, Mr. Gardner. Anderson is our other boy. He'll be along soon."

Sarah took the muddy boots out into the yard, and the rest of us stood in the living room, prolonging an awkward pause. Margaret hurried back to the kitchen to tend to the chicken, and Reuben Jones took charge of his young namesake, and plopped down in an old easy chair near the fireplace, motioning for me to pull up a chair and join him. His wife, lingering at the entrance to the kitchen, said, "Mr. Gardner is representing Mr. Trout Shue at his trial."

Reuben Jones nodded to me, but his expression gave nothing away. "Is that right?" he said, still polite but noncommittal. I detected a shade less warmth in his demeanor.

"To be exact, I am assisting the lead attorney in the case—Dr. William Rucker."

"I see."

"Dr. Rucker is white," I finished lamely.

"Figured that." He allowed the child to play pat-a-cake against one of his callused hands, but despite that I could tell that he was attending me closely, perhaps listening for the click of a springing trap.

"So I came out here to speak to you folks—and especially to your son Anderson—to see what you can tell me about the people involved."

"They kept to themselves."

"Why do you think that was?"

"They didn't say."

Mr. Jones was not precisely uncivil, but he made it plain that he did not intend to say anything that could be twisted by lawyers into an accusation toward anyone. Perhaps he was protecting his son, or maybe he was just naturally cautious. It must have been a quarter of an hour before Anderson Jones returned home, and in that time I learned nothing at all from Reuben Jones.

I confess that I was relieved when I heard the clatter of boots on the little wooden porch. Sarah hurried to the door to collect this brother's shoes for cleaning, and Anderson came into the house in his stocking feet. He was grinning broadly until he saw me, and then the happy expression faded, and he cast an anxious look at his father, awaiting instructions.

"Pull up a chair, son," said Reuben Jones. "This here gentleman is a lawyer from town, and he's wanting to ask you some questions. Nothing hard. Don't worry. Just tell the truth."

I had not spoken, nor risen to shake his hand, because I was trying to master my consternation at the sight of him. All the accounts I had heard of the case had described Anderson Jones as a young boy, and I had been expecting to meet a child, but this strapping youth, as tall as I was, must have been nearly twenty.

His father's quiet words of reassurance did nothing to allay the young man's fear of being questioned. Although I did my best to smile and make him feel at ease, he would not meet my eyes. He kept glancing this way and that, as if the slightest provocation would send him darting from the room in terror.

"I don't know nothin' 'bout none of it—sir," he said, eying me like a cornered rabbit.

"But surely since you found the body of Mrs. Shue, you must know a little bit."

He shook his head. "He told me to go. Three times he came and told me. So along about eleven o'clock I went, and there she was—the lady—cold and dead in the hall. Folk already asked me all that, and I told 'em."

I realized then why young Anderson Jones had been characterized as a child in all the accounts of the case. In every respect save the corporeal, he was indeed a child, what people in those days referred to as a simpleton. The unworthy thought occurred to me then that if I were a murderer who wished to have the body of my victim discovered by someone other than myself, this harmless fellow would be the perfect choice. Both his color and his mental condition would mitigate against his standing in court as a credible witness, and he might well be too befuddled by his discovery to remember much of what he had seen.

I could also see why his parents were uneasy at the thought of an investigation into the death of Mrs. Shue. Who could be more easily incriminated than this poor hapless youth? Who except his family would care what became of him?

I asked a few more desultory questions, but I learned nothing that would either help or hurt the defense of Edward Shue when the case went to trial. Then Martha Jones appeared in the doorway, hands on her hips, observing our conversation for a few moments. She frowned at the sight of her son shifting from one foot to the other in silent misery. At last she summoned a false smile, clapped her hands, and said, "Supper's ready! Won't you stay and join us, Mr. Gardner?"

Nothing is so sure to speed a lingering guest as a perfunctory offer of hospitality. Besides, I knew that the flesh of a single chicken and a few beans and potatoes would hardly stretch to feed all the hungry mouths in the Jones household as it was, even without the addition of an unwanted guest. Thanking them profusely for their patience and kindness, and pleading the lateness of the hour, I retrieved my hat and coat, and fled.

twenty

GREENBRIER COUNTY, WEST VIRGINIA

1897

DEATH IS QUICK, but retribution moves at a snail's pace. My Zona died near the end of January, but June will be nearly over by the time Edward Shue is finally made to stand trial for killing her. I hope he has had a sorry time of it, languishing in jail in Lewisburg. I hope he's cold and pent up in a tiny cage, big as he is. I hope they aren't feeding him enough, for there never was such a fool over victuals as Edward Shue. I hope he has to eat rats.

I have not seen Zona again since those times she came to me a little while after her passing, but I still talk to her, for now I know for a certainty that her spirit lives on somewhere, and I hope she knows what is going on in the world that she left behind. I pray that she can hear me. When we go to church on Sunday, I still stop by her grave with a few flowers or a pretty pebble from down by the creek, and as I lay the gift on her grave, I tell her that her brute of a husband is locked away in a box not much bigger than the one she's in. I have never seen the jail in Lewisburg, but I hope this is true, and I hope that once the trial is over and done with, they send him to hell at the end of a rope. I have stood at Zona's grave and promised her out loud that if they hang him, I will go and watch. Jacob would probably say that it wouldn't be proper for a God-fearing woman to witness such a spectacle, but I have lived on a farm all my life. I have wrung chicken's necks and seen hogs killed, and I bore that without tears, even though some were pets and their deaths came through no fault of their own. Edward Shue has earned his execution. I hope he gets it.

Anyhow, I know I will see him in a few weeks, for I am to testify at his trial, and Jacob cannot stop me from going to that, because I have been summoned as a witness and the law says I must go. They wouldn't have to force me, though. Why, if I had to, I'd walk all the way to town for the privilege of telling what I know about Mr. Edward Shue. The prosecutor, Mr. Preston, has written me to say that he would like to see me a few days before the trial so that we can go over my testimony. He thinks I will be nervous or frightened appearing before all those people in court, but even if I were, it wouldn't stop me. I know Zona wants me to do this; she came back from the dead to tell me so. I must do whatever I can to help Mr. Preston put that monster away.

I hear that Edward Shue has got himself a lawyer now, though I don't know how that came about. He is a no-account blacksmith who never had two nickels to rub together, so it's strange that he can afford to pay for the services of a lawyer, much as he needs one. My brother-in-law Johnson Heaster says there is some provision made by the courts to provide counsel for them that cannot afford it, so maybe that's it. Perhaps the county lawyers take it in turn to work for free, as a kind of charity.

So I don't know exactly how Edward came to be represented by Dr. William P. Rucker, but I'd say it's a coin toss as to which of them is the worse villain. I remember people talking about Dr. Rucker when I was a young girl back during the war—how he burned the Cowpasture bridge, and led the soldiers to people's homes to steal their food and their livestock, and to burn whatever they didn't feel like taking. They came through Meadow Bluff. Folks never forgot it. Mamas would scare their children by saying that if they didn't behave, Dr. Rucker would come and get them.

They also say that Dr. Rucker killed a man his own self over in Covington in the early days of the war, and he never served a day in prison for that murder, so perhaps he doesn't think anybody else should be punished for doing away with someone, either. But Jacob says that maybe if a judge appointed Dr. Rucker to defend Edward Shue as a charity case, he would not have been allowed to refuse.

Whatever the rights of it, I think Dr. Rucker will have a hard time defending Edward Shue. Ever since the story came out in the newspaper about him being charged with Zona's murder, people have begun to talk about Shue's past, and every story that comes out of Pocahontas County just makes him sound worse. No one here had any idea about the wickedness he had got up to before he moved to Greenbrier County. Zona knew about his two previous wives, but I'll bet he told her a pack of lies about what really happened to those poor women. His first wife, Allie, who is now Mrs. Todd McMillion, lives over here in Greenbrier with her new husband, and she's not shy about telling folks how Edward Shue beat her when they were married and living in Pocahontas

County. It's a pity she couldn't have made free with that information before more women fell prey to his wickedness.

People say that his ill-treatment of Allie Cutlip was so widely known about the settlement that one winter night some of the neighbors went over to their place, lured Edward out of the house, and then threw him in the icy creek to teach him a lesson about beating up on women. I'm sorry for the poor woman, having to go through all that at the hands of a brute, but compared to Zona, she was lucky. She lived to tell the tale. Then Edward got caught stealing horses, and got sent to Moundsville for a couple of years. She divorced him while he was in prison. They had a daughter that he didn't seem to care anything about, either, which shows you what a coldhearted devil he was.

They say Moundsville is a terrible place—cold, dark cells that stay damp all winter, so that more men die of sickness than ever see the hangman. Still, if you do something bad enough to warrant going to prison—like beating and killing your wife—then I guess you don't deserve any better treatment. Still, seeing what a dreadful place it was, you wouldn't think he'd risk going back there, after experiencing it firsthand. I don't suppose he gave it any thought, though. Either he struck Zona in anger, not thinking of the consequences, or else he was so cocky he thought he'd get away with it.

Well, he *had* got away with it before. There's even more talk about his second wife. Lucy Tritt, I think her name was. She was about the same age as Zona when she passed. Edward Shue claimed that she fell down and hit her head on a rock, but folks now figure that either the rock was in his hand when it hit her or else he killed her some other way and lied about it, like he did with Zona.

I wish we had known all that before Zona up and married him. Maybe if we had known, we could have saved her.

John Alfred Preston stared at the page of notes he'd made for the upcoming trial of Edward Erasmus Shue: summary of the case, notes regarding the evidence, a list of witnesses. It seemed straightforward. The man had obviously killed his young wife, and according to the authorities over in Pocahontas County, where Shue had grown up, he had a history of violence toward two previous wives there, too. Violence seemed to be very much in character for the defendant. Preston could not imagine a jury doubting the evidence in the case.

Besides, the prisoner's attitude told against him at every turn. Even before the autopsy had provided physical evidence, people had been grumbling about the insouciance with which Shue had met with the death of his wife. People said that he had been laughing and making jests, even while he accompanied the dead woman's body back to her parents' farm. That, coupled with his attitude of defiance when he was forced to attend the autopsy, evincing not one trace of grief or shock at the sight of the corpse of his bride of three months, had turned the community against him. His reaction when they found the finger marks on her broken neck had been *You'll never prove it!*— not a protestation of innocence but a brazen boast, daring the authorities to convict him.

Preston hoped that Shue would prove equally repellent in the witness box. Sometimes juries made up their minds not on the evidence, but on their impressions of the accused. The defendant was a handsome fellow, but fortunately ladies did not serve on juries. Before the all-male jury, Shue's arrogance and bluster would win him no sympathy, and his history of violence toward his wives would make the jurors despise him as a cowardly bully.

Preston didn't envy the lawyer who had the task of defending the wretched fellow. If the attorney knew his business, he would do his utmost to persuade Shue to adopt a pose of humility on the stand and to play the grief-stricken widower at every turn. If he could weep in front of the jury, it might save him. William Rucker was defending him, though, and Rucker would win no prizes himself for humility, so would he think to counsel such behavior for his client? Probably not, which meant that the business of bringing the heartless wife-killer to justice ought to be plain sailing for the prosecution.

There was only one snag that Preston could see in the whole matter of convicting Edward Shue. One question that he hoped no one would think to ask. *How did Mrs. Heaster know to request an autopsy?*

twenty-one

LAKIN, WEST VIRGINIA

1931

JAMES P. D. GARDNER WAS STARING through the window bars and the rain-spattered panes at the leaden sky. Back home, his mother would have called it a "clabbered sky," because the clusters of thick clouds reminded her of the lumps that form in milk when it is being churned into butter. He drew no comfort from the sight, though, nor from the memory of his mother. He was so far from that life-time, both in years and experience, that it might as well have happened to someone else. This dead time of gray institutional life seemed to stretch backward and forward until it encompassed the whole of his life.

The damp chill had seeped into his bones. He took the thin gray blanket from his bed and wrapped it around his shoulders, hoping to ward off the aches that invariably followed the cold. He had not left his cell, even for breakfast, and the prospect of wandering the halls or sitting in the dayroom, blanketed by the aimless noise of his fellow patients, did not appeal to him.

He turned to look at the woods that bordered the grounds of the asylum. The sight of them was his only respite from the metal and concrete surrounding him. Those scrubby weed trees looked nothing like the soaring oaks and chestnuts back in the eastern part of the state, but he found them soothing, even in the winter months, when their bare twisted branches made them look like frozen dancers. A red-tailed hawk was hunting somewhere on the edge of that cluster of trees beside the overgrown field separating the forest and the close-cropped grass of the asylum lawn. The hawk—he thought of it as a she—would sit motionless on a high branch, watching the tall brown grass for a sign of movement. When she lifted her broad rounded wings and plunged downward in a deliberate, purposeful dive, he knew that she had spotted her quarry—a field mouse, perhaps, or a young rabbit that would not live to learn caution.

He wondered if Boozer watched him that way—staring with those expressionless black eyes in a face that was the same brown as the hawk's, preternaturally alert, waiting for some slip that would lead to a useful revelation. He conceded to himself that Boozer meant well, wanting only to help. No doubt it would grieve the earnest young doctor to be compared to a bird of prey, but help is only a benevolence if the recipient wants it, and Gardner wasn't sure that he did. Dying would be easier than trying to keep thinking up reasons not to.

The hawk must have missed her target, for she flew back to her accustomed branch to begin again the ritual of staring and waiting.

Gardner found himself thinking about Dr. Rucker, but not because the hawk in any way resembled him. Rucker was never one to bide his time and wait patiently for favorable circumstances. He made things happen, and whether they worked or not seemed to matter little, because he would go charging off to the next thing with very little regard or regret for the results of his last endeavor. A Rucker hawk would fly down to the field and beat at the long grass with his wings, trying to force the mice to panic and run. Perhaps they would escape or perhaps he would snatch them up, but either way, there would be no long stretches of silent waiting.

Rucker had certainly beaten his wings against the weeds in the preparations for the trial of Edward Shue.

He remembered the bright day in June, a few weeks before the trial, when Dr. Rucker had summoned him to his law office to discuss their strategy for the defense. On his desk a mason jar of pink cabbage roses sweetened the air with their heavy perfume, and for a long time the only breach of silence was the drone of a lone housefly hovering near the open window. After the briefest of greetings, a mere acknowledgment of his presence, really, Rucker had returned to studying the notes in front of him, his lips moving silently as he reviewed them.

Gardner, who had not been invited to sit down, stood there, clutching his straw hat, and wiped his forehead with a linen handkerchief. He waited another two minutes for Rucker's attention, and then, as unobtrusively as possible, he sat down in the chair beside the desk, facing the window. Outside, a trio of scruffy neighborhood boys, two white and one colored, were taking turns pulling a homemade toy wagon. A shaggy collie-mix mongrel rode in the back of the wagon, its tongue lolling happily as the triumphant procession passed along, trailing dust in its wake. He thought of a prisoner riding in a cart on the way to the gallows, and he closed his eyes until the boys and the wagon were out of sight.

Finally Dr. Rucker reared back, swiveled his chair, and slapped the case notes with the flat of his hand. "Wake up, James! We have a lot of work to do in the next few weeks. A miracle wouldn't come amiss, either."

Gardner sighed and bit back the hasty retort that was lodged in his throat. "No, Dr. Rucker, I wasn't asleep. I was just collecting my thoughts while I waited for you to finish." He set his satchel on the floor, and took out a notebook and his fountain pen. He assumed his most alert expression, waiting for Dr. Rucker to initiate the discussion.

"Well, what are your thoughts in the matter then? You're a capable fellow, James. How do we save this foolish client of ours?"

Gardner shook his head, knowing better than to take the lead in a discussion of strategy, especially since this was a defense of chicanery rather than a belief in the innocence of the accused. Rucker was much better at that sort of strategy than he was. "I was hoping you knew, because it sure looks to the rest of the world like Mr. Shue is guilty."

Rucker fixed him with a cold stare, and the seconds passed in such silence that the fly's buzzing sounded loud again. "The community has taken against Mr. Shue? I suppose they have. What about you then? Do you think the client is guilty? That he ought to be strung up?"

The right answer was also the wrong answer. He knew that. "I don't think anything, Dr. Rucker. You're the one getting paid to do the thinking. I'm just here to do whatever it is you think needs doing.

I talked to the Jones family awhile back at your behest."

Rucker grinned at the word *behest*. He was highly diverted when James Gardner "talked white," as he put it. "All right then, let me tell you what *I* think. I think that somebody else killed that little lady. Somebody other than her devoted husband. He was away at work, wasn't he? And she was there alone in that house. No way to defend herself."

"Defend herself?"

"That's right. I think somebody broke in, maybe a stranger, maybe not."

"Mr. Shue never said anything about signs of a break-in. I don't think they had much to steal, anyway."

Rucker stared at him for a moment, eyes wide and mouth open, and then he broke into a braying laugh and slapped the desk again. "There you go, James! You should go back on over there and count the jars of green beans in the pantry, or wherever the lady kept them. *Not much to steal!* What about her virtue, huh? Have you considered that?"

Gardner thought about saying that, having heard the rumors about her, he wasn't aware that Mrs. Shue had any virtue to steal, but to say such a thing would be impolitic, especially when the woman in question was not of his race. He was not supposed to have any speculations whatever about the sexual behavior of white women. After a pause that was almost too long, he said, "I confess that it did not occur to me. If there were a shred of evidence . . . Was her clothing in any way disturbed?"

Rucker scowled. "Not that anybody noticed. But that doesn't stop us from bringing up the suggestion."

"Reasonable doubt. I suppose if you're going to argue that the husband did not kill her, then you have to suggest an alternative."

Rucker smiled. "The mysterious cloaked stranger. Yes, indeed. I almost got Kenos Douglas off with that one three years ago. Got myself a hung jury in the first trial, but for some reason, the next bunch in the jury box wasn't having any. You can never tell what people will cotton to. I like to give them some choices, because of course nobody can know what really happened. All we're doing is guessing."

We're guessing that the sun will come up, too, thought Gardner, but he assumed a solemn expression and nodded in agreement. "Do you have any other choices, Dr. Rucker?"

"Well, I was hoping you'd have a thought or two about it, James."

What could he say that Dr. Rucker couldn't use to ruin someone else's life? "Well, I suppose it might have been just what Mr. Shue always said it was: an accident."

Rucker nodded and pulled at a few stray hairs of his beard, which meant that he was cogitating. "Came over faint, you mean? The lady had been attended by George Knapp in the weeks before her death. That's true. I don't suppose we can be so indelicate as to talk about female trouble before the court, but it certainly does make a lot of sense."

"Yes, sir, it does." Sometimes Gardner made a game of seeing how few times he could say "sir" in the course of his conversation with Rucker, but at times the honorific was unavoidable, particularly when he was forced to voice an objection. "Except that Dr. Knapp said he found that Mrs. Shue had a broken neck, and there were fingerprints and bruising there."

"Oh, he *says*." Rucker waved away the objection. "She was his patient, though, wasn't she? He might have had all kinds of reasons for wanting people to believe that her death was a result of foul play. Maybe he gave her the wrong medicine. Maybe she fainted on account of something he prescribed in error."

"I wouldn't know, but since you are a physician yourself, perhaps you can suggest something?"

Rucker scowled. "Not offhand. Besides, Knapp is a decent enough fellow. No call to cast aspersions on him if I can help it."

"And remember that he had two other doctors with him during the autopsy. Surely they would testify to the veracity of his claim about her injuries. Even if you could persuade a jury to believe that Dr. Knapp is lying, Dr. Rupert and Dr. McClung would have no reason to do so."

Dr. Rucker shrugged. "*Corvus oculum corvi non eruit.*" He said it in an offhand way, but he was watching Gardner through lowered eyelids to see if his bit of erudition had been understood.

It had. Gardner paused only to wonder what would give Rucker greater satisfaction: for him to feign ignorance so that the old man could show off his learning, or to prove that he understood the quote, thus reassuring the old man that he was getting his money's worth in a legal associate. He decided to risk the latter. Money was always important to William Rucker.

"Yes, sir, I take your point. Crows will not pull out one another's eyes, and doctors will not destroy the reputation of a colleague even if they know he made an error."

Rucker grunted, but Gardner couldn't tell if that indicated satisfaction or disappointment. He tapped the case notes with the end of a pencil. "That's it, James. Doctors are notorious about hanging together—to keep from hanging separately, as Benjamin Franklin so aptly put it. I reckon the other two would lie for him if he needed them to, but since they seem to have hauled in half the county to watch that autopsy and no one disputed the findings, I suppose we will have to accept the examiners' word for it that the woman's neck had indeed been broken, and that finger marks were present on the skin around her throat."

Gardner scribbled something in his own notebook, to underscore his diligence. "And you wish to persuade the jury that someone other than Mr. Shue was responsible for this."

"I want them to concede the possibility, anyhow. No one can know for certain that Edward Shue killed his wife—though it doesn't help our case that his first wife is going around telling all and sundry how he beat her. He served two years in Moundsville for horse-thievery, did you know that?"

Gardner sighed. He had not known it, because his gossip was often filtered through the household help and delivered to him at church, but he supposed that most of the county had already been apprised of the fact. The client's criminal record would complicate matters for them. "That is unfortunate. A previous legal transgression speaks ill of his character."

"*No smoke without fire*, people will say. Damn their eyes." The pencil had been tapping steadily for a minute now, and Dr. Rucker seemed to become aware of it, because he shoved it back into the pencil cup, knocking it over in the process.

Gardner saw him begin to put the cup back to rights, but he busied himself with his notebook, so that he had an excuse for not scurrying to help.

"I must take care to remind the court that larceny is a far cry from murder." The buzzing fly sailed close to Rucker's nose, and he made a halfhearted lunge at it with one of the pencils, but it soared out of his reach, and he threw the pencil back into the cup. Sinking down in his chair, he went back to staring at the trial notes. After another minute of silence, his head snapped up, and he looked at Gardner, his eyes alight with inspiration.

Gardner caught the look and leaned forward. "Has something occurred to you . . . sir?"

"By Jove, it has! I was looking over this account of the events, and I noticed that the body of Mrs. Shue was discovered by the boy that Shue had asked to gather the eggs, and to look in on his wife. What was his name again?"

There was a long pause before Gardner said, "Anderson Jones."

"That's it! And you interviewed the boy and his family. What age is he?"

"About eighteen—sir—but—"

"*Eighteen!* The way people talk about him, I was picturing a lad of ten. Well, there you are! An eighteen-year-old colored boy goes into the house where a pretty young white woman is alone and ailing. No neighbors nearby to hear her cries for help—"

"*No!*" He had said it with such force that the "sir" would have to be added, probably more than once to soften the opposition, but he did not intend to give way on that point. He restored the cap to his fountain pen, giving all his concentration to the process, while he took deep breaths and marshaled his thoughts. More calmly then, "No, sir, Dr. Rucker. Andy Jones did not interfere with Mrs. E. Z. Shue, and he had nothing to do with her death."

Rucker's avid expression wavered, but he rallied. "Now what makes you say that, James? Not everybody is as cold-blooded as you are, you know."

Gardner stiffened. By *cold-blooded*, Rucker had meant *indifferent to sex*, an impression that was partly true and partly the result of Gardner's efforts to seem so, by ignoring risqué humor and salacious comments in badinage with the other attorneys. He could not afford to do otherwise. He could have disputed the charge by pointing out that he was engaged to be married, but he knew better than to bring up personal matters. In the world of the court-house, he was happy to be regarded as an automaton in a suit. It simplified matters. Keeping his voice low and his face expressionless, he said, "Anderson Jones is what you might call simple, sir. He is not an ordi-nary eighteen-year-old youth. People talk about him as if he were ten because that's about what he is in his mind. Still a child. I talked to him, and I know."

Dr. Rucker gave him the cold smile of one who much prefers his pet theory to the facts. "Never mind the boy's brain, James; his body is eighteen years old. The mind may be trapped in eternal child-hood, but the urges of the flesh grow just the same as they would in a normal person. He could have felt lust right enough, and not have the wit to control himself or to foresee the consequences of his actions. Perhaps he didn't mean to hurt her. Certainly not to kill her. Just a tragic accident."

Rucker's tone was soothing, promising that nothing dire would happen to this poor afflicted youth, that everyone would be sympathetic and understanding, but Gardner knew better. When it came to matters of sex between the races, the whole world was full of simpletons who could not be rea-soned with. If Rucker proceeded with this ploy, which to him was no more than an ingenious ruse to deflect attention from the client, Anderson Jones would surely hang for it. Not legally, perhaps; not after due process in a court of law; but, trial or no trial, one dark night a mob would lynch him from a tree somewhere out in the country. Even the sugges-tion of such an incident might be enough to get him killed.

Gardner stiffened. He was polite and temperate

in the face of all slights and discourtesies because he saved up his resistance for times when it mattered. He leaned forward—to stand would be threatening—still calm, still speaking softly, but with an intensity that made itself felt. "*Anderson Jones did not do this*, Dr. Rucker. No one has even suggested such a thing, not even the man about to go on trial for his life. That child—for he is a child in his mind—is innocent. And you know he is innocent. I know this is just a legal maneuver to you. You want to use Anderson Jones as a smoke screen to protect this wife-killing scoundrel we are defending. It's just a move in a legal chess game to you, but you have to see what the result might very well be."

"And what is that?" Dr. Rucker would have looked just the same if the fly had started talking: skeptical, but interested.

"Why, it would get that poor boy lynched. People feel that they have to bring *somebody* to justice over the death of this woman, and if it's somebody who doesn't matter to them, they would consider that all to the good. Even if they didn't believe Anderson Jones killed that woman, they might hang him anyway, just for good measure. And don't talk to me about evidence and the protection of the law, *sir*, because we both know that even if he were acquitted, or never even charged, the mere suggestion of sexual impropriety of that sort would cost him his life. Not in a legal execution, but he'd be dead all the same. *You cannot do this* . . . sir. It would be the cruel murder of an innocent, just as much so as the killing of Mrs. Shue."

The fly buzzed close to Dr. Rucker's face, and he picked up another sheaf of papers from the pile on his desk and folded them over. Instead of swatting the fly, though, he used the rolled-up paper to shoo it toward the open window. He waited as it hovered near the sill. Then it picked up a breeze and sailed off into the shrubbery. Dr. Rucker lowered the window, and tossed the papers back onto the stack. He took out an oversized handkerchief and mopped his brow before sitting down again. He studied Gardner's face for a few moments, but Gardner couldn't tell what he was thinking because the silvery thicket of a beard concealed much of his face. Only his eyes might give him away, but now they were blank, as they often were.

Finally he shrugged and scribbled a note on the topmost paper. "Well, perhaps you're right, James. It might not save the client, anyhow. I suppose the prosecution would argue that Shue had expressly sent young Jones to check on his wife to ensure that someone other than himself would find the body."

Which is exactly what he did. Gardner managed to hold back the words, but his expression said them anyway.

Dr. Rucker nodded. "I take your point about putting the Jones boy in danger with such a suggestion. Mobs do not possess the sum of their members' intelligence; they replace intellect with passion, and nobody thinks at all, so things might indeed transpire just as you suppose."

"Yes, sir," said Gardner when he could trust himself to speak. "It would be unconscionable to risk it."

"Perhaps it would, James. Perhaps it would." Rucker stroked his beard. "You know, in my youth I was trained as a doctor. Physicians take an oath that begins, *First, do no harm.* Now that I am practicing law, I don't know that the oath applies to my activities outside the field of medicine, but perhaps in this case, it ought to. To be responsible for a death, even indirectly, is a solemn matter. Sometimes, perhaps in war, such an act may be necessary, but in a trial, where the sacrifice may not even make any difference—yes, perhaps it is too great a charge upon my conscience."

Gardner did not move or breathe, but he listened very carefully, hoping that Dr. Rucker would not talk himself out of this merciful impulse. He tried to think about other things—the bloom on the roses in the jar on the desk, the film of road dust on his freshly shined shoes—while he waited without a flicker of expression to see how the old man's reasoning fetched up.

Rucker stood up now and began to pace while he thought. "I suppose that if Anderson Jones had given any appearance at all of a threat, Shue would never have sent him to the house to begin with. And if he perceived the boy to be harmless, then surely all of the residents of Livesay's Mill would have been of the same opinion."

Gardner nodded. "And I'm sure that Mr. Preston could summon any amount of them to testify to the fact that young Jones is a blameless innocent. But it mustn't come to that, Dr. Rucker. We mustn't cast aspersions on him in a public forum. Why, even if the angels themselves sang his praises, there are likely to be some hard-hearted souls who would doubt his innocence, and they might well harm him on the off chance that he did something wrong."

"*First do no harm.*" Rucker exhaled a deep breath, puffing out his cheeks while he thought about it. "Well, I wish I could come up with a better idea for casting doubt on Mr. Shue's guilt. Anderson Jones would have been a perfect alternative for the role of culprit, but I take your point, James. Have you a better suggestion for a defense strategy?"

"Can't we just say that Mrs. Shue's death was a tragic accident, sir? That would get our client acquitted without harming anyone else."

"But the finger marks on her throat?"

"Perhaps they occurred shortly after her death. Perhaps her distraught husband attempted to revive her when he found her insensible and inflicted those injuries unintentionally. And as for his apparent lack of grief, one could argue that he was not one to show his feelings: still waters run deep. I think Mr. Preston would find it more difficult to find witnesses to refute that."

Rucker's lips moved, and he paced back and forth, as if constructing an argument. He turned on his heel and smiled at Gardner. "Well done, James. That reasoning does you credit. I recall that I used the mysterious-stranger defense in a murder case once before, and I did not carry the day that time, so perhaps it would be wise not to try that gambit again. Very well, let us call it a tragic accident, and implore the jury not to compound the tragedy by convicting an innocent man in a misplaced quest for revenge. Do you think they might bring themselves to believe that?"

"Yes, sir, I do. I'm sure you could persuade them to see it that way." Gardner breathed a sigh of relief. Yes, given a fervent, well-crafted argument, an unsophisticated jury might very well believe that construction of the events. He, of course, did not.

"There's something else," he said. Rucker would hear about it sooner or later. It might as well be from him. "Mrs. Jones says that the mother of Mrs. Shue claims to have seen her daughter's ghost, and that the daughter told her that she was murdered by Shue. That's why Mrs. Heaster went to Mr. Preston and requested an autopsy."

Rucker was speechless for a moment, and then he threw back his head and roared with laughter. "Did she, by God? And Preston fell for that?"

"I wouldn't say that, sir. More likely, he figured

he had nothing to lose by granting the request of a grieving and suspicious mother."

Rucker shook his head, still grinning. "He'll be laughed out of court."

"Remember the results of the autopsy, sir. He got his proof. The doctors will swear to that. I don't suppose Mr. Preston will introduce the ghost story into the trial testimony."

"I daresay he won't. But I will."

Despite the heat of the day James Gardner felt a stab of cold beneath his ribs. "But, Dr. Rucker, suppose the jury believes it."

Rucker gave him a pitying smile. "Give them some credit, James. The jurors may be indifferently educated fellows, but they're not fools. They won't fall for superstitious nonsense. After all, there will be no ladies on the jury—or darkies."

twenty-two

GREENBRIER COUNTY, WEST VIRGINIA

1897

"IT'S NICE TO SEE YOU AGAIN, Mrs. Heaster. I'm sorry to have kept you waiting."

"That's all right, Mr. Preston. I passed the time of day with your wife, since she was waiting to see you, too."

"Yes, just a question about hiring a carpenter for some household repairs. Fortunately, it didn't take long."

"Mrs. Preston was kind enough to say that she remembered my father," she said with a trace of a smile.

"Ah. Well, now we can begin our conference. I trust you are well?" Preston smiled back reassuringly at the stern-faced woman in black.

She was sitting ramrod straight in the visitor's chair in his courthouse office, and now that the discussion had begun she wore a grim expression more appropriate for facing a firing squad than for engag-

ing in a witness discussion with a friendly attorney.
Her homemade high-necked dress and the straw
bonnet that put him in mind of a dinner plate were
unfashionable, but there was a fierce dignity about
her that made her attire irrelevant. He thought she
looked thinner than when he had seen her in February; her cheekbones seemed more prominent,
and the dress seemed to hang on her angular frame.
Asking in general after her health was as close as he
could come to mentioning it, though, and really it
wasn't any of his affair. He could do nothing about
private grief. All he could promise her was his earnest effort to secure a conviction of her daughter's
killer. Maybe that would alleviate the poor woman's
grief and maybe it wouldn't, but it was all he had to
offer.

She managed another tight smile, for form's
sake. "I'm tolerable, thank you for asking, Mr. Preston. And yourself?"

He dabbed at his temples with a handkerchief.
"I don't mind working hard, but I could wish for
cooler weather to do it in. Opening the window just
seems to let in more hot air. Can I fetch you a glass of
water? You must have had a hot, dusty journey over
from Meadow Bluff."

She shook her head. "I'm all right. I don't seem
to mind the heat as much as I used to. Seems like
it takes me all summer to get the chill out of my
bones."

Preston smiled again. "You're right. I shouldn't
complain. Now that summer has arrived, I notice
that my knee isn't hurting anymore. Is your husband
in good health? I see that he didn't come with you."

"No." She was twisting her wedding ring up and
down between the knobby knuckle and the base of
the finger. The ring was loose, but Preston doubted
that she could get it past that swollen joint. He won-

dered if she ever took it off, or if she wanted to. "My husband wants no truck with this court business."

Preston nodded. He had encountered such reluctance before, especially among country folk. Even if they led blameless lives, they seemed intimidated by the prospect of appearing in court before a room full of strangers. "Is Mr. Heaster shy about appearing before a crowd? We won't call him as a witness, you know. He can sit in the courtroom as silently as he pleases to give you moral support, and no one will bother him. Does he understand that?"

Her lips tightened. "He knows. But you're putting me on the witness stand, and he doesn't want that to happen, either. If he could forbid me to testify, he would. But I told him that it was my duty to speak my piece. Besides, I promised Zona that I would."

"But surely, as the father of the poor murdered young woman, Mr. Heaster will want to see the killer brought to justice. Any grieving father would want the satisfaction of seeing Edward Shue pay for his crimes."

She looked down at her lap, twisting the ring again. "My husband says that nothing the law can do will bring Zona back. I reckon he thinks she brought it down on her own head, marrying him quick as she did and knowing next to nothing about him."

Her voice quavered, and Preston felt deeply sorry for her. Bad enough to have to face the death of one's only daughter and the ordeal of a public trial without having to face family opposition in one's efforts to get justice. He said gently, "Perhaps his own grief has caused him to speak harshly. Even if we concede that your daughter acted with the rashness of youth, she did not deserve to die. Why, from what you have told me, Mrs. Shue herself came back from the grave to ask for justice."

Mrs. Heaster took a deep breath, and again she looked down at her hands. "As far as Jacob is concerned, that's the worst of it, I think. My husband does not believe that Zona did come back. He thinks I made up the whole story out of grief and spite, for all along I made no secret of the fact that I had no use for Edward Shue. Jacob is embarrassed by all of it. He's a simple man, and he wants a quiet life and the respect of his neighbors. He says he doesn't want to be laughed at in public for having a foolish, wayward daughter and a wife who claims she sees ghosts."

"He doesn't believe you?" Preston began to draw circles on a scrap of paper on his desk. He wasn't sure he believed Mary Jane Heaster, either, but the autopsy report had proved her suspicions were correct. Preston could hardly blame her husband for his skepticism, but he thought that a grieving parent should want to believe it, even if a pragmatic prosecutor had doubts. "Well, perhaps I can understand his feelings on that score. I had a hard time crediting it myself when you first came here back in February with the tale of your daughter's murder and her testimony from beyond the grave. But he cannot dispute the fact that you were right about your daughter's being murdered. She was strangled, with the finger marks still on her throat weeks after her burial. The autopsy proved it. Dr. Knapp will swear to it. Does Mr. Heaster doubt him, too?"

"He hasn't said. I don't think he sets much store by doctors, though—or lawyers."

"Had it not been for you, ma'am, Shue might have got away with murder—again. We think he also killed his second wife back in Pocahontas County. Don't let your husband's attitude make you ashamed, Mrs. Heaster. Your bravery in speaking out allowed us to stop a murderer before he could prey upon still more trusting women."

"I don't think Jacob cares about that. He just doesn't want people pointing at us and laughing."

He could hear the catch in her voice, and he was afraid that she would give way to tears. He wished he had a clean handkerchief to offer her, and indeed he usually kept one in his desk for just such emergencies, but the heat of the day had caused him to use his own and the spare to mop the perspiration from his brow. "Laughing, Mrs. Heaster? I don't believe they will. The people in court could not be so heartless as that. At least, I hope not. In fact, the trial will be rather cut-and-dried. I shall call young Anderson Jones, who discovered the body, and his mother, Mrs. Martha Jones, and they will testify to the condition of the body upon discovery. Dr. Knapp and perhaps Dr. Rupert will give an account of the autopsy and what they learned from it. When you are called to the witness box, you've only got to say what you observed about Mr. Shue's manner when your daughter's body was brought back to Meadow Bluff, and describe his behavior at the funeral."

She nodded. "I am ready. And then you'll want me to tell the court about Zona coming to me a few nights after the burying to tell me what really happened to her."

Preston sighed and set down his pen. He had been dreading this conversation, and he hoped that he could convey his message with sufficient tact to keep from distressing his witness. "Perhaps I should have mentioned this before, but I won't be asking you any questions about your—er—encounter with your daughter's spirit."

Mary Jane Heaster blinked, and her lips moved soundlessly for a moment before she could marshal her thoughts. "You won't be asking— But how could you not? Why, that is how we knew to request the autopsy! The jury must hear that."

"Mr. Gilmer and I don't deem it necessary for you to go into all that. We think that we have sufficient evidence to convict the accused, relying on the accounts given by the physicians, and that of the Jones family, and the testimony of various persons, including yourself, about Mr. Shue's callous behavior after his wife's death. We are afraid that introducing the supernatural element into the proceedings would only confuse and distract the gentlemen of the jury." He ventured a gentle smile. "After all, in a murder trial one does not expect to hear the testimony of the deceased."

Mrs. Heaster narrowed her eyes and gave him a scornful look. "You sound like my husband. I thought you believed me."

"I did order the autopsy, remember. But my personal feelings in the matter are of no consequence. We think that an astounding tale of a spirit seeking vengeance might confuse the jurors and obscure the other facts in the case. The jury might mistakenly vote according to whether or not they personally believe in ghosts, and that is not the issue here. We want them to concentrate on the more mundane evidence proving the guilt of Edward Shue, and Mr. Gilmer and I feel that the extraneous matter of your, er, visitation is unnecessary. After all, we cannot put the victim's ghost on the witness stand."

"I see." She was staring past him at the treetops and the bright blue sky framed in his office window, but her jaw was tight and her face was set in a grimace.

He sighed. "Mrs. Heaster, you mustn't lose sight of the fact that our purpose here is to see Edward Shue convicted for his crime. That is the most important thing, surely. That is what your daughter wanted, is it not?"

She glanced at him, and then went back to staring out the window, as if losing herself in the view was the only way that she could escape from the room. "I suppose so."

He breathed a sigh of relief. He could see that the woman still felt angry, but because she also felt powerless to interfere in the decisions of prosperous male attorneys, she would make no further objections. Now the awkward interview could end. Preston came out from behind his desk and ushered her to the door. "Then let us set our sights on making it as simple as possible for the jury to see that Edward Shue is guilty, and to have no qualms about seeing him hanged. The trial begins on Tuesday, the twenty-second of June."

"That will be five months nearly to the day since Zona died. Well, I hope you hang him, Mr. Preston. He's lived a good deal longer than he deserved to already." She swept out of his office without waiting for him to frame a reply.

James P. D. Gardner wondered why lawyers always seemed bored when they were in court. Was it because they had been through the formula so many times that it had ceased to make an impression on them at all, or was it an attempt to mask their competitive feelings on such a solemn occasion by feigning a dignified indifference? *He* was excited; indeed, he had scarcely been able to sleep the night before for anticipating the drama and the awful significance of the coming trial.

A murder case! Not many of those would come the way of a country lawyer in the course of his career. Deeds and wills and petty squabbles between neighbors—that was the meat and potatoes of a village law practice. He looked forward to the trial of

Edward Shue as a rare opportunity to test his skills of argument and persuasion—if, that is, Mr. Rucker allowed him to take any active part in the case. Perhaps he would only be allowed to sit at the defense table and make notes of the proceedings, but in any case he would now be able to boast that he had participated in a murder trial. He fancied that his acquaintances—and, most importantly, Miss Eliza Myles—regarded him with a new respect because of it.

He had dressed that morning with the utmost care, despite the summer weather, donning his newest white shirt, freshly laundered and ironed; his black wool suit, twice brushed; and his church shoes, polished until they gleamed. Perhaps he was more carefully attired than the other three attorneys appearing in the case, but then he had to be. The other three were white. Still, it wasn't only his fear of being mistaken for a lackey that made him dress so formally; a man was on trial for his life, and there could be no more somber occasion than that, even if the formula of a trial had become so routine for the more experienced attorneys that they barely noticed its import.

He wondered how Edward Erasmus Stribbling Shue felt about the proceedings. He had seemed restless, as if he were unused to sitting still for long stretches, but he had a ready smile for anyone he recognized. Gardner supposed that, like most people who are confident of their physical beauty, Edward Shue expected people to be glad to see him, never anticipating slights or snubs. Gardner wondered what that would feel like.

Given the informality of his attire, though, the defendant might have been attending a horse race or a picnic. He wore a simple white shirt, without a coat or necktie, and the same cheap, worn trousers and

brown work shoes he might have put on for a day at
the blacksmith shop. Gardner wondered if the man
hadn't known any better, or if his lack of coat and
necktie had been a concession to the stifling heat of
the courtroom. Two other possibilities also occurred
to him: one, that the only suit the man owned was
the one in which he had got married seven months
earlier, and he was loath to wear it to stand trial
for the murder of his bride; or two, that he was so
indifferent to her death, and so arrogantly certain of
being acquitted of the murder, that he couldn't be
bothered to feign grief or concern. Gardner felt a
twinge of guilt for this last judgment, for after all he
was defending the man, and he felt honor-bound to
believe in his innocence. All the same, if he could
think so uncharitably about Edward Shue, what
impression must the man be making on the spectators and jurors?

Gardner took his place on the far end of the
defense table, to the right of Dr. Rucker and the
defendant, who sat between them. As he sat down,
murmuring a greeting to Shue and returning a brisk
nod from Dr. Rucker, he recoiled from the sour
smell of stale sweat that came from the defendant.
The rank odor surrounded Shue like a wall, and
Gardner had to force himself to maintain a calm and
neutral expression. Fighting the urge to retch, he
took his handkerchief out of his coat pocket, wishing
he had thought to soak it in lavender water to coun-
teract the stench. Tomorrow he would.

The genial and smiling Shue seemed unaware
of the situation, and Gardner wondered whether
the odor was due to the stifling heat of the crowded
courtroom or the anxiety of the trial itself. The inad-
equate sanitary facilities of the jail were probably to
blame as well. His stomach lurched, and he wished
he could move his chair farther away from the defen-

dant, but he knew that to do so might be seen as a moral judgment of the man. He must not allow his actions to prejudice the court. He glanced over at Dr. Rucker, but there was no indication that Rucker detected anything amiss. He was looking around the courtroom like a fox sizing up a henhouse, occasionally offering a polite nod to someone who caught his eye and then looking down again to scribble more notes.

After a moment Shue leaned toward him and murmured, "They'll never prove anything, you know. All they've got to go on is suspicion and spite."

Gardner gave him what he hoped was a reassuring smile and nodded, but the gesture came from politeness rather than conviction. In fact, he felt far from confident about the fellow's chances with the court. Had there been more time to talk and less at stake, he might have explained to Shue that juries' decisions did not necessarily depend on facts. Sometimes a jury would acquit in the face of solid evidence simply because they liked the look of the defendant, or because the man's lawyer had charmed them into benevolence; at other times, they might base their verdict on a gut feeling unsupported by any proof at all. At times a trial came very close to being a game of chance, and Gardner earnestly hoped he would never have to bet his life on the whims of a dozen random citizens.

"All rise."

And so it began.

The evidence was circumstantial, but there was a lot of it. One by one, Preston or Gilmer summoned witnesses to add to the slow-forming mosaic that would depict the death of Zona Heaster Shue.

On the witness stand, Anderson Jones, well scrubbed and somber in his Sunday go-to-meeting best, stared out at the crowded courtroom with the eyes of a frightened child. Once his gaze fixed on Gardner, who nodded and ventured a brief smile so that the anxious witness would see at least one friendly face in the sea of strangers.

Judge McWhorter, too, seemed aware of the witness's unease. He leaned down and said, "Now, young fella, you have no call to be nervous at all up here on the witness stand. You are in no wise in trouble. You just answer these gentlemen's questions as truthfully as you can, and we'll all be much obliged for your help. Can you do that?"

Anderson Jones still looked wary at being before a crowd of strangers, but he nodded to the judge, and managed a faint "Yes, sir."

Judge McWhorter smiled. "Well, that's fine then. Yonder comes Mr. John Alfred Preston, who is one of those lawyers I told you about. You don't have to be scared of him. He just wants to have a conversation."

Preston approached the chair, trying to summon a reassuring expression for the witness, but his thoughts were mainly on the business at hand. He started off gently, intent upon putting the witness at ease before they had to talk about the horrors of that day. A brief series of questions established that the young man was Anderson Jones, that he lived with his parents and brothers and sisters at Livesay's Mill, and that they were neighbors of Mr. and Mrs. Shue. When Preston decided that Anderson Jones was sufficiently relaxed and focused on the conversation, he drew his attention to the events of January 23.

"Now you said that you and your family were neighbors of Mr. Shue. Did you often run errands for him or do little jobs about the place?"

"Yes, sir, whenever he was to ask me, I did."

"And on January twenty-third, did Mr. Shue stop by your house and ask you to do something for him?"

"Yes, sir. He came from the blacksmith shop about ten o'clock, looking for me."

"What did he want you to do?"

"He asked me to go hunt eggs over at his place, and then to go to the house and ask Miz Shue did she need anything from the store that she wanted me to fetch."

"And what did you do?"

"I took me a basket and went over there looking for the eggs, but I didn't find none."

"What did you do after that?"

"Well, like he told me to, I rapped on the door to see if Miz Shue needed anything. But she didn't come to the door."

"No? What did you do then?"

"Well, when nobody answered, I pushed open the door and went in. Miz Shue had been feeling poorly lately, and I thought she might be took sick."

"And what did you see when you went in?"

Anderson Jones squirmed in his chair and tugged at the collar of his shirt. "You know that, sir. You asked me about that the other day, and I told you. Do we have to go over it again?"

There was a ripple of laughter in the gallery, and Mr. Preston glanced at them with a perfunctory smile. "That's true, I did, but you see, those twelve gentlemen over there in the jury box need to know exactly what you saw and heard, and they have to hear it directly from you. So perhaps you could tell it again for them?"

"Yes, sir, all right. But it's a terrible thing. Gives me frights to think of it."

"Indeed it is terrible, but you must tell them nonetheless. When you opened the door and walked into the hall of Mr. Shue's house that day, what did you see?"

"I saw Miz Shue, there on the floor of the hall, near the stairs."

Preston nodded. "That's fine, Mr. Jones. You're doing well. Now do you remember how the body of Mrs. Shue was lying? The position of her limbs and so on?"

"I do. At first I thought she might have passed out and pitched down the stairs, but she was too tidy for that."

"Tidy. Can you tell us what you mean by that?"

"Well, she was stretched out straight with her feet together, just like she was already in a coffin, only she wasn't. One of her hands was down by her side, and the other one was on her tummy. Her head was tilted a little to one side. And thank the Lord her eyes were closed. Else I might have dropped dead with fright myself, right then and there."

"Did you make certain that Mrs. Shue was dead?"

Anderson Jones regarded the attorney with horror. "No, sir! I didn't get no closer to her than two paces from the front door, and when I saw her stretched out like that, I knew there wasn't no use in getting any nearer. I turned right around and ran out the door and back home to tell my mama what I had found."

"What did your mother do?"

"She told me to run on over to Mr. Crook-shanks's blacksmith shop and tell Mr. Shue. Then she started putting her coat on, and getting ready to go on over there herself to see if there was anything she could do."

"To the house, you mean?"

"Yes, sir. I told her that lady was dead, but she wouldn't take my word for it."

"Thank you, Mr. Jones. The court appreciates your account of this tragic event. Now I think we must hear the rest of the story from your mother."

Preston looked expectantly at the defense counsel, but Mr. Rucker waved him away, and Judge McWhorter told the witness that he could stand down.

Anderson Jones hurried down the aisle of the courtroom just as his mother's name was called as the next witness. When they met in the doorway of the courtroom, Martha Jones touched her son's cheek, and her anxious eyes sought out Mr. Preston. The prosecutor gave her a faint nod of reassurance, and she paused for a moment. "Now you sit out there in the hall and wait for me, you hear?" she said to Anderson.

"All right, Mama." As she turned to go, he added, "Wasn't too bad."

Thus satisfied that all was well with her family, she made her way down the aisle, and took the oath somberly, but without a trace of nervousness.

Henry Gilmer, Preston's predecessor and his second chair for the trial, undertook the questioning of the new witness, establishing more details about the events of Saturday, January 23. Mrs. Jones echoed her son's statements that, yes, they were neighbors of Edward Shue, and were acquainted with the newlyweds.

"And did you visit the residence of Mr. Edward Shue on the afternoon of January twenty-third?"

She sat up straighter and gave Mr. Gilmer a stern look. "I did."

"What prompted you to do so?"

"Mr. Shue asked my son—the one who just left outta here—to go over to his house and gather some eggs that morning, and then to see did Miz Shue need any errands run. Anderson left the house in the early afternoon, when we had done eating dinner, and went on over to their house, but before I could even get started on the washing up, he came tearing back in the house, hollering that Miz Shue was laid out dead in the front hall. So I thought I better get on over there, and see what was the matter. I sent my boy to tell Mr. Shue he better get on home. Then I took my apron off, put my coat on, and hurried over there myself. I got there the same time as he did."

"Can you tell us what you saw inside the house?"

Martha Jones glanced at the defense table and looked away again. "That poor lady was dead, just like Anderson had told me. Mr. Shue, he pushed on in past me and stood over her body, and he says, *Oh, no! Oh, no! My poor wife has fallen down the stairs.*"

"Did he sound distraught about it—in your opinion?"

She shook her head. "He came out with it real quick—like he had already planned what he was going to say. And he sounded like somebody in a Christmas play, reciting a piece they had off by heart."

"And what did you say?"

"Me? I didn't say nothin', but I didn't think she had pitched down those stairs, neither."

Mr. Gilmer affected a look of surprise and faced the jury for a moment before he resumed his questioning. "Despite the fact that the body was lying lifeless on the floor of the downstairs hall, you did not believe that Mrs. Shue had fallen down the stairs?"

"No, sir."

"Whyever not?"

"I've seen a fair number of dead folks, and I've never yet seen one die posed like a statue."

"Please tell us what you mean."

Martha Jones thought for a moment. "She looked like dead folks look when they've already been laid out for the funeral by one of the neighbor women. I have done it myself for folks, so I know. People die every which way. Eyes open sometimes, mouth agape, arms and legs all twisted, clothing askew from the death throes now and again. Mrs. Shue, though, looked so perfect that they could have had the funeral right that minute. Her eyes were closed; her dress was smooth and in place all the way around; her feet were together. But it was her hands that struck me as the queerest part of it all."

"The position of her hands? How so?"

"Well, one of them was stretched out neatly at her side—just like you'd arrange it if you laid her out for burial—and the other hand was placed just below her heart. There only needed to be a lily curled in her fingers to make her look like a Sunday school picture of the dearly departed. People look like that when they're set in their coffins at the funeral, sir, but they don't *die* like that."

"So you think it likely that someone placed her in that position after her demise?"

Before she answered, Martha Jones glanced again at Edward Shue and then back at Mr. Gilmer. "Do I think someone had laid her out that way on purpose? Yes, sir, I surely do."

This time when the defense was invited to cross-examine, Dr. Rucker heaved his bulk out of his chair and lumbered toward the witness stand, mopping his brow with a flowing white handkerchief. "Now then, you have said that you have seen a fair few deceased persons, and a good many of their grieving relations in consequence of that. Is that correct?"

Martha Jones eyed him warily. His manner was mild enough, but it lacked the cordiality of Mr. Gilmer's questioning. After a moment's pause, she said, "Yes, sir, I reckon that's so."

"Well, then, is it your observation that all grieving relatives mourn in exactly the same way? Do they all give way to floods of tears and shouted lamentations?"

"No, sir, they don't."

"What sorts of reactions to grief have you seen in your experience?"

"Well, like you just said, some people give way entirely, crying like little babies, and others get mad as hornets, looking for somebody they can blame for their sorrow. And some people don't show their hurt at all. They look like they're sleepwalking, some of 'em."

Dr. Rucker nodded. "So when you say that Mr. Edward Shue did not seem to be upset by the death of his wife, is it not possible that he was one of the last sort of mourners? The ones who make no great display of their feelings?"

Mrs. Jones took on a mulish expression, and her eyes flashed, but if she had considered making a sharp retort to this question, she thought better of it. "It could be," she said, in a tone of voice that proclaimed her disbelief of such a notion.

"Yes, it could. Now let us proceed to another statement you made. You said that when you and Edward Shue entered the house, you saw the body of Mrs. Shue positioned in a formal way, did you not?"

"She was laid out, same as an undertaker would do it."

"And because she would not have fallen to her death and ended up in such a composed position, you believe that someone had rearranged the body?"

She nodded. "They had to."

"But you said that you and Mr. Edward Shue arrived at the house at the same time, did you not? Did you see him arrange his wife's body?"

"He didn't do it—not right then. She was already like that when we opened the front door."

"I see. And had anyone else set foot in the house that day?"

"I don't know. I wasn't there. I just went over when . . ."

"When what, Mrs. Jones? Please finish your statement."

". . . when my son came and told me that Mrs. Shue was dead."

"And how did he know?"

"He saw her."

"So your son Anderson Jones entered the house sometime before you and Mr. Shue arrived?"

"Only because Mr. Shue asked him to."

"Yes, of course. But is it not possible that Anderson, upon finding the poor lady dead and in disarray . . . Is it possible that your son Anderson rearranged the body to a more seemly state, out of respect and pity for Mrs. Shue? There is no crime in that, after all, Mrs. Jones. It would be an act of charity, surely. Might your helpful lad have done that, as a final favor for his neighbor?"

"No, sir." A stone-faced Mrs. Jones had folded her arms, and although she replied to the question, she would not look at the attorney, fixing her gaze instead on a blank wall in the back of the courtroom. "*No, sir.*"

Ignoring the hostile expression of the witness, Dr. Rucker spoke to her softly, in a tone of sympathy and sweet reason. "Perhaps he would be embarrassed or afraid to admit such a thing later, but surely in the shock of the moment, a charitable impulse might have moved him to set the remains of the deceased to rights?"

She gave him a blistering glance and looked away again. "Don't you try to trap me with big words, sir. My Anderson never touched the lady. He wouldn't touch a dead body for a hatful of nickels. Anderson said she was like that when he went inside and caught sight of her. He saw her dead on the floor, and he lit right out of there, and no one can make him or me say different. My boy is simple, sir. Too simple to think up any lies."

Dr. Rucker paused for a moment, and then, more in sorrow than in anger, he said, "A man's life is at stake here, you know. A poor grieving widower risks being hanged on mere circumstantial evidence, in part because you contend that no one but he could have rearranged the body. Are you so sure of what you are saying that you would swear a man's life away on the strength of it?"

If the defense attorney had expected Martha Jones to falter at the grave consequences of her testimony, he had mistaken his witness. She turned to look for the last time at Edward Erasmus Shue, seated next to James Gardner at the defense table. He met her eyes, and for once the jaunty, cocksure look in them faded, and he seemed to be silently pleading with her to relent and let there be a shadow of doubt about the events of that day. When the moment passed, Martha Jones turned back to the attorney. "No, sir. I am not mistaken."

Dr. George Knapp took the stand with the slightly exasperated air of a man who has better things to do. Since most of the officers of the court were members of his social circle, he was not fazed by appearing before them, and no testimony or interrogation that took place there would affect those friendships in any way. A day in court for him was little more than an annoying distraction from the more pressing business of tending to the sick of Greenbrier County. He wore a coat and tie, as he invariably did, but his attire was not his Sunday best, and he had taken no pains to impress the court with his appearance.

He took the oath midstride, and heaved himself into the witness chair with a brief nod to Judge McWhorter, who wished him good morning.

Preston was in charge of questioning the doctor, and although they had known each other since childhood, he went through the necessary formality of establishing the physician's name and profession before he got down to the business of discussing the case of Zona Heaster Shue.

"Was the deceased a patient of yours, Doctor?"

"Briefly. She moved to Livesay's Mill upon the occasion of her marriage last fall, and shortly thereafter she became a patient of mine."

"What was the nature of her illness?"

Knapp shrugged. "Nothing much, as far as I could tell. She felt seedy, suffered from headaches, and from nerves. I thought it might sort itself out by the end of the winter, but I gave her a tonic anyhow."

"And you did not feel that her illness was life-threatening?"

"Certainly not. She wasn't much past twenty, and a sturdy farmer's daughter to boot. She could have outlived us all. But, of course, you never can tell with human beings. A person can outlive a catastrophic illness that ought to have carried them off, only to be felled by a trifle that no one would have thought twice about. After all the years I've been practicing medicine, nothing surprises me anymore."

"Now on Saturday, the twenty-third of January, you were summoned to the home of Mr. and Mrs. E. S. Shue, were you not?"

"That's right. I was told that Mrs. Shue had been found dead, and I went to their home as requested."

"And what did you find, sir?"

"Mrs. Shue was indeed deceased. Since both her husband and Aunt Martha Jones were present when I arrived, I assumed that one of them had laid out the body, because it looked ready for the undertaker."

"Would you be more precise in your description, please?"

"Well, the poor woman was stretched out as if she were already in a coffin, one arm at her side, one on her breast. And she was clad in a dress with a high stiff collar. I noticed her head lay a little to one side. When I checked for signs of life, I noticed some discolorations on the right side of her throat and cheek. I unfastened that high collar and looked at the front of the neck. I was about to examine the back of Mrs. Shue's neck when her husband became distraught, and requested that I leave. He contended that he could not bear to have his wife's remains touched, and that if I was satisfied that she was deceased and would sign a certificate to that effect, then my services were no longer required." He took a deep breath and glared at the defendant. "So I left."

"Did you think Mrs. Shue had died of natural causes?"

"I hardly had time to think anything. The woman was dead, and her husband appeared to be beside himself with shock or grief or both. I thought she might have come over faint and fallen down the stairs. Obviously the body had been arranged since the time of her demise, so I was unable to tell much from its position when I observed it."

"But you had no suspicions of anything untoward?"

"Not at the time, no. One doesn't expect to find murder in such mundane circumstances. A respectable newlywed in her own home? Hardly. Most violent deaths around here are straightforward and in no wise mysterious. A drunken shootout or a stabbing in the course of a quarrel. We don't have to go looking for crimes, as a rule; not only is it as plain as day, half the time we could have seen it coming."

"*Not at the time*," Preston repeated. "But later, had you cause to reconsider?"

Dr. Knapp frowned. "I was encouraged to reconsider. A few weeks after Mrs. Shue was buried at Meadow Bluff, there was a lot of talk in the county. The husband's attitude struck folks as peculiar, for one thing. So we thought it best to proceed with a postmortem . . ." Here he looked up sharply at Preston, who had, after all, ordered the autopsy, but the doctor forbore to point this out. ". . . just to make sure one way or the other."

"And you conducted the autopsy?"

Here Dr. Knapp became formal and precise. "I was in charge of the proceedings, with the assistance of my fellow physicians Dr. Rupert and Dr. McClung."

"Would that be Dr. William McClung?" Preston had noticed that the recorder had paused in his note taking and looked in question at the prosecutor.

"No, sir. Dr. Houston McClung."

The recorder nodded and went back to his notes.

"The postmortem examination took place on Monday, February twenty-second, in the Nickells schoolhouse, near the Soule Chapel burying ground in Meadow Bluff. In addition to the two other doctors and myself, we had a number of witnesses, including the accused, Mr. Edward Shue, who was compelled by law to be there."

"And can you summarize your findings for the jury, please, Doctor?"

"I can. The remains of Mrs. E. S. Shue were in

an adequate state of preservation, owing to the sea-
sonably cold temperatures we had experienced in the
four weeks since the body was interred, and we were
able to make a thorough examination—undeterred
by any interference from the defendant." His voice
took on an edge of sarcasm, and he scowled at the
defendant, but without further comment on the
antics of obfuscating wife-killers, he continued,
"When we removed the high collar from the neck of
the deceased, we found that the neck was dislocated
between the first and second cervical vertebrae. The
ligaments thereabout were torn and ruptured. The
deceased's windpipe had been crushed at a point in
the front of the throat."

"From these wounds, what would you conclude
to be the cause of death?"

"Oh, manual strangulation, most certainly."

"Not an accidental fall down a flight of stairs?"

"No."

"And aside from the neck wounds, what were
your findings upon autopsy?"

"All other portions and organs of the body were
apparently in a perfectly healthy state."

"When you were conducting your examination,
Dr. Knapp, did the defendant make any comments
that you were able to hear?"

"I heard him say, *You'll never be able to prove it.*"

As soon as Preston walked away from the witness box, most of those in the courtroom turned to
look at Dr. Rucker at the defense table. It was well-
known in the community that, before he turned to
the practice of law, Dr. Rucker had been a physician.
He stared for a moment at Knapp on the witness
stand, scribbled a note to his assistant, and leaned
back in his chair, seemingly unconcerned with the
proceedings.

James P. D. Gardner read the note twice and

then approached the witness. Dr. Knapp looked back impatiently, took out his watch, frowned at it, and slowly replaced it in the pocket of his suit.

"I won't keep you long, Dr. Knapp, sir," said the defense attorney. "Just one or two questions. On the day of the death of Mrs. E. S. Shue, did you sign a death certificate for her?"

"I did."

"And what did you list as the cause of death, sir?"

"I believe I said she died from an everlasting faint."

With a trace of a smile, Mr. Gardner paused for a few seconds longer than usual to allow time for the court to realize that an everlasting faint was a fairly accurate description of death in general.

Dr. Knapp added, "Later I amended that to complications from childbirth."

Gardner made sure the jury saw his wide-eyed look of surprise. "Mrs. Shue was with child, Doctor?"

George Knapp scowled. "I thought she might have been. Women sometimes come over faint when they are expecting. It was an educated guess on my part, though in the event, it seems I was mistaken."

"But at the time you were satisfied that Mrs. Shue had died a natural death?"

"Upon a cursory examination, yes." He glared at the defendant. "And a cursory examination was all I was allowed to make."

"But why did you decide to perform an autopsy nearly a month after the death of Mrs. Shue?"

Still scowling, Dr. Knapp said, "People got to talking. Said the defendant was behaving oddly, and what with one thing and another, we thought we ought to make sure of the findings."

"And so you found broken . . . cervical vertebrae, I believe you said . . . and bruising, a month after death?"

"That is correct."

"But in that time, the body could have been handled by any number of persons. Undertakers, those who transported the body to Meadow Bluff, the men who exhumed the body for autopsy. Is it not possible that the injuries you noted during the autopsy occurred after your original examination?"

"The injuries were consistent with manual strangulation. I believe that woman was murdered."

Mr. Gardner raised his eyebrows and asked mildly, "Just as you originally believed in natural causes, Doctor?"

twenty-three

THE TRIAL CONTINUED through that week and into the next one with a procession of witnesses contributing to the picture of Edward Shue's guilt like pieces of a jigsaw puzzle falling into place one by one. First came the details of the finding of the body, and the medical opinions on the cause of death. Then witnesses from Pocahontas County informed the court of Edward Shue's mistreatment of his first wife, Allie Cutlip—now Mrs. Todd McMillion of Greenbrier County—and his subsequent imprisonment for stealing horses. Most tellingly, they testified that Shue's second wife, Lucy Ann Tritt, aged twenty-five and a citizen of Greenbrier County, had died in 1895, less than a year after her marriage to Edward Shue, supposedly by hitting her head upon a rock.

Doggedly, the defense attorneys attempted to counter each bit of damaging testimony, casting doubt here, offering alternative explanations there, but the mosaic being assembled with all these bits of information showed a callous, violent man who was attractive to women, but by no means kind to his conquests.

The jurors' expressions over the course of the trial had changed from frank curiosity to a stony disapproval. They looked at the defendant with increasing animosity, and finally they ceased to look at him at all.

Early in the second week of the trial, John Alfred Preston finally put Mary Jane Heaster on the stand. He had waited to do so until a solid case had been built up against the defendant, because he knew that the fantastic testimony of the grieving mother might prove dangerous to his case. As he had told her before the trial began, he did not propose to question her about her encounter with the ghost of her murdered daughter, but in a small, sparsely populated place like Greenbrier County, word inevitably got around. She had made no secret of the incident. Still, he reasoned that if he did not allow her to testify, people would wonder why, and the rumors about that might do more damage than the testimony itself. So, with some misgivings, on Tuesday, June 29, Preston finally called Mrs. Heaster to the stand.

After the steady drumbeat of condemnation of Shue that had taken place over the previous days of the trial, Mrs. Heaster's account added very little, except to reinforce the opinions of the previous witnesses. Yes, she said in response to questioning, Edward Shue had been jaunty and cheerful when he accompanied his wife's body back to her parents' home. He had been secretive and controlling, not allowing the family to visit Mrs. Shue in their new home. At the funeral, he had shown no indication of grief.

Preston's questioning of the grieving mother was routine, but most of those present had heard the rumors, and the courtroom was unnaturally quiet, with the jurors and the spectators concentrating on Mrs. Heaster's testimony. At last, the precise recital came to an end, and with a sigh of resignation, Preston turned to the defense table. "Your witness."

Dr. Rucker hauled himself up from his chair, mopped his brow, and grinned at the jury, as if to say, *Watch this*. Then he inclined his head toward Mrs. Heaster with a feral smile, and the attack began.

"I have heard that you had some dream or vision which led to this postmortem examination?"

"They saw enough themselves without me telling them. It was no dream—she came back and told me that he was mad that she didn't have no meat cooked for supper. But she said she had plenty, and said that she had butter and apple butter, apples, and named over two or three kinds of jellies—pears, and cherries, and raspberry jelly—and she says, *I had plenty*, and she says, *Don't you think he was mad, and just took down all my nice things and packed them away, and just ruined them.*"

Dr. Rucker was looking at the jury, inviting them to share his amusement at the little lady's prattle.

"And she told me where I could look, down back of Aunt Martha Jones's, in the meadow, in a rocky place; that I could look in a cellar behind some loose plank and see. It was a square log house, and it was hewed up to the square, and she said for me to look right at the right-hand side of the door as you go in, and at the right-hand corner as you go in. Well, I saw the place, just exactly as she told me, and I saw blood right there where she told me, and she told me something about that meat every time she came, just as she did the first night. She came three or four times, and four nights, but the second night she told me that her neck was squeezed off at the first joint, and it was just as she told me."

"Now, Mrs. Heaster, this sad affair was very particularly impressed upon your mind, and there was not a moment during your waking hours that you did not dwell upon it?"

"No, sir, and there is not yet, either."

"And was this not a dream founded upon your distressed condition of mind?"

"No, sir, it was not a dream, for I was as wide-awake as I ever was."

"Then if not a dream or dreams, what do you call it?"

"I prayed to the Lord that she might come back and tell me what happened, and I prayed that she might come herself and tell on him."

"Do you think that you actually saw her in flesh and blood?"

"Yes, sir, I do. I told them the very dress that she was killed in, and when she went to leave me, she turned her head completely around, and looked at me like she wanted me to know all about it. The first time she came, she seemed that she did not want to tell me as much about it as she did afterwards. The last night she was there, she told me that she did everything she could do, and I am satisfied that she did do all that, too."

"Now, Mrs. Heaster, don't you know that these visions, as you term them or describe them, were nothing more or less than four dreams founded upon your distress?"

"No, I don't know it. The Lord sent her to me to tell it. I was the only friend that she knew she could tell and put any confidence in it. I was the nearest one to her. He gave me a ring that he pretended she wanted me to have, but I don't know what dead woman he might have taken it off of. I wanted her own ring, and he would not let me have it."

"Mrs. Heaster, are you positively sure that these are not four dreams?"

"Yes, sir, it was not a dream. I don't dream when

I am wide-awake, to be sure, and I know I saw her right there with me."

"Are you not considerably superstitious?"

"No, sir, I'm not. I was never that way before, and am not now."

"Do you believe the scriptures?"

"Yes, sir, I have no reason not to believe it."

"And do you believe the scriptures contain the words of God and His Son?"

"Yes, sir, I do. Don't *you* believe it?"

"Now I would like, if I could, to get you to say that these were four dreams, and not four visions or appearances of your daughter in flesh and blood?"

"I am not going to say that, for I am not going to lie."

"Then you insist that she actually appeared in flesh and blood to you upon four different occasions?"

"Yes, sir."

"Did she not have any other conversation with you other than upon the matter of her death?"

"Yes, sir, some other little things. Some things I have forgotten—just a few words. I just wanted the particulars about her death, and I got them."

"When she came, did you touch her?"

"Yes, sir. I got up on my elbows and reached out a little further, as I wanted to see if people came in their coffins, and I sat up and leaned on my elbow, and there was light in the house. It was not a lamplight. I wanted to see if there was a coffin, but there was not. She was just like she was when she left this world. It was just after I went to bed, and I wanted her to come and talk to me, and she did. This was before the inquest, and I told my neighbors. They said she was exactly as I told them she was."

"Had you ever seen the premises where your daughter lived?"

"No, sir, I had not, but I found them just exactly as she told me they were, and I never laid eyes on that house until her death. She told me this before I knew anything of the buildings at all."

"How long after this when you had these interviews with your daughter until you did see these buildings?"

"It was a month or more after the examination. It had been a little over a month since I saw her."

At this point, Dr. Rucker retired from the field and indicated to the prosecution that they might redirect questions to the witness. Preston approached the box. "Mrs. Heaster, you said your daughter told you that down by the fence in a rocky place you would find some things?"

"She said for me to look there. She didn't say I would find some things, but for me to look there."

"Did she tell you what to look for?"

"No, she did not. I was so glad to see her I forgot to ask her."

"Have you ever examined that place since?"

"Yes, we looked at the fence a little, but didn't find anything."

The jury waited for more, for some sort of final statement that would make sense of the convoluted story of the search for unspecified items in the little shack near the rocks, but there was no enlightening explanation, no result to the odd little quest. Mary Jane Heaster simply answered the final question and sat there in the witness box with folded hands, waiting for further instructions from Mr. Preston.

The court fell silent, waiting with her. At last he seemed to give up the idea of rebutting the cross-examination altogether, as though belaboring the grieving mother's ghost story no longer mattered. He finished lamely, by murmuring, "Thank you, Mrs. Heaster, you may step down now."

With one last meaningful look at the jury, she stood up and made her way out of the silent courtroom. Only when the doors closed behind her did the buzz of voices break out among the spectators, punctuated by the pounding of the judge's gavel.

Another witness was called, and the trial ground onward in the breathless heat of the little courtroom.

The chief witness for the defense was Edward Erasmus Stribbling Shue himself. He wore a white shirt cleaner than the one he had worn on the previous days, with a clumsily knotted necktie at his throat, apparently meant to show that he evinced the proper respect for the authority of the court. His lawyers regarded him with the wary misgivings of parents watching a small child mount a skittish horse. He wiped his right hand on the side of his trousers before placing it on the Bible, obscuring it completely with a sweaty palm and thick, stubby fingers that curled over the edge. When he took the oath, looking as carefully solemn as a choirboy, he looked up at the jury and nodded, smiling, as if to say, *No hard feelings, fellas.*

No one smiled back.

There were no questions. The defendant had taken the stand on this last day of the trial in order to make a statement, and no doubt his attorneys had impressed upon him the necessity of impressing the court with his sincerity and his wholesome charm.

He offered to shake hands with the judge, who politely indicated that Mr. Shue should be seated in the witness chair and get on with it. Shue sat, composed himself for a moment, and then he faced the jury with the earnest look of a horse trader. "I'll be honest with you . . ." he began.

Nobody could remember much of what he said after that. He rambled on for most of the afternoon, talking about what a poor, hardworking fellow he was, and claiming that the prosecution had taken against him, bolstering their case with lies and coincidences. He said that his wife (he never called her by name) had died of natural causes, and that all the evidence against him had either been invented or misconstrued by people who were out to get him. He smirked at the outlandish claim of Mrs. Heaster that her daughter's ghost had accused him of murder, tacitly inviting the jury to have a chuckle at the foolishness of fanciful older ladies.

His tanned face beamed with sweat, and one black curl dangled just over his right eyebrow, giving him the look of a boyish rascal.

He had dearly loved his wife, he said, and he swore that even though he had indeed served time in the pen at Moundsville, he was once again an honest, upstanding citizen.

He could have made all these points in a quarter of an hour, but apparently he realized that his life depended on what he would say, and he seemed determined to use every minute he was allowed in order to waste no opportunity to charm the court, and to leave no argument unspoken. He mopped his brow with a soiled red bandana and kept on talking. Once, when his voice faltered, Mr. Gardner got up from the defense table and took him a glass of water from the lawyers' pitcher. Shue gulped it down, coughed a bit to clear his throat, and launched into speech again, making the same points he had already made twice before.

At one point, he broke off in his declaration of love for his dead wife to look over at the jury. "Look at this face, gentlemen," he said, big-eyed and solemn. "Look in my eyes. Do I look like a murderer to you? Do I look like a heartless killer?" He seemed on the verge of tears, and his voice quavered. The jurors squirmed in their seats and looked away, perhaps embarrassed at such a fervid display of emotion in the otherwise staid and somber courtroom.

All his life "Trout" Shue had been a virile, handsome man, relying on his easy smile and a lazy charm to make people willing to give him his own way. Mostly his manner had served him well. He had managed to acquire three wives, a host of friends, and a decent job, despite his criminal record. He must have reasoned that his good looks and affable personality would impress the jury so much that they would be loath to convict him of such a terrible crime.

In this, he was not entirely wrong.

After lengthy closing arguments, the twelve men retired to deliberate on Thursday afternoon, July 1. One hour and ten minutes later, they came back and filed into the jury box, ready to render their verdict.

Judge McWhorter poured himself a glass of water from the pitcher beside him, and drank deeply while he waited for the courtroom to settle down. The foreman stood at his place, twisting the paper with sweaty fingers and licking his lips in anticipation of his big moment.

At a nod from the judge, Rucker and Gardner stood, helping their client to his feet. Shue swayed a little, and the color drained from his face. He glanced first at the jury, but they were resolutely looking in any direction except at him. Next he seemed to be searching out the exits to the courtroom, but the bailiff moved closer to the defense table, his hand on his pistol. Rucker stood at attention, a soldier awaiting grim orders, but James Gardner touched his client's arm and leaned over to murmur soothing words to him.

In a tired voice, Judge McWhorter uttered the formula: "Has the jury reached a verdict?"

"Reckon we have, your honor." The wiry little man in a worn black suit jacket and a string tie held up the scrap of paper, and his fellow jurors folded their arms, nodding in agreement.

"Well, let's have it then."

"We find the defendant guilty of first degree murder. Guilty as charged." He paused for a moment, cleared his throat, and added, "But we recommend that instead of hanging him, that the judge sentence him to the penitentiary for the rest of his natural life."

When the spectators heard the verdict, a clamor broke out in the courtroom, but Dr. Rucker shouted them all down. "Motion for a new trial, your honor!"

Judge McWhorter nodded in his direction, just to indicate that he had heard him above the din. Then he thanked the jury and adjourned the court.

Edward Shue allowed himself to be manacled and led away by the officers. He stumbled from the courtroom like a sleepwalker, without a word to his attorneys or a glance at anyone present.

Dr. Rucker gathered up his papers and prepared to leave.

James Gardner pushed his chair back and stood up. "Well, at least he wasn't sentenced to death."

Rucker nodded, apparently unmoved by the outcome of the trial. "It was a sensible verdict, really. The jury believed that he did it, but we managed to make them understand that the evidence was only circumstantial, and apparently they felt that there was just enough of a sliver of doubt to keep them from ordering him hanged."

"What about Mrs. Heaster's testimony?"

He laughed. "The ghost of his dead wife claiming that he did her in? I think the jury saw through that quick enough. A spiteful old woman out for revenge, that's all that was. You notice that Mr. Preston did not question her about it himself when he had her on the stand. Perhaps I should have let well enough alone and not mentioned it, but I thought it would show the court how vindictive and unreliable she was. I had hoped that her testimony might sway the jury to favor Mr. Shue, but perhaps they were a credulous bunch."

"She was most steadfast on the witness stand. I think the jurors were impressed."

"I know. I was surprised. Who'd have thought that a backwoods farmwife would have had so much composure in a court of law?" Rucker picked up his white straw hat and placed it on top of the stack of papers he was carrying. "Ah, well! I don't suppose we could have got him off, James, no matter what we did. A defendant with two dead wives and a prison record for horse-stealing has too much baggage to receive an acquittal even if he had a pair of archangels defending him. Don't take it to heart. We did all we could."

Gardner nodded. "And I suppose there's always another chance for him, since you've requested a new trial."

"Oh, that!" Rucker gave him a cold smile. "Lawyers have to claim to be unhappy with a guilty verdict. It's good for business. Remember that. But I shall have a talk with our client about the prospect of a new trial, and I believe he will agree that it would be best to abandon that idea. After all, this jury did spare his life. The next one might not be so accommodating."

A few days after the trial ended, John Alfred Preston and his wife joined a dinner party at the Old White

Hotel, at the request of an old friend and fellow board member at Washington and Lee University. A number of his acquaintances were summering at the hotel in White Sulphur Springs, always a popular alternative to the heat and miasmas of the lower elevations. The dinner party was by no means a celebration of his victory in court, he told Mrs. Preston, for to celebrate another man's ruin would be unseemly, but the prospect of wearing evening clothes and dining with people of taste and refinement was most gratifying. It would be a pleasant change from the crowded courtroom, reeking with the sulfurous smell of sweating, unwashed bodies.

The dinner party was quite elaborate. In the Old White's beautifully appointed dining room, the last rays of the July sun shimmered in the long windows. Places for fourteen were set around the banquet table, an expanse of starched white damask, twinkling in candlelight with fine crystal and gleaming silver serving dishes. Preston greeted his old friends and exchanged pleasantries with the new acquaintances before they settled in to dine. He had noticed, however, that one of the gentlemen had a copy of the *Greenbrier Independent* folded next to his plate. He steeled himself, suspecting that he was to furnish the evening's topic of discussion.

The party had nearly finished the soup course, an interval dominated by remarks about fashion and the weather, before the gentleman with the newspaper cleared his throat and addressed the attorney across the table.

"I have just been reading about your latest achievements in the *Independent*, Mr. Preston. Quite an unusual case, I should say."

"Achievements?" Several of the ladies at the table—apparently not local newspaper readers—looked puzzled.

"Mr. Preston is Greenbrier County's prosecuting attorney, and he has just emerged victorious from a sensational murder trial."

Preston took a sip of sherry as he marshaled his thoughts. He had a brief respite while the soup plates were whisked away, and the fish course—West Virginia brook trout à la meunière—was set before them, but the polite murmurs of interest all around the table indicated that the conversation had only begun.

"A murderer?" echoed a fashionable young woman, regarding him with interest. He thought he detected a trace of an English accent, but she might still be American. Many of the upper class these days divided their time between America and Britain, and the British accent was fashionable. "Do tell us about it, Mr. Preston."

He smiled. After all, he supposed, it was better than having to refight the war with maudlin old veterans over the brandy. "Well, it wasn't much of a case. All quite straightforward. The fellow was a blacksmith, newly settled in the county. In January his bride of two months was found dead in the front hall of their house, and an autopsy eventually showed that the poor woman had been strangled."

"And the husband confessed?" asked another guest.

After some hesitation, Preston gave his dinner companions a more detailed account of the incident. When he finished his account of the case, eschewing the most unsavory details, an interval of silence fell on the dinner party as the guests contemplated this grim story. But before anyone could introduce a more pleasant topic, the man with the newspaper spoke up again. "Mr. Preston is being too modest, I think. Too reticent, anyhow. There was indeed a sensational element to the case, was there not? Testimony from the murdered woman herself?"

Amid the murmurs and exclamations around the table, Preston took another sip of wine. He had been afraid of this.

Across the table, Lillie spoke up. "Oh, do tell them about it, John. Don't worry about shocking us. In Lewisburg, the ladies have been talking of nothing else for days."

Preston managed a tight smile. "Well, make of it what you will. The mother of the murdered woman came to me several weeks after the funeral, claiming that her dead daughter had appeared to her during the night—not in a dream, but in the flesh. The mother—a Mrs. Heaster—insisted that the apparition, Mrs. Zona Shue, told her that the husband had murdered her. The mother had no proof, of course, but some rumors of suspicion had already come to my attention. Apparently, some of the neighbors at Livesay's Mill felt that the husband was not sufficiently bereaved. They also remembered his odd behavior in not allowing anyone to come near the body of his wife. I thought we might as well make sure, so I consulted the attending physician, and we arranged for an autopsy. Fortunately, the winter weather had preserved the remains sufficiently for a determination to be made as to the cause of death."

"And she had been murdered?"

"Oh, yes. I'm afraid this isn't a seemly topic for the dinner table, but if you are all sure . . . ?" He looked at each of his dinner companions, but they were all nodding, some solemnly and some with avid interest. The woman with the English accent had a secretive smile.

"Yes? Well, then: the poor woman's neck was broken, and fingerprints were still visible on her throat."

A stout older woman, her forkful of pigeon pie poised midway to her mouth, was still thinking about the extraordinary circumstances of Mr. Preston's case. "So the ghost came back to seek justice. Such feelings can prevent people from moving on to the next plane, you know."

"*The next plane?*" said Preston, in what he hoped was a neutral voice.

The woman fixed him with an icy stare. "A great many prominent people are believers in spiritualism, Mr. Preston. In England Sir Arthur Conan Doyle is a leader in the movement. And I have heard that in New York, Commodore Vanderbilt once consulted mediums, did he not? How else can you explain the dead woman's mother knowing the circumstances of her murder?"

Preston sighed, hoping the dinner conversation would not devolve into a discussion of spiritualism. "I like to think that a grieving mother's intuition led her to imagine the supernatural visitation, confirming what she already suspected to be true."

One of the gentleman guests chuckled. "Do you think the mother made up the story out of whole cloth?"

"I couldn't say, sir. I did not bring the matter up in court. I felt that the circumstantial evidence against the man was sufficient to secure a conviction. He had a prison record, and another young wife of his had died approximately one year before, which seemed entirely too coincidental for my liking. And I feel we did convict him on that evidence, but the defense attorney, attempting to make mischief, brought the ghost matter up in cross-examination. He tried to make sport of the grieving mother, inviting her to concede that her preoccupation with her daughter's death had given her nightmares, which she mistook for actual events. I will say this for her, though: she never flinched from his questioning, and she never gave an inch. I don't know if the jury believed her supernatural tale or not, but they were impressed by her courage and her steadfastness."

The man with the newspaper steepled his fingers together and smiled. "A ghost in Greenbrier testifying at the trial of her killer. I never heard the like!"

"Oh, but I have!" The young Englishwoman's smile was wider now, and she inclined her head, tilting her wineglass toward him in a mock toast. "Most of Britain knows that story, I should think, or one like enough to it to be its twin."

Her companion stared at her for a moment. "Jennie, are you talking about that play? What was it called?"

"*The Murder in the Red Barn.*" She gave her table partner a satisfied smile. "I thought someone else here would know it. It's a dreadful old melodrama, but it's been staged more or less continuously in Britain for half a century, at least. It's based on a true story, of course. Have none of you ever heard of Maria Marten? No?"

"I should be glad to hear of it," said Preston quietly.

Jennie's eyes sparkled in the candlelight. "Maria Marten was a mole catcher's daughter in Suffolk in the 1820s—and no better than she should be, I might add, though I believe the play does not elaborate on that point. She had two children by two different men by the time she was in her twenties. Well, those men wanted nothing more to do with her, but the brother of one of them, William Corder, took up with Maria Marten. He was already known to be a wrong'un, dallying with various women in the community and engaging in sharp practice with business dealings. I believe he stole a pig once, and he had forged a check as well."

"A wrong'un. That certainly sounds like your fellow, Preston," said the man with the newspaper.

"So it does. Our Mr. Shue was convicted of stealing horses, though. Do go on, ma'am. What happened next?"

The lady sighed. "Oh, the usual old-as-the-hills story, I'm afraid. Maria Marten fell for the ne'er-do-well William Corder, and she believed him when he told her they were going to elope. At the appointed time, she met him in the red barn, and then she vanished. Corder left the area, and even went so far as to send the Martens letters claiming that Maria was with him and in good health, but then . . ." Here she paused and looked around the table for effect. "*Then Maria Marten's stepmother had a dream.* In the dream, Maria said that William Corder had shot her and buried her body in a storage bin for grain in the red barn. After that, the family and their neighbors searched the barn, and sure enough, Maria's body was found in a sack, just where she said it would be."

The man with the newspaper was aghast. "You astound me, young lady. Why, it's nearly the same story that's reported about the trial of Edward Shue here in the *Independent*."

Another gentleman nodded. "Mighty like, indeed. Mr. Preston, do you suppose your witness could have heard this story?"

"I don't see how."

The Englishwoman shrugged. "It was made into a play, remember. Dreadful rot—pure melodrama—but my stars, it was popular! There's hardly anybody in England who hasn't at least heard of it, if they haven't seen it on stage. I expect you could find a dozen people in this hotel who are familiar with the story."

John Alfred Preston smiled. "In this hotel perhaps we could, but Mrs. Heaster is a farmer's wife, living all the way over in the mountainous part of the county, near Little Sewell. She has lived there the whole of her life. I cannot imagine her ever frequenting this hotel, and she lives much too far away to have ever worked here or to know anyone who has."

Lillie Preston spoke up. "But, John, Mary Jane Heaster was a Miss Robinson before her marriage. I was talking to her only a few weeks ago, outside your office, before the trial, and she happened to mention that her father, John Robinson, *was from England*."

"Was he?" murmured Preston. "I'm afraid I've never heard of the play, but perhaps he had. I wonder if he ever told that story to his daughter?"

"Well, never mind about that," said one of the older ladies. "What happened to William Corder— and to his Greenbrier counterpart, for that matter?"

Preston was running his finger along the rim of his wineglass, lost in thought, but the lady beside him touched his arm and repeated the question.

"Edward Shue? Oh, the jury found him guilty, of course. But they recommended life in prison instead of the death penalty. He will stay in the penitentiary at Moundsville for the rest of his days, where he can do no more harm to trusting but foolish young ladies."

"Mr. William Corder wasn't so fortunate," said Jennie. "They took him back to Suffolk for trial and promptly hanged him."

"And that was the end of that," said the man with the newspaper.

Jennie and the other woman who had remembered the story looked at each other and shrugged. "No, I'm afraid it wasn't. On the gallows, he did confess to the crime, but after the execution, they cut him down, took his corpse back to the courtroom, and made an incision in the body—I don't know why—and they allowed thousands of people to file past and view his remains."

"I expect they were medical students dissecting him," said Preston. "I believe that was customary."

"It was, but the formal autopsy was done on the following day with students from Cambridge in attendance. One of my brothers is a surgeon, which is how I came to know the part about the execution and the aftermath." She looked down at her unfinished dinner and sighed. "The story gets quite grisly after that."

"I for one should like to hear it," said the man with the newspaper. "But if the ladies would prefer to be excused?"

Apparently, the irony that it was one of the ladies who was telling the story was lost on him. In any case, no one left the table. Mr. Preston reflected that in his day well-bred young ladies were not so outspoken, and he suspected that if Jennie were not very rich indeed, she would do well to learn to be more circumspect before her beauty began to fade.

"I suppose after they'd finished cutting him up, they didn't think it worth the bother to reassemble all the bits again. In any case, they didn't. William Corder's skeleton went on display at the Royal College of Surgeons at Lincoln's Inn Fields, and they made several death masks, some of which are exhibited in various places. To me the most unsettling thing is that one of the surgeons tanned a bit of William Corder's skin, and he used the . . . the human leather . . . to bind a written account of the murder." She shivered. "I told you it was grisly."

"So it was," said Lillie Preston, with a glance at her husband. "But it makes me glad that our legal system here is more merciful. I could never really pity Edward Shue, for we know he deserves his fate, but at least I know how fortunate he is, and how much worse it could have been."

John Alfred Preston, who knew a great deal about Moundsville and resolved that his wife never would, stared into the candle flame and said nothing.

twenty-four

LAKIN, WEST VIRGINIA

1931

"SO YOU LOST the case, did you?"

The days were warmer now, and Dr. Boozer had left off wearing his suit jacket under his white coat. He had persuaded Mr. Gardner, who still felt the chill in his old bones, to take a walk with him around the grounds. The two men inspected the flower beds, where petunias and thrift bloomed purple and white. They began to walk to the higher ground away from the road, hoping for a glimpse of tall barges along the river, if not the river itself. An occasional gust of wind scattered last fall's dead leaves in their path, and they crunched them underfoot, scarcely noticing.

Savoring the afternoon sunshine, James Gardner considered the question. "Lose the case? I'll grant you that the jury convicted Edward Shue of murder, but I think we got them to see that the evidence was purely circumstantial, and that may have made a difference."

"Do you think the mother's testimony about her daughter's ghost made the difference?"

"Oh, I think there were enough nails in his coffin without her testimony. The abused first wife, the second wife dying in peculiar circumstances, his prison record—it all added up. I don't think Clarence Darrow himself could have got the man acquitted, but we did spare him the death penalty. At least the legal one."

"The *legal* one?"

Mr. Gardner smiled. "Edward Shue was sentenced to life in prison, but Moundsville is up that river over there, and a mighty long way from Greenbrier County. I don't suppose he ever got to see the river, either. Anyhow, they had to get him from Lewisburg to Moundsville. Fortunately, the lawyer's responsibility stops at the end of the trial, so I wasn't a witness to what came next, but everybody knew the particulars.

"As soon as the jury came back with that guilty verdict, Dr. Rucker stood up and requested a new trial, but he withdrew that motion the next morning."

"Why? If I had been convicted, I'd want a second chance with a different jury, if I could get one."

Mr. Gardner stopped looking up at the sky and regarded the doctor with raised eyebrows. "Would you?"

"Well, I'd assume that I had nothing to lose."

"You would be mistaken then. Dr. Rucker had asked for a new trial without consulting the client, without even a second thought, apparently. I think it was just a natural impulse on his part. The man hated to lose. But later that afternoon, once the excitement of the courtroom had faded away, we had to consult with Edward Shue and to consider the matter with cold logic. Then we had three factors to take into account. One: Life in prison was not the worst verdict he could have received. If he were granted a new trial, a second jury might well give him the death penalty instead. Two: The man had no money, and we weren't anxious to keep representing him pro bono when there was so little chance of accomplishing anything. Three: Awaiting a new trial would mean that Shue would remain in the county jail in Lewisburg, where his safety would be threatened by a populace who hated him and resented his escape from the gallows."

Boozer stuffed his hands into the pockets of his white coat and began to walk again. "Moundsville is a hellish place, isn't it? I would have been in no hurry to get there."

"Well, he had been incarcerated there before, remember. *Better the devil you know . . .*" Mr. Gardner stood on tiptoe, peering out over the field and the treetops, searching for the glint of sunlight on water, but all he saw were the bare rock cliffs on the Ohio side of the river. "Anyhow, we persuaded Edward Shue not to risk his life on the uncertainty of a new trial, and Dr. Rucker withdrew the motion the following morning. Shue thanked us for our help, and we parted from him on cordial terms.

"They kept him in the Lewisburg jail for another ten days, getting ready to transfer him by train to Moundsville, but because the jury had not sentenced him to death, the local feelings against him were still strong—especially in the Meadow Bluff area, the home of the Heasters. People felt that Shue had deserved to be hanged, and there were rumors going around that if the state couldn't dispense justice in a satisfactory manner, then the local citizens would have to see to it themselves.

"On the Sunday after the trial ended, a group of vigilantes in Meadow Bluff decided that they were going to meet at a campground about eight miles west of town about ten o'clock that evening. From there they planned to converge on the county jail, seize Edward Shue, take him out, and lynch him."

"I wonder why they didn't trust the jury. They were the ones who heard the evidence."

"Oh, what does evidence have to do with vigilante justice? Some men get mean when they're liquored up, and they're mighty glad to find some deserving soul to take it out on. Edward Shue was the perfect target—a stranger and a wife-killer. The evidence against him was all circumstantial, but that didn't matter to them."

Boozer was silent for a moment. "Circumstantial doesn't necessarily mean false. My belief that the sun will come up in the morning is purely circumstantial, but I believe it all the same. Don't you believe that Shue was guilty?"

"I expect he was, but he wasn't getting off scot-free, you know. I wouldn't wish Moundsville on anybody. I think I'd rather be dead than shut in that hellhole, knowing I'd spend the rest of my life in a cage." He glanced back at the brick building looming behind them at the top of the rise. "On the other hand, maybe it's quieter in Moundsville."

"Let's come back to that in a little while, Mr. Gardner, because it is a talk we ought to have, but go ahead with your story about the lynch mob. So they were going to storm the jail and take care of Shue themselves?"

"That was the plan, but another problem with liquored-up lynch mobs is that they talk too much. The sheriff at that time was S. Hill Nickell, and he lived out in Meadow Bluff. One of his neighbors, a fellow named Harrah, got wind of the mob's intentions, and he rode over to the sheriff's house and told him what they were planning.

"The sheriff and Harrah started for Lewisburg that evening, but they had to pass the campground in order to get there. They rode past about an hour before the mob was set to assemble there, but some men were there already, and although the sheriff and Harrah got by without incident, somebody in the crowd recognized them, and four of the vigilantes gave chase, caught up with them, and, pistols drawn, they ordered the sheriff to stop."

Boozer shook his head. "Sounds like a Saturday morning Western. *Did* he stop?"

"He did, and they almost had that Western-movie shootout you're picturing, but Sheriff Nickell talked about it later. He said he had his pistol out of the holster and was getting ready to shoot the nearest man when he recognized the fellow. He never would say who it was, but apparently it was a close friend or neighbor—maybe even a kinsman. Anyhow, he decided to try moral suasion instead of hot lead to resolve the matter."

"I wouldn't want to lecture somebody who was holding a gun on me."

"Neither did Sheriff Nickell. He and Harrah surrendered and let themselves be taken to the nearby home of a Mr. Dwyer. The vigilantes gathered in Dwyer's parlor, and maybe some of them had sobered up in the interval. Anyhow, the sheriff managed to talk them into disbanding the lynching party and going home."

"So the sheriff saved his prisoner's life."

"He never thought so. Sheriff Nickell always said that his deputy back in Lewisburg had already been warned about the lynch mob. Some fishermen on their way home had spotted the well-armed crowd at the campground, and they headed straight into town and warned the deputy. That deputy's name was Dwyer, too, now I come to think of it. Wonder if he was kin to the man who held the meeting in his parlor? Well, they're stingy with surnames in Greenbrier County—there's not that many to go around."

Boozer chuckled. "What did Deputy Dwyer do? Circle the wagons?"

"No, and he didn't feel like sitting out a siege in the county jail, either. As soon as he heard that there might be a lynch mob coming, he put Shue in irons and took him out of his cell. Then he and another deputy bundled him into a wagon and took him a mile or two out of town to wait until the storm blew over."

"And did that work?"

"One way or another. Sheriff Nickell talked the mob into disbanding, and somebody fetched Dwyer and the prisoner back the next morning, so it all ended peacefully. The day after that, the sheriff and Dwyer boarded a northbound train with the prisoner, and off they went to Moundsville."

"Did you see them off?"

James Gardner shook his head. "Maybe if it were happening now, I would. Now that I know what it's like to be shut up in a cage. But in 1897, I was a young man, full of myself and busy courting my Eliza, so I had no thoughts to spare for a man we defended two weeks earlier. I suppose it would have been a kindness to take him a sack of biscuits and a tomato or two, but, you know, he did kill two of his wives, as far as we could tell, so perhaps he didn't deserve any more mercy than he showed them. You're the age that I was then. Would you have gone, Boozer?"

The doctor took a deep breath and looked for an answer in a cloud scudding past the ridge. "I'd like to think I would. But to be honest, I'd have been more likely to do him a kindness if he hadn't been white. People might have thought I was being arrogant offering him something, and I wouldn't risk my neck to do any favors for a murderer."

"Maybe that's what I thought, too. Besides, I wouldn't have risked my life just then for anything. I was too full of myself—new career as a lawyer, new fiancée." He looked down at the shoots of spring grass just visible among the dead leaves. "It was a long time ago. I guess if I had been of a mind to help anybody, it would have been Martha Jones."

"The woman whose son found the body? What became of her?"

It was a bleak day in late December 1897, when the leaden sky seemed close enough to snag on the church steeple. James Gardner, bundled into his black wool overcoat with a white silk scarf at his throat, had just come into the courthouse on some errand of legal business when he saw Martha Jones, gaunt and tired-looking in a shabby brown coat, coming down the hallway from the clerks' offices. He was glad to see her. In his current mood of jubilation, he was glad to see everybody. Freed from his customary reserve by the immediate prospect of happiness, Gardner hurried up to her with an open smile and an outstretched hand.

"Mrs. Jones! I never thought to see you in town. I haven't seen you since the trial, but I'm glad of the chance to wish you a merry Christmas."

She shivered a little, and he thought she must have been in the path of the gust of wind that swept through when someone opened the front door. "Good day to you, Mr. Gardner. I hope you don't hold it against me that I testified for the other side, seeing as how y'all lost the case."

Gardner laughed. "That was six months ago, and anyhow the jury agreed with you. Besides, this is a small county—if we lawyers took umbrage at everybody who opposed us in court, we'd get mighty lonely."

"That's so, I reckon." A flicker of a smile lit her face, but only for a moment. "Are you keeping well, Mr. Gardner?"

"Oh, better than that, Mrs. Jones. I'm getting married on Christmas Day—to Miss Eliza Myles." He wondered if he sounded drunk, if this was what being drunk would feel like. He wanted to share his news with everyone; the slightest pretext set him off. "Miss Myles is a lovely lady. I don't know if you're acquainted with her . . ."

"No, sir. I don't know too many folks outside of Livesay's Mill. But I wish the both of you well."

"Thank you. I hope you can meet her. All of you. We're having a big old-fashioned wedding at our church in White Sulphur Springs on Satur-day next—Christmas Day, that is—and I wanted to invite all of your family to come along to the celebration. It's a bit far to travel from Livesay's Mill, perhaps, but we're hoping that the weather will be fine. There'll be a big reception afterward in the church hall, and Miss Myles's mama and my sisters have all been cooking nineteen to the dozen all this month—cakes, pies, and I don't know what all—so we'll have enough to feed the heavenly host if they should happen to drop by. You're more than welcome to come. All of you. There'll be plenty."

Her face creased with bewilderment, but after a moment she nodded to herself, and the bleak expres-sion returned. "You don't know, do you?"

Something in her tone stopped his babbling. He blinked. "I beg your pardon? Don't know?"

"Well, that's not to be wondered at. I reckon you couldn't have known. They're all gone, Mr. Gardner. All except me and Anderson and the baby Reuben."

"All gone? Your family?" At first he thought of

asking if they were traveling and when they were expected to return, but her solemn expression made her meaning clear. Dead. He tried to think of some sympathetic rejoinder, but he had been taken by surprise, and the words caught in his throat. All he could think of was that there had been a house fire. Should he ask? He had finally mastered the polite nothings of ordinary conversation, but awkward discussions with people he did not know well were difficult for him. He could chop a cord of firewood and not be as tired as he got from making civil conversation. It was hard to change from his own joyful preoccupations to make the proper responses to an unexpected tragedy.

Martha Jones wiped her eyes. "I reckon they're all together in heaven now, and happy with the Lord, but sometimes I wish I could just lay my burdens down right here and now and join them. But the two that are left can't do without me, so I am keeping on."

"But what happened?"

"Fever. The first one took was Reuben—my husband, that is. Not the baby—the Lord in His mercy spared the little one. My husband came down with the typhoid back in late summer, and we lost him on the twenty-eighth of September. Then Samuel got it, too, and he passed four days after his daddy. I was worn out with nursing by then, but I thought we'd gotten through it. Then Sarah took sick, and she was gone by the end of October. Last of all was my poor Margaret. She had helped me tend the others night and day until she was worn to a shadow, and she came down with it about the time Sarah died. She passed on the eighth of this month, not two weeks ago." She tried to smile. "Mary Ellen was spared, though. You remember, she got married back in May, so she's doing all right with her

new husband over at their place. Sometimes thinking about her, and hoping for grandbabies, is all that
keeps me going."

James Gardner stared at her, trying to shift his
feelings from his joy to her great sorrow, and failing
to find any words to say. Finally he managed to murmur, "Typhoid? All of them?" The line from *Mac-
beth* jangled in his mind: *What, all my pretty chickens?
At one fell swoop?*

Martha Jones nodded. "I reckon the water was
bad. I don't know why me and Anderson and little
Reuben were spared. Seems like the others might
have been more needed in this world than us: an
old woman, a lap baby, and a boy who's never quite
going to grow up."

Gardner thought of the happy, laughing family
crowded into that little house in Livesay's Mill back
in the spring. Gone now. He couldn't take it in. "I'm
sorry, Mrs. Jones. I hardly know what to say except
just that, and it doesn't seem like enough."

She patted the sleeve of his overcoat. "It's a lot
for a body to hear all at once. I've had three months
to get used to it, but I'm sorry for springing it on
you all of a sudden when you were so happy there,
talking about your wedding and all. I didn't mean to
cast cold on your joy, Mr. Gardner. I'm real glad for
the good news about you and your wife-to-be. Real
glad. A Christmas wedding."

"You're . . . you're all still welcome to come, of
course."

She shook her head. "Reckon we'd just be spec-
ters at the feast. I ain't done with my mourning
yet, and maybe I never will be, but I'll get through
it somehow. I'm glad to hear your good news, Mr.
Gardner. I shore nuff am. It's a fine thing to know
that there's weddings and babies and joy to offset all
the rest."

Still at a loss for words, Mr. Gardner dug into his pocket and found a crumpled dollar bill. "Christmas is coming, too, Mrs. Jones. I'd be glad if you'd take this and buy your two boys a present and something good to eat for the holiday. And yourself, too, of course. It isn't much, but—"

"It's a kindness, Mr. Gardner, and that means the most to me." She put the bill in the pocket of her coat. "You know, every now and then I get to thinking about Mr. Trout Shue, shut up there in that cold, dark prison. Have you had any word lately about him?"

"No. I doubt that we ever will. He declined a new trial, you know, and we did not appeal the verdict, so I don't suppose there is anything more to be said. As far as the world is concerned, he is as dead as . . . as his wife," he finished hastily, thinking it would be rude to connect the convicted felon with her own recent losses.

"He was such a strapping fellow, so fond of the outdoors and near to bursting with health. I don't say he didn't deserve it, but it seems a waste to shut him away in the dark for the rest of his days. I wonder if he would rather be dead and buried himself."

"I don't think he has much to look forward to in the hereafter, Mrs. Jones."

Again someone opened the outside door of the courthouse, hitting them with another blast of cold air. Martha Jones shivered, seeming to shrink down into her cloth coat. "It's getting late. I need to be heading home before we lose the light. I wish you joy and sunshine for your wedding, Mr. Gardner. Joy and sunshine."

She looked up at him with a tremulous smile, and then she was gone.

❖

"So that was it then?" Dr. Boozer gazed at the burning tip of his cigarette.

James P. D. Gardner nodded, staring at a bare patch of ground in the grass near the bench. "That was it. I never saw her again. Eliza and I got married on Christmas Day, but none of the Joneses came to the wedding. A little while later, we moved to Bramwell over in Mercer County, and I started my own law practice there. Later on, we moved to Bluefield, and I've been there ever since—well, except for now. But the law practice prospered, and I never regretted the move from Greenbrier. I lost Eliza, though. She passed on Valentine's Day in 1911. Holidays make me sad now. I don't care to celebrate any of them. I thought the feeling might go away after I married Alice, but I still get restive before a holiday, even if it takes me awhile to realize why."

"I married Dorothy on the day *before* Valentine's Day. That didn't work well, either. But let's stop looking backward. Dr. Barnett summoned me to his office today to tell me that he got a big brown envelope in the mail yesterday. It was full of letters of recommendation from people petitioning for your release."

Mr. Gardner struggled to keep from smiling. "Went over your head, did they?"

"Straight to the boss man himself. He wasn't too happy about it."

"Those letters—did they come from lawyers?"

"Some of them. They threatened to sue on your behalf, of course, but I think Dr. Barnett was more concerned about some of the politicians in Charleston who championed your cause. He very pointedly asked me if I thought you were well enough to leave, the implication being that I would be wise to say yes."

Now Gardner did smile. "Well, don't be too hard on your boss. He has to be a bit of a politician himself to run this place. He's probably afraid that if he doesn't cooperate, the powers-that-be in the state government will remember that when it comes time to vote on the funding of this fine establishment."

"Your brother Masons are behind this, aren't they?"

"Some people think they're behind everything."

"Don't try to palm off a persecution complex on me. You're still the patient. I'm glad you have friends looking out for you, but surely your health ought to come first."

"You've had a good many months to *minister to a mind diseased*, Boozer. I may not be the happy-go-lucky man you seem to want me to be, but then I never was. It will be better for both of us if you just sign the forms and trust me to look after myself from here on out."

Boozer sighed. "Well, we do need the bed space. But I don't want you on my conscience, Mr. Gardner. Can you give me your word that you won't try suicide again?"

"In fact, I can, Doctor. I am a cautious man, and suicide attempts run the risk of failure. Much as I've enjoyed your company, I don't want to end up here again." He glanced out the window, at the view that never changed except for the seasons.

Mr. Gardner struggled to his feet. "Let's go find those papers, Dr. Boozer. You've got some forms to sign."

James Boozer nodded. "We'll do that, Mr. Gardner, but first, why don't we go across the road and take a look at the river?"

James P. D. Gardner was released from the hospital in Lakin after 1930, and returned to Bluefield, West

Virginia, to resume the practice of law. In 1935 he was elected corresponding secretary of the Ancient Arabic Order of the Mystic Shrine and the Mountain State Consistory 32nd degree FAAY Masons. He died on August 13, 1951, at Welch State Hospital, McDowell County, West Virginia. He is buried in an unmarked grave in the Old Lewisburg Cemetery, Lewisburg, West Virginia, across the street from the graves of his fellow attorneys John Alfred Preston and William P. Rucker.

Dr. James Boozer died in July 1978 in New Rochelle, New York.

twenty-five

STATE PENITENTIARY, MOUNDSVILLE,

WEST VIRGINIA

1898

THE OHIO RIVER was only a couple of blocks west of the prison, but he knew he would never see it. The exercise yard, surrounded by high walls anyhow, faced the hills in the other direction. The staff offices and living quarters on the upper floors of the prison might have windows offering views of the river, but he would never go there. It seemed little enough to wish for: just a glimpse of that broad flat stretch of water, conveying boats and ore barges to faraway places. Imagining the peaceful river scene helped to take his mind off his hunger, but he might as well dream about a South Sea island or even the moon; he would never see any of them. For him, the river's only presence was a faint stench on the hottest days of summer, and the bone-chilling dampness that seeped into everything in the icy winter air.

Somehow he had forgotten the stupefying cold. Strange that the memory of the prison had faded from his mind after a decade. At the time his sentence had seemed to last forever. Two years for horse-stealing, and every day in Moundsville then had felt like a month. He had paced the tiny cell like a caged bear, trying to keep track of the dates, counting the days until he would be free again. He hadn't missed Allie and the baby while he was inside; in fact, he had hardly thought about them. What he had missed most were the wide green meadows and the wooded hills of home, the taste of apples and cold clear water from a mountain stream.

All he really remembered about his previous stint in prison was the constant, gnawing hunger. There was never enough food, and what they were given was hog swill. Foul as it was, though, he could never get enough, and when he was finally released, he could become enraged simply by having hunger pangs because that feeling brought back the nightmares.

Now that he was entering his second winter of a life sentence, he had become well acquainted again with all the things he had mercifully forgotten before. The darkness for sixteen hours a day, when the prisoners were locked in small stone cells with barred metal doors. When the door slammed shut at dusk, the rising panic of knowing that he was trapped in a dark space scarcely longer than his body and only the width of his outspread arms made him want to scream and throw himself against the door until they came and let him out. Except that they wouldn't.

Sometimes men did go mad in the cold darkness, and they shouted until their throats bled, silenced only by exhaustion. After a few days, those men would be gone. Word spread among the prisoners that there was a worse place of confinement in the prison. From the exercise yard, you could see a flight of narrow steps leading down to a locked door. The old-timers claimed the passage led to a windowless cellar, forever dark and cold, and that if they put you there, you stayed there around the clock—no tasks to perform during the daylight hours, no meals in the mess hall, no brief stretches in the exercise yard with its view of a rounded green hill against the sky. Nothing but darkness until they let you out again— if they did.

How could he have forgotten the cold? The cells had no heat and no light. In summer the prisoners sweltered in the humid, airless stench, and in the winter, the cold seeped into their bones until even their thoughts slowed down, and they couldn't sleep because every movement under the thin blanket was a reminder that no matter what you did, how you turned or lay or tried to wrap your arms around yourself, you would still be cold.

Too bone-chilled and hungry to sleep, and nothing to stay awake for. He had managed to endure it when he knew that he had only to survive for a stretch of months before the nightmare ended and he could go back into the world. But this time there was nothing to look forward to except the same endless round of hunger and misery for as long as he lived.

There was some consolation in knowing that the rest of his life wasn't going to be that long. He hadn't minded the fever, because at least it kept him from feeling the cold, but the blood disgusted and frightened him. He couldn't see it when he coughed at night, but he could feel the thick, warm fluid on his thumb and forefinger, and even in the dark he knew it was not phlegm. In the daytime, when he worked and ate in the company of the other prisoners, he heard the coughing and saw the pink-stained rags with which they staunched it. Consumption. The prison doctors, helpless to treat it, solved the problem by ignoring it. "It's only a bad cold," they would say. "Come spring, you'll feel better." He knew better, though. He'd heard about somebody back in Greenbrier County, who, contracting consumption in Moundsville and sent home to die, nevertheless recovered in the pure mountain air of that beautiful place. But staying here with consumption just meant a quicker way to die than waiting for your heart to give out.

He didn't suppose it mattered. He was, for all intents and purposes, dead already. Immured here in a tomb-sized cell, alone in the dark. It was worse than dying, really, because he could still feel things, still shiver, and starve, and suffer. The dead knew nothing, felt no pain, and had nothing more to fear.

It didn't seem fair. Here he was, shut away in the cold dark in a stone coffin, while Zona, who was supposed to be dead and gone, was apparently out and about, talking to people and appearing wherever she wanted to.

Where was the justice in that?

He even saw her himself sometimes. In the quietest hours before dawn, when his thin and weakened body was shrouded in sweat and his fever raged, shapes took form in the utter blackness of his cell. It was only a sign of delirium; he knew it was. He had heard other men talk about the night terrors that tormented consumptives. It wasn't only the madmen who screamed in the darkness. Those who coughed up blood saw harrowing visions of their past crimes or of tortures to come in the hereafter.

Sometimes he saw Zona.

He would be lying on the bunk, staring off into nothing and willing sleep to come, and there she would be, standing an arm's length away against the cell wall, watching him, her headed tilted and a faint smile playing on her lips.

On her first appearance, he had wiped the sweat away from his eyes, thinking that she must surely be a fever dream but not caring much one way or the other because, after all, what was there left for him to fear? She was wearing that brown dress, the one she was wearing when she died, and which he hid and later burned. Idly he wondered why she wasn't wearing the dress he'd put on her to be buried in. The crooked smile was beginning to irritate him, and he closed his eyes, hoping she'd be gone when he opened them, but she was still there, watching him with a vaguely curious expression. He could have understood anger or a smirking triumph, but the calm contemplation puzzled and annoyed him.

When the silent staring became unbearable, he muttered, "I didn't mean to kill you, Zona."

Her eyes widened and her smile became broader now. She put her hand over her mouth as if she were afraid she'd laugh aloud.

"You're thinking about Lucy, aren't you? And maybe Allie, too. I don't reckon I was a good husband to any of you, ever. I always meant to start fresh, and to make things different every time, but you and Lucy were so besotted with me, so eager to please and so much like cringing cur dogs when I lost my temper that it made me want to kick you. And when I did raise my hand to you, instead of fighting back, you just crept about, trying even harder to please me, until I swear I began to want to see what it would take to get a rise out of you."

He looked at Zona, still watching him with that half smile and eyes like flint, so solid-looking that he felt he could reach out and touch her, but if he did, then he might discover that she was real, and somehow he couldn't face that.

"I guess what it took to get a rise out of you was being throttled to death. Wouldn't say boo to a goose while you were still alive, but once we put you in the ground, you found you had plenty to say, didn't you?

"I didn't mean to do it, though, Zona. I was hungry that night. I had worked all day in Crookshanks's blacksmith shop, and I came home ravenous. Then when you stood there and told me in your whiny little voice that there was no meat to be had for supper, but only those puny salted vegetables in jars left over from summer, why, I felt the black rage swallow me up like a swarm of bees. I had starved before, Zona, when I was here in Moundsville last time, and I swore back then that I would never endure hunger again. Didn't you know that? Nothing ever set me off like an empty stomach. I swear, Zona, if you had bothered to kill one of our chickens and put it in the stewpot, it would have saved your life."

He thought he saw her shake her head, ever so slightly. "Well, it would have saved it that night, anyhow. Maybe it would have happened sooner or later, anyway. I'd already got away with wife-killing once, and that made it easier. I wasn't as afraid with you as I had been with Lucy.

"Poor mousy little Lucy. She used to creep about the house as if I were a rattlesnake that she might tread on if she weren't careful. Well, you've come back, Zona, but I wonder where she is? Still afraid to come near me, even after she's dead? Or has she gone through the pearly gates already?" He was hit by a spasm of coughing and felt the thick, warm blood on his clenched fist. He wiped his hand on the sweat-soaked blanket that was as thin as a bedsheet. "Well, I don't reckon I'll be seeing *her* in the hereafter. I'm headed elsewhere, I suppose. I wonder if they'll let you slip down into hell to watch me roasting over the coals? I bet that would be heaven for you, Zona.

You couldn't leave off chasing men while you were alive—oh, yes, I heard about George Woldridge!—and now that you're dead, you are still coming after me. Well, I'll be dead, too, soon enough, and I hope I can get away from you then. I thought you'd be sorry that they didn't hang me . . ."

Did he imagine it, or was there a slight shake of her head? *No.*

"I don't think you mind, though, that I escaped the noose. Hanging would have been quick and merciful: a few seconds of pain and then a broken neck—same as you got. Now that I think on it, I reckon that would have been fair. A neck for a neck. But wearing my life away year after year, starving in this cold darkness, in a cage too small for a hog pen, why, I'm getting far worse than I gave. You didn't suffer long, Zona; you'll have to allow that. And I have. Oh, I have. Day after day, with nothing to look forward to but more of the same until the consumption finally wears me away. And now you come and stand here, with a little girlish smile on your face, and watch my torment. You are dead and I am alive, but I'm the one in the tomb and you are free."

The fit of coughing began again, wracking his body with the force of it. He lay facedown on the blanket, and coughed until his throat was once more clear enough to let him breathe. When he looked up again into the darkness, he was alone.

Edward Erasmus Stribbling "Trout" Shue died in the tuberculosis epidemic in the West Virginia State Penitentiary at Moundsville, on March 1, 1900. He was buried within the grounds of the prison in an unmarked grave, now situated beneath a more recently constructed building.

twenty-six

GREENBRIER COUNTY, WEST VIRGINIA

1897

NEARLY SIX MONTHS since Zona died, and the churchyard was green and shady. There was still no headstone on Zona's grave—probably never would be, if Jacob had his way, but I needed no marker, for I would never forget where my daughter was buried. Every time the family came to church, I'd go around to the side yard just past the end of the church and up the slope a bit, and I'd put some little token of remembrance on her grave, just as I had from the beginning. In July, I brought pink cabbage roses from the bush out by the back porch. I wish I could have brought white blooms, which would have been the proper color to honor the dead, but we only had the one rosebush.

I would talk to Zona, too, if nobody was nearby to overhear and think I'd taken leave of my senses. I didn't know if she was still this side of heaven, or if she cared about earthly things anymore, but it gave me comfort to say my thoughts out loud, whether or not she was lingering here to listen.

"Well, Zona, the trial is over and done with, and the jury had no trouble in finding that worthless husband of yours guilty of murder. I wonder if you have been waiting for him at the gates of death to have your say—though I'm sure he will not be spending eternity in the same place as you. That's what I came to tell you, though: don't expect him to be crossing over into the hereafter anytime soon. That worthless jury recommended life in prison, and shipped him off to Moundsville a week after the trial. A lynch mob from here in Meadow Bluff almost put the matter to rights, but Sheriff Nickell got wind of it, and Deputy Dwyer hid Edward Shue outside town somewhere until the danger had passed. So now he's in prison over on the other side of the state, and I guess we've heard the last of him. You may know when he dies before we do, though I think I may feel a weight lifted off my heart when he finally departs this world.

"It doesn't seem fair, does it, for him to be walking around, eating and sleeping and seeing the sun shine and the grass growing, while you have had all the pleasures of this world taken away from you forever. I hope it's better where you are now, Zona. I hope heaven is splendid enough to make up for what you lost here.

"And I hope he has found his hell on earth. I hope he is cold and friendless and miserable. And above all, Zona, I hope he's hungry.

"I did what I could to get you justice. I hope the Lord will forgive me for the lie I told—about seeing your ghost and all—but I knew in my heart that devil had murdered you. It was the only way I could make them look for proof. I was right, after all, and I don't suppose it matters what method I used to get them to find out the truth, but even if heaven faults me for the sin of telling a falsehood, it was worth it.

"Rest in peace, Zona. I did all I could for you, and you are not forgotten."

I was there, Mama. You couldn't hear me, but I was there.

You were so tangled up in your own grief and anger that I couldn't make you hear me.

You were locked inside your own thoughts tighter than I was in Handley's wooden coffin. I was sorry to have put you through so much anguish, and sorrier still that Daddy hardened his heart to keep from feeling anything at all. I wish I could tell him that it doesn't matter about a tombstone. All a grave marker is for is to make sure that the person will be remembered, but I think you made sure that people won't forget me ever, Mama.

Zona Heaster Shue finally did get a tombstone erected on her grave in the Soule Chapel Cemetery by local citizens of Greenbrier County in 1979.

Mary Jane Robinson Heaster died on September 6, 1916, without ever recanting her story of seeing her daughter's ghost. She is buried with her husband in the churchyard of Soule Chapel, near the grave of Zona.

Author's Note

THE STORY OF ZONA HEASTER SHUE, "The Greenbrier Ghost," is West Virginia's best-known tale of the supernatural, but the incident has always been treated as folklore, a jumble of hearsay and supposition built on a handful of facts. When I first requested information on the Greenbrier Ghost, I was referred to a book of regional folktales, in which Zona's story took up all of a page and a half. Two years later, with the help of a number of generous and scholarly people, I had amassed a pile of documents six inches thick—census records, birth and death certificates, property records, maps, photographs—a wealth of evidence to bring the folktale back into the real world.

As I uncovered more and more facts about the incident, the story became more than an account of a mother's search for justice for her murdered daughter. The Greenbrier County of the Gilded Age came to life, and I have tried to enlarge the narrative into a portrait of that time and place.

I am grateful to Jim Talbert of the North House Museum in Lewisburg, West Virginia, who was patient and helpful in the earliest days of my research. Mr. Talbert pored over maps with me and gave me pointers in county geography, so that I could locate the places where the events took place and the sites of the residences of most of the key figures. Early on, Mr. Talbert directed me to the museum's material relating to the Greenbrier Ghost, located a photo of John Alfred Preston, and suggested helpful source material on the attorneys. Greenbrier County physician Kendall Wilson spent a summer afternoon giving me a guided tour of Greenbrier County, helping me to get a sense of the local geography, including the Soule Chapel Cemetery, the house occupied by Edward and Zona Shue, and the place where the community of Livesay's Mill once stood—it is now open fields with no signs of human habitation.

Raymond and Lynn Tuckwiller, owners of a beautiful farm not far from where Livesay's Mill would have been, generously gave me a tour of their home, which is similar in age and construction to the one Edward and Zona Shue once lived in, so that I could visualize the setting—especially the steep flight of stairs leading to the front hall. The Tuckwillers, accomplished drivers of horse-drawn coaches, own an impressive collection of antique vehicles, and their advice was invaluable in helping me to decide what sort of transportation each person would have used in 1897 Greenbrier County.

Sandra Menders, a native of Greenbrier County, and an expert at finding obscure documents, was my guide and fellow time-traveler, helping me to reconstruct the lives of long-forgotten county residents. As I assembled the list of people who were the major players in the incident, I would fire off questions to Sandra asking for biographical data on each one, and she would track them down through a maze of century-old records. One of the most poignant moments of our research happened when Sandra was examining the birth and death records of the family of Anderson Jones, the youth who discovered Zona's body. "I think I have just uncovered a tragedy," Sandra informed me, sending me the paper trail detailing the fate of the Jones family in the fall of 1897. The scene in which Martha Jones tells Mr. Gardner what happened to her family is based on information from their death certificates.

By tracking these people through half a century of official records, we were able to draw some conclusions about their behavior and personalities. For example, in the folklore accounts of this incident, Anderson Jones is variously described as a child or a young boy—the impression the reader gets is that he was about twelve years old. According to census records, though, Anderson Jones was eighteen years old in January 1897 when he discovered the body of Zona Heaster Shue. Why, we wondered, did the tales depict him as a child, and even more to the point: in a rural Southern community in 1897 why was an eighteen-year-old black man never suspected in the murder of a twenty-three-year-old white woman whose body he discovered? We followed Anderson Jones through census records and county documents until his death in Lewisburg on June 17, 1953, and we learned that he worked at handyman jobs; he never married; and he lived with his mother for most of his life. Putting all these facts together, we concluded that Anderson Jones was developmentally disabled. The folktales depict him as a child because in that era he would have been considered one.

Sandra Menders and I went from paper trails and library archives to the roads of Greenbrier County, in search of the key places in the story, and for the graves of all the people who by then we felt we knew. We went round and round about the timing of Zona's death and funeral. The (now defunct) local newspaper, the *Greenbrier Independent*, listed her death as occurring on Sunday, January 24 (in the paper's January 28, 1897, edition), but in an article published on February 25, announcing the autopsy,

Zona Shue's date of death is given as Saturday, January 23, which is also the date written on her death certificate. Later accounts from other sources say that she was buried on Sunday, January 24. An interval of eighteen hours from death to burial seems improbably quick, given the distances involved and the weather in January. We spent many hours trying to make sense of the chronology.

It is approximately twenty miles from Livesay's Mill to Meadow Bluff, where the Heasters lived and where they buried their daughter. In 1897 the journey would involve unpaved roads and horse-drawn conveyances. On January 23, in West Virginia, sunset comes around 5:30. If Zona died on Saturday, January 23, and was buried on Sunday, the following things have to take place within twenty-four hours:

Saturday ca. 11:00 a.m. Anderson Jones finds the body, and notifies his mother and Edward Shue.

Saturday ca. 11:45 a.m. Someone travels the five miles to Lewisburg to summon Dr. Knapp to examine the body. *(Is the coffin ordered from the Lewisburg undertakers at this time? If not, there would be a further delay waiting for it.)*

Saturday ca. 1:00 p.m. Riders set out for Meadow Bluff to inform the Heasters of their daughter's death.

Saturday ca. 1:45 p.m. Dr. Knapp arrives and is permitted only a cursory examination of the body.

Saturday ca. 2:15 p.m. Dr. Knapp leaves, and Edward Shue alone dresses his wife's body for burial. The coffin must have arrived about this time, because Shue had time to put padding into it to support Zona's head.

Saturday ca. 3:30 p.m. Riders reach the Heaster farm with the news of Zona's death. They now have just over two hours of daylight left to make a return journey of twenty miles.

Saturday ca. 3:15 p.m. In a wagon borrowed from Crookshanks's smithy, Shue and a group of neighbors set out for the Heaster farm, at a slower pace than that of the riders, with just over two hours of daylight remaining, on a cold January evening. *(This is a bit hard to believe. Why not wait until the next day?)*

Saturday ca. 7:30 p.m. Assuming the loaded wagon can travel five miles an hour over dark winter roads, the party will arrive at the Heasters' place. *(Do they go back that night to Livesay's Mill, twenty miles in the freezing dark, or do they spend the night at the Heaster farm—despite the fact that Zona's parents dislike and distrust Shue? Or do they not set out on Saturday night, but instead deliver the body on Sunday when they have daylight and warmer temperatures? This would also limit the Heasters' time with the body and obviate the need for an overnight stay.)*

Sunday afternoon—Funeral? The Meadow Bluff community could be notified at the morning church service that the burial will take place that afternoon.

The weather and time of year make all this seem improbable—an unnecessary hardship for the travelers with no real urgency to accomplish their mission so quickly. The arguments in favor of the undue haste are: 1) Shue wants Zona's body buried before anyone has a chance to examine it too closely; 2) If the funeral is delayed until Monday, he would miss a day of work and either have to spend more time with the Heasters or make the twenty-mile journey twice.

Lacking evidence to the contrary, and trying for the most logical sequence of events, I opted for the Sunday funeral, with the body arriving that morning by wagon.

Sandra and I hashed out every possible alternative for the events of January 23–24 before agreeing on this one. Our correspondence of analysis, fact-checking, and speculation on all the people and events we examined would outnumber the pages of the novel itself. Having the documentary evidence to substantiate the details of the lives of everyone involved transformed the vague folktale back into a story about real people. It was extremely helpful to be able to talk over the case with Sandra as I worked on the novel. She was a kindred spirit who shared my enthusiasm for that time and place, while bringing her own opinions and expertise to bear on the story.

As Louis Pasteur said, "Chance favors the prepared mind." Because I have spent years studying nineteenth-century England, I was fortunate to come to this story with an arcane fact that no one else who had studied the Greenbrier Ghost seemed to know: the precedent—the story of Maria Marten/ *The Murder in the Red Barn*. Was there a connection? Although the stories were eerily similar, the murder of Maria Marten occurred in Suffolk, England, in 1827. Could Mary Jane Heaster, poor, ill-educated, and living on a remote mountain farm in Appalachia, have known about that earlier incident that happened an ocean away? It took more than a year, and many hours of Sandra's diligent and wide-ranging document searches, to confirm my hunches, but we finally found the connection. In the last chapter of the book, John Alfred Preston, the prosecuting attorney, learns this fact at a dinner party at the Old White Hotel. I don't know that Preston ever did hear of it, but it is likely that the cosmopolitan guests at the hotel would have known the story because *The Murder in the Red Barn,* based on the Marten case, was one of the most popular plays in Victorian England. The explanation Preston was given in that scene and the evidence for Mary Jane Heaster's knowledge of the Marten case is all true.

Much of the biographical information on William Parks Rucker, attorney for the defense, came from *Bridge Burner: The Full and Factual Story of Dr. William Parks Rucker Slave-owning Union Partisan* by Michael Rucker (Quarrier Press, 2014). John Alfred Preston was never the subject of a biography, but a brief reminiscence of his life appeared in J. R. Cole's *History of Greenbrier County* (1917).

James P. D. Gardner, who is buried in an unmarked grave in Lewisburg, proved particularly difficult to track, even though he practiced law in Bluefield, West Virginia, for more than thirty years. My thanks to the Craft Memorial Library in Bluefield for allowing me access to their archives on Bluefield's past, and especially to Ramona Fletcher of Bluefield, who was able to locate important pieces of information about Mr. Gardner's college education and his social activities in Mercer County. I'm grateful for all her help. Thanks also to Jason Riffle for his guidance on the West Virginia Masons.

Background on the psychiatrist Dr. James Boozer was provided by Peggy Mack Roach, who visited Pennsylvania's Lincoln University, Boozer's alma mater, in search of more information about him. In New York, Karen Chapman found the site of Boozer's boyhood home in Mt. Kisco (now a parking lot), and she discovered the only photograph we have of him: his yearbook photo from Howard University Medical School, taken only a year or two before he joined the staff of the West Virginia Asylum at Lakin.

My thanks to Dr. Robert Sevier for his advice on some of the medical aspects in the narrative, and to my old school friend, attorney Jim McAdams, for giving me the benefit of his expertise regarding matters of law in the story, particularly for explaining to me why the nineteenth-century attorneys took turns serving as county prosecutor.

I am grateful as always to my friend Susan Richards, for accompanying me to the Moundsville prison and an old asylum (both now tourist sites) in the early stages of my research; to North Carolina Civil War historian Michael Hardy for his advice on the war experiences of attorneys Preston and Rucker; and to Professor Elizabeth Baird Hardy for sharing her expertise in the clothing styles of the nineteenth century.

—Sharyn McCrumb

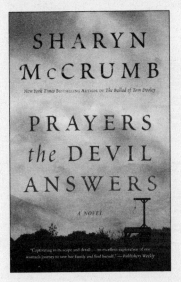